Somebody's Child

A Novel

Dennis A. Williams

SIMON & SCHUSTER

SIMON & SCHUSTER
Rockefeller Center
1230 Avenue of the Americas
New York, NY 10020

SIMON & SCHUSTER and colophon are registered trademarks
of Simon & Schuster Inc.

Designed by Irving Perkins Associates
Manufactured in the United States of America

1 2 3 4 5 6 7 8 9 10

Library of Congress Cataloging-in-Publication Data

Williams, Dennis A.
Somebody's child: a novel/Dennis A. Williams
p. cm.
I. Title.
PS3573.I448455S65   1997
813'.54—dc21   97-9173
                                        CIP

ISBN 0-684-82713-1

To Eagle, from Hawk
In memory of Willis Hall,
Godfather of Soul

Acknowledgments

Thanks to my agent, Faith—the name says it all—and to my editors, Dominick Anfuso and Bob Asahina

To Plotmeister Pacha, my own Ezra Pound

To Herb Jackson, Karen Koshner, Dr. Eldridge Anderson, D.J. Tashir Lee, Greg Gary, and Tom King for technical assistance, and to Jim Knudsen, my extra pair of eyes

To my Daddybuddies Squirrel, Starr, Spero, Cakes, Fred, and the rest, and all the friends whose encouragement got me over

To Adam, for letting me play the big brother

To Cat & Gert, for everything

To John A., for showing me how to do it, on the page and off

To Maleficent, for making it all happen

And to The Fantastic Four—Margo, John Gregory, Nancy, and D.J.—who will take care of everything.

De Voodoo Spell

A Short Story by Quincy Crawford

Greg Jackson looked up from the barber chair and blew the hair up out his eye so he could see. Frank Drew, he swept floors down at the music hall, had just came into the shop grinnin and lookin like new money. He had on a red suit with a matchin derby hat and was totin a cane. And his gold tooth look like it had a piece of diamond in it.

"Well looka here!" Sonny the barber say in a big voice. "Somebody tried to *tell* me you done hit the number, but I didn't wanna believe em. Ain't nobody seen you in a week."

"Thas right," Drew say and he strike a pose in the middle of the shop. "Hit it big, too! Ain't been back to work since. Took me a little trip down home—in my new Cadillac."

"Man, you mean you jus walk off your job? If that don't beat all!"

"Huh! Weren't much of a job nohow. I get another one—when I decide to go back to work, that is. I'm a man of leisure now."

"Drew, you somethin else," Sonny say. The other men in the shop was crackin up but Greg only stared at the new Drew, thinkin about how a man's life could change so fast. But his thoughts was interrupted by his brother makin noise in the other chair.

"Boy, you sho is tenderhead," say JoJo's barber. "Now jus hold on a minute. I'm almost done but I can't do nothin less you set still."

"Almos finish?" Greg ask Sonny.

"Ack like you in a hurry, son. You mus be goin to slip it to yo gal fo her mama get home, ain't that right?" The striped cloth come loose from around Greg's neck and he jumped down, not payin no mind to the laughin barber. On his feet, he immediately checked in his right pocket to see did he have his good luck charm his grandmother had gave him.

"You got the money for both?" ask the barber. Greg nodded and gave up the $4, just as JoJo was bein let down from his chair.

"C'mon, I paid awready," he say to his brother as he start out the shop.

"Say there, Jackson!" Sonny call after him. "Tell yo daddy I wanna see him. Got somethin for him."

"Okay," Greg say and the two of them shoot through the door into the Saturday morning bustle of Grove Hall, the busiest part of Roxbury. It was September and people was sportin up and down the street in the new '61 model cars. Drew's white Caddy was standin out in front of the shop.

"Greg!" JoJo shout, watchin the parade. "Lookit that Thunderbird!" Greg didn't look. He started up Blue Hill Avenue in a hurry and JoJo he have to almost run to catch up. Greg had just started to grow real fast— he had grew three inches over the summer—so JoJo's legs was a lot shorter. Plus, he didn't know where they was goin.

"Why we goin this way?" he ask after a couple of blocks.

"Goin up to the park."

"What for?"

"Mr. Drew gimme a idea. We gotta collect some things."

"But Mama say come right home, cause we gotta watch Tina while she go to the beauty parlor."

"We got time. She don't hafta go till one o'clock."

"But she say—"

"Well go on, then, simple! You tell her I be home after while."

Hurt by the suggestion, JoJo went even faster to keep up with his brother, just like Greg knew he would.

"You member when Mama say she like us to move up here?" Greg say while they was passin the houses that border the park.

"She don't like it where we live at now, do she?"

"Course not. It's fallin apart. Daddy say so all the time. Know what we gonna do?"

"Huh?"

"We gonna help em move."

"How we gonna do that, Greg? Daddy say we can't afford to move yet. That's why he be drivin the cab at night."

"You saw what happen to Mr. Drew when he hit the number, right? Well Mama play all the time. If she hit, we be able to move."

"What we gonna do?"

"You'll see."

Since he wasn't gettin no more answers, JoJo didn't ask no more questions. When they got to Franklin Park, they climbed over the hills and past the picnic areas. It looked to JoJo like Greg goin someplace in particular, so he just followed along. Until they got to the basketball courts. JoJo stopped to watch then, his little eyes growin big as they took in the action. The players was movin up and down the court like they could do it forever, legs pumpin, shoulders dippin. And all the time talkin trash. JoJo was thinkin that he wanted to be that good one day. Dribble all around people into the corner, fake his man right off the court, and jump way up and shoot a pretty jumper wouldn't nobody be able to stop. It would be like magic, just like Elgin Baylor.

"JoJo!" Greg's voice came from behind some bushes. JoJo went in the direction of the voice and stumbled down a slope.

"You sho is clumsy, JoJo," his brother say. He was walkin around the small pocket of woods lookin at the ground.

"How I'm supposed to know that stupid hill was there?" He got up and brushed himself off. "What we doin, Greg?"

"Okay, look here. You member when we was down in South Carolina and Big Mama was talkin bout voodoo?"

"Ye-e-e-ah," JoJo say, gettin excited. "Workin roots and castin spells and stuff."

Greg pulled the small pouch out his pocket. "See, I still got that John de Conquer powder Big Mama give me. I'ma really try it out now."

"We gonna make a spell so Mama can hit the number!" JoJo exclaimed.

"See there, you ain't so stupid. Now c'mon, we gotta find some stuff to do the spell with."

"What kinda stuff?"

Greg scratched his head and squinched up his face. "I'on know, exactly. Big Mama was talkin bout herbs and cattails and goat eyes and all funny kinda things. We ain't got none of that."

"We gotta kill somethin?"

"Naw, she say you don't hafta do that no more. Sides, we'd need owls and goats. I don't think dogs and squirrels work. Let's just get some roots and bark offa some trees—maybe some leaves and stones and dirt to throw in, too. It's gotta come from round here is all, since this is where we wanna move to."

They gathered up all the stuff they can fit into their pockets or carry, then hustled on home. JoJo kept askin when was they gonna do the spell. Their parents was supposed to go out that night, so Greg decided they would do it then.

Later that night, in the first floor apartment that still smelled like cabbage and ham hocks, Greg and JoJo's parents was gettin ready to leave.

"Be careful not to wake up the baby," their mother say. "Greg, you know how to change her if she need it. And please don't start no who struck John and tear the place up like last time. JoJo, if he try to start somethin, just go on bout your business."

"Y'all just set in front of the TV and look at Paladin," their father say. "If I hear any mess I'ma be on both your butts like a hawk on a rabbit, you hear me?"

The two boys nodded solemnly through the instructions.

"Daddy," Greg say, remembering. "Sonny down at the barber shop say he got somethin to tell you."

"Maybe he heard somethin from that man he usedta work for. I'll call him tomorrow."

"Good night," their mother say and kissed them both. "Don't let us find you up when we get back."

"You finish the cards yet?" say Greg when the door close.

"I gotta do all of em?"

"Naw, you can leave out the face cards. We just want em for the numbers." JoJo went off to finish markin up the cards, and Greg went into their parents' bedroom. The spell have to have somethin that belong to the person, so he took his mother dusting powder. Powder was good for spells. Some smelly somethin be good too, but it was only a little perfume left so he took that and his father aftershave, and carried all the potions out to the back porch. Then he went back for the stuff from the park and brought along his Bat Masterson cane cause a priest got to carry a stick.

Outside, Greg walked anxiously up and down the driveway lookin for the moon. For a while he was afraid it wasn't there and he wondered should he call off the spell. But then the clouds moved out the way and there it was, almost full, too. JoJo came out the back door with his deck of cards.

"You do em all?" Greg ask.

"Just like you tol me."

"Okay, I gotta set this up, make it look like somethin. Oh yeah, we gotta have a fire, too. Get the matches out the kitchen. And bring a candle and some paper."

JoJo dashed off again and Greg laid out the cards—with a woman face and the word "Mama" drawn on—in a circle in the driveway, near the stairs. He covered all the cards with stones to keep them from blowin away cause the wind be blowin hard, then he put the pieces of tree root and branches in the middle of the circle. By the time JoJo came back Greg was grinnin like a fool cause he was so proud of himself.

"Look what I found!" JoJo say, trippin down the stairs. "That ol drum we got. I can play it while you make the spell."

"Hey, yeah, good idea. I knew you'd catch on, boy. Okay, let's go."

Greg carefully set up the candle in the middle of the circle with the roots and paper all around it. Then he stepped back and grandly hung the magic John de Conquer pouch around his neck.

"If this work, can we do one for me?" JoJo ask as he get down on his knee with the drum.

"Whaddayou want?"

"I want you to make me Elgin Baylor."

"Shoot, JoJo, I ain't gonna waste my power on no foolishness like that." He lit the stubby candle and picked up his cane. "Now you just start playin and hush."

JoJo he started to thumpin on that old toy drum like he was doin somethin. "Ain't you gonna do nothin?" he ask his brother.

"I said hush up, man. Wait a minute, I gotta get into the spirit." Slowly, Greg lifted both arms up to the sky, then he started in to stompin and dancin around the circle, gruntin like the Indian medicine men in the movies. On his third time around, the paper caught fire, and he stopped to pick up the dusting powder.

"You member the words Big Mama tol us?"

"Uh . . . oh yeah.

"AG-WE! IMMAMOO!"

He threw the powder on the fire and it commence to hiss and jump.

"OOM-GOWA
OO-POO-PA-DOO

MUMBO JUMBO
DOO-WOP SH-BOOM!"

He tossed in the perfume and the fire began to twist.

"Baby need a new pair of shoes!" JoJo screamed, poundin on his drum.

"Shut up! I'm doin this." In went the aftershave and Greg hollered
louder:

"KADA DAMBALLA
MAMA JUJU
HEY BOP A REEBOP
AND VOODOO TOO!"

The wood began to catch and it sputtered and popped. The fire
raised up and leaped from side to side.

"Cut out that racket!" somebody called down from the house next
door. People passin on the sidewalk paused and looked at the two boys
cuttin a fool, but didn't nobody interfere.

Suddenly, Greg stopped and chanted:

"Fire, fire, burnin bright,
Give our mama luck tonight."

"Go head, Greg!" JoJo yell, goin to town on his drum.

"Fire, fire, with the big old flame,
Help us make our fortune change."

Greg turned and danced around the driveway, hoppin and turnin
and wavin the cane around his head. He didn't even notice when the
drum stop.

"Greg . . . ," JoJo say quietly.

His brother kept on dancin.

"GREG!"

The voodoo priest came out his trance and looked around. Sparks
from their flame had started a fire on the porch steps.

Greg dropped his cane and ran to his brother side. A strong blast of
wind made the fire almost bend over double, and a line of flame
started to run up the steps and nibble on the porch posts.

"Jesus, Greg, the house is on fire! What do we do, what do we do?"

"Come on, we gotta get Tina."

They climbed over the porch railing and raced into the house. Their two-year-old sister was still asleep in her bed outside their parents' room.

"Hurry, Greg, I'm scared."

"Okay, don't panic," he say as he lifted the girl into his arms. "I'ma call the fire department. You go next door and get Mr. Adams. Go on now, it's gonna be okay."

JoJo ran back to the porch but the fire was makin a steady advance toward the back door. Thinkin maybe he can keep it from gettin inside, he grabbed a bucket that set in the corner on the porch and carried it to the kitchen sink to fill it. He didn't know water would be that heavy, but he dragged it back outside and heaved it at the flames. It was a splash and some smoke, and the fire shrank back for a minute. JoJo tried it again, and while he was goin back and forth Greg came up the driveway with Tina in his arms.

"JoJo! Hey, Jo, where you at?"

"Up here! I'm puttin out the fire."

"Get off the porch, fool! You can't put it out!"

A stocky man in his socks and undershirt and stocking cap came huffin through the next yard toward Greg.

"What the hell happened, boy?" he ask.

A crash came from the porch; one of the posts had collapsed.

"Here, Mr. Adams," say Greg, giving his still-sleeping baby sister to the man.

"Hey, wait! Where you think you goin?"

Greg ran around in back of the porch, but it was almost covered with fire now and he couldn't see JoJo. He try to get close but it like a oven. A bucket rolled off the porch by his feet.

"JoJo!" He grabbed tight on to the magic pouch around his neck and closed his eyes, ready to leap into the fire to save his brother.

Then he heard something hit the ground around the corner of the house, and he saw JoJo scramblin toward him like he seen the devil himself.

"It's all right. I gotcha," Greg say as JoJo ran into him shakin and sweatin.

"It started to come inside . . . I had to jump out the kitchen window. I thought it was gonna get me, Greg."

Sirens screamed in their direction.

"You done good, Jo. Take it easy now."

"Come on, you two, get back away from there," shouted Mr. Adams.

The lights from the fire truck flashed down the driveway and white men in black raincoats began to surround the house. Mr. Adams, still holdin Tina, led Greg and JoJo out to the curb, and they watched the powerful sprouts of water from the hoses rain down on the house. Neighbors gathered around and a car charged up like it might go right into the house. Greg and JoJo parents jumped out.

"Everybody out?" their father shouted.

"Got em right here," say Mr. Adams. "They all okay."

Their father rushed to the back and their mother hurried over to them.

"We was over Alice house and somebody said it was a fire in this block. I called and didn't get no answer so we came right back." She took Tina then look at Greg and JoJo. "How'd it start?"

JoJo looked at his brother, who didn't have his story together yet.

"JoJo . . . ," she prodded.

"Well, uh . . . we was doin a spell and the fire got too big . . ." He had hung his head down low and rolled his eyes up like a periscope to watch his mother's reaction. Greg had a disgusted look on his face.

"A spell! What kinda spell?"

"Voodoo. We made it so you could—"

"*Voodoo!* Oh my God, you don't be playin with that stuff. Boy! What's wrong with you? Who taught you that?"

"Big Mama."

"Oh Lord. Greg, this was your idea, wasn't it?"

"You gonna hit the number now, Mama."

"*What?*"

Their father come back to the curb, looking impatient. "They say they got it under control. Didn't get much past the back door. All right, now what happened?"

"They was playin voodoo."

"Voodoo!" He grabbed Greg by one arm and almost lifted him off the ground. "You mean you set that fire?" he thundered.

"No, Dad—it was a accident . . . We just had one little bitty candle in the driveway and—no, no wait! It's gonna work. We don't need that house no more."

"I'll take em over my place till you get everything straight, Jackson," Mr. Adams said to spare Greg's life.

"Awright, but don't you all get too comfortable cause I'll be back for you later and I'ma put a voodoo on your black behinds so bad you won't *ever* forget it!" As Greg and JoJo went off with Mr. Adams and Tina to wait for their execution, they heard their father grumblin. "Goddamn shack . . . Knew somethin like this was gonna happen one day . . ."

A week later Greg and JoJo was in they room with the lights out.

"JoJo, you sleep?" Greg called in a loud whisper.

"Uh-uh."

"You heard what Mama and Daddy was talkin about after supper?"

"Naw, what?"

"Daddy say we gonna move. He don't wanna live here no more."

"Really? But Mama ain't hit no number."

The door of they room opened quietly and their mother stood framed in the light of the hall outside.

"You boys spose to be asleep. We fixin to go to bed now, so you bet not let your daddy hear you. You know he ain't forgot bout last week yet."

"Mama?"

"What, JoJo?"

"We gonna move?"

She stepped inside the room a little more and softened her voice.

"Well, your father gonna make a little more money on that new job and we gotta get outta here, so we thinkin bout maybe buyin a house over in Dorchester."

"A whole house?"

"Maybe. We'll see. Don't tell him I told you—he want it to be a surprise when we decide. And remember what I said before—Big Mama was foolin when she told you bout that voodoo, so I don't wanna hear no more bout it, okay."

"Uh-huh."

"Now go to sleep," she said and left.

"See, I told you it worked!" Greg said even before her footsteps had faded away.

"You mean the spell?"

"Yeah. We movin, ain't we?"

"But what about the numbers?"

"That ain't important. We did what we wanda do."

"Naw, Greg. You messed up."

"Well we used Daddy's aftershave, right? I probly just said the wrong spell."

"But he was gonna get that job anyway."

"I had the pouch with me at the barber shop when Sonny told us bout it. Sides, we movin cause a the fire. It just didn't work the way I spected it to."

"Yeah . . . I guess you right. Hey, does that mean we can do more?"

"Aw, you just want me to make you a basketball player or somethin stupid."

"Naw, I change my mind. I wanna Thunderbird."

"A Thunderbird! That ain't no car, simple. You need a Corvette, you wanna car."

"You crazy, Greg. A Corvette—"

"Shh!"

The door swung open again, more violently this time, and their father stood for a moment glarin at the two silent bodies buried under the covers.

"Y'all ain't slick," he said in a low voice. "I know you awake, but just keep pretendin like this and everything be fine." He paused on the way out. "Now please don't make me come in here no more. I'm still tired from whippin y'all last week."

The door closed and it wasn't no sound for a while. Then the footsteps started trailin away.

"Greg?" JoJo whispered after five minutes.

"Yeah?"

"Think we could do one to make Daddy a little nicer?"

Greg thought about it. "I don't think I'm that good yet."

Part One

MAY 1976

One

Quincy

"**G**ood morning, Crawdaddy."

"Fox! That you?" Quincy surprised himself with his own voice. He had been ready to chat awhile with whoever it was—that's why he settled into the seat before lifting the receiver—but he was genuinely happy to hear her.

"Who else but your conscience would be bothering you this time of night? What are you doing up?"

"Now when have you known me to go to bed early? What time is it, anyway?" He squinted at the clock on the bookshelf but couldn't make it out in the dark.

"It's quarter to three. Who is she?"

"Nikki Giovanni. We're doing the sixties in class next week." He wondered if Max was listening but didn't really give a shit. Other than dropping into the soothing Barry White tone he always used on the phone, he made no effort to conceal the conversation. "So what is it, midnight out there? You must be back to drinkin coffee."

"I don't know about out there, but it's quarter to three in Jersey, and I'm on a natural high."

"You're back? Oh shit, when'd you get in? How long you gonna be around? *Talk* to me, girl." As he spoke, he grabbed the pack by the typewriter on the desk and lit up. That he could do in the dark.

"I heard that," she said. "You still tryin to kill yourself?"

"Fuck you."

"You wish."

"I'll live. So what's up?"

"Well," she said, "I got in a few hours ago, and I'm here to stay, I guess."

"What happened to the institute and artistic freedom? What happened to what's-his-name?"

"Why something gotta happen? I can't come home if I want? Maybe I just wanna look at the sky from a different direction for a while."

"Hey, yo. Uh-uh. This is me, remember? I was supposed to shoot you if you ever thought about setting foot in Jersey again."

"A girl can change her mind, can't she?

"Yeah, but not every six months. I done told you about that."

"You've told me about a lot of things, Mr. Crawford."

"Well, if it makes you feel any better, I'm thinking about going to Boston for a hot minute in a few weeks."

"Hey, stop the presses."

"Okay, so one can go home again. But what about your sculpturing?"

"Photography."

"I forgot. You changed your mind."

"It's okay. I just need to regroup. What about you? You getting any writing done?"

"Not much. You gettin any?"

"What?"

"You heard me."

"I don't want to talk about that."

He hadn't expected her to fold that easily. Even when she was bummed out, she usually managed to stay aloft for a few more rounds.

"Fontelle, is something wrong?" he asked.

"I don't know, Quince. Not really. But I need to talk to you, okay? Not right now. I just wanted you to know I was back. You still got the number out here? I mean, that was probably two or three black books ago."

"Like I said, fuck you."

"Yeah, right. I thought you'd gotten over that."

"Who told you that lie?"

Silence. He'd misjudged her altitude again.

"Yeah, I got it," he said softly.

"Soon," she said, almost in a whisper. "You know how dead it is out here."

"Okay. Soon."

"Night, Crawdaddy."

He eased the receiver into place and held it there for a moment with both hands, feeling a tingle ease down through his body. Then he lit another cigarette from the smoldering butt and closed his eyes with the intake. *Call* soon, or . . . ? Still throwing him curves after, what, six years? Seemed like forever. Definitely more of a diversion than he'd bargained for.

But a diversion nonetheless. Stabbing out in the dark after a few puffs, he kept hitting filters from earlier in the evening and knew he'd exceeded his limit. Fuck it. He peeled himself from the fake leather chair, like ripping a Band-Aid from his naked behind, and stood. He was in no hurry to get back to Max, but that had nothing to do with her. He cherished these moments. Even as a kid, lying in the dark talking to Bubb long after they were supposed to be asleep. Here the light from the street lamp on Morningside, when it was working, arced upward to illuminate the slimmest corner of his curtainless room. When no one was with him, he liked moving around naked through his one-and-a-half-room kingdom, plucking just the right record from a shelf, or even a book that he might hold, unseeing, standing or sitting at the cluttered desk, hearing the real or imagined voices, replaying or forecasting intimacies that were always truer when he was alone.

Maybe she was asleep.

He could lie still with one leg and one arm draped over her, holding on as much as holding her, and watch their ghosts till the sun rose. He had always done that, even when it was all good. In the dark he could see them, over and over again. Cooking Chinese food in the tiny kitchenette. Watching the good stuff on Channel 13 when they begged for money. Watching the anchor puppets mouth her words while she critiqued their delivery. Him grading papers. Her reading the paper. Reading books to each other. And fucking every which way, anytime, for any reason or for no reason. Her ghost was always clearer than any of the others, her presence in the apartment more pervasive. When she was there, in fact, he never saw the others, but she used to turn up when he was with somebody else. That had been a while. Would she still be there when she was gone?

"That your friend from California?"

He almost wished there'd been an edge to her voice, but that wasn't her style. And she knew better. The phone calls, the nights he insisted on being alone, were intended to create the illusion that she did not hold a monopoly.

"Yeah, she just got back for a while."

"Are you going to see her?"

"Of course," he said, surprised that she'd asked. Maybe there'd be a fight after all.

"Good." She was entirely awake and beginning to dimple. "You can tell her all about me. About us."

"Really? Just what should I tell her?"

"About this," she said and reached out to where he was already rising to meet her.

He couldn't help it. He wanted no more, but she knew what she was doing, believed as always that she had him where she wanted him. She drew him in quickly, overwhelmed him, and talked, more than usual, deep, dirty talk that fueled their struggle for dominance. Pushing against her to set himself free, he slipped into double exposure. Their ghosts were right there with them; it was the night, more than three years ago, when they bent his old bed frame, which was why his mattress remained on the floor. When she first enthralled him with her fierce desires and frightening promises. She was everywhere, all around him. Taking control. It was all happening again. Finally, tortured by the merging of past and present, he exploded in a howl of desperation.

"Tell her that," she said, penetrating the brief silence.

"You're dangerous," he said, exhausted and stuck inside her.

"No, I'm not. I can't hurt you, Quince. This is the worst thing that can happen, me being here with you, making you feel good. That's not so bad, is it?"

It was the same promotion as before, as always. *It's all right. I'll stay with you. We'll be happy together.* She did. They were. Now what?

"Is it?" she repeated.

Refusing to answer, he extricated himself and rolled onto his back. She rolled with him, placed her head on his chest, reached a hand to the side of his face, and slid a thigh across his groin. Surrounded.

"Why don't you tell your friend that you're going to be a father?"

Her bright eyes beamed into his, requiring, as always, a response. The goddamn red light never went off.

"Don't play that, Max," he said, and cut to the ceiling, where he wouldn't find her. "That's serious shit."

"I'm not playing."

He came back to her eyes and found no hint of a punch line. He pushed her aside and rolled off the mattress.

"What the fuck are you talking about?" he demanded from his knees.

She turned to face him, not laughing but pleased, like a girl who'd tricked the teacher. The dimples she seemed to control at will creased her cheeks. Her relaxed Afro drooped sexily on her forehead.

"I'm going to have a baby," she said with the kind of dramatic reading that made her cringe on newscasts.

He stood, spun, and stalked across the room to the desk, where he swiped at his pack and matches.

"*Whose* baby?"

She started giggling, and he knew the question was lame; this was part of the plot, like the frenzied father in the delivery room. He tried to light up but had a handful of cigarettes and no matches. Like rubbing two sticks together. She laughed some more. He was being cute.

"Whose do you think?" she said, rolling lazily onto her back. "I know it's sooner than we planned—we haven't talked that much about it. But I figure it'll just give us a reason to work that much harder."

He reached her in two strides and flung the crumbled cigarettes at her face.

"What the *fuck* do you think you're doing?" he yelled, standing astride her on the mattress. "This ain't no *show,* Max. You can't write a script for this shit. How you gonna get pregnant?"

"How the hell do you *think* I got pregnant?" She drew herself up, instantly on the defensive. The dimples disappeared. "You *fucked* me and made a baby. I *thought* you'd be happy."

"*Happy?*"

"Don't you touch me!"

"Little late for that, don't you think?" he asked and sank beside her. "You want me to be happy? You tell me I'm gonna be a father, *you're* gonna be a mother, we're supposed to have a baby, and you want me to be happy?"

"Look, I didn't plan this, okay?" she said. "It was an accident. I just found out a couple of days ago, and it threw me at first, too. But I thought it all out. I was just waiting for a good time to tell you."

"I can't believe this," he said. "You know what *I* was waiting for? I was waiting for a good time to tell you to get the fuck out of here. I never asked for this, Max. I never asked you to come in here and take over my life, tell me who I'm supposed to be. I don't need this shit."

Quicker than he could see, she planted a foot in his chest and pushed him hard into the wall. A framed Alvin Ailey poster bounced on its wire, danced off its hook, and crashed to the floor.

"Goddamn you, Quincy, goddamn you to fucking hell, you weak son of a bitch. You can't take it, can you? You're just like all the rest of those sorry motherfuckers. I thought you were special. Always talking about your precious kids."

"Hey—"

"I thought you had what it takes, thought you wanted something, but you just want the pussy, don't you? You just wanna fuck, fuck *this*, nigger." She threw a pillow in his face. "It's about love. It's about going someplace. I thought you could see that. I thought you *knew!*"

"*I* know. I know that kids are real. I know what it's like not to have a father. I know this isn't some goddamn fantasy, and it's *not* gonna happen."

"That's what you think. Talk about too late, well listen up, *Crawdaddy*—isn't that what she calls you?—you're gonna be a sure-nuff daddy now, 'cause I'm having this baby whether you like it or not."

He lunged across the mattress and slapped her hard in the face. "No, I don't think so. I get to vote on this, and I'm not having it."

". . . shit."

"No, listen, cause I'm serious about this. It's no good, Max. We shouldn't even be together anymore, and you can't do this alone."

"You already voted, Quincy. You don't want any part of this, fine. But don't you even think about telling me what I can't do." She began to lift from the bed.

He pitched forward and grabbed her arm. "Max, I'm tellin you—"

"Get the fuck *off* me!" She broke down as she tried to pull free. "You want me out, I'm going," she cried, and then, in his face: "I'll send you a picture."

"*No*, goddammit!"

Her arm came loose, and she took a step away. His leg lashed out, and his shin smacked her stomach. She hit the wooden floor sprawled. He felt the rumble, but the sound was drowned out by one of those piercing Melba Moore screams that plummeted into a growl.

"You *bastard!*"

He stopped, let her voice work him, and stared at her writhing form in the light that floated from the ceiling. He was excited, and didn't move when she turned over in slow motion, reached out for the wine bottle on the floor, and banged it against his knee. He seized her wrist and bent it away from him, pulling her toward him, locked a hand on her neck, watched her face gasp and moan as the pain arrived in his leg and crept up his thigh. She continued to struggle. He brought the arm still holding the bottle down across his throbbing knee and heard the bottle fall. The sweat on their skin loosened his grasp. When she began to fall away, he kicked her and felt his toes caress her. Her feet flailed at him as she retreated, scooting like a crab down the hallway toward the door. He snatched up her clothes, whatever he could grab from the pile near the bed, and threw them down the hall. Then he seized her legs, feeling their strength, and dragged her the rest of the way. He had to let go with one hand to open the door, and she scrambled away. He tackled her from behind. Lifting from where they fell, he pressed against her more tightly than ever, strangling whatever life there was in her smooth stomach and helplessly nibbling her satin back with his panting mouth. There was no yield. He turned her just as she parted his slippery hands, and she fell stumbling into the hallway. Not daring to look at her, he turned, gathered her clothes, dropped them softly onto her, and shut the door.

The darkness dizzied him. He hobbled deeper into it. In the middle of his room, at the point where he could see everything, he paused and focused carefully. She was gone, all of her, three years of her, leaving only distant crying, like a baby's, which drew him to the window. The pain radiating from his leg dropped him into his chair. He lit a cigarette and gazed across the park to the east, toward his son.

He felt the reassuring pressure of the hand on his hip and leaned into the thrill of the brief, sweet tension. Then he was rising, straight and strong, almost magnetically. The release, as always, mesmerized him, until the slap on his arm, which he knew would be coming, broke the spell. He smiled kindly at the kid as he landed—noticing, but not acknowledging, the pain in his ankle—and listened for the soft *chink* as the ball settled, spinning, into the back of the chain net. Two fouls, not worth calling, and the hoop. Next time he'd spin left from the pressure and find out what the tall skinny one could do underneath. And what his ankle could do.

Or maybe not. Gliding backward, he could see that the kid he'd beat wanted to take him. Pounding the ball high and crouching low as he came across the line. Stupid. Elliott offered a path to his right. The kid's eyes grew big, and he damn near palmed the ball in his haste to get by. He got by all right, but by then Elliott had already taken his eager dribble the other way. At the foul line Elliott slowed to consider his options. No point drawing contact, nobody would call it, but that Unseld-looking dude on his team oughtta be chugging up on his left. He started to leave it behind his back on a high bounce, give the boy a moment, but thought to glance over his shoulder first. Son of a bitch had fallen down, so he had to pull it back, jump, spin, pump to gather himself, and toss it up off the board. Ugly. They wouldn't think so, they liked that dipsy-doo shit, but he also knew he was going to have to come down off-balance on his right foot.

Quick-stepping through the landing helped, but not enough. He grabbed the basket support to keep from stumbling and eased back toward the other end, breaking a new sweat. *Play, goddammit. Move!* His kid showed no mercy. In fact, they came at him more than before. Smart. But not a problem. Boy didn't have no outside shot, and he was greedy, so Elliott packed it in, letting himself be posted up. Farther under he went, the less he'd have to make quick moves out front. And though he'd never been a banger, he could lay enough body on the boy to mess with him. He didn't have to jump much for the misses, either, since nobody taught blocking out anymore. Just like doin the bump.

The hard part was on offense. Once it became clear he wasn't interested in driving and wasn't going to take the jay right off, his teammates went crazy dashing out to the wings or camping underneath for a pass. But he wouldn't give it to them unless they got to the right spot, where they could shoot, not play Doctor. He'd hoped for more of a workout for himself, but since the wheels weren't cooperating, he settled for a clinic. Which was cool. The next best thing to getting his own shit off, and sometimes better, was watching somebody's face when he gets a step and, just as he's raising his hand for a pass, finds the ball in it, ready to be launched. If he could make Glenda a shooter, after all, he oughtta be able to do something with these clowns.

But enough was enough. He wouldn't want them to get spoiled. So when they were two baskets from winning, and he had them all cutting across the lane like Havlicek, he faked a lob, all heads turned, and he raced in to throw it down. His shit was sore, it wasn't broke. Then he slacked off on D, the kid went up lazy, and he slapped it out of the air, ran around him, and pushed it up. Top of the key, one more time. Since he couldn't just turn and walk off, his favorite trick—it was his ball—he knelt to retie his sneaker nonchalantly as it rattled the chains and bounced to the ground.

They slapped hands all around, and one even fetched the ball for him. He thanked them, complimented them, and eased on off, knowing at least a few would produce another ball from someplace and stick around—the ones who, next time he found them there, would know better how to make their cuts and maybe even block out some.

He almost forgot his sweatshirt. He was used to having it brought to him, lately by the ball boys but first by Glenda. Right here, day after day after day. She'd rebound his straight-up jumpers for him until she got tired, then sit on the grass, square behind the basket, and he'd chase it down himself, shooting on the run, working the angles like a pool shark. After a while, it got so that when he went up, before he sighted the rim, he would locate the outline of her 'Fro in the dusk—and he could tell whether it would be good by the bush nodding up and down or moving side to side. Strictly speaking, though, her biggest help began when she decided she wanted to shoot, too, and after a couple of weeks of working on her form, then finding her most comfortable spots, he would have her run to them from the other side of the court and hit her with a pass she could handle. That's what made the difference in his game, feeding her and caring that she made the shot. If it hadn't been for her, it never would've happened for him. He never would've left. And where did it get him? Pro arenas and network TV. NIT and Final Four. Sure. And a bogus bust, a fucked-up ankle, and walking papers disguised as a diploma. Lotta shit to end up back in the damn park. With no map.

He dribbled down the hill toward home, mostly with his left—Glenda always told him he didn't use it enough, and she was right. But he didn't know what the hell the point was now. The game could go down as exercise, but this was force of habit. Vanity. No one was going to call. He wasn't even sure if he wanted them to, since he didn't know what he'd do if they did, and didn't believe it would last anyway. The job was the sure thing, and if he wanted a long shot, he should stick to school. That's why he was glad none of the older guys were around, still wearing their college sweats or the gear they'd picked up from training camps and ten-day contracts. Still stuck in the fantasy. A call now would only confuse things, and he didn't need any more choices to make.

He bounced one hard dribble on the wooden front steps to mess with his mother. She'd been telling him since he started playing, at fourteen, not to bounce that ball into the house, but he also knew that she liked the fact that she could hear him coming in. So the game was to see how many dribbles he could get in between the announcement of his arrival and the time she started fussing at him. As an afterthought, he gave it another bounce just inside the door, so he could hear her voice.

"Bubba, didn't I—"

"Think fast, Ma."

He flipped the ball at the figure standing in the hall in a floured apron, which probably meant smothered chops for dinner, and she expertly deflected it with her elbow. Nice move. He grabbed it just before it hit the floor at his feet, tucked it under his arm, and made a great show of bending down to kiss her.

"Get away from me, boy. Act like you got to get down on your knees to kiss me. You know you're not even that tall."

"I know, but you're that short. Where's himself?"

"You know where he is. Game's already started. But wait a minute, honey, we've got to talk. I know you just got home and you want to relax awhile, but when are you going to go talk to the man about that job?"

"Can't talk now, Ma, the game's on. Besides, it's a holiday weekend. Can't do anything for a couple of days anyway."

"All right, go on, but if you see your sister, send her on back to the kitchen. Maybe she can learn something."

Elliott loped into the living room, set the ball down on the floor in front of the sofa, and made himself comfortable, using the ball as a footstool.

"What's fat, man?" Davis said from deep in the easy chair beside the sofa.

"You got it, Big Daddy."

"I thought I was going to have to watch this mess by myself."

"Sorry. It took me a little longer than I thought to teach those boys a lesson."

"It's just that I don't want your mother to think I'm crazy sitting in here by myself talking back to the television set. If you're here, at least it sounds like conversation."

The truth was that Davis didn't really even like basketball. He was a football man at heart. The only basketball player he knew by name, before Elliott started playing, was Wilt Chamberlain, because he was so big and strong. Davis always said he believed that Wilt could have given Ali a good fight, just like Chamberlain had boasted. When Elliott took up the game, though, Davis did, too. He would see that Elliott got to practice, and then he went to all the games. He even took Elliott to the Garden, which Davis hated. It smelled like beer and cigars filtered through stupid white people who he always said would rather watch a bunch of foreigners sliding into one another on the ice with sticks, even when they were losing, than watch black men winning.

Along the way, he had become quite an expert. Of course, he always thought he was an expert about anything he turned his mind to, but Elliott had to admit that the old boy had a pretty good feel for the game. He paid attention to things like setting picks and making outlet passes and working the clock, and even when Elliott's coaches told him to look for his shot, Davis always insisted that a guard's first job was to give it up inside. It was all football strategy, basically: give it to your baddest cat, block for him, and see if they got one can stop him. But it worked, especially in the last few years, when everybody just wanted to jump through the damn hoop, and Elliott sometimes seemed the only one who knew when to keep his feet on the ground. His freshman coach had called him old-fashioned and meant it as a compliment. So it seemed strange that Davis never watched a game unless Elliott was home.

"I still can't believe this team beat Golden State," Davis said during a lull. "They showed nothing all year. And this center they've got is a cream puff."

"The Warriors fell apart, though. You could just see it comin. Bad chemistry. Barry's a punk anyway, and besides, they miss Butch Beard. I told you that was a bad move."

"That Westphal is a smart one, though. I told you that when we had him. I believe they'll take this one. The Celtics appear rather overconfident."

"They might as well take it. It's all they'll get."

"You know what Phoenix's mistake was?"

"Yeah, I know," Elliott said. He'd heard this one before. "They never should have given up Paul Silas."

"That's right. That's a man, right there. You can tell, anybody who looks that foolish in shorts and sneakers, that's a man playing with boys. You can say what you want about Cowens, Silas is the man that makes the Celtics winners. Anyway," he added, glancing over at Elliott, "Phoenix needs another guard."

"I'm too short."

"Who's talking about you? And what about Tiny Archibald? He's no taller than you."

"Yeah, right. He's faster than I was before. With this ankle I'm not even close."

"Well, you could always sue your brother."

Elliott had first broken the ankle, at age ten, swinging from the roof of the back porch on a Spiderman web devised by Quincy.

"What for? He ain't got nothin."

"Well, then."

"Hey, you brought it up, I'm just watchin the game."

"All right, then. I just want to be sure you don't have any regrets."

"No," Elliott mumbled. "Not about that, anyway."

With that, they lapsed back into the easy silence, punctuated by comments on particular plays, that often dominated their sessions—and had always driven Quincy crazy. Whenever he was around and they were watching a game together, he just had to say something. Primitive male bonding, he called it. What were they doing, getting ready to hunt for lions and tigers and bears? Go knock women over the head and drag them back to the cave? You could at least say something once in a while, grunt to let Ma know you're still breathing and whatnot. But Quincy was a fucking mutant anyway—a space alien, Davis called him. What did he know?

Elliott definitely enjoyed the game of basketball, but watching on TV for him was like homework, dating from the time when Davis made him watch in order to learn how to play properly. And Davis loved him some football. But in a way the best times were when they watched baseball, which neither of them cared much for. On slow summer nights, without even thinking about it, they would end up catching a few innings together, Davis with the newspaper and Elliott with a magazine, silently rooting against the Red Nex and soaking in each other's company in a way that nobody else in the house understood. It was like curling up in his father's lap, which Elliott had never done because he had pouted through the years when he could have, while Phine took his place. After spending his first twelve years in Quincy's parallel universe, it felt good to soak up the gestures and inflections of a real man—except for the Barbadian accent, which came and went depending on how serious he was.

Elliott also knew that his time with Davis was a reward for his loyalty after Quincy tried to tear the family apart. Everybody knew that Davis adored Quincy—everybody but Quincy, that is—and wanted his approval, and not just because he was supposedly the man of the house at age eight, when Davis showed up. With that, and Phine being the baby of the family, Elliott was the one left out in the cold, and he'd done everything in his power to drive Davis away. That was the real reason he'd gone along with all of Quincy's crazy schemes that had injured himself, worried their mother, and once damn near burned the house down with Phine in it. But when Quincy took off and Elliott quit fighting, it was like Davis transferred all his energy to Elliott. He was glad for that, but he never completely understood it, either.

"Why'd you put up with all that crap anyway?" Elliott said out of nowhere near the end of the game.

Davis said nothing for a while, as if he hadn't heard the question. "That was a long time ago, son," he finally answered.

Elliott liked the way he never had to explain what he was thinking about. It was still the same way with Quincy, when it happened. "Yeah, but didn't you ever just wanna get away from all this? I know I gave you a pretty hard time, and it's not like you were stuck with me or anything."

"Actually I rather enjoyed it, you know. It could have been worse."

"Yeah, sure."

"Elliott?"

He'd always liked the way Davis said his name. He remembered that from the very beginning, it was a more delicate sound than you expected coming from a man his size. He managed to put the accent on all three syllables at once, and it always came out like a question, usually, What did you do this time? Now it was, So what are you going to do?

"I don't know," he said, fidgeting on the sofa. "I mean, I guess I'll just get a job and settle into the grind. Isn't that the way it's supposed to work?"

"You're supposed to do whatever makes you happy."

"Is that right? Tell you what, I'll be happy if the Celts take it in five. That's about as far ahead as I can figure."

"Better make it six. That white boy knows too much."

"Okay, six, whatever you say. Where's Phine?"

"She better be upstairs getting ready for work."

As the clock ran down on a Phoenix win, Elliott palmed the ball and bounded upstairs. Kool & the Gang were funking from the same box he'd used to blast James Brown in high school, in the room he had all to himself when Quincy moved out. Delphine had moved in when Elliott went off to school five years ago, and now she was about on her way.

"Gimme a bucket of extra crispy," he said when she answered the knock, looking like a magazine ad in her Kentucky Fried Chicken suit. Even though he'd been home for two weeks, he still hadn't gotten used to how grown she looked. She was tall—five seven, easy—and Davis's Indian features, which had messed with her face in adolescence, had actually made her kind of elegant. She'd do all right.

"Game must be over," she said by way of acknowledgment and turned away.

"What you hidin up here for?" he asked, stepping uninvited into the room. Posters of the Jacksons, Reggie and young Michael, hung on the walls, along with the signed Doc J he'd gotten for her. A stack of newspapers sagged in the corner. In fact, it looked like everything to read that came into the house had crawled up in there and died. That was Quincy's influence. Elliott got his comics, but he used to read the girl two books a night. Every night. "Got a lot of homework? I've hardly seen you."

"Some of us have real lives to lead you know, Bubba. Besides, it's not worth it to come down when you and Daddy are playing along with the TV. I might as well be invisible, and Mommy'll just yank me into the kitchen. It's safer up here, thanks. I had some phone calls to make."

Elliott rolled his eyes.

"No, not like that. About the prom."

"Oh yeah, I heard. What's goin on with all that?"

"I'll tell you later. I'm late. I have to ask Daddy for a ride."

"I'll run you over."

"You ready now?"

"Yeah, I was just gonna get a quick shower."

"Never mind."

"Okay. Let's go. I'll just roll down the window."

"Too late, you already stunk up my room."

"Hey, it's still mine, Miss Thing. And you behind on your rent."

Easing down Dorchester Avenue in his Trans Am, he noticed her checking her watch.

"Don't worry, you're on time. So tell me, why is this prom thing so important?"

"You don't understand."

He hated that blasé stuff, but couldn't blame it on her age. She was always like that.

"I know I don't understand, that's why I'm asking. Ma says you've been through hell this year. Personally, I don't know why you bothered."

"I explained all that to you last summer, Elliott. And it's been two years."

"Okay, and I'm real proud of you and everything. Hey, you did it. You got through all that busing crap, did good in school, so why not just walk away?"

"All of us aren't so good at walking away from things."

"Hey, I didn't leave home, remember? That was your other brother. I grew up. I went to school. Big deal, that's what you want."

"That's not what I mean."

"What then?"

"Ask Glenda. You call her yet?"

"Whoa, girl. That's my business. We're talkin about you."

"And that's my business, if you don't mind. Tell Daddy I'll call when I get off."

Three
Delphine

It was only after she had rushed through the door, snatched up her time card without looking, and hit the clock right on the dot that she realized Bubb had spoiled her plan. She had meant to use the ride down to give Daddy a hard time about not letting her drive. It was ridiculous that she had to always wait around for somebody to take her wherever she needed to go. It's not like she was asking for her own car or anything. It probably wouldn't have made a difference anyway, but she would have felt better if she'd tried.

"Can I help someone, please?" she asked, opening the register as quickly as she could. She was supposed to get all squared away before she said anything, especially when it was busy. But that didn't make any sense. If it was her waiting in line she'd just get burned up to see somebody fiddling around like they didn't know what they were doing and not even looking up, like they couldn't see her standing there hungry. Besides, Charlene was cutting her eyes and muttering under her breath, like she was actually late instead of right on time, and like Charlene had never left her for dead on those half-hour-supposedly-fifteen-minute breaks. She just knew one of the boys they kept back in the kitchen or out sweeping the floor could do a better job than Charlene, just like she knew after only six months that she'd make a better manager than that swaggering, pasty-faced fool Frank. But that was policy. Only girls at the counter—like Charlene with her big-tittie self was gonna make somebody order more chicken breasts—black boys out of sight, and white boys in charge. No time to think about that foolishness now, though.

"Uh, lemme see, I'll have, hmm, what come with that three-piece, baby?"

Delphine smiled patiently at the elderly woman who had come over from Charlene's line. Nine times out of ten the first person up wasn't quite ready, which gave her time to collect herself. "Mashed potatoes, biscuit, and cole slaw," she answered.

"Okay, I believe I'll have that, in original recipe. That crispy got too much crisp for me."

"Yes, ma'am. Would you care for anything to drink?"

"No, that's all right, I got me some lemonade at home, you know."

"Coming right up."

As she rang up the order she noticed a few more people switch over to her line.

"Girl, you can have 'em all," a sweating Charlene whispered as they turned to fill their orders.

"Rough day?"

"It's just hot, and I'm tired. I need a break."

"After this rush I'll cover for you, okay?"

"You don't have to tell me twice."

Maybe that was it, the heat. It did get busier when the weather was nice, but even in winter Mommy was always surprised that people would come here on a Sunday, when they should have been at home, cooking and eating with their families. And every time she said it Daddy reminded her that those days were gone, or at least going. People didn't do that stuff anymore, they didn't have enough willpower or whatever to hold it together like before. They'd rather give the white man twice as much money to cook some bad food for them and not have to sit at home and deal with one another. When he talked like that Delphine could never tell for sure if he was saying it was the white man's fault or their own. Probably both, since he was the only one who was right about everything.

Even this job. It took her a while to figure out that he had tricked her into it. She thought it was her idea. Well, it sort of was. She just got tired of begging him for things she needed. A hen would get off her eggs before he'd get up off a dollar. So she went on and got herself this job on weekends and two school nights, still pretty much in the neighborhood, which was good, but not exactly anything fancy, which she figured would bother him. After two pay periods she came home with the sweater of life from Jordan Marsh and a most fly pair of boots, paid for with her own money, thank you, *and* her best report card in two years. And all he said was: "Feels good, doesn't it? I knew you could do it." Damn. She was so mad she *almost* wanted to take the sweater back.

It was a good move anyway, even if he did approve. Besides the money, she got to be out among the folks, the same people Daddy worked with all the time, which was why he probably tried to keep her under wraps. All he saw was their problems, and the worse their problems got, the stricter he got. She always knew things were getting bad when he came home and laid down a whole bunch of new rules that didn't make any sense. Like when he was dealing with a teenage mother and Mommy had to intervene to let her have anything that vaguely resembled some kind of date. Even then he'd show up early to pick her up from wherever, or stand by the front door with the light on if he hadn't insisted on driving himself. Or worse. It took her months to live down the time he actually *came into the theater* and snatched her out of *The Exorcist*. And he had this huge thing about violence against women. Part of the catechism of responsibility he drilled into her was that a woman should do nothing to provoke a man's anger. She of course thought that was incredibly unfair. Just judging from the way he talked about men in the cases he dealt with, it seemed like everything was their fault. He always said there was no excuse for a man attacking a woman, so how was it supposed to be her job to keep it from happening? He told her not to worry about what was fair, and to remember that if she ever let some man misuse her, he would kill her first. That was a nice sentiment.

But what he didn't know wouldn't hurt him—or her—and having this job meant there was more he wouldn't have to know. Like the fact that in a couple of hours Chris would be strolling in with his dimples and freckles and big hair and step to the counter lightly licking his lips and take about fifteen minutes, looking more at her than the board behind her, figuring out an order that was more than one person could eat. Charlene knew she better have her behind in place then, because Delphine was going to take her break eating with her man—and it didn't matter what Frank said, either. Her man . . . Daddy would have a conniption fit. Especially since Chris looked like the kind of mongrel who represented the bastardization of the race and all that other do-wah-diddy. But he was also the one who had helped her through hell on the Other Side, where Daddy didn't want her to be in the first place and where he couldn't have saved her even if she'd wanted him to.

The very first day on the bus to Hyde Park, she remembered, a cho-rus of the O'Jays' slavery song "Ship Ahoy" went up from the back, and they all joined in to break the tension. It became a password for the first few months, something they would say to one another for strength and recognition each day as they were carried off into a new world. It was never like Southie or Charlestown, as Mommy kept reminding her, but it was bad enough. There was a fight about every week for a while. A white boy would get stabbed, a brother stomped, somebody sus-pended, and everybody would protest. There was the everyday harass-ment, the "niggers" and "coons" jumping out of passing mouths between classes, and the bumps and glares and blank stares that were even worse. A whole half year fighting about the pledge of allegiance, which none of the brothers and sisters wanted to say, and you'd think they were spitting on white folks' mothers' graves, as if that crap had meant anything to them before the black folks showed up and re-minded them they were white and therefore American, which didn't mean shit until they could point to somebody else and say they must not be. Coming or going, you could be looking out the window, imag-ining it was just a ride, and have an egg splatter across the window, right before your eyes, painting your view in an ugly yellow ooze, and end up feeling grateful it wasn't a rock, cause then the boys would want to charge off the bus and get into it and the bus driver would have a fit, speed up, and keep the door closed, and you just knew you wouldn't be saying anything to your parents that night and damn sure wouldn't get any work done.

For her, the hardest part was the invisibility. She maintained her status in the tribe, but the tribe had no status and so she didn't, either. No record, no background, no identity. Ten years of report cards, certifi-cates, glee club, volleyball, track, drill team, honor society, all washed away in the land of pink-zit, straggly-head, know-nothing, I-am-God motherfuckers. By spring the first year she was losing weight bad cause she couldn't eat at school, couldn't stand the questions that came with the food at home, and spent every night in a sheet-twisting, teeth-grinding sleep that brought no rest. The doctor said she was working on an ulcer, which, her mother said, was what the same doctor had said about Bubba when he was ten, but this time Delphine knew he was right.

That's when she decided to make her move. Her health improved, but her life got real funky. Everybody wanted to know why she was try-ing to act white all of a sudden, joining clubs, sitting in front of the class with her hand up all of the time (like she had always done before), and generally making a spectacle of herself. And that's when Chris came back in the picture. They'd gone together for a while in ninth grade, one of those one-month things that went bad as soon as he found her hands too strong and somebody else's hair too straight. She'd always liked that kind of silly, young, and safe look about him. Mostly what she liked, and hated, was that he was smarter than he bothered to show, which was not unusual. The kind of guy you thought maybe would be ready on the real side some day but couldn't be bothered waiting for cause someday could be a long, long time. But he was acting like he figured he knew what was going on with her, and he offered his protection on the bus and started walking her home from the stop. He knew she'd always had her mind set on college like her brother and wanted to get her shit together, he told her all big-time and confidential. That was cool with him, cause he had plans too. He was definitely getting out of this bullshit town. Had family in Baltimore and was thinking about Morgan. But he knew she could go just about anywhere and had to play the game to get over. That's what he said.

But that wasn't it, she told him on the steps that afternoon, must have been like November cause it was starting to get dark for no good reason. He wasn't wrong, anyway, that was part of it, but that wasn't the way she was thinking. They didn't have a school anymore—she knew he'd understand cause he wasn't one of those knuckleheads who never had one in the first place. But they needed one. It wasn't just her and college, they used to have like a whole life, teams, colors, traditions, all that stuff. And it was cool, they needed that. If they gave it all up just cause they were in a white school now, they'd be the ones to suffer. Cause they weren't going back to the way it used to be, not anytime soon anyway.

He was nodding but he wasn't getting it. "That's *our* school," she said louder than she meant to. He made one of those shit-it-ain't-none-of-my-school faces and she surprised them both by grabbing his hands. "Look, we remember what we used to have but in a couple of years they won't, the kids behind us. They'll just be like on somebody's plantation and they won't care about anything the way we used to. And then what'll happen?"

"I see, so you wanna like take over?"

"Get our foot in the door anyway. Show em what we got. Let em know we're not goin anyplace, you see what I mean?"

"You somethin else, you know that?"

She squeezed his hands and kissed him. Right on the freckles. Someday can sneak up on you sometime. "So are you. Gotta go. Thanks."

It was easy after that, well, not easy, but not as hard as it had been, cause she wasn't alone. Chris started acting more at home, too, joining things and asserting himself in class, and so did some of the others. She started working on the newspaper, ran for student council, and reorganized the drill team, but this time it had to be integrated. Beth, a perky little pain-in-the-ass blonde, became their token. The only white girl who dared to hang, she got to be something like a friend to Delphine, which kind of surprised everybody but Beth herself. Delphine had to admit that Beth had helped to make life tolerable, even though Chris didn't have much use for her.

Charlene returned from her second Salem break still muttering, with Frank barking at her because the evening lines were already forming. But that was all right because he was there, easing his way toward her with his floppy cap slung low over his right eye.

"And something for you, young man?"

"Yeah, let's see. Whatcha got good?"

"Everything you see."

"Well all right. I definitely want me some dark meat—lotta leg and thigh, you know. I could use a couple of those hot biscuits, too, you know what I mean?"

"Anything else?"

"You all are too much," Charlene said, rolling her eyes.

"We're here to serve the customers, Charlene," Delphine said, still staring at Chris.

"Yeah, yeah, just feed the boy already. And I ain't talkin bout no chicken," she added.

After she prepared his order, Delphine closed down her register and joined him at the far-corner table she preferred, by the window, where she could keep an eye out just in case Daddy came early. He never had, but you never knew. They ate mostly with sly smiles and small talk and legs rubbing under the table. Chris was still waiting to hear from Bowie State about financial aid; if they didn't come through he was looking at Suffolk Community and a part-time job. Delphine thought he'd be playing himself cheap if he did that, but they'd already had that argument. Also, part of her thought that he might be willing to settle because she was staying in town to go to BU, and she wasn't sure how she felt about that. It turned out they were both going to be tied up with family stuff on Memorial Day—and she was going to put in some overtime with the Colonel—so he asked what she was doing after school on Tuesday. She confessed that she was getting together with Beth about the prom. His face turned sour, as she knew it would.

"Delphine, do you hafta still be messin with that business?" he nearly whined.

"Just a little while longer. It's going to be good, you'll see. We'll have fun."

"Yeah. If it happens. And if I go."

She hated to see him sulking that way, and didn't like the idea that school politics messed with their own thing so close to the end. But dammit, this was important, and everything was happening so fast. He ought to understand.

Beth was the one who had clued her in that the white kids were planning it all by themselves, like nobody else was graduating. So Delphine got herself right on the committee and let everybody know that this here was going to be a two-tone affair. They didn't like it, but she had the backing of the administration, some of them anyway, who didn't want the publicity if the blacks raised hell about getting left out, because things had finally settled down and the school wanted to play the same at-least-it-ain't-Charlestown tune Mommy had been humming all year. The white kids thought the blacks wouldn't show anyway, and judging from Chris's first reaction, they had a case. At least he didn't try to stop her, and he finally agreed to help talk it up and mumbled a promise to take her if it came to that, which he obviously hoped it wouldn't.

He almost got his wish, too. Toward the middle of May, a brother who sometimes hung with Chris, a pretty good student who never made any trouble, was stopped coming out of class by the physics teacher, who accused him of stealing somebody's super-duper slide rule. Didn't matter that Randy had his own. The kid who lost it swore that Randy, the only brother in the class, must've took it cause he had let him check it out a few days before. Randy was about to give up his bag to prove it, cause he knew he didn't have the doggone thing and wanted to put a stop to the fuss, but the teacher snatched it away first and started pawin at it. That was too much even for Randy. He grabbed the bag back, the teacher went for it again and caught him upside the head, and Randy smacked him in the mouth. Just as the vice principal was coming by.

Randy was suspended, but not for stealing. The slide rule turned up in somebody else's locker—the owner forgot he had told a friend he could use it. He was suspended for assaulting a teacher, which was more serious, and at that point in the term would mean he probably couldn't graduate. When word got out, all the black students walked out of class, marched through the school, and threatened to boycott the rest of the year. But that wasn't half of it.

A few days later a bunch of the whites skipped school to go to some antibusing rally downtown and got arrested for chasing a black man on his way to work—a lawyer, no less, dressed up and probably making better money than they ever would—and beating up on him. Didn't happen on school property, though, so they didn't get suspended, just detention for skipping. That about did it. The black parents got into it, went to a big meeting at the school, first time some of them had ever seen the place, and said they would not only support the boycott but help keep the white kids out, too. Shut down the whole place for the rest of the year. The school couldn't deal with all that. They reinstated Randy and suspended the white kids for a week, and they still had to face criminal charges, which probably wouldn't amount to much, but the blacks were hoping that brother lawyer would sue their asses off for the next two, three generations.

By the time all that went down the white kids were ready to call off the prom altogether, they were so pissed, but Delphine knew they'd still manage to work something out on the side and the blacks would get shafted. That's when she and Beth came to each other with the plan. Beth was one of those girls who had always thought about her prom like her wedding and couldn't stand the thought of doing without, she didn't care who did what to who. She wanted the real thing, too, not some little after-hours on-the-side. Delphine felt sort of the same way, but it was more, really, the principle of getting her due like she'd been working for the whole time. Beth knew enough other white girls who wanted the prom regardless, and Delphine figured she could get the black kids to go for something if it would mess with the white kids' plans. So the girls got together and did it themselves, for themselves—they were the ones who were going to do all the work anyway.

On the phone, in lunchroom huddles, and at drill team practice they worked out a simple plan. To avoid trouble and keep everybody happy, they would have two proms, one white and one black, at the same place on the same night: two shifts, with pretty much the same decorations but two different servings and separate bands. The cost was a bigger strain on the blacks, cause there weren't as many of them and they had less money. But Chris had the idea to get in touch with the lawyer they'd messed over, and he gave a little. And Daddy, bless his heart, got in touch with some civil rights folks who came up with a little bit more to support the idea, even though they wanted it kept quiet cause the separation thing wasn't really supposed to be where they were at.

She started getting some grief from white kids at school then. Scary looks, a shove here and there, even a threatening note in her English book. She didn't tell Chris or Beth or anybody about that part. It would only mess everything up. Meanwhile, in order to make the white boys go along with the plan, Beth organized her own boycott. No dates, no nookie, no nothin unless the boys played ball. The brothers didn't want to hear about that part, but by then most, like Chris, had more or less agreed to go anyway.

"You're really gonna like my dress," she coaxed as he sullenly finished off his apple pie.

"You know my partners think I'm some kinda idiot for gettin caught up in all your stuff," he said.

"They do?"

"Yeah." He slid his eyes over her and then couldn't help smiling. "But I just tell em don't be puttin no badmouth on my baby, now. If she says that's the right move, she must know what she's talkin about."

"Really?" She took hold of his hand.

"I don't always believe it, mind you. But that's what I say."

They both laughed and she snuggled in close to him. He really was a sweet thing, and moments like this always brought the words of that Chaka Khan song into her head: *Love me now or I'll go crazy.*

Most of her friends already thought she and Chris had made that move, so she didn't want to talk to any of them about it. But the expectation, his and hers, weighed on her. Having Bubb back at home just made things worse. He liked to try playing big brother sometimes, but that mostly meant just asking a lot of questions, not listening. Besides, he had his own problems in that department. At least she had Quincy. He'd already heard the call of the wild and freed himself. He understood all of her longings; she could tell him anything. God, what would she do without him?

Four
Quincy

When the sun began to appear, Quincy finally rose from the chair and began to clean out the apartment. He stripped the sheets off the bed. He gathered the clothes she left there for after work and weekends— jeans, shoes, tops, a few pieces of underwear—and jammed them in a paper bag, topped off with her toothbrush and various potions that had worked their way from the rim of his bathroom sink into his medicine cabinet. A long shower washed her smell from his body.

Then, depositing the paper bag in the trash can by the front steps, he crossed Morningside and started down through the park. It was safer than most thought, sometimes even at night. The secret was to look like you belonged—and like you didn't have anything worth taking. Then it became simply a backdoor passage, his own Batcave. He worked his way south and east, to the edge of Central Park and around, behind the hospital, under the tracks, all the way over to First Avenue. And as he made his way, the lightness of his step reminded him that he had been treading in quicksand for three and a half years.

It was never what he wanted. He just kind of fell into it, cruising down Broadway when he caught sight of her ass easing around the corner. It had kind of a lazy, country sway to it—out of place even in an area full of non-natives, where most attempted a version of the typical uptown hustle or somehow called attention to themselves (like Fontelle's, which he had discovered near that very spot). It was nice enough, by itself not worth much more than a few steps' worth of hard looking. But she carried all of herself that way, and that's why he slowed down to identify the species. Too tight to be called sassy, not bold enough to be regal. Casually precious. Fully formed, and content, for the moment, to be out of step. A first-year grad student, he decided as he fell into her wake. Maybe from a black college, definitely from some all-black, non-ghetto environment. Someplace she'd be known as medium brown, which meant a little on the dark side, and where her restrained voluptuousness would count as both character and charm. He tried to figure whether, if he talked to her, she would straight-up ig him or offer some chilly, slightly too proper put-down. It would be one or the other, neither particularly interesting, and he wasn't sure he wanted to talk to her anyway yet, so he watched her on down a ways.

When she paused at the bookstore, he knew what play to run. He hadn't done that since his freshman year when, using a technique he'd developed at Harvard Square, he cornered a slight, exotic-Jewish sensitive type in the poetry section. The hit was good for a couple of transition weekends before they both moved on. He had known he didn't want to get sidetracked in a white thing anyway (was that his Sly or his Huey period?), and she turned out later to be gay—and a pretty good poet, actually—so it was cool all around. In a way, he was a freshman again, a month into Teachers College, back in the fishbowl after a treacherous year out on the open seas, a year that had convinced Fontelle, who had cut him adrift in the first place, that he was some kind of pussy pirate.

He could never see it that way himself and wasn't intent on plunder when he reached out ahead of the sashaying stranger to open the bookstore door. It was not an anonymous gesture; he gave it enough personality—yes, this is for *you*—to invite a pleasant acknowledgment, which might have been enough to send him on his way. Nothing doing, we wanted to be a hinkty bitch today, so he recommitted to the mission. Checking her direction, he looped around and took up a position by the magazines, blocking the aisle she'd be coming through, so she'd have to say "Excuse me" or "Kiss my ass" or something to prove she had a voice. Instead, it was a testy (but surprisingly resonant) "Do you mind?" He stepped forward without looking up and noted her destination. He gave her almost ten minutes before he followed. Luckily, he wanted to check out *Mumbo Jumbo* as a funky example of literature as history and so didn't feel entirely depraved. He found her in political science, working the shelves like a researcher, trying to locate information, not just a book. He liked that and stood at the end of the aisle openly admiring her diligence. The moment he forgot he was stalking—he should have been scheming a way to force a conversation—she turned as if expecting him and spread a dimpled, front-porch smile. That was enough, too much, and by the time she made her choice he had fled with Ishmael Reed and some funny hoodoo vibes.

A few weeks later, depressed by Nixon's easy victory and a half semester's teachings that contradicted most of what he knew about children and schools, he went down to check out Roy Ayers at Mikell's on the Upper West Side, where Fine Young Negroes with Good Jobs had begun to cluster in increasing numbers, bumping up against the older, intellectual crowd. He was also pissed about what he'd heard had gone down with Bubb and his girl. The kid didn't say it straight out—he'd had to read between the lines on the phone, and Phine filled in the blanks in a letter. It shouldn't have been that big a deal, but it *was* to his baby brother, who had a heart like Jell-O and didn't deserve a kick in the ass like that. He was thinking about borrowing a car and running up to Amherst to check the kid out. Maybe he could do something to make it better. Like he used to.

First things first, though. Between sets, he noticed a honey-hued newcomer at the bar, black-stockinged legs snaking out of a tight, short skirt. I got your four more years, Tricky. Maybe it won't be so bad after all. He slid into a convenient vacancy beside her, signaled David for another Dewar's, and asked if he could get her something. She looked doll eyed at him and back to her half-full wineglass, considered her options like a child choosing a toy, and finally (before the impatient but considerate bartender moved away) nodded yes. She turned toward Quincy and thanked him. As he responded, preparing to build his case for repayment, he noticed her eyes shift away, behind him.

"Do you mind?"

Quincy took a step back from the bar, yielding the space to its rightful owner, Miss Lazybutt from the bookstore herself.

"I think my friend would like another vodka tonic," the first said both to the bartender, delivering her wine, and to Quincy.

"Of course," he said, surrounded.

"Max, will you watch my drink, uh, drinks? I'll be back."

Quincy breathed deeply and watched the skirt call attention to itself bopping away from the bar. Tag team. He paid for the three drinks. Put his wallet back calmly. Sipped his scotch. Watched number two settle into her seat and study her vodka. Ignoring him, as he thought the first time, but then, he hadn't said anything yet. And he was less sure than before if he cared to. Her friend's skirt sure was working.

"You're welcome," he said at last, on general principle.

"Thank you." She spoke over her shoulder. He didn't need this. "So how was it?"

"A little draggy," he mumbled, surveying the crowd. "They sounded like I feel."

"No, not the band. I mean the book. *Mumbo Jumbo.*"

"Damn, you've got good eyes," he said and, looking at them as they now measured him, decided he meant it.

"I'm in journalism. I notice things. I tried to read him before but it was too freaky for me."

Yeah, but not for your friend, I bet. He stole a glance toward the ladies' room. "Well, then don't bother. It's more of the same. But better. What else do you notice?"

"Are you in English?"

"No. I was. I teach high school. Taking a break to get my master's."

"You don't look like a high school teacher."

"Oh yeah? What do I look like?"

She repositioned herself to take all of him in. The smile that had startled him in the aisle of the bookstore made a quick appearance, but he knew it was less for him than for the guessing game. She crossed one leg smoothly over the other and held it. Her skirt, not as short as her friend's, crawled up her medium-brown thigh. A delicate hand with clear-polished nails rested there a moment and rose to the side of her head, drawing his eyes back to hers. It was a steady gaze, not playful or even challenging. Neutral, like a camera.

"A writer," she said.

He blinked. Drank some scotch. She was waiting.

"Why would you say that?"

"The way you held the book. The way you look at things and see something else."

"Like what?"

"Like me."

"Max, was it?"

"Maxine Love." She held out her hand.

"Quincy Crawford." He took it.

The glass and a half of wine remained on the bar when they retreated from the noise of the second set. He needed to hear her better because she wanted information, not conversation, and he felt compelled to give it. It had been more than a year since he had spoken to anyone but Fontelle about the stories, longer since he'd mentioned the more expansive writer's dreams that seemed lost forever in his hunt for experiences to justify them. She absorbed all he said, without judgment, and added little about herself except the certainty that she would become a White House correspondent. And she spoke, for the record, about the election and politics in general and the way they were covered, and about education and literature. All the things he knew her friend would not have talked about, and that he hadn't known he wanted to.

The conversation continued without the slightest overt sign of flirtation, right up to the moment in his room when she took the book he'd been reading aloud, Morrison's *The Bluest Eye,* from his hand and unbuttoned his shirt and kissed his nipple. And he tasted the medium brown of her shoulder and the peekaboo thigh. And he wondered for the first time where everybody had gone, the ghosts of seductions past who always came out to greet a new playmate. When he fell into her she spoke again. Her precise pronunciations melted to a near-demonic whisper that asked no questions but told him what she was going to do to him and for him, conjuring up a ready-made vision of some jointly ambitious future, and the more she said the deeper he drove to find the source of the spell that banished all others and held him fast. The bed frame groaned; he thought it was him. She wrapped him up like a baby and cushioned the impact when the mattress dropped. She cried out, he cried, and she held his face with both hands an inch from hers.

"Tell me what you see," she demanded.

He had never been able to, had never really known what kind of answer she wanted. But it didn't seem to matter. Things were nice and easy between them for the rest of that year. She obviously had some kind of agenda but was mostly cool with it. She knew he was still frying other fish. But her presence had been useful. It continually reinforced the question What do you see? and reminded him that he ought to be seeing something, that his life should have more clarity. It had allowed him to concentrate on his studies and, at the same time, on his writing: she was big on that. And there were those bottom-soil thighs to till, although planting seeds had never been part of the plan.

It was when she left at the end of the school year to take that job in Cleveland that he had realized how much the hypnosis had worked on him. The apartment filled again with ethereal, unseeing strangers—including her eel-hipped roommate from Mikell's—who provided late-night distraction but no daylight focus. Even others who came to be more, like Mariela and Bernie, ultimately failed to satisfy him because, ironically, they never bothered to lie about a future he didn't believe in anyway.

And then, just as Max returned, the past ran up on him on a Saturday twilight here on First Avenue. He was on his way to meet her for their first reunion date, though he had no idea how he had wandered over that way. He paused to use the pay phone to confirm their plans or to see if she had left yet—he remembered being anxious to see her. As she spoke into the phone, he glanced down the street and saw them, the woman and the boy. And he knew, but he froze. Panicked. Chose the siren voice in his ear over the unimaginable testimony of his eyes. Completed the conversation—"Good to hear you too, baby," blasé, blasé—and when he hung up and looked back they were gone. There was still time, of course, to search and confront, and he did in fact force himself to walk to the end of the block and gaze into the project maze. Then he looked to his watch, remembered the fresh promise and the hypnotic voice and the casually precious ass, and headed downtown.

It was easy enough to blame it on Max and not think about it. Maybe he hadn't seen what he knew he had seen, and in any case it wasn't really his problem. No contract, no obligation. He didn't even know her name. Maybe that was why he let Max in deeper the second time around, allowed himself to become more vulnerable to her hoodoo. So he could forget. She had already moved into a sublet in walking distance of Lincoln Center and the TV station, but he soon found himself, under her direction, rearranging the furniture that had been left behind and setting up new stuff, like the bed. Which meant that her place had the potential to become theirs, as it threatened to during the first few weeks, when he would meet her at the station after the late news and spend the night. It didn't take long for him to determine that they should spend more time uptown, in the undomesticated space that he wanted to believe remained his own, even after she parked her toothbrush and chased the other spirits away.

And all that time, he let himself think that she could help once again to sharpen his vision. That she would be good for his work. Hadn't Reeves called about the stories right after her reappearance? Soon, though, he could see all too clearly that the question could not also be the answer. Though neither her presence nor his desire had faded, his attention had. Good as they were together, they were too often out of phase. She thought he was wasting his time and talent teaching dead-end kids; he should start work on a real book, maybe go for a Ph.D. to teach at the college level. She was intent on taking him somewhere that he didn't want to go. And he couldn't make her understand his reluctance because he didn't understand it himself. All he knew was that he was determined to keep moving, to maintain the trajectory he had established when he blasted out of Dorchester vowing to avoid domestic entanglements—including the unmentioned vision on First Avenue—which could only lead to disappointment because nothing was forever.

He had to make her see that. It wasn't personal. Maybe her dreams and schemes could work. For her. But not with him, and not, ever, at the point of a shotgun. If there was anything positive in this alleged accidental—and additional—germination, it was that it had forced his hand and freed him once and for all from her spell.

It was still early when he plunged through the bottle-littered courtyard of the projects, past the spare little metal climbing structures and the beat-to-death basketball court. He himself would have had little use for either; he always wanted more space or less, either a yard or a park with views or a quiet room where his mind could go where it wanted. In fact, it was only sometime after he left, he couldn't say when, that Bubb had joined that strange cult of little men who measured their space and time on paved plots and never looked higher than the rusted orange rim.

The thought depressed him as he crossed the pocket parking lots and climbed the steps over the FDR to the bridge spanning the East River, where he could meet the sun halfway as it pulled free of Queens. As a teenager in Boston, he used to wander over to the strip of grass by Memorial Drive, watch the carefree scullers on the Charles, and marvel at the distance from that world to the 'Bury, Dorchester, and Franklin Park. At how little those worlds knew of each other and how simple geography and architecture could enforce such a gap. It was more frustrating here because everything seemed even closer—he had just crossed over within blocks of the Columbia campus—but at the same time more confining. From the stultifying aeries behind him, Rikers was both a more visible and more likely destination than the spires of midtown.

Satisfied that the day had begun and he was where he needed to be, he submerged himself in the waking-up sounds of the neighborhood, went back to the avenue to pick up a *Daily News* from the corner bodega (Max could never understand that there were some times that didn't call for the *Times*), and staked out a bench by one of the project entrances. The spot was near a pay phone, the same one he'd used to call Max that evening more than a year ago.

He read inside out, starting with the funnies and taking his time, and listening. To the grocers setting up across the street, the winos stirring, the women heading out to downtown cleaning jobs, the kids flooding the street in search of nothing in particular, all to the background of cars, cabs, trucks, and buses flocking up First like large, noxious birds. Until finally, he looked up as if someone had called his name. There, racing toward him as energetically and recklessly as a puppy, was a little boy, the same boy, wearing tiny jeans, red sneakers, a navy jacket, and one of those blue "Little Slugger" baseball caps that all little boys seemed to grow like hair. His had been red, Bubb's blue. The small eyes did not come his way—they were fixed on the Canaan land of the far side of the avenue—but Quincy's locked on him like a tracking beam. He had made creation, in some form, his life's work, but not creating life. How could he finish a story he had never intended to begin?

"Easy," he said softly but anxiously as the child hurtled past.

But it was another sound, a sharp *"Hold it!"* from around the corner of the building, that projected an invisible force field in front of the boy; he stopped as if the air were solid.

"Told you," Quincy said.

The boy turned then to Quincy for the first time with an annoyed, no-fair look. Then, rather than stand still in shame, he got the inspired notion of going back to where his mother was cruising into view. But first he grinned at Quincy and shrugged: it was worth a shot. The woman moved with the slow, hippy confidence that nothing important would get away from her and that nothing she feared would catch up. That was one way to survive among so many people in such cramped quarters, by existing deliberately within your own space/time continuum, rather than dashing in and out of everybody else's as most did. And because of that, she seemed just as old and as young as she wanted to be, the probable lack of a future balanced by the nonburden of past. She glanced at Quincy briefly, too, long enough to judge him not a threat. He was still staring when she looked a second time, like maybe he almost reminded her of somebody she thought she'd seen, once, and the look jolted him into uncertain readiness, but she ignored him in favor of the blue bundle bounding back up into her arms. Pretending anger, she hauled the boy past Quincy, who had gone back into his paper, then pointedly set him down at the curb, took his hand, and waited for the light.

As they stepped off, Quincy lowered the paper. They were almost to the other side before the boy, who had already pulled, dragged, and looked around in every direction, cast a thoughtless, smiling look back over his shoulder, toward the bench. Barely two, the boy knew his way around his world well, and was looking for other ways. And he was only one child. How many others knew what they wanted and didn't know that they couldn't have it? And what would happen when they found out? Quincy twitched with an urge to rise, dash across the street, and say something. Isn't that what he had come here for? But this time, with no distraction to pull him away, it was also clear that he had little to offer. He hadn't been able to protect Bubb, had all but lost Carlos. Hell, he was still looking around for ways out himself. No, the best he could do—all he could do—was to keep it from happening again. And so he sat, without breath or strength, until mother and child disappeared down the street, the truth again gone from view. Then slowly he stood, wiped his eyes, left the paper on the bench, and set out for the West Side, determined to stop history from repeating itself.

When he reached Max's building, he charged up the stoop and buzzed. No answer. He leaned on the buzzer for a full ten seconds. Nothing. He stepped out into the middle of the street, eyed the turquoise Levolor blinds they'd special-ordered from Bloomingdale's, and shouted her name. As if she were simply late for a date, or he had lost his key, or hadn't kicked the crap out of her the night before.

"What're you, Marlon Brando?" kibbitzed a bemused middle-aged man parking his car nearby. "Rehearsing for *A Streetcar Named Desire?*"

Quincy shrugged and called up again. Maybe she wasn't there. But where else would she have gone at that hour? He would have felt better if she had yelled back, or even thrown a plant at him. He was starting to get pissed and scanned the curb for a rock.

"If she's there, I don't think she's going for it, my friend," the nosy parker offered. "Why don't you let the neighbors have some peace? Listen, you try flowers? Works for me."

Defeated for the moment, Quincy wandered back up Broadway, retracing the fifty-block route he had sometimes walked to meet Max. At his end, he would move easily among the people for whom it was still early, who didn't give a shit about the news she was preparing; midway, he could tell which citizens were heading home precisely so they could see it. By the time he got to this point, where the West Side flowed into midtown, the city had changed completely—it was whiter, quieter, and slower, although still with enough upscale party people and hustlers, illegal and legal, to make it a far cry from the Back Bay. This morning it was even quieter, the first holiday weekend of summer having pulled away whole layers of people who believed in being elsewhere whenever possible, even if it took them half the weekend to get there and back.

He paused, as always, to check the window of Charivari, a clothing store that was for him the symbol of the New Broadway of the Pretty People, a Walt Frazier, Studio 54, fuck-you-if-you-can't-hang kind of place. It was hard enough to imagine people wearing these vines to work, harder to imagine *where* they worked in order to afford the shit. Studying a full-length leather coat draped on a disdainful-looking mannequin, he recognized a tall, light-skinned, handsome man emerge from the store with a classy black plastic bag containing a shoe box. And wondered how much they cost. And whether they'd been bought with any of his money.

"Hey, Sheldon."

"Crawford, how you doin, man?" he said, greeting Quincy as warmly as if they'd planned to meet for brunch. "I've been trying to call you."

He said it as if he actually believed it. Maybe he'd been thinking about trying, but he sure as hell hadn't dialed. They hadn't spoken since March, and Quincy had been calling him every week for a month then. Soon, he'd said. He'd have everything together.

"Okay, so what were you gonna tell me?"

Sheldon grinned and patted Quincy on the shoulder. "Hey, don't look at me like that, man. What, you think I was gonna tell you the warehouse burned down or something? Come on up to the crib and I'll show you."

Sheldon Reeves had been an editor, agent, would-be independent publisher, and jive-time motherfucker-about-town. But maddening as his too-smooth manner could be, he was always about business, always hustling. The shoes he carried in the Charivari bag, a write-off for sure, were presumably intended to dazzle some prospective client as much as to satisfy his own vanity. Quincy had gotten his name from a guy at school, back when they all believed they were going to take the Second

Black Renaissance to higher ground. Reeves was just starting out as an agent then, having shucked the bonds of junior editorship at Random House. Quincy knew *he* was bad, so he sent his stuff just to see if the dude could handle it and was surprised when Reeves called in two weeks and invited him to lunch. They did Hunam at Broadway and 100th and Reeves didn't play him cheap, even though he was still an undergraduate. They talked for two hours about writing and the business, where things were heading, and how only a handful of agents and even fewer editors understood what was happening.

But Reeves also told him there was probably nothing he could do then. The stories were terrific, but nobody was ready for youth-oriented stuff coming from a black man. Unless it was Superfly shit, which was getting old anyway. Everybody wanted women. And the Black English thing was probably too far out, wouldn't play. If Quincy wanted to get something out there, he should think about changing his approach. But Reeves's advice was to fuck it and keep writing; he was young and the future would take care of itself. What Quincy remembered most about the conversation was that it took him a few days to get mad. Getting screwed and being made to feel good about it at the same time was a new experience, but he knew from practice on the other end that it took skill.

For that reason he respected Reeves and was ready to bend over again when he called out of the blue two years later. He was about to gear up his own line, he said, and wanted to take another look at those stories if Quincy would be willing to fix them up a little. Quincy hesitated; had the market changed that much? Reeves, he remembered, laughed into the phone. "Hey, I was talking about selling then," he'd said. "Now I'm talking about buying. It doesn't matter what anybody else thinks as long as I like the shit, you know what I mean?" Max was in the picture then, and her ambition coupled with Reeves's casual flattery pushed him into action. He polished the whole manuscript, adding in some new stuff, revising the old, in six weeks. Then Reeves disappeared. Took him two months to acknowledge receipt of the manuscript, six months more before he offered half a piss-ass advance to tie up the rights. He knew Quincy didn't have any other options, and Quincy realized he was stockpiling. Reeves wasn't about to publish his own phone number, let alone anybody's goddamn book. By the time Max faded to Cleveland, they never even mentioned the manuscript anymore.

Then, last year, she brought him back, almost as if she had made him up in the first place. She'd been in town maybe a month when he called. He'd started teaching at City when things were slow to get off the ground, and he chatted on about the Jews pulling up the ladder, lowering standards, and charging tuition. Like they talked about shit in general all the time. When Quincy asked about the manuscript, Reeves said no problem, he was ready to get on with it if Quincy still wanted to deal. He'd pay the rest of the advance when the book was ready. Quincy wanted to think that, if not for Max's renewed enthusiasm, he would have told Reeves to take a hike. But he knew that was a lie.

It didn't surprise him, then, that he would run into Reeves now, when he'd been out looking for Max. It meant that she was still working him, but he didn't know if it was supposed to be good karma or payback. He didn't know what to expect anymore, and Reeves had done nothing to relieve his anxiety. He walked the way he did business: slowly, with frequent stops and much talk. Every time Quincy tried to force the pace, the back of Reeves's hand caught his upper arm, blocking him as Reeves gestured to make a point.

"We're almost there, man. Relax."

Quincy shot an annoyed look at him. He hadn't known he was being that obvious, but he didn't care.

Reeves laughed and slapped him on the back. "Say this cat got my *money*, right? You want me to shut the fuck up, don't you?"

"Sheldon?" Quincy said, breaking down. "Shut the fuck up and show me what you got."

Sheldon laughed harder, squeezed Quincy's arm, and steered him into the lobby. Quincy had been to his place once, three years before when he dropped off the manuscript. It hadn't changed. A large, prewar building, it still harbored faint pretensions that linked it to its grander cousins on Central Park West and kept it above the others fading fast on Amsterdam. The key feature was the elevator, which had to be operated manually by an employee, who therefore doubled as a half-assed doorman. But the game was exposed by the man on duty, who resembled a raggedy Sammy Davis in a greasy wig and seemed like the kind of person he should be trying to keep out.

"Nice day, huh?" he said, pocketing the cigarette he'd been about to light. He shuffled with a slight limp to join them in the elevator and took his time closing the polished metal door, then the inner grate. "Maybe I get over to the park this afternoon. Thought you'd be gone this weekend, Mr. Reeves. Everybody takin off, you know."

"Too much work to do, Hector," Sheldon said and winked at Quincy. "Step on it, my man's in a hurry."

"You wanna step, better take the stairs," Hector said, staring ahead and chuckling. "You know this thing don't go but so fast."

Sheldon's apartment was a large mess, which Quincy took as a sign of encouragement. At least he was working, even if he hadn't made enough to put all this shit somewhere. The living room was filled with cartons, the table in the middle of it spread with bookkeeping crap, and the sofa weighted with manuscripts and page proofs. Underneath, it was the kind of sturdy, spacious apartment Quincy supposed he would want if he ever thought about those things, and back when Reeves was an editor it had probably looked as good as he did.

"This is what happens when you do business at home, man. It ain't pretty, but it saves money. I know you can appreciate that."

"What is all this?"

"That's a report on world hunger. Got a foundation contract to produce it, now I just gotta move it out of here. That's what solved the cash flow, but it held up everything else—your stories, got a collection of black feminist poetry, and a thing on South Africa. Brother at Michigan did it for his dissertation but the traditional academic press wouldn't touch it. It's pretty hot. I knew I wanted it but it took some persuading. He wasn't sure how it would look, you know. I told him, hey, a book's a book, and if I do it, it won't die up there in the library. People will read the motherfucker."

"Now this over here is what'll probably interest you the most." He high-stepped over to one of the smaller cartons, which was open, and plucked a slim volume off the top. "There you go, my man. It's real."

Quincy held the paperback in awestruck silence. Only six by nine and less than an inch thick, it had the weight of a Norton anthology. In bold yellow type on a solid red background were the words he'd seen so often in simple black-and-white he'd never pictured them any other way: *De Voodoo Spell and Other Stories by Quincy Crawford*. On the back, the faces of him and Bubb stared out at him from twenty years ago as if they'd been waiting to meet him here, at this moment. Quincy sat straight down, crushing the corner of a carton, set the book down to dry his hands, then gingerly picked it up again.

"So say something, man. You like it? Sorry I didn't get a chance to run the cover by you. I had a tight deadline with the presses."

"Goddamn, Sheldon, you did it."

"Yeah, how about that? You are a published motherfucker, man. You know I told you before, none of this may show up in B. Dalton and Brentano's for a while, but there's a good network of independent bookstores out here that can sell this stuff. That's what you want anyway, people who aren't just shoppin for magazines and calendars. Nobody's gettin rich here, but that's not the point, right?"

"I don't believe it," Quincy said, and looked into the carton.

"Yeah, there's more all right. I must've printed at least a dozen."

"What?"

"I'm kidding, man, there's plenty. I'll have a few sent over to your place. Meanwhile, come on over here."

From the pile on the table, Reeves produced a large, bound checkbook and began filling a check out. He was still on the first page—not a good sign. But Quincy had no cynicism left when Reeves handed him the check for $500. It didn't even matter that fame and fortune amounted to just two months' rent.

"You know I'm at the bank with this at eight o'clock on Tuesday," he said.

"Tuesday's good. Don't wait till next week, though," Reeves replied with a wink that no longer irritated. "Congratulations, Quincy."

"I don't know what to say, Sheldon."

"Just go tell your lady she was right to believe in you. And have a good time. I'll be in touch."

It was all Quincy could do to keep from running all the way home like a thief with a hot diamond in his pocket. Besides not wanting to seem a fool, it helped that he wanted to move slowly enough for passersby to read the title he carefully held visible between spread fingers. Inside, the book reactivated the vibes he'd cleaned out that morning, and he went straight to the desk to call Max. It couldn't change anything about last night, he knew—that would be a mistake. But maybe it meant something. She was the one who had made it happen, in a way. This was the vision of him she'd had in the bookstore that afternoon, the recollection that seduced him the night they hooked up at Mikell's. *Be there, dammit.* It had to be now. This was the sign, the fulfillment of the spell.

Twenty rings later, he knew he had it wrong. It wasn't happening. A tree falls in the forest, and it doesn't mean shit. With his hand still covering the receiver, he thought to call Bubb. The stories were their story, after all, and after the kid had pretended not to be impressed with the first piece Quincy had shown him years back, he'd never mentioned the collection. Or how he hoped, subconsciously, that the telling could reach back over the last ten years of confusion and resentment. But the phone wouldn't do it. He'd have to put the book in the boy's hand, maybe even sit on him and read the damn thing to him to make him understand. Quincy sat back, flipped the pages of the book, and glanced up at the heroic oil portrait of himself on the wall. And then he knew what to do. The message had been there all along, through all the writing, the revision, the negotiation. Even before Max's vision. Without pausing to recall the number, he leaned forward to dial Jersey.

Five

Elliott

"**K**night to king's bishop three."

It had taken a full week, after Elliott had finally decided to call, to figure out what to say. And then Erika answered. What's a three-year-old
kid doing answering the phone? he wondered. What kind of mother is
she anyway? Maybe this was all a mistake; she wasn't who he thought she
was. Turned into one of those women passed out on the sofa with a bottle of vodka. In the bedroom humping "Uncle" somebody while the
child sat watching shoot-em-ups on TV. Or worse, out somewhere, and
the girl would stick her finger in a socket or end up on the front page
of the *Herald* as a charred body when the place went up in flames and
nobody knew where the mother was and why she left the child alone.
Or maybe she was hurt, choked on a bone or left bleeding by a mugger
who took pity on the child (or couldn't find her because she was clever
enough to hide in the closet), and she was scared and alone and didn't
know how to dial out so she was waiting for someone to call so she
could ask for help. All those possibilities sped through his mind in the
instant he sat frozen by the sound of her voice. Unable, or unwilling, to
sort them out, he simply hung up and spent another two days concentrating on how *old* she sounded. The last time he had spoken to
Glenda, the child was minus six months, barely conceived. Since then
she had not only been born but had learned a language, or at least a lot
of it, because nobody started out with "hello," not with that kind of confidence that made you know she was ready to start a conversation. She
had a whole life. The world had started again and begun to revolve.
Amazing. Paralyzing. Next time he'd call later.

"Stupid move," Glenda had said when he did and spoke the words Erika had stifled before. That's all, and he realized just after she said it that that was the reaction he'd been hoping for, not excitement, not anger, not hurt, just a straight response, though as usual she managed to imply more (he remembered telling Quincy once that she was better than he was with words that way). Yeah, he said to himself, it was a stupid move, but it wasn't the first, and he was in it now.

"You think so?" he'd asked.

"Takes too long. As usual."

"Well, maybe we could play it out anyway."

"Are you drinking, Elliott? I gotta get up and go to work in the morning."

"No. She sounds real grown, Erika does. That's her name, right?"

"Three last month. Was that you hung up the other night?"

"I'm sorry. That was a stupid move. I didn't think she'd be answering."

"Look, Elliott—"

"Glenda, please. Do you have some time?" He heard a faint sigh and some sounds of settling in.

"How's the leg?"

"Ankle. Bad enough. Same thing as high school but worse." She had been his crutch then. He didn't want word to get around how bad he was hurt, a week before his second varsity season, so he ignored the doctor's orders and leaned heavily on Glenda. And she helped him work it back in shape the next time, when it wasn't so bad and he knew the UMass coach was coming to the game. "That doesn't matter, though. How are you?"

"Same as always. Living. Working."

"Yeah, but Erika must make a difference."

"Yes, she does. She's great. You know she saw the game where you got hurt. Just by chance. She was watching, and she noticed you cause they'd just done ten on *Sesame Street* that morning. She called me in to see when they carried you off. She was upset and I guess I must've said something cause she asked me, 'You know him?'"

She stopped talking. That meant she had either said too much or was afraid she was about to. She'd always been like that. Straight, simple answers, then after a while she got rolling and was like another person altogether till something inside her pulled the plug, just like that, as if she'd exceeded her quota of words or blown a fuse. Sometimes it happened in the middle of a sentence. And her face, Elliott recalled on the other end of the silent phone, would go perfectly blank for a few seconds, and then she quickly nibbled her fingernail, third finger, right hand.

"I'd like to meet her," he said.

"She has a father," she said (and, Elliott imagined, clenched a bit of nail in her front teeth). "We're fine."

"I'm not."

"Bored? No TV, no tournaments, no scouts?"

"I don't need that. I never did. You know that. Yeah, it was nice, I won't lie. It got good to me. But that was only because . . . I didn't have anything else."

"That was your choice. I'm right here where I always was."

"Yeah. You're right." Why start? She was one move ahead. He could go off about his reasons, if he dared (though he knew she'd have a counter for that, too), but the fact was that she had been there. And they both knew it. "Choices don't have to be final, though," he said.

"Some are."

"I think I got a job offer," he said. A new opening.

"What you mean, you think?"

"Well, it's not definite. First I gotta finish up. I guess that's one good thing about missing the tournament, I should make it on time. And then I gotta do a final interview. Sounds good, though."

"Yeah? Where?"

"Boston."

"Mm. I see. That's convenient."

"Glenda."

"What?"

"It's not like that."

"It's not?"

"Listen. I'll be home around the third week of May. I'd like to come see you if that's okay."

"What for?" she asked, as if the notion really did come as a complete surprise. As if she couldn't imagine what they could possibly have to see each other about.

"To see you, girl, what do you think?"

"Oh. All right, well, call me when you get in. I'll be around."

"That's great. I'm really looking forward to it."

"Bye."

Tyrone couldn't understand why he was so anxious the next day—but then, T had pretty much given up on him by then. Couldn't understand why he didn't get a real agent to bogart the pros. Couldn't understand why he'd consider that half-ass, off-the-street engineering gig back home instead of going back out to the coast with him. And definitely couldn't understand why he'd ice some fine pussy like he'd been getting on account of a bitch who dogged *him* out big-time four years ago.

Delphine understood, and from his mother's looks and Davis's signifying, it seemed that they all did. His sister had nagged him from the minute he got in the house until he confessed that, yes, he'd made that call they'd talked about when he came through for the BC game around Christmas. Out of spite, mostly—and to avoid their questions—he didn't mention until just this morning, very casually, that he'd be dropping by Glenda's.

Good timing. Holidays were a general pain in the ass anyway, and Memorial Day was especially useless. Why tease? Let's just finish out the school year and be done with it. The first five years were probably okay, when it was just the three of them. But after that those special days when the family was supposed to enjoy being together were just fucked up, first by him resenting Davis for being there, then by him hating Quincy for not being there. Seemed like they just never got it right, and thanks to the basketball season, a lot of the time since he'd been at school he didn't even have to deal with Thanksgiving or Christmas. The only really good times, looking back, didn't have anything to do with the family. They were when he and Glenda just hung out together, avoiding everyone else so completely that it never occurred to them they were hiding from anything. It was just the way it was supposed to be.

The way he never thought it would be again—and maybe it wouldn't—but here he was taking the same old route he could follow blindfolded and backwards, dribbling with his left hand. He could imagine Quincy going on about the significance of history repeating itself, like time travel and shit, to see if you could change the outcome. But it wasn't all that. More like going home.

And he was there before he knew it, took the porch steps in a single bound, and rang the bell without thinking first about what to say or do. It was only when there was no answer that he became self-conscious, and when he saw the little table where they used to play chess that the memories came. *"You play?" "Huh?"* Before he'd had a chance to misunderstand she'd nodded to the table where the board was set up, waiting. "Yeah," he'd said. "You know, some." Quincy had gone through a phase and had sat him down for three or four draggy Sunday afternoons trying to teach him. It had actually appealed to him a little bit, but because he thought it was lame to think so, and because he had already pretty much had it with Quincy's phases by then, he'd become easily distracted and cut short the lessons. But as Glenda's face brightened and she grabbed his hand to pull him to the table he had wondered again how Quincy knew.

But Elliott wanted to deal in the present, and to do that he had to keep moving, so he scanned the street and stepped down from the porch, guessing which direction she might be coming from. He guessed right. As he approached the corner, she came around it. Right at him, carrying a grocery bag. Except for her curled hair and big-lens glasses, she looked more the way he remembered her—dressed in shorts and a Celtics T-shirt—than she did the last time he saw her. The big difference was the brown leprechaun skipping alongside in jean overall shorts, with her hair braids fastened by a squadron of airplane barrettes. "That him?" he heard her ask as he approached.

"Looks like."

Uncertain how to greet them, Elliott stood for a moment and extended his arms toward the bag. She let him have it.

"You number ten?" Erika asked loudly with a squint-smile.

"Yeah, that's me."

"Hi, ten!"

"Hi yourself. And hello."

"You're movin pretty good."

"Yeah, I can walk all right. You're in pretty good shape yourself." It was a shape he could pick out of any crowd, with shoulders too wide for her small frame and the muscular legs he'd always envied, except that they were so damn short. She used to swear that she was going to get bigger someday, to which he usually replied that she must be going to get fat cause she sure wasn't getting any taller. He was glad they were both wrong.

"Try keepin up with this one. That'll do it."

"Mommy, I have the key?"

"Okay, Rikitiki. Wait for us, hear?"

"Okay!" she hollered and dashed up the porch steps.

"See what I mean?"

Elliott followed Glenda's deliberate, bowlegged strut into the house.

Without even looking around to see how anything had changed, he went straight to the kitchen, set the bag down on the table, and began to help her unpack. Erika skipped into the room with a miniature green-and-white basketball.

"Hey, ten," she said.

"His name's Elliott."

"Elliott?"

"That's right," he said. "Nice ball you got there. You know what to do with it?"

"Yeah, wanna play? I show you."

"I'm just gonna get some stuff together to take over to the park," Glenda said. "It'll take a few minutes."

"Come on," Erika yelled and pulled Elliott into the living room. "See, I dwibble. My mommy teach me."

"Hey, not bad," Elliott said, noticing that she was careful to use both hands as she bounced the ball across the room.

"Catch!"

A strong pass flew toward his face. He bobbled it but held on as Erika rushed at him with unexpected force, pulled on his sore ankle, and took him down.

"Touchdown!" she cried, pulling the ball from his hands, spiking it on the floor, and going into a wobble-kneed celebration. "Mommy, I touchdownded Elliott!"

"Yeah, I heard," Glenda said from the kitchen. "Give him another chance, but don't hurt him, okay? I want him to carry the cooler."

The kid was all right, pretty and bouncy and fun and smart, but Elliott didn't trust himself. He couldn't play her off, even if he wanted to, just because she didn't look as much like Glenda as he'd hoped. But the last thing he wanted to do was seem like he was using her to get in good with Glenda. He knew what that felt like, and besides, he knew Glenda wouldn't be having it anyway. So he went ahead and played with her and let her show him her books and her *Sesame Street* stuff, but he was glad when it was time to get out of the house.

Of course, that meant dealing with her mother, which was hard just because it didn't seem to be. They strolled and talked easily enough, just like everything was the same, which felt good and drove him crazy at the same time, but, shit, you had to start somewhere. At least she took the lead, talking about her changes like he was an old cousin from out of town or something. Talked about her mother going back to

South Carolina with her kid brother, who, Elliott remembered, had begun to snap out of his zombie thing by cutting school, shoplifting, and
generally going berserk. It never got any better so Moms took him
down home and left the place to Glenda. Didn't want to have to worry
about hers and her daughter's too. Glenda's father had been gone—
"like a ghost," she said, after that night they drove him out. He had
been in and out before Elliott himself disappeared and, Glenda said,
had come around a few times to see the baby. But only when he got
himself together—she had made that clear the first time, along with
the fact that it was her house now, although that wasn't entirely true
legally. He hadn't gone far, though, so sometimes she and Erika saw
him hanging out on the avenue looking like hell. She never lied about
it, but wouldn't let him talk to Erika those times.

In the park, they went to a spot on a small hill half encircled with
trees and spread a blanket—something they'd never bothered with before, but the grass made Erika itchy. They made sandwiches from
chicken she'd fried up the night before, pulled out the chips and soda,
and Glenda asked him about Phine. The two of them had gotten to
know the park well by taking her there on outings, trying to lose her,
and then looking to find her in time for Elliott to get her home.

"I was hopin you could clue me in," he said. "She's so busy bein
grown, she doesn't tell me anything." He didn't bother to say that their
few conversations since he'd been home had ended with her bothering
him to call Glenda.

"Haven't seen much of her lately, that's why I asked. She was a big
help with Erika in the beginning, still calls maybe every couple
months. I think that school's keepin her pretty busy."

"Yeah, what's up with that anyway? First Ma said she was totally depressed, now she stays on the phone all night plannin the damn prom
and organizing graduation. Like suddenly she's supposed to be in
charge of everthing."

"She's changed her attitude, all right, but I think it's good. She always was one to set her mind, you know, but she's never been pushed
this hard. Might be she's just learnin to push back. I say go ahead. If it
don't kill her it'll make her stronger."

"I suppose. It's just, first Quincy goes off and becomes a different
person, and now Phine's gone weird on me."

"Like you haven't changed since you were twelve, right? What you
think they think about you?"

"You know what, Glenda, I honestly don't know. I never did. I always just tried to be what they wanted. Somebody's baby brother and somebody's big brother." And somebody's boyfriend.

"Well, if Phine don't need a big brother right now, that gives you a chance to figure out what you want you to be. Doesn't it?"

"Hey, Elliott. You take me to the playground?"

He was watching Glenda's eyes. They seemed larger and rounder behind the new glasses. Or maybe that was just the way they magnified the question he was still trying to figure out.

"Elliott!" Erika repeated.

"Huh? What is it?"

"Elliott wasn't paying attention, sweetie," Glenda said, still staring at him. "Come on, I'll take you."

From a distance, he watched the little girl make her rounds from the swings to the slide to the jungle gym, like a regular practice routine. The girl had endurance, like her mother, who stood watching from the perimeter, taking everything in, calling out encouragement, and guarding against any interruptions. Just like she used to stand by the court and watch him.

When they returned to the blanket, she seemed to forget that she had put him on the spot, which made him wonder if it was just his imagination. She played catch with Erika and talked about her job, while he tried to avoid talking about basketball or school or any of the last five years. Which didn't leave much.

And all the while he wondered if she remembered, if she could possibly not remember, that this was also the scene of their next-to-last fight. Not really a fight—he just thought of it that way now—but one of those moments when she was so stubbornly herself that she ceased to make any sense to him. There had actually been quite a few of those along the way, and this one he would have forgotten the next day just like all the rest except that the next day he was leaving for school. And she was still refusing to ride up with him, even though he had it all arranged for her to come back with his family and it wasn't like she didn't get along with them or anything. She'd practically adopted Phine in place of her own mystery brother by then.

She just said it was his show and she didn't want to be part of it. He would have felt better if she had just admitted that she would miss him too much or didn't want to go through a big scene. But because she wouldn't say it that way, he couldn't be sure that that was it. But then what? It wasn't like they hadn't known the day was coming. She was the one who damn near planned it—helped him develop his game, sort through the few scholarship offers, worked with him to plan a curriculum, even helped shop for his wardrobe. His mother had even complained that it looked like Glenda was the one sending her son to school, not her. It wasn't that she resented him for getting to go. She could have escaped, too, if she'd wanted to, and he had tried to convince her to apply and go with him. Desperate, he tried that day in the park to accuse her of living through him, not having the guts to pursue her own dreams. But he knew that wasn't it either, and he didn't even try suggesting that she was eager to get rid of him, because he knew that wasn't true. She had another strategy working, but he couldn't see what it was. Still couldn't.

"I'm not going anywhere, you know," he told her. "It's just like a long road trip. I'll be back. Nothing's going to change."

And she stood there, her back against a tree and her arms folded, and didn't answer. She wasn't sad, and she wasn't mad, she was just Glenda, and she wasn't moving.

He hung there trying everything he could think of to reassure himself, mostly, because she wasn't giving any sign that she needed it. Finally, when he was all pleaded out and just leaning his face into the bush of her hair, breathing her in and prolonging the moment, she looked at him through those little granny wire-rims and said: "It's getting dark, Elliott."

That was all: it's getting dark. Knowing when a game was lost, he kissed her a polite good-bye—not the deep, warm, clingy one that he had hoped for—and stomped off through the park toward his future.

Over the next six weeks they talked on the phone and wrote letters back and forth, and everything was pretty cool. But when she finally agreed to visit campus for homecoming weekend, she seemed uncomfortable, in a way he never would have expected. He took her to parties and the football game and whatever else was going on with the folks he had gotten to know, but he could tell right away that she wasn't all there. Like she didn't want to claim him, or didn't approve of the company he was keeping, or felt out of place, or something. But like he kept saying, these people weren't anybody, just folks, and they weren't more important to him than she was. And she was as smart as any of them, definitely smarter than him, and looked as good as any of the women. But if she wasn't feeling inferior, it wasn't like she thought she was any better, either. Just different, that's all. It showed in the way she looked at this one girl who kept hanging around every time they were out with people and who kept bugging him to dance with her. He wouldn't, but Glenda kept acting like she didn't care one way or the other. If she had just been jealous, he was ready for that, but this was more like curiosity, like examining an odd species at the zoo, but only for a minute, like uh-huh, so that's what one of those looks like, what else they got? That it? Shit, where the monkeys?

So after that he just came home to see her. A lot. She never asked him to, but it was clear she wasn't interested in going up, not even for the games, and sometimes he wondered if she wanted him to make the effort, but he thought he was supposed to, and wanted to. Like, that was the deal, right? And when he got back after that first year, he just chalked it all up to transition and was ready for everything to be like before.

That was when he first heard about this guy Walter, somebody Glenda had met while he was at school. They'd gone around together a bit, but she told him all about it, and he didn't make anything of it. Besides, he'd figured he could count on Phine, she was old enough and nosy enough to know what was going on. As long as this Walter wasn't in the way, Elliott decided he wouldn't even say anything about it. They did okay, then, him and Glenda, even though their time together wasn't the same as when summer meant complete freedom or little half-ass jobs for pocket money. She was working full-time at the phone company, so summer was really nothing different to her—vacation was a two-week luxury, not a full-season license to screw around. They weren't kids anymore, and he respected that, kind of dug it, so when he spent sit-around evenings at her place, he had no problem with leaving early because he knew she had to get up. Even on weekends she wasn't as free as she might have been, since she had housework and shopping and all that to do, things that became more important when this was your life and not just a break from schoolwork. Sometimes he hung around and watched or helped—kind of playing house—but sometimes he played ball or took Phine to the movies or helped around his own house. All righteous and responsible.

So righteous that, before he headed back to Amherst, he hinted around about getting married. Maybe that was what she'd had in mind, proving that she could give him some freedom and that she could get along by herself, that they could get past being a couple of horny kids looking to the future. She said she didn't think it was such a good idea right then, so he figured the experiment was still on, and he left planning ways to get her more involved in his life at the university.

Her next visit was her last, homecoming again. It had worked once before to get her there, why not? A little tradition. The basketball season was still more than a month off, so it wouldn't have to be about watching him, but he felt good and knew he was going to have a monster year. Felt so good he'd turned down Erving's number 32 to keep Frazier's number 10, which was less of a betrayal now because Jo Jo White was wearing it for the Celts. He met her at the bus stop on the village green across from the Lord Jeff—that shit was so high toned it killed him, but he liked it—and she looked the proper new up-North schoolteacher coming to some quaint old Southern town. (Take away the long-nose bullshit and there was a lot of Mayberry in a place like Amherst.) He'd never thought of her in that way before, but maybe that's what happened when a regular bush-jean, big-'Fro sister from Dorchester takes the gray dog to preppyville, and maybe that's why she didn't want to come. Shit wasn't natural, but he was there, after all, and that should have counted for something. She said she was cool, so he whisked her off to the Polynesian place in the Cutlass he'd borrowed from the brother who was starting at center.

She didn't waste any time dropping the bomb. Between her sloe gin fizz and the pupu platter, she told him she was going to have a baby. And it was probably merciful, although she was just being herself, that before he finished his sip of Brass Monkey and figured out how to react, she added that the baby wasn't his. At that moment the platter arrived, but neither of them made a move as she eyed him across the table and waited for him to ask who.

"Walter," she said.

"You mean that guy from last year you told me about? You said there was nothin goin on."

"Wasn't, much. It was an accident."

"Aw, shit. So what you gonna do?"

"I told you. I'm gonna have a baby."

"Glenda! Shit, what you doin here? I mean—gotdamn."

"You asked me to come up."

"I didn't know about this shit! How you gonna sit here with me and . . . you and me supposed to be together and whatnot, and you know how I feel about you, I even said I wanted to *marry* you, and you gonna tell me this shit?"

"I thought you'd want to know."

"You goddamn right I wanna know. This is *outrageous!* I don't believe this shit!"

"Elliott, listen. It just happened, that's all. You can't tell me you haven't been screwin around up here."

"No, I—"

"Don't lie. I don't care. I left you alone and I expected that would happen, but I was alone, too, you see. But I don't love Walter. I'm not going to marry him."

"That's too damn bad. You might as well, now."

"No, I'm not going to, no matter what. I love you. I always have, you know that. Walter knows it, too."

"Shit." It didn't help that it was only maybe the second or third time she'd said the magic words. It had been so obvious for so long they'd never really needed to say it, and now, on top of everything else, he wanted to slap her just for using the words. "That your idea of love?"

"I want to have a baby, and—"

"You don't think I could give you one? Something wrong with me now?"

"And you know the trouble my mother had. I'm going to keep this one. It just means there'll be two of me waiting for you, that's all. I don't want to hurt your feelings, but that's the way it is. I'm here because you need to know that I still want to be with you. Nothing's going to change that, not even this."

"Yeah, that's what you think. I gotta get out of here." He stood from the table and fumbled in his wallet for money to pay for the uneaten dinner. And realized as she sat there, not looking repentant but not defiant either—just herself—that he couldn't just leave her there. Much as he wanted to get away from her. "Come on," he said.

They drove in silence to his dorm, because if he spoke he'd curse her out, hit her, wreck the car or something, none of which seemed like a bad idea, but he didn't have the energy. Instead, he parked in front, took her shit out of the trunk, led her to his room, and left. Slammed the door out of frustration because she wouldn't even cry or beg or apologize. In fact, he knew the only reason she didn't protest the treatment wasn't because she knew she was wrong but because she didn't have anyplace else to go.

He drove way the hell out past the tobacco fields, trying to go as fast as pissed-off people always did in the movies, but he wasn't used to that kind of where'd-the-road-go country darkness, and almost running off the road twice made him realize he didn't want to die even if he thought that's what it would take to make her sorry, so he just got himself good and lost instead. He thought about going to the gym to work it off, which he'd started doing his first year, mostly when he missed her, but he didn't want to miss her. He wanted to go back to Franklin Park and have her ask him not to go. He wanted her to need him as much as he needed her. When he knew he didn't want to go any farther but didn't know which way to turn, he simply stopped the car and turned on the radio. He forgot that he'd asked his buddy to play a dedication on his show, timing it for when he and Glenda would be in the room together, between rounds, talking. A delfonic interlude. Don't you want to live this moment again and again and again and again and again and again and again and again?

He didn't know what time it was when he walked into the room. She looked like a little girl, like Phine, wrapped under the covers in her nightgown, lost and out of place. But content. Why the hell not? She got what she wanted. But the resentment was drained out of him, and he knew he couldn't hate her, because he'd tried. Her eyes fluttered open and made him feel that he'd just come out of a bad dream.

"You came back."

"Yeah."

"I'm glad."

"I could probably think of a hundred things to do. It's Friday night, probably not even that late. I know there's a couple of parties, card game, movies, somethin goin on."

Her face asked, not unkindly, What's keeping you?

"It doesn't work with you here. It's like, there ain't nothin out there. And I don't like the idea of leavin you here in a strange place alone."

"That's sweet."

"No, it ain't. It's fucked up. I can't deal with this, Cooz."

"You could if you wanted to."

"I shouldn't have to. This is your choice, girl. Look what you're doin to me. You're messin up everything. Everything we always talked about."

"You said you wanted to marry me when you finished school, maybe even before. And I remember you always talked about babies. You even wanted girls, I always thought that was nice, cause most guys don't even think about that. And if you got a pro contract you'd put Phine through school, maybe someplace near where we were so she could baby-sit and I could come on the road with you."

"Stop it. I know what I said. It's not the same now. It can't be. Every time I looked at her, I'd see him."

"And me. She'll still be my child, Elliott. Could be yours, too. Isn't Mr. Davis your daddy?"

"That's different. My father's dead."

"That's your brother talking. It doesn't have to be any different. He loves your mother and he loves you just like Phine. Quincy too."

"Well maybe he's a better man than I am. I can't do it, Glenda. I don't know if I can ever get past it."

"I understand. But what's done is done, and I can't take a chance. I don't know if I'd be able to have another baby. Then maybe you wouldn't want me anyway. This way I know I get something, part of what I want."

"Yeah. You know, you're wrong about me, Cooz. It's not like you said. There hasn't been anybody else."

"I know. I just said that. I'm sorry, Elliott. I'm sorry about everything. I really do love you."

"Me too. I love you. And I'm sorry."

He curled up beside her and fell asleep with his clothes on, and when he woke up she was gone.

"So?" he said.

"So what?"

Erika was asleep, and they were sitting on the porch. "So don't you have anything to say?"

"Like what?"

"Like where have I been."

"I know where you've been. Basically."

"That's not what I mean."

"What do you mean?"

"Oh, here we go."

"Where we goin?"

"Okay, hold up. Let me back up a minute. This is great. I had a really nice time."

"Thank you. So where we goin?"

"I mean, doesn't this seem strange to you? Sitting out here, just like when we were kids, like I haven't been *gone* for five years?"

"Oh, I see."

"You do? I'm glad."

"You want me to like dog you for abandoning me or something?"

"Well?"

"You don't listen very good. I meant everything I said the last time I saw you, Elliott. I told you it was my decision and I knew what I was doing. You remember what else I said?"

"What, about loving me?"

"You didn't believe me, did you?"

"Why should I?"

"Because I said so. Look, it's not like I've been pining away or anything stupid like that. I've been goin on about my business just like I would have if you'd never called. And I'll keep doing that, cause frankly, I have no idea when you'll show up again."

"Hey, it's not like that."

"You have to understand that we're fine, me and Erika."

"I can see that."

"Then why are you here, Elliott?"

"I don't know. I guess I just wanted to see you."

"So, here I am. Satisfied?"

"No."

"Well, I can't help that, now can I?"

"No, I guess not," he said, and stared glumly out at the street.

"Hey, you okay?" she asked at last, placing her tiny hand on his forearm.

"I really missed you, Cooz."

Six

Quincy

The first time he saw her hotfooting down Broadway she reminded him of one of those loose-limbed wooden puppets that collapses, arms and legs falling every which way, when you press the button on the bottom, relieving the tension of the string holding it together. She was all shoulders and elbows and hipbones cranked into motion by her bowlegged, pigeon-toed gait. She had a large canvas tote bag over her shoulder, which added to the herky-jerky motion, and she looked in a hurry, but uncertain about where to. As she ambled toward him, she seemed to notice him and he thought she might want to ask directions. Instead she stopped, tugged at the scarf on her head, and turned around. She had a nice little Popsicle ass, too—her stick legs set wide apart—and he paused to watch her locomotion until she crossed over to Barnard.

Two months later he noticed her again, spotted her immediately in a crowd waiting for the doors to open for a rare campus concert—rare for a black happening anyway, a benefit for some community center in Harlem, so everybody was out there. She was off to the side, alone, staring upward as if watching the clouds her breath formed in the chilly air. Her hair was out in a big, shaggy Afro that curled into wispy strands, the kind only light-skinned sisters could manage. He worked his way closer and saw, now that she was standing still in profile, that she had somebody else's tits, not huge but almost too much for her thin back and shoulders to bear. But because they seemed insignificant to her, they did not hold his gaze. Instead, he focused on the way light from a street lamp fell across her small, angular face. He'd been wrong; she wasn't watching her breath. She wasn't watching anything. Her eyes were closed. She was sunbathing, tipping her head so that her hair did not shade the softly humming blue-white light that fixed her like a transporter beam. Like this time she knew where she wanted to get to. Quincy stepped close, almost touching her because he thought he might like to go, too. An old Smokey lyric: *I will carry you away with me as far as I can, to Venus or Mars.* Too close: her eyes snapped open and found him—they were tiny and dark, a sparkling indigo reflecting the streetlight at him, and Quincy stood ready to be beamed away. But she moved her head and shadow fell across her face, except for her mouth, which flashed a little smile of shiny braces. The doors opened behind them, and she disappeared again.

For maybe five months. Perhaps it had been a delayed reaction thing, and she had been drawn into another dimension. He had stopped looking and stopped wondering by the time he strode into the big lounge for what was, in effect, the spring coming-out party. Two years before, his first, the white boys had gone apeshit while the brothers and sisters were still trying to cope with King's assassination and the "real" revolution down the hill and around the country. This time, although he and others were still up to their asses in meetings and projects, everybody felt a need for a less complicated release. So the place was jumping, and there she was, the queen of the stars back from Earth-Two or Alpha Centauri or wherever, all her strings being pulled at once by some celestial puppet master—or perhaps by herself. She had on boots, a mid-length skirt, and some kind of ruffly Gypsy-ass top, and she was just shaking, spinning, hopping, and popping, giving it all up without turning any of it aloose.

He set about doing what he had come to do, dancing and flirting and dancing some more. But he kept turning so he could keep her in view, and when one of his partners, a woman he had gone out with the year before, caught him staring over her shoulder and rolled her eyes, he gave in and went to confront the mystery child. At first she seemed not to recognize him, intent on her own ecstasy, but when she fixed him with the beam—same glow, without the streetlight—and smiled the same little braces smile, he thought maybe she did. Didn't matter; he had determined to reel her in when the music stopped.

"Come on, take a break," he said and grabbed her wrist.

There was no place to sit, so they leaned against the wall. She crossed her arms.

"Yes," she said noncommittally, not quite with a question mark.

He shook his head. This was not supposed to be difficult.

"Hello. I just want to talk to you. My name's Quincy."

She gave him a peek of braces.

"I know. You do a lot of talking, don't you?"

"Excuse me?"

"Well, you hang out with all those serious political and literary types, right? That's what you all do, talk about things."

"Yeah, I guess so."

"Oh don't get me wrong, I'm not tryin to snap on you or nothin, I mean if that's what you wanna do, that's cool."

"Thank you. Well, let me see, you're a freshman, and you're some kind of artist."

"That's right. I'm Fontelle." She gave him an exaggerated hand-shake, her elbow stuck out at an odd angle, a parody of a glad-handing businessman.

"Hello, Fontelle. So what do you like to do, besides hypnotizing yourself in a streetlight?"

"Oh wow, you remember that, huh? I was tripping, boy. I think you were, too."

"Yes, I was," he said, pleased that *she* remembered. "I think I might be again."

"Well, you know what, Mr. Quincy? What I like to do right now is dance, so if you'll excuse me. They're playing my song."

Shit, girl, they're all your song.

It was clear soon enough that she wasn't coming back. He mingled, smoked, danced, drank, and wondered why he was letting this silly child work on his mind. There were other women in the room, many better looking, some he had dated, a couple who had indicated some interest. Maybe it was just the challenge. She obviously knew who he was and knew he'd been watching her. She wasn't cooperating, but he had to see this through and get it out of his system, one or the other.

"Let's take a walk," he said, having transported himself to her side between records. His body language was nonthreatening but insistent. He was already moving, ever so slightly, toward the door, with his shoulder gently pressing hers.

"Sure," she said. "I bet you want to talk some more."

"That's right. That's what I do, you know."

He could tell it was spring because the air outside was beginning to carry all those funky, thawed-out city smells that would become over-whelming in July. And because the sky was still clear enough to make out some stars. He lit a joint, inhaled, and held it toward her.

"Uh-oh, we're gonna get deep now, I see."

"Where've you been all semester?"

"Venus," she said, and took a drag.

"That's what I thought."

"I'm surprised you missed me."

"So am I. But I did."

"Are you like trying to hit on me or something?"

"I don't know. You want me to?"

"This is freak. Is this how it works, all this bobbing and weaving and playing games?"

"Hey, I'm not playing. I don't even know what the game is. I'm just talkin."

"I see. Okay, Mr. Quincy, what do you want to talk about?"

"You."

"But there is no me, not really. See I'm an alien life force sent to this planet to bring joy and laughter, especially to this lost tribe of Negroes that lost their sense of humor in de rebolooshun."

"Good, then I can be your special assignment."

"I don't think I'm supposed to specialize."

"Sure you are. Otherwise you could have appeared as a flower or some of this herb, something for everybody to enjoy together."

"Or maybe a man, huh?"

"Yeah, maybe. You can check with home base right now on that transmitter in your mouth. All those metal wires and shit."

She gave him a sneaky giggle-grin and took another hit.

"You know, what I really think is that you're some kind of fox."

"Oh, here we go again with the rap."

"Yeah, that's it. You've got these beady little eyes and a kind of pointy nose. Pointy ears, too. And reddish complexion. A fox in human form."

"Like a werewolf? Good thing the moon's not full."

"Dig it. You might eat me up."

"Don't count on it."

He didn't tell her then, and didn't for a couple of years, that she re-minded him that night of the white chicks in Cambridge, the ones who'd let him try out all kinds of things, sexually and politically. It was all playacting. Nothing counted. He was living on his own, light-years from Dorchester, and trying on different costumes, anything to confound expectations—hippie, stud, revolutionary, poet. What had begun as unusual, however, had become routine, until Fontelle opened her magic trunk and made him see he'd been wearing the same outfit for a couple of years.

When the joint was spent, he lit a cigarette and they sat on the steps for a while, naming constellations. He gave her his jacket as the night turned cooler and put his arm around her without thinking about it. His dick hardened, which surprised him, but he ignored it, which surprised him even more. When he finally offered to walk her to her room, it was as if he had touched a switch, reactivating her body. She wanted to go back and dance some more. Joy time, she said.

"What about me?" he asked.

She bared her metal fangs and tossed him his jacket. "Don't worry," she called back. "I've got your scent."

And a few weeks later she sniffed him out, on a sunny Friday morning while he was sipping coffee in a spot on Broadway where he'd never seen her before. She sat right down next to him like he was supposed to be expecting her.

"Well, if it ain't the fox," he said. "What brings you? Couldn't get me out of your mind, huh?"

"As a matter of fact, I have been thinking about you. And I just happened to be walking by, and here you are. What are you doing today? I want to paint your picture."

"Just like that? I've got class."

"Oh, come on. I just get these urges, you know what I mean?"

"Yeah, I've been known to have a few urges."

"I feel like I need to paint today, and I've been thinking about how perfect you'd be for my portrait project. When's the last time anybody offered to make you immortal?"

"Can't say."

"Then let's go. You go to class all the time. This'll be an experience to remember. God, I'm glad I found you. It's so beautiful out, if I didn't find the right subject I'm afraid I'd just waste the whole day."

"I bet you're one of those people goes skipping around barefoot when the sun comes out."

"I might, but you wouldn't understand. You're too serious."

"Then how come you want to paint my picture?"

"That's why. Come on."

Hours later, Quincy sat in a large studio watching her long rainbow fingers making delicate movements on the canvas. The streaked work shirt she wore, with an old scarf on her head and pretty, clownish smudges on her cheeks, transformed her into something more than the hippie parody she usually presented. But it was the expressions on her face since she'd stopped chatting and gotten into it that most intrigued him. At times she looked like a barber in the mirror worrying the edges, and at times she seemed to be mimicking him like a zoo monkey. It was probably a good thing, he realized, that nobody had to be staring back at him when he was trying to write.

"Keep your eyes on the window, please. And hold still, you're getting out of position."

"When do I get a break?"

"Hang on. I want to get this somber thing you've got happening around your eyes."

"Hurry up. I need a cigarette."

"Good. Keep frowning like that. Just a little while longer. This is going to be good. Okay, relax."

"About time," Quincy said, craning the crick out of his neck and reaching for his last cigarette. "Let's see what you been doin to me."

She set down her palette and ushered him around the canvas with a confidence he admired. The image startled him; it was larger than he expected, and intense.

"Damn, do I really look that evil?"

"Sometimes. That's the quality I wanted to capture, you know, the intellectual warrior."

"Yeah, right. Say," he said, surveying the work on the walls, "doesn't anybody paint anything but naked white chicks up here?"

"Well, I could fill up the walls with pictures of nude black men, but I don't know who I'd get to model for me."

"Don't be smilin at me. These people don't deserve to see that much of me. Besides, it's drafty up in here—unless you're talkin about private sessions."

"That's all right, thanks. I won't be able to finish today, but I would like to try to get your coloring down a little better. How long can you keep it up—I mean, can you stay awhile longer?"

"Depends. What's in it for me? I already blew two classes and I probably won't make my meeting this afternoon."

"Why, the pleasure of my company, of course. Come on, just sit in the light." She steered him back to the other side of the easel. "You don't have to hold a pose right now. Say, listen, there's this movie playing on campus I want to see tonight. Wanna go with me?"

"What is it," he asked, settling back into position.

"*Yellow Submarine.*"

"The Beatles cartoon?"

"See, I knew it. It's probably not heavy enough for a deep brother like you, right? Like you'd rather see some documentary on Angola or whatever."

"I'd love to."

"You serious? Great. You know, maybe I should soften this frown just a little bit."

As she predicted, they were the only black students in the auditorium that night, but he did impress her with his knowledge not only of the Beatles but of animation as well—though he didn't care much for that style. He preferred the classic Warner Brothers look. Satisfied that he wasn't such a Blue Meanie, she agreed to get some food and drink afterward.

The time together stripped her of some her mystery but none of her appeal. She was wide open in a way he kind of hoped Delphine might turn out. But his sister, a woman from birth who had been here before and didn't like the way things turned out, was already becoming jaded. And he was probably as much to blame for that as anyone. There was definitely a lot of evasion in Fontelle's carefree attitude, but at least her mask was one she had designed herself. That was enough to get him to take his off as he sipped wine and watched her inhale a burger-and-fries platter that had nowhere to go on her skinny body.

"So when do you want to finish up the portrait?" he asked, after they'd compared notes on movies and music and intolerant Negroes.

"You're not sick of me yet, huh?"

"Not hardly."

"Does that mean you're going to try to get me to go to bed with you now?"

"I was thinkin about it, actually."

"Now why *is* that?"

He shrugged. "Well, it's getting too late to call anybody else."

"No, I mean, like—we've been hanging out all day getting to know each other and having a good time and everything. Why do men always want to mess that up with sex? It makes everything so complicated, and being friends with someone is complicated enough, you know?"

"But why would I want a friend that I *didn't* want to sleep with? I don't know why anybody would. The things that make me like somebody are the same things that make me want them."

"Even a man?"

"Good question. I don't have any men friends, but who knows?"

"No, but you can't be really open and honest with someone if you're always scheming to get them to go to bed with you."

"Sure, you kidding? That's when the truth comes out. No holdin back, man. When your nose is open and the sap's risin, you don't have time to make shit up, it just comes. So to speak. Women always accuse men of lying then, but that's just cause they can't deal with the truth. Most women don't believe they're beautiful and sweet and precious and all the shit we be saying when we want some. You ever see a group of men talking? Standing around with their hands in their pockets or their arms crossed or grabbin their joints, talkin out the side of their mouths, gruntin and carryin on. Their body language just screams bullshit. That ain't real."

"Oh, I see."

"Yeah, but to be with somebody you want, that's like walking around naked, constantly turned on, all your senses sharp, tingling down in your soul. You can't help but tell the truth. Every moment is pure and intimate, like foreplay."

"That's beautiful, I never thought of it like that before. Tell you what I'm gonna do for you, Crawdaddy. I'm gonna give you the biggest turn-on you ever had. We'll just stay friends, and that way I'll blow your mind every time we're together. How's that?"

It was close to 11 P.M. as Quincy paced in line outside the club, Deuteronomy, in the shadow of the Empire State Building. It seemed at least a week since the nightmare with Max the night before and the odyssey of that morning. The memories of Fontelle had filled the evening and altered his spirits so that he felt like bursting into flame and soaring around the spire above—more than a torch, a human firecracker. Whether he was excited more about the book or the reunion he couldn't say, and it didn't really matter. The convergence made perfect karmic sense. She had been so disdainful at first about his literary pretensions.

They all just wanted to be Amiri Baraka or Last Poets, she said, yelling angry fuck-whitey poems that were really meant to help them fuck black, or sometimes white, women. That changed when he mentioned during an argument after a campus poetry reading that he'd started out writing his own comic books and thought he might try it professionally. She got a big kick out of that; it seemed so unlike what she expected him, but didn't want him, to be like: like she'd caught him pulling apart his shirt and tie in the *Daily Planet* stockroom. He let her read the story he'd been working on then, about him and Bubb, which dealt with voodoo and was written in Black English—two more unorthodoxies that she loved. She offered to illustrate it for the campus black-lit mag, and they spent his senior year discussing plans for a black children's book, words by him, pictures by her. It never happened, but the idea had led to the completion of the stories he eventually sold to Reeves.

As the crowd inched closer to the small, wrought-iron gateway that led down into the club, he heard a quick click-scrape on the pavement behind him, a pace utterly different from that of others moving past on the sidewalk. He turned, grinning, and opened his arms to the creature in the shiny short dress, long gloves, and high-heel boots that made her look like she just got off the Mothership with George Clinton. She did a little Diana-Ross-here-I-am shimmy and head toss and jumped to his embrace, shrieking "Crawdaddy" in an exaggerated Southern-belle voice.

The greeting was interrupted by a commotion up ahead. "What do you mean I can't come in here?" a woman demanded. The notorious club bouncer, *sensei* of a karate school favored by what Fontelle used to call Baby Muslims, floated his eyes over her denim jumpsuit and dismissed it with a gesture. "Say look here, man," said her escort. "I paid my money and I'm comin in. You can't pull that shit." The bouncer stepped in front of the couple, slipped a crisp twenty out of his pocket, and said good night. The escort snatched up the money, muttering all the proper denunciations for his girl's benefit, and turned away. The bouncer told him to drive safely.

Fontelle blinked the exaggerated incredulity that always made her look high when she wasn't. "Oh wow, that's embarrassing. And I was gonna wear my old jeans and a leather jacket."

"Good thing you didn't, cause I wouldn't know you when my man put you out."

"What's with all this impeccability?" she asked when they made their entrance into the dark, colorful swirl of Harold Melvin suits and Love Unlimited dresses. "Why you gotta look like a magazine cover to have a good time?"

"Look who's talking. You got more costumes than the circus. Besides, I never had anything against being clean, myself." That, in fact, was what he liked about these clubs: with their dress code, along with the $10 cover and twenty-five-year-old limit, they rewarded adult behavior. He was getting too old for the rowdy shit.

Because it was still relatively early, they were able to get a table for two, but closer to the dance floor and the music than Quincy would have liked.

"So, what's up?" he asked, drawing his chair close to hers.

She stared into his lap and pronounced: "Nothing, I guess."

"Where's Antoinette?" he asked meanly, stung by the tease.

She ignored the put-down. "He's still in San Francisco, putting together an exhibit," she said. "I don't believe this," she added, shifting her attention to the fashion show around them. "It's all so . . . *mannered*. And what about Miss Anchor Lady?"

Quincy was used to sudden swerves in her conversation, but this time he knew there was a connection: she equated Max with the kind of bourgie hypocrisy she had decided was on display in this place. And she hadn't, obviously, missed the "Antoinette" crack.

"We don't need to discuss that."

"Whatsamatta?" she said in Jerseyese. "You have a fight last night? Was it about me, sugar?" For the last phrase she switched back to Southern, an intonation she had picked up from Antoine.

"Don't flatter yourself. Besides, what makes you think I was with anybody?"

"Dear, please, this is me, remember? I'm the one . . ."

Quincy waved off her comment. "Never mind. Listen, I've got big news."

"You're getting married. Oh, can I be the flower girl?"

"Shut up, Fontelle." He missed that shit when he wasn't with her. When he was, it often pissed him off. "It's the book. I got paid today. It'll be out soon."

"Fantastic!" she cried and pumped his hand in the same corny shake she'd given him when he first introduced himself. "Let's dance."

His disappointment was brief; it was as much congratulations as he could reasonably expect—and it confirmed that she was the main event after all. On the floor he abandoned his normal reserve in a show of solidarity with her. Perversely, they ignored the precision movements of the dancers swirling prettily on the flashing, throbbing square, motions pitched as much to the loud, swooping strings—and the effect of their clothing—as to the thumping bass. Quincy and Fontelle, in contrast, looked like white people goofing at a black party, having a stylelessly good time.

"Hey, check that out," Quincy called to her.

A man with a glistening, neatly cropped beard stood alone on the floor facing the room-length mirror, combing his hair and swaying to the music like an oak in the breeze. Fontelle spun over to him; touched up his beard, his hair, her hair; stuck the comb in her teeth like a pirate's dagger; and jumped into his arms with her legs wrapped around him. She rode him to the song's end, when Quincy finally came and got her and led her to the bar.

There he ordered a celebratory scotch. She got a mimosa, and they toasted his success.

"I had to take out the Black English. Except in the title story, the first one, with the voodoo."

"Sellout."

"That's not the worst part. Remember that illustration you did? We couldn't use that either."

"Thank God. It was terrible. I wouldn't want anybody to think I was still doing that stuff."

"Well, I always liked it."

"Next time I'll do your author's photo. Very artistic and surreal."

"Bet."

Back at the table, he started scoring the women who passed by. Their Miss America routine: when Fontelle announced, "There she is," he would try to pick up the winner, but he had only ten minutes before Fontelle would break it up. Her heart wasn't in it, though, and since she didn't want to play he began to feel a little awkward, like this was the kind of date they'd never really had. She had steadfastly resisted the characterization in Columbia days. When she transferred to Pratt and he started teaching, they were both busy but kept in touch with periodic "undates" to revival movie houses, art exhibits, Off-Broadway shows, and new night spots. And random, middle-of-the-night phone calls. She was determined not to be added to his lengthening chain-chainchain of fools, and they never got the timing right anyway. When he went back to school and hooked up with Max the first time, he basically left her for dead; by the time Max left for Cleveland, Fontelle had taken up with Antoine.

"Okay," he said finally. "Thanks for sharing my good news, but you had something on your mind. What did you want to talk about?"

"Nothing special. I'm just kind of confused right now."

What else is new? he didn't say.

"How do you know that you're in the right place? That you're who you're supposed to be? You always seem so centered."

"Me? You cured me of that, remember? I never know what's goin on."

"You know what I mean. You've got the teaching. You've been doing that for a long time. You've had at least one long-term relationship. And you're still here. Like you know you're supposed to be. That blows my mind, you know? Like, I don't know, I might as well be in Timbuktu as in California. It doesn't seem to make any difference."

"Well, I like what I do, most of the time. And you're right, I've made a home here. But that was almost by accident. I escaped from Boston by coming here and I just haven't found any reason to move on yet. And I've got you, you know? Even when you're not around. That's part of it, knowing who your friends are and knowing you can get to them if you need them. Doesn't matter where you are."

"That's nice. Thanks. I didn't know that."

"Yes you did." Every once in a while she stopped teasing and challenging and running and allowed him to feel wise, not like the older man he often played but like a big brother. That, he realized, had always been part of the attraction, now more than ever as it occurred to him that Delphine had gotten to be nearly as old as Fontelle was when they met. Although he'd done his best to prepare his sister, Fontelle's persistent confusion made him wonder if it would ever be enough.

"How are things at home?" he asked suddenly. "Your father okay?"

"He's fine, glad to have me back. For a while, anyway. Can we dance?"

Marvin Gaye had begun to croon, the very song that had been floating through Quincy's mind on the train downtown. She had never asked to dance a slow record with him; that was his thing.

But I want you to want me too. Just like I want you . . .

"I know there are still some funkier places we could go after this," he said, trying to speak normally as he held her hand to his chest and clutched her still-tiny waist. "I'm not sure where, though. I don't get around much anymore." Then, not wanting her to think he had become too domesticated, he added: "Teachers have to maintain a little respectability, you know."

"No more picking up students in Brooklyn clubs?"

He felt the smile on his collarbone. "She wasn't *my* student. If you want, we can always do Times Square again. This time *I'll* approach the cars and you can be the pimp."

"No, that's all right." She released his hand to hug him tight as the record faded. "Maybe, after a while, we could just go to your place and hang out," she said. She looked up at him with eyes rounder, fuller, than ever, no darting or flashing.

She immediately spotted the portrait hanging above his desk, on the wall beside the window. He was afraid that, since she had already disparaged her work from that period, she might command him to get rid of it. But she didn't. It was, she said, something she had always liked. The only good thing she had done at Barnard. He didn't think she would lie about something like that, although he would, under the circumstances. Either way, he was glad. It helped establish a common ground for them in this new territory. She had been to the apartment only once after dark. That was when she'd finished Pratt and had given up her place in Brooklyn to move back home. But one night, in no hurry to get there, she had insisted on stopping by. They got high, and she missed the last bus to Englewood, clearly on purpose despite his good intentions, and she spent a hands-off night on his sofa. Quincy had slept unusually well that night, and ironically, their sexual innuendoes had been freer since, as if sleeping together without sleeping together had moved them beyond the simple question of having had sex.

Tonight was another story. They sat on the floor, leaning against the grounded bed—she didn't ask—while he spun Columbia-time discs and she repeatedly, and uncharacteristically, held out her wineglass for refills. Midway through the second joint, third glass, and fourth side, she made the move he'd been dreading for several hours and hoping for, off and on, for several years. It was a fairly clumsy advance. He opened his eyes from an intake of herb and found her face lurching toward his. It landed somewhere near his ear, and instinctively he turned so their lips could meet. The last time she had been there, maybe four years ago, he had become resigned to the fact that this was never going to happen. He thought about it only when he saw her, and not always then. No memory, no fantasy, no ghost. He knew he had kissed her sometime, a purposeful kiss, not just memory or affection, but he couldn't remember when or how it felt; whenever it was, she'd still had her braces, and her tongue had not wrestled his so vigorously—he'd had to probe for it, quickly—and her hands had not been *on* him this way, in a scramble of desire that forced him to search blindly for the ashtray.

Nimbly—and almost embarrassedly, aware of the practice it betrayed—he lifted her onto the bed, her lips still working indiscriminately, established his position above her, and began to work her out of her dress. An overeager pupil, she helped, shrugging off the fabric in Houdini fashion and attacking his buckle and zipper.

Too fast. He had always, especially in the most fleeting couplings, indulged himself in quick comparisons, with the last one, with Max, with what his radar scan had suggested for that night's target. But this was someone he knew as well as he knew any woman, though bodily he did not know her at all and had stopped guessing years ago. He needed to get acquainted. Seizing her forearms tightly, he began his tour: the points of her shoulders, down her thin arms with the wispy-haired and nearly white-thin skin, her surprisingly taut stomach with the inny he expected, the sharp slope from her prominent hipbones to the silky hair between. He briefly tasted smoothness and salt inside, but no dampness, as her legs worked to dislodge him. Because his hands had slid to her thighs, hers were free to grab his head—they were long and strong, Lincolnesque, he'd noted when she painted his picture years ago—and led it back to hers. On the way he dipped to her breasts, which he'd avoided before, assuming from experience that women with large ones didn't appreciate obsession. He managed only a few kisses on the small, indistinct nipples before she pulled him off, shaking her head vehemently.

There was nothing left to do but to do. He let her help him peel his pants and briefs and felt her hand roughly on his joint as she jabbed it toward herself. At that moment he quickly scanned the apartment, still illuminated by the lamp on the desk. Max was not there, but the little boy in the baseball cap ran laughing across the mattress, and he worried that she hadn't said anything about being on the pill. It didn't matter. He was soft and she was dry, and the almost frantic pumping of her hips could not help. He wrapped both arms tightly about her shoulders, kissed his way to a neutral spot on her neck, and covered her with his weight in a moment of frightful stillness.

"That's it?" she said.

He felt panic and shame, but mostly sorrow. After all this time, she had taken the risk he had, many times in many ways, asked for, and he had failed her.

"Mr. Big Stuff," she said, and laughed a knew-it-all-the-time giggle that relieved and bothered him. She was okay, maybe, but was this a test, his bluff called?

She extricated herself, kissed him on the side of the head, and patted his back.

"It's okay, Crawdaddy," she whispered. And as she rolled out from under him: "I'll be back."

He lay still, a stranger in the place he knew best. He thought to turn out the light while she was gone, vanished into the bathroom, but he worried that that might be taken as a sign of . . . something. Should he refill the glasses? Put on another record? Get dressed? He had no idea. The sound of flushing sharpened his anxiety. She'd be back soon. How should he play it? But this was Fontelle, his fox, his unloved lover. Why should he play at all, even though playing was what they did best?

She did not return. He sat up, listening. Even she couldn't get out the small window in there. She'd have to come back by here. He'd wait, start over, try again if she wanted, or pretend nothing had happened. Or take the abuse. But where was she? He didn't like people hiding in his space. Max had long ago gotten used to him walking in on her in the bathroom, and even women he'd never seen before or since learned they could not depend on privacy here. She was no different, though out of respect and caution, he pulled his briefs back on before pushing through the door.

He found her kneeling on the white-and-black tile floor, between the claw-foot tub, over which one arm was draped, and the toilet, which she grasped with the other hand. Pale, thin, and pathetically beautiful, she sobbed and trembled and muttered through teary eyes: "It's me, it's me." He turned off the light and sat to hold her, for as long as he could.

Seven

Maxine

This thing with the missing Katz kid was going to run all through the week, maybe longer if he wasn't found soon, or if nothing else broke before time for the Bicentennial and convention warm-ups in a few weeks. The boy had disappeared on the way to school Friday before the holiday weekend, hadn't turned up in five days, and they were all milking it like it was the last story on earth. The parents' tearful pleas, shots of the older brother tacking flyers up all around the neighborhood, and today the anguish and anxiety of his classmates. At first it seemed like just another sob story from the naked city, but this one had struck a nerve. The *News* and *Post* were screaming daily. Of course, the Puerto Rican girl who was raped and thrown off the roof in a Spanish Harlem project was good for only a day.

Max had tried to get Karla to ask about the kid's habits. How did he and his friends get to and from school? What kind of precautions did people in the neighborhood take—before the horse was out of the barn? At the very least, it could stretch the story for another day with helpful information, instead of the same old boo-hoo. But no. It wouldn't play, she said. Be like blaming the victim. This was a good kid—there was nothing suspicious or reckless about his behavior—and his parents were suffering enough. Karla was right, of course; it wouldn't be entirely fair. But that's how Max would have pitched it now.

It wasn't often that the familiar frustrations came to the surface, and when they did, usually the story had something to do with black folks; this one must be getting to her, too. Always it was people like Karla, shaping the world according to their own warped view, no matter how hip and worldly they thought they were. And in the end, they were only talking to themselves, really, although they'd deny it (or worse yet, not see anything wrong with it—no demographics and they'd all be out of work). But Max knew she was a better reporter—a real reporter, that is—and a better writer than nearly all of them staring evenly into the camera, trying to look like they hadn't been up all night fucking some powder-snorting moose they'd picked up at the Apple. Problem was that the first didn't count for much on TV, even though it paid a hell of a lot better. Other than a handful of designated or self-styled reporters, like old hound-faced Abe with his deskful of contacts and Jack Daniel's, or Baby Moose Julio, who liked to jump up in people's faces and climb trees or mud-wrestle or whatever, it was mostly chasing fire trucks and being spoon-fed. And parading your ego. The money would be nice, no question about that, and so would the influence. But that wasn't real. Unless you were Cronkite himself, or maybe Mike Wallace, it was mostly just celebrity. And the truth was, they'd never let her get there anyway, so why sell her soul?

She was a *much* better writer, though, and that was really why she was in it. Even if they were third-grade words coming out of fourth-grade mouths at the desk, they were words, and even though everyone from the messenger to the network brass knelt to the picture god, she knew that it all started and ended with words. Yeah, all right, so that White House correspondent bit had seduced her a little, and she had driven her sister and her parents crazy summing up the day's events with her hairbrush mike and sending it back to Walter in New York. She knew that was just playing around, and it wasn't until she got to Columbia and started sizing up the opportunities (for jobs, black jobs and black women jobs) that she'd given in. So she veered increasingly into TV, and when it came time to apply, the responses seemed to justify her choice.

Cleveland was happy to have her. She figured she could thank Carl Stokes for that, or the force that had put him in office in the first place; it was ironic that he ended up anchoring in New York while she was out there. And it surprised her that they wanted her to try out on camera, which reinforced the notion that she was an affirmative-action pickup and that they didn't have a clear plan for her. They wanted black faces—with no doubt about it, not the lighter hues that were begin-ning to turn up all over now—and they wouldn't get credit in the community for hiring her if nobody could see her. Given that, it did not surprise her that they gave her a black-youth piece to do. What she hadn't counted on was that the South Portico style she'd honed with the hairbrush and perfected in school was deemed too stagey for Euclid Avenue. They wanted her to act as well as look like Cleopatra Jones. She should have known what was up when they suggested the leather jacket and boots. Did Barbara Walters ever wear a leather jacket? Did anybody ever see Norma Quarles in *boots*, for God's sake? Loosen up, Harry said, shifting his weight to one hip and jiggling his shoulders, and she knew like she knew her own name that this was a man who'd never got no brown sugar but believed Mick Jagger's every leering word. She didn't know whether to laugh, cry, slap his pocked face, or kick his turkey-skin balls the way Tamara Dobson would (no, he'd like that). This fool wants me to be a goddamn whore, she thought, picturing herself, with alarm that overrode her indignation, in front of her mother's grade school class, and knowing that she had to find a way to make it work.

Why not try Nina? she asked. Her first production decision. Nina? Harry didn't see it. He thought Nina was like his cousin or something, a suburban-Midwest-Jewish-Oberlin mousy thing best suited for school news and perky shit. He may have suspected that she was also a cutthroat hussy—they all were, to some extent—but he didn't know that she was also a hard-rockin' broad who liked her some chocolate. Give her that gang feature—make it a series—and she'd send off sparks that would titillate without offending. He knew Max could write, and because they were shorthanded, number three, and had nothing to lose, he let her produce the piece, which he didn't care that much about anyway. Maybe he thought she'd fuck up. Certainly, he figured she'd owe him. But it clicked. Nina was even tougher than Max thought, and she generated just the right amount of street heat confronting the sly-eyed young gangsters (who could have been *Max's* cousins). The ratings jumped. Nina became a star in the making. And Max's career path was set. Harry needed her writing, he said, and she knew that was true but insisted, with the temporary leverage of her success and her color, that she be allowed to produce an occasional piece as well.

Freed from the prison of her face, she found, she could be more herself, or as much of herself as the medium allowed. Nobody knew, or cared, who wrote the copy for a mayoral race or political scandal, or who produced a piece on hospital mismanagement. And when Nina showed up on the weekend anchor desk, Max determined to make her

her puppet, to feed her words as she herself would say them. Of course, she couldn't do anything about the veiled eyes or tossed head—those little celebrity touches to let everyone know this was Nina Kaufman, six o'clock heroine—but she could set parameters and try to highlight the intellect the bitch was trying to leave behind. The downside, however, was that Harry found her funky-prep casual newsroom persona closer to his fantasy than her oracular on-camera pose had been, and he got in the habit of positioning himself ever closer while she, shackled to the typewriter, had less room to escape.

But escape she did, after a total of eighteen months in the hinterlands, back to New York, while Nina took her hot mama routine upmarket to Detroit. It seemed like a good idea at the time. It *was* a good idea. Even if she wasn't going to be a personality, she harbored network ambitions that would never be fulfilled in Cleveland, and her talent and color could still push open some doors if she didn't let herself get too comfortable. Besides, she was lonely and depressed, and she knew that, whatever else he had gotten into, she would be able to get most of what she needed personally from Quincy, with whom she had corresponded sporadically but with increasing intensity as Harry pressed closer and Nina flaunted her nocturnal gymnastics with an alderman all the sisters in her Thursday night group had the hots for.

Here, though, she had much less influence, and the off-camera role-playing was even more rigid. How could she tell Karla that her concerns, her fears about the Katz kid, were real? Karla and others passed it off as black cynicism, and there was some of that, but Max also wanted to know how you could keep a child safe out here. There must have been something, even the most innocent bit of carelessness, that had singled him out for destructive attention. Something that a good mother—not that the woman was negligent by any means—a mother who both cared and knew, could have prevented. The devil was definitely loose in the city, but he couldn't just be devouring random children for the pure hell of it. And this was a kid big enough to run, yell, and fight. How would she protect her baby?

"Don't cry, baby." It was Julio, gliding up beside her on an oil slick, preceded by his Givenchy. "Wanna come down to the office and let Daddy make it all better?" Several months before, the story had gone around that someone had caught Julio humping Becky, one of the film editors, in an editing booth; since then it had become known as Julio's office, and no one had worked harder to sustain the fantasy than Julio himself.

"Kiss my ass," she snapped.

"Ooh," he said, uncoiling his tongue. "Should I take that as a yes?"

"You better put that back before you lose it," she said and walked away to hand in her latest installment of the tearjerker. Now she was pissed. Because she hadn't known she was visibly upset, and because she really liked Julio. She'd tried to have several conversations with him about not reinforcing stereotypes. He was a genuinely talented reporter, she told him, and a nice guy, which she didn't tell him. It was one thing to act a fool on camera—somebody had to, she supposed, and he was good at it—but he could at least keep it professional and can the uptown Casanova shit. Couldn't he just fuck civilians and keep his mouth shut about it and not bring all that hey-mama crap to work? But he would never play it straight, too insecure or full of himself, or more likely both, to let his guard down even to her, and she usually ended up playing his game despite herself. Brushing him off like that, like some righteous priss, was something of a betrayal, but maybe now he'd get it. Probably not. But really, she couldn't be so bothered. Not now.

When Julio had cleared the area to get made up for his studio piece, she returned to her desk and banged out a California primary update as the broadcast began. On the nearest monitor, Rex began his lead-in to Karla's piece, to the inevitable cracks about his likelihood as a boy-snatching suspect. That's when Max suddenly lost it.

Striding purposefully, as if she'd just remembered to make an important call, she charged out of the newsroom and whirled down the hall. The framed photos of local and network personalities whizzed past her line of view, mingling with the startled faces of real-life coworkers. It was like the camera-eye view of the chase scene in one of Julio's pieces. Hey, c'mere, I wanna talk to you! This is Julio Lopez, *Channel 6 News*. What are you trying to hide? But since this wasn't an ambush, why were the faces so leery, even the framed ones? It occurred to her to turn around and see what was going on. But she seemed to be in a hurry. Near the end of the hall, the camera jerked sharply to the right, its focus dissolving on a black metal door.

Her momentum shot her past the sinks she knew were standing unused to her right and to the door of the last stall. No, God, not that one: she didn't even stop to think it until she locked a different stall door and slammed down both toilet lids in a single motion, sat, and pulled her legs beneath her lotuslike, out of view. That one was the throne of sorrow, the torture chamber. Little sneezing sighs, great hillbilly-sounding whoops of despair, and sick, snotty moans had been heard from there. Those were the worst cases, or sometimes just the beginning before the wretched creature could be coaxed out to sing her blues. They all sang, and others always listened with sympathy, even Max, because, after all, they were sisters bucking the odds in a man's world—and they could hang because they both were sympathetic and wanted the dirt. Especially each other's, knowing as they did, but never thinking it, that their time would come. The blues even had a standard refrain, once overheard from behind the door of the last stall and ritually quoted in times of crisis: There are just no rules in this fucking business.

Max never sang. She was in fact the toughest audience. Clear, practical advice was her thing. Tell him. Sue him. Call the union. Kick his ass. She had little tolerance for the professional shit, the overperceived slights, reassignments, sharp words, and missed opportunities that filled their lives like the blaring, cacophonous noise of the newsroom. But she had absolutely no patience with the personal stuff she felt people should have left behind in high school, or at least at home. He didn't call, he thinks I'm too fat, he left me waiting, he called me somebody else's name, he fucked me, he didn't fuck me, blah blah. All of that didn't make it to the throne; some was just whining that blocked the way to the sink.

But there were some real doozies: the unrenewed contract after seven months of dick sucking, the speed freak-out, the nervous breakdown brought on by official harassment, wandering husband, and dying mother. If Max was genuinely moved, they all knew it was *really* bad, and that meant a particularly long dinner with lots of drinks or serious coffee time or, if it went the other way, more pills and powder and personal days.

Actually, this could be a good time, an opportunity, to leave those blues behind. There was that hint of an opening at the D.C. affiliate her college mentor and lover had been telling her about. The network connections could be nearly as good, and it would have to be more sane. She knew that the staffs bore little resemblance to the localities, but these goddamn prima donnas, even if mostly imported, had to be different than everywhere else, just as Columbia had brought out the neuroses in the presumably most down-to-earth heartlanders.

Besides, D.C. was home, and home sounded like an even better idea than New York had a year ago. She knew her way around. She had friends. The devil didn't gobble up children for no reason—he was busy gobbling up Third World countries and Democrats. And she had family, a network of support for a single career mother. That was the key: she had a career, she could pay her own way, she knew what she was doing, but it would be nice to have a little help.

It was not the same as with Brenda, with whom she had pleaded to get that abortion during her junior year at Virginia, and who had gotten married and knocked right up again anyway before the ink was dry on her diploma. Max thought their mother would be pissed even then, but she was cool; the guy made good money at Du Pont, and Brenda was set to go to become a social worker as soon as Trey was in school. Max should have known. Really, Brenda could have done anything she wanted to, within reason, and it would have been okay, because she wasn't supposed to do shit but smile and breed anyway. The first pregnancy would have been something of a scandal, all right, but Max's urgency in arguing for the abortion was all projection, and she knew it at the time.

Max didn't want Brenda to give up, to settle too soon, on the off chance that she might come through and take some of the weight. There was still the possibility then that she might get herself into a management training program, become the star, and no one would have bothered her, Max, about her unusual choices. Since she was not going to follow a safe path and become a teacher—she'd made that clear enough—and wasn't going to be a conventional professional, either, a lawyer or manager, she'd have to do it right. She damn well better *be* Barbara Walters. No half-stepping.

But a baby and no husband and no on-screen presence either? Who was she kidding? Watch the baby, Mama, while I go work the night shift? No, that she'd have to manage alone, couldn't take that mess home, not yet, and she *couldn't* do it alone, not scripting intros for Julio's D.C. counterpart, some skinny-hipped big-hair brother, at six and eleven, while the whole federal government had their pick of smooth-skinned, articulate, and childless sisters, not to mention the flat-out ho's with money to dress and not a thought in their heads but civil-service dick, and Mama pursing her lips and Daddy pretending to be busy and Brenda cruising in from Wilmington with annual additions to her own Jackson Five. She just wasn't ready.

The broadcast had ended, she knew, because she heard the pre-dinner traffic filing into the room, highlighted by Karla's gloating over the reaction she'd gotten on film from one of Katz's little friends. The tremble Max felt made her lose her balance and fall against the metal wall of the stall, and she could sense the faces turning in her direction. Quickly, she flushed, dabbed her face with toilet paper, and emerged.

"You okay?"

"Why wouldn't I be?"

"It's seven o'clock, do you know where your kids are?"

"That's a stupid thing to say."

"Hey, what's eating you? Anybody up for Szechuan?"

"I'll pass," Max said as she stepped to the sink. As soon as they all cleared out, she was going to call her doctor. She didn't have the time—or the heart—for this shit. Enough already.

Eight

Quincy

Quincy spent the first day back at school trying to think about Max. Should he go by at dinner break? Maybe he should send a copy of the book as an icebreaker—if Sheldon ever gets around to mailing them. That could take weeks. He'd have to get to her before then. Talk some sense into her, let her know he really wanted the best for both of them. She'd never listen, though. Shit, why should she? He'd already told her the real deal, and then made it clear even if she wasn't listening. Nice wouldn't get it. Maybe a lawyer.

Or a shrink. It wasn't just him. He could tell when he took Fontelle to the bus station Sunday morning. Could it be she was still afraid of her old man? She ought to be too old for that shit, but you never know. But why'd she come back to Jersey in the first place? Then again, it could be Antoine, who might have gone native in San Francisco and left her stranded. Doubting herself. Did she think she could straighten him out or something? She'd been around, she should know better. She always had me. Well, no she didn't. And when she tried . . .

"Yo, Mr. Crawford. I gotta talk to you." The familiar voice cut through the hallway hubbub as he was going back to his room after a lunchtime smoke in the teachers' lounge.

"Can it wait till after the meeting, Carlos?"

"Awright, but don't forget. I been tryin to catch up to you all day, but you been like in outer space somewhere. Just cause we don't be hangin out no more you don't got to do me like that, man. This is important."

"Yeah okay. I'll be here." At least Carlos still remembered to call him

Mr. Crawford in school; that was about the only deference he showed. It must have been something important, because usually Quincy was the one trying to get his attention, to make sure he didn't fuck up in his last year and blow college.

Right now, though, Quincy didn't want any distractions until he got through the after-school lit club meeting. Times like today, when it seemed that his whole life was rushing together and falling apart simultaneously, he needed to remember that this was the good stuff, the real teaching. It reminded him that their shit was deeper than what he'd run away from in Boston, and that his current troubles at least came from an excess of love (or something like that), not the want of it. All in all, dealing with their tortured metaphors and painfully compressed worldviews was probably the best thing for him to be doing right now. Because you could never begin to deal with the shit unless you had the words for it. In the lit club he helped them find their voices, which included encouraging them to explore their bilingualism: the depth and structure of their own patois. So they could use all the language available to them to name their demons and define themselves.

Fontelle was right: he had always known that this was where he should be. Known it since Bubb came along and he was the one who looked after him when their mother was working, who told the kid about their father and protected him from the impostor. He'd known it when he taught Phine to read and continued her correspondence course through all the years he began to fancy himself a writer. Fontelle had been surprised at first when he showed no interest in law school or a graduate writing program; that was because she didn't understand that in his jive pursuit of her he had always been playing the smitten tutor as much as the decadent artiste.

And among these kids he'd pulled together, Carlos was the real thing. For all the kid's talent, Quincy never would have imagined him taking control like this, editing the magazine and even persuading a couple of hard cases to come out of the closet with their poetry. Carlos was tougher than he had been but with less armor, smarter about people but perfectly dumb about the world. And had a sweet voice, on paper at least, that matched his face and could break your heart.

At three-ten, as students and teachers both fled the old building more quickly than in any fire drill, Carlos promptly appeared and began pulling chairs into a circle as others trudged into the classroom and Quincy tried to look busy. Most in the club, the first to arrive after

Carlos, were girls, who put down most of their corridor feistiness like a heavy load once inside because they knew this was a safe place to dream. Quincy had banned stories or poems about babies, though; over the years he had lost too many students who had decided that life should imitate art.

Their longings were so palpable that in his first year out of college he had to remember to keep his to himself. But that didn't stop him from sharing his reveries with Fontelle. It was, he said, like being born again in pubescent heaven. All those short skirts not hardly doing anything to hide the legs, not fully formed but growing like Jack's beanstalk, leading to unseen, uncontemplated riches. And despite their sly eyes and foul mouths that projected knowing attitudes, they really had very little idea of the assaults being planned against them. Oh, they knew it was coming—to be aware was part of the ritual—but the sheer relentlessness, the carelessness, the infinite deviousness of those assaults was as beyond their knowing as the consequences of underestimating them. Or succumbing to them. How could a child, after all, comprehend the incomprehensible wants of others?

"Others like you?" Fontelle asked. "Wanting and climbing are two different things," he replied. "That's why I try to stay busy with that which has been previously harvested"—meaning, at that time, fellow teachers mostly. "Why are you telling me this?" she asked in what he took for disgust.

By the time he started in Brooklyn, after he finished Teachers College and Max had gone off to Cleveland, he was not seriously tempted, not by the students, anyway, who had become the same age as Phine. But during the sparsely attended open house that fall, he couldn't help noticing one stunning young woman who looked like somebody's sister and came up to him after his brief presentation to ask about her son, Carlos. At first he couldn't put the student's face together with the name, but the phrase from a classroom poem came to him, almost audibly—*virgin of the valley of the shadow of death*—and he knew that he was standing in the presence of the virgin herself. And he knew that he wanted to know what kind of woman could inspire such a vision in such an apparently uninspired kid. Was Mr. Perez here tonight as well? No, Carlos's father died five years ago. Sirens blared in his head, the sound of somebody breaking into a car that should never have been parked in the neighborhood in the first place. Carlos had a lot of potential, he said. Some of his creative writing was very good, but he showed little interest in his other work. It was difficult to talk right then, though. There were so many students, they were supposed to keep these things pretty general. He did appreciate her concern and wanted to help. Maybe there was sometime they could meet—talk more about Carlos?

They met for coffee after school a week later at a diner a few blocks from the bulding. Carlos was playing ball, or pretending to; even for those who had no game, that was the standard pretense for hanging out, checking the girls, and not going home. His mother had managed to get off an hour early from Gimbel's—lingerie, as it turned out appealingly—so she'd arrive home at the same time. Actually, Quincy had thought it would be easier just to meet her in Manhattan, since he would be heading that way, but as this was supposed to be school business he decided to keep it close to the office, as it were. Not too close, though; the diner was out of sight in the opposite direction from the way Carlos's crowd drifted.

"I am very concerned about my son," she said just after placing her order for a cup of black. Quincy, already sipping his cream-no-sugar and puffing his second cotton-mouth True, locked on to her chocolate eyes. "Of course, I want him to do well in school, and English is the most important subject. He should do well in that."

"He does. He's a little shy in class. I try to get him to open up more. But even when he seems not to be paying attention . . ."

"Believe me, I know the look. He's a thousand miles away right in front of you."

"Yeah, that's the one. But he must have a good connection because he seems to hear me, you know. When I do get him to talk he knows what I've been saying." As she turned her head to thank the waitress, Quincy quickly scanned down the line of her neck to the delicate gold chain and contemplated the lightly tanned skin below that disappeared behind the rayon turquoise blouse.

"The Spanish is not so much of a problem for him, he reads all the time and all the time is writing things down, you know?" She may have caught him measuring the gentle heave of her chest as she began to speak, but he thought he recovered nicely, making it as far back as the violet lips that had been trained to let her words pass with a minimum of emotion. "He writes about everything and nothing. I ask him if he is doing his other homework and he says yes, but he's staring at the wall and writing in his notebook. In your class, he gets to do more of his writing than before, and you like his poems, yes?"

"Especially the one about you. I thought he made all that up, but I guess he has a stronger sense of reality than I gave him credit for." The lips relaxed wordlessly, and for a moment he felt himself neither customer nor teacher, which had been his goal. She sipped her coffee, went blank and looked out the window, got to maybe five hundred miles, and came back.

"He likes you very much. He says you are very smart and funny. And kind."

"I try. It's hard to get to know all the kids well—there's so many of them. Carlos kind of draws you in. He's more interesting doing nothing than most are talking all the time. He's a deep kid." The phrase briefly puzzled then pleased her.

"You like him?"

"I do. I like him and I like his work."

"You'll look after him, then? As you say, there are so many children, and to most teachers my Carlos is invisible. Because he has no father and he looks up to you, it would hurt him if you did not pay attention to him."

"I'll look after him. I would have anyway, but most parents don't ask."

"Good. Thank you. I have to go now. But there is one more thing I want you to know. I know you didn't ask me here to talk about Carlos. Maybe next time we can talk about some other things. Can you come to my house next Friday for dinner? I think Carlos would like that."

"What about Carlos's mother?"

"She's the one who asked you. What do you think?"

The next week Quincy had dinner in a smallish, second-floor Brooklyn apartment with Carlos, his mother, and his two younger sisters. Arroz con pollo. Quincy expected some dutiful school talk, with Carlos in a classroom-bored stupor on account of the intrusion, while he tried to slip meaningful glances at Mama on the sly. Instead, Carlos dominated the evening with observations on the Knicks, Langston Hughes (the Ornette Coleman period), and jazz fusion. Mama chatted it up pretty good too, and Quincy was surprised when she kept talking while Carlos put the girls to bed. Then, when Quincy figured it was time for him to slide, Carlos got his hat and went off to a buddy's place, so he sat back down for another hour.

They repeated the ritual twice more in a month, and although Carlos seemed perfectly happy to see him, nobody pretended any longer that he was the reason for the visits. In fact, he volunteered to stay with the girls while Quincy and his mother took in a showing of *The Way We Were*. He had seen it earlier that year with Max, who had little tolerance for Streisand's fawning and took issue with the depiction of the blacklist period. This time he emerged holding hands with Mariela, appreciating the sheer cinematic sentimentality. The pacing of all this fascinated him, like one of those long-simmering high school romances he'd never had, or needed, the patience for. He and Max, the year before, had fucked his bed to the floor the second time he'd laid eyes on her, which he considered a more typical courtship.

But enough was enough. Around mid-November, he borrowed an apartment from a Brooklyn colleague who was out of town for the weekend and lured Mariela away from the kids on the pretense of dinner and another movie. She did not resist, but simply stated, as he let them into the apartment, "This is not yours." Undressing her—nervously, to his surprise—he replayed the record *Jungle Fever* in his mind, full of sensuous moaning leading up to uncontrollable screaming in Spanish. But she was quiet, meditative, and at the end simply whispered his name, with a slight accent. It was enough, though, to make him start writing poetry, too, inspired by the fruity scent and smooth feel of her.

After that they all spent weekends, like a family, at museums, *The Nutcracker*, a BAM children's show. She was unfailingly respectful, deferring to him despite his age, at least six years younger than hers. Not because he was the teacher or even, he realized, because he was a man. Because she wanted to. For his part, he refused even to consider making love in their apartment, with the kids around, even if she'd been willing, and a few lingering, nonfurtive good night kisses suggested she might have been, although he knew enough not to trust that.

They did end up at his place, once, near Christmas—late Manhattan shopping provided the cover—almost as a matter of pride. They'd been together only a handful of times, mostly because he didn't like asking his friend, and it was okay. He actually enjoyed doing toys in Macy's with her and looked forward to coming back to see Santa with the girls, and there was an awkward sense of getting it over with when they hit the number 1 for the run up to Morningside. They danced naked in the dark to Coltrane's "My Favorite Things" between lovemaking, and as they dressed afterward she confided that she felt bad for him because it was a very lonely place and he felt so comfortable in it. She called later that night. He had asked her to so he'd know she got home safely, but it came later than he'd expected and the message was bad news. Carlos had left the girls alone and had just returned. He was upset and wouldn't talk about it. Could Quincy try to find out what was wrong? He put Coltrane back on and tried to write what he guessed would be his last poem for a long time.

The denouement was quick. Carlos didn't show for class. Quincy cornered him after school and offered to take him to a Knicks game, to placate him and get a chance to find out what was bugging him.

"You fuckin my mother," Carlos stated, too loudly.

Quincy immediately thought of an old comic book story, where a college-age Clark Kent was caught in a lie-detector test and asked if he was Superboy. He denied it, truthfully, because he had just then decided that it was time to be known as Superman.

"No, I'm not," Quincy told the boy, honestly, because he knew at that moment he would never again lie between those golden thighs and hear his name sighed like a soft, tropical breeze. Instead, he found himself in possession of a new little brother, one as insolent as Bubb tried to be and as improbably intellectual as Quincy had vainly hoped he would become. They did go to the Knicks game, as well as college games. They were the first sporting events Quincy had attended since he had gone to see Bubb play once in the Garden. Carlos converted him into a casual fan, and Quincy turned him on to poetry readings and real-jazz concerts. They were almost like dates, and Quincy enjoyed his company, looked forward to it, even if Carlos did have some weird habits like throwing things at rats on subway tracks with such enthusiasm that Quincy always feared he was going to fall off the platform. But he also had his mother's grace and reserve, the same fluid motion that was most apparent when he was not moving, and the same generous hands and cautious eyes. If Carlos were a girl, instead of a fatherless, knife-wielding "little brother," Quincy might have been fired.

Spring fever got to him, though, as it always did, and one weekend he finally had to beg off and go for himself. His Brooklyn connection had told him about a nasty little club with some good scenery, so he headed back out, though he usually didn't like to work the boroughs because it was a hassle to get back to his place. But Manhattan was increasingly requiring a different kind of effort, a level of conversation and styling he didn't always feel like being bothered with, either. So he took his chances. And it paid off. The place, the music, and the women were raw; it had a Latin-Caribbean, butt-naked feel to it, and he soaked through his shirt in an hour without ever going for the Trues in his sock to profile and strategize. When he did pause for a moment, a precocious gymnast in skintights and a halter wiggled her butt in his face and engaged him for a half-hour hands-on workout. This was the one, he thought, and knew it when he asked her name and she slipped her tongue in his ear and smiled. "Glory." Without another word he pulled her aside, cupped a hand under her tight bottom, and returned the favor, plumbing her throat with his own tongue; her leg lifted and curled around his; his hand ran up under her halter; hers worked under his shirt. When he started to ease her toward the exit, she seized his wrist and led him deeper into the darkness, through a door he hadn't noticed, to an unseeing place that smelled of reefer. He had some of that in his sock, too, but it wasn't necessary. In an instant he was sitting on wooden steps that carried the suddenly muffled sound of the music straight to his bones, and Glory was upon him. He snatched up her halter and fed on her nipples as she shook her head wildly, clawed at his chest, and rotated her crotch against his; she had never stopped dancing. A quick, thigh-trembling yelp distracted him long enough for her to reach his belt. Slippery tongue and tumbling hair tickled across his midsection, and he felt a sweet moment of freedom before she had him in her gasping mouth. Not all at once, he noticed with fleeting satisfaction, but she moved quickly, worked hard, and it didn't take long. "They were right." "Who?" "The girls in the front row of your English class. They said they bet you had a big, tasty one." "You know people at Prospect?" He went for the smokes then. "I go there." The striking match and initial draw covered his panic. "How old are you?" "Sixteen yesterday. I'm celebrating." "Happy birthday," he said and stepped uncertainly for the door to the accompaniment of her chilling, childish giggle.

He waited grimly for the bomb to explode the next Monday in school, but she never told, at least not anybody who mattered. She did turn up in the halls cooing at Carlos and winking insinuations at Quincy, but she transferred out at the end of the year, dropping from memory as quickly as from sight.

That summer, Quincy convinced Carlos to take math in summer school so that he might get himself in position for college. Quincy had planned to invite Bubb to the city, but he was out on the coast, so Carlos filled in, spending hours in his apartment on homework—Quincy had no interest in confronting Mariela in Brooklyn—and accompanying him to the beach and the movies. The cache of vintage Spiderman comics Carlos found on Quincy's bookshelf opened a new avenue of diversion, and they began making the rounds of specialty shops, where Quincy offered advice on classic collectibles and Carlos updated him on current trends as Bubb once had, in effect maintaining Quincy's hobby for him while he was too busy being grown to bother.

The arrangement was mutually advantageous, as Quincy discovered one late-summer Sunday afternoon at a midtown hotel comic convention. He had left Carlos on his own while he chatted with some folks about the writing end of the business; he had never completely let go the fantasy of developing stories for minority kids with some educational benefits.

"Hey, Quince, you got to check this out, man," Carlos said running up to him with a huge smile.

"What's up?"

"I was lookin at this fierce artwork, you know, with all these great bodies in wild poses and a lotta spooky shit like Conan with the dark colors and everything, and there's this fly chick sittin at the table watchin me dig it, you know. I mean she's really watchin me, like she's checkin me out and everything."

"Oh yeah, I bet."

"No, really. She starts askin me how I like the stuff, and tells me she worked on it. Then she aks me how I'd like to take a tour and see how they put it together."

"No shit. Really?"

"I told you, man. Come on, I'll show you."

They worked their way to the booth of a marginal company called Nimrod, which specialized in sword and sorcery, and Quincy saw right away that Carlos was right. About the artwork too, but the woman was fly. Light skinned with a mass of reddish brown hair that looked almost Rastafarian: definitely not the comic-geek type.

"Hey, I'm back. This is—"

"Quincy Crawford. Pleased to meet you."

"Hi, I'm Bernie Lieber."

"Colorist, right? I've seen your stuff, it's terrific. I had no idea. Didn't you do a *Vampire Slayer?*"

"Yeah, I been around. Thanks. I usually surprise people, they expect me to be Stan Lee's nephew or something. So, you with my new friend here?"

"Yeah, I'm his keeper. You really got him excited."

"Hey, what am I, invisible? You don't hafta talk about me like I'm not here, you know."

"Sorry, Carlos." She stood and touched his shoulder in a gesture that reassured Quincy as well. She was big, nearly as tall as Carlos, and solid: the blade-wielding heroine on her Nimrod T-shirt seemed not such a stretch from reality. "We need all the fans we can get. We may not be around by next year's show, frankly. So like I said, you're welcome to drop by, for what it's worth. Would you care to come?" She shifted her hazel eyes to Quincy's legs and up to his face.

"Yeah," he said. "I would."

The tour itself was disappointing. The seedy, lower-Broadway office was primarily for business, and most of the work was farmed out. It could have been a place that produced girlie calendars for Queens service stations. But Carlos was made content with a packet of back issues and original artwork and Bernie's touchy attention. Quincy wanted more, and he came up with a plan. The Met was doing a three-week pop art exhibit; would she join him and Carlos?

She did, and after that the only problem was getting her alone. Carlos helped with that, too. He was in the habit of quoting liberally from a Richard Pryor record he'd heard at Quincy's; Bernie was a huge fan, and a comedy freak in general. So Quincy asked her out to the new stand-up club on Second—which didn't allow minors.

He loved to watch her laugh. Robust was the word. Her head reared back, her bust heaved, and she actually slapped the table with her open palm. Part of her tough-broad thing, which included smoking even more than Quincy and wearing a wide leather wristband that made her look like an archer. And she was quick: some of her punch lines were better than the comedians', and usually raunchier. Those were the nerdier ones who built their routines on old TV shows, which Quincy thought was kind of cute because he remembered them all. Bernie grew up on Riverside digging Lenny Bruce, was hip to Redd Foxx and even Moms Mabley. Said she had gotten her taste for the outrageous from her father, who had shocked his family with her *schvarze* mother and wondered why it had taken Bernie so long to drop out of Ethical Culture. And while she enjoyed most of the performers, she was concerned that the smug, smart-ass white guys, especially the goyim, would win in the long run.

The analysis carried them to Quincy's floored mattress, where she did an equally robust she-devil impersonation—he was almost expecting whips and whatnot—and they played Pryor and laughed and fucked into the night. It turned out not to be a regular thing, which was just as well because she was more than he could handle (he'd have to tell Fontelle *that*). She was often otherwise engaged, and neither of them wanted to shut out Carlos. In fact, when the three of them hung out together throughout that school year—she was into hoops, too—Quincy began to wonder if she wasn't giving him some. But he never asked.

For a while, he suspected that was why Carlos was pissed off when he abruptly stopped seeing Bernie months later. It was easier than taking responsibility for having broken up some kind of nuclear unit that the kid had grown attached to, even though he knew it was a nonexclusive relationship. When Carlos found out the reason, though, he really freaked, and everything still wasn't cool between them when Glory returned to school for Carlos's senior year. Quincy told him she was bad news; he couldn't say why he thought so. The disapproval only forced Carlos's hand. She became his declaration of independence, and with Max back in the picture by then claiming more of his attention, it was nearly impossible to repair the damage. Watching Carlos and Glory become more deeply involved, Quincy had felt less a disappointed mentor than a jilted lover.

"Okay, Carlos, what's so important?" The boy sat slumped at a desk as the lit club meeting broke up, looking annoyed at the exasperated tone that Quincy now took with him all the time.

"It's about Bimington. I ain't goin."

"Binghamton. You *ain't* got any business going if you can't even pronounce it." Quincy didn't like the sound of the reproach himself, but they'd been through this a hundred times, and it was getting old. "All right, time out." He put his foot up on the next desk and leaned in close. "No teacher shit. I'm listening. What is it?"

"It's Glory. We're gonna have a baby. I can't go. I'm gonna stick around and get a job."

"Are you fuckin crazy? You gonna fall for that?"

"No, I ain't 'fallin' for nothin."

"Are you sure she's pregnant?"

"Course I'm sure. You think I'm stupid? We went to the doctor together."

"You worked hard for this, Carlos."

"So? It ain't nothin but school."

"Oh, right. What about your future? What kind of job you supposed to get?"

"I'll manage. We'll do okay."

"Yeah, for how long? Listen, if you really wanna go through with this, why don't you both go up? You can still be a student."

"Forget it. You're the one told me I wouldn't have much money, how I'm gonna support a family and shit in school? Besides, I ain't gonna drag her way the fuck up there, away from both our families. No way."

"Dammit, Carlos, don't you understand? You can't just give up everything and settle down to play house the first time you think you're in love. Besides, it's not that easy, and I don't think you're ready."

"No, *you* don't get it, man. It ain't just about love. I do love her, but if it was just the two of us it wouldn't be no problem. You just can't stand it, can you?"

"What, seeing you ruin your life?"

"No, you can't stand it that *I'm* doin what a man's *supposed* to do. Later, Mr. Crawford."

Nine

Elliott

Number 10 owned the snakepit his sophomore year. That was all he had. The rest of his life had disappeared on a bus. And Quince had been gone so long that the guinea-pig sidekick part of himself had gone the way of *Bonanza*. Talking to Quincy had helped when Glenda made her move, Elliott had to admit that. And showing up at his dorm in that borrowed Batmobile the night before his first varsity game to settle him down, that was pretty cool. Especially since they hadn't talked through the night like that in years, and he never once mentioned the old man. Holy nostalgia and shit. But that's all it was, really, a blast from the past, and he still had to get through this bad boy on his own. Ma and Davis knew all about it but kept their distance, the way he wanted it. He wasn't about to be spending time at home anyway. Phine was just starting high school, he didn't expect anything from her, but she turned into a real pain in the ass, like she was Glenda's sister. As far as the rest of the world was concerned, it was none of their fucking business. Guys on the squad, he just told them he let her go so he could concentrate on the season. And dared them to tell him he was lying; they knew they'd never see the damn ball.

He owned that, too. Like Willis Reed once said about Clyde: "He just lets the rest of us play with it once in a while." But you had to be good to get some sugar. Don't be wavin your hand with somebody hangin all over you. Elliott would just hold it, pull it back out, or take it to the hole himself. If the sucker was dumb enough to come over and try to block it, and you kept your hands up, then Elliott would let you have it—

maybe hand it to you in midair from behind his back—and let you do some monster shit. If you got it off the defensive board, gave it to Elliott right away, and busted some booty down the floor, you'd get it back again. But not till the last minute; he didn't like to see anybody else dribbling his ball much. And if nothing else worked, he'd just airmail the shit in himself, but usually not till deep in the second half. Davis was right. This was basically a very simple game.

Which was good, because the rest of life was a stone cold mother-fucking bitch.

All through his first year, with the anticipation building, he'd thought that starting and starring and making the pit rock would be magic. It was, for the fans and the team, but Elliott didn't care, except that getting everybody excited made his job easier. He'd made up his mind by the time Quince got back in that black Buick and yelled, "Atomic batteries to power" (and he couldn't stop himself from re-sponding, "Atomic turbines to speed"), that all this would be contin-ued elsewhere. So when he left the court he went his own way, left the parties, pot, and pussy alone, and booked. He called home with news about midterms, not wins or assists; that shit was in the paper. And af-ter they'd captured the conference and lost in the second round of the NIT, before anybody could even start some next-year shit in the locker room, he told everybody he was moving on.

He knew he'd have to sit out a year but there wasn't shit else to do. That was one of the reasons he concentrated on the books. The coaches at Syracuse didn't want him to enroll in engineering, because they thought it would take up too much of his time. They did want him to play, though, and they couldn't stop him from actually going to school while he waited. Even though he'd lose some credits he'd be able to get a lot done in his year off and be in good shape with two years of eligibility to turn the place out. He even stayed in Amherst over the summer with no scholarship—Davis paid, he didn't even have to ask—to take two courses. And to stay his ass out of Boston. Phine had called in the spring to tell him when the baby was born. In the middle of the damn tournament, no less. He hung up. Not right in her ear and all, he wasn't really mad at her, but he just kind of grunted and said he had to go. Later she sent a picture of Glenda and the baby, Erika. He didn't want it, but he slipped it into one of his books and took it with him when he left.

One advantage to spending two years in Mayberry, Massachusetts, was that Syracuse didn't seem that bad. A lot of the students were from New York City, and the general word was that this was a dipshit town. It actually reminded him of Springfield, which he'd visited several times as a freshman in search of blood life—and because that's where his father had come from, though he'd never told Quincy about that part of it. Studying faces in Woolworth's or walking through the neighborhoods, he'd tried to picture what that earlier life was like. Once he'd used a trip to the Basketball Hall of Fame as an excuse and had deliberately misdirected the driver so he'd have more time to soak up the vibes from the streets that he'd finally decided looked just like anywhere else. He probably wouldn't have wanted to give Quince the satisfaction if he had found something of him, meaning of them, there, but he didn't.

Here it was like the same drill for a different reason, he wasn't looking for some past that he never really believed in but for a here and now that he'd fit into. And so in addition to the team meetings and practices at which he was primarily a visitor, and the classes in which he surprised people by being serious, he spent time off the Hill checking out the native habitat.

That's where he found T, shooting pool in a nasty little club on the colored side. Pushing past the recollection that that too was something he'd learned with Glenda, he watched the tall blood who looked like a hinged cue—he'd never seen anybody that bony this side of Biafra—work the table. Elliott knew the guy was an outsider, by his posturing behavior as well as his dress: he was sported all in black, with a cowboy hat and boots, wraparound shades, and a long, thin Kojak cigarette. His victims, on the other hand, were remarkable only in that they didn't seem to know that's all they were, like they were supposed to have some kind of home-court advantage by looking like part of the furniture and hiding their other lives as workers or sons or fathers or whatever they turned into when the sun came up. Maybe they just disappeared. If so, the Lone Ranger here was speeding up the process by null-and-voiding them one by one.

"Get a stick, man, you want some?"

Elliott knew he was being addressed although the hustler had not turned around.

"No thanks. I don't go in for garbage time."

The player nodded and put his cue away, then stepped to the bar, drawing Elliott magnetically along.

"You pretty smart. Must be from the Hill."

"I'm from Boston. I'm up there for a while now, though."

Another nod and a smile as a bottle of Miller's slid into his hand. "You Davis, right?"

"Elliott."

"Yeah, we'll have to do somethin about that," he said and clinked bottles in a salute. "Tyrone Tillman. Welcome to the dark side."

T spent just about every night in those shadows. Mostly he was scouting for business. A freelance disc jockey—have turntable, will travel—he was steady lining up dates in the colored clubs and bars that didn't quite deserve the name around town. He'd do weekend gigs for the regular clientele, special events for fraternal organizations, or offer promotions guaranteed to bring in the college crowd. And in the meantime, he just hung out, making himself known, measuring the musical tastes of the customers, shooting pool, playing cards, talking shit, and drinking like a goddamn fish.

He was more heard than seen on campus, known first for his ten-to-twelve weeknight radio spot and secondarily for his Paladin silhouette slouching downhill after dark. Few ever claimed to have seen him in class, but that was because, as Elliott discovered after visiting his off-campus apartment, he had a secret identity. It never occurred to most people that the T-Man would occasionally change clothes and put in some book time under his given first name, Stanley.

The Darknight DJ was a perfect companion for the year because he didn't give a shit about sports and helped keep Elliott's mind off not playing. He thought jocks were fools and seemed to tolerate Elliott at first only because he was a jock in exile. In fact he thought most people were fools, including the nonstudents whose company he preferred. Except musicians; he was a fool for them. T could sing a little bit, not as well as he thought, and couldn't play any instrument. But he could play the musicians themselves. In the studio, where Elliott took to hanging out, and especially on the weekend gigs that Elliott assisted, T saw himself as an artist, like Count Basie or James Brown conducting his band, made up of everybody on wax, with body English.

He wasn't hung up on genres, which surprised Elliott, a straight-up soul man who'd always thought Quincy's more varied tastes on the weird side. T would play the Doobies and Bowie as well as James and Kool & the Gang because he saw it all as the same shit, wherever it came out, and gave the white boys credit for knowing a groove when they fell into it. "Groove don't care who's in it, man," he'd say, slipping a taste of Stones into the mix. In fact, though he seemed to worship the cool above all, he sometimes gave points to the white boys who didn't worry about it, cause they couldn't, and let it lay out there, busting a gut and trying real hard to get to the Real Thang. Too much cool can kill, you know. Free your mind and whatnot. Elliott chalked it up to T's being from California but had to admit that the shit got over. Everybody tuned to T-Man on school nights, and his parties jumped.

Elliott didn't need much of a life to get him through those days. Aside from doing his schoolwork, eating, and working out on his own and in pick-up games, T was plenty. By the end of spring, he had put in enough time at the studio to become a valuable part of the operation, and though he was never heard on air he became known as Sweet D, the T-Man's trusted companion and silent partner. When T got a brainstorm for a mix, Elliott would pull the record from the floor-to-ceiling shelves in the back room. He stacked the tapes for PSAs and commercials and screened phone calls, because T didn't want to be bothered with most requests; he came with a playlist in his head every night.

On Friday nights, the show often served as a lead-in for a campus party featuring the one and only T-Man, guru of the boogie. While he finished up in the studio, Elliott would be putting in the black lights, lugging the amp, attaching the speakers, rearranging furniture, and stacking the sides. Everybody else on campus was yawning out of their evening naps, clearing up the dinner dishes, playing cards, or getting high to the smooth tones of T and his midtempo tunes. About ten-thirty-five the movies were letting out, and Mister T jacked up the pulse a little. At eleven-fifteen, he turned it loose, and all those folks pulling on their party clothes, combing out their 'Fros, firing up the third jay, pouring out another round of wine, vodka, or tequila, clapped their hands and cut barefoot warm-up steps. At midnight, the Terrible T had them where he wanted them and wheeled back from the console to tighten himself up just a bit. By twelve-thirty they were falling into the pad and Elliott was there, holding the temperature just right. Let them stay loose, but no sweating yet. Wind sprints. At one, Tyrone the Cyclone blew down the door. He took the mike and Elliott was free to go for himself a while. Sometime after two—you could never be sure when—the party would be there. Maximum people, maximum motion, maximum magic. On cue, Elliott returned to the table and Tyrone jumped up, like James Brown out of control, like Sly on the good nights, like anybody's preacher stepping away from the pulpit, and hit the floor, fronting his electronic all-star band with splits, twirls, and chants. They were a hit.

At the end of the year they took it on the road, sort of. Elliott got a summer job offer from an engineering outfit in L.A., and T, who couldn't be bothered making plans in advance, was going home to kick back, knock on doors, and see what was happening in the music business. He invited Elliott to stay at his place, but it was a shaky invite. They had always respected each other's privacy, spending remarkably little time in each other's rooms, considering they spent so much time together. So they compromised, and Elliott got just four days of Stanley Tillman's strained Crenshaw District home life before landing an apartment out near LAX that allowed them to maintain their roles. Elliott went to work each day, Tyrone did what he did and showed up most evenings in full costume for a seamless round of bars, nightclubs, Fatburgers, chicken shacks, and concerts for which T had mysteriously obtained tickets. It didn't take long for Elliott to figure out that T-Man knew a lot of people and had no friends. Even stranger, he knew the summer would not have gone any differently if he hadn't been there; T would make the same rounds with someone else he'd found somewhere, or alone, it didn't much matter. He was glad to be along for the ride, though, having never been out of the Northeast, and it amused him to learn that black folks could be so different, so *California,* and at the same time so perfectly country. It was as Quincy, who had never been out there but didn't mind passing judgment anyway, had predicted: niggers on a beach.

In any case, the timing was about right. It was early August before Elliott finally met a woman T had been talking about all summer, some kind of mysterious player named Hortense he had gone out with in high school, who sported a huge platinum blond Afro wig and battery-lit earrings. She and a Korean girlfriend got them in to see Rufus at the Whiskey A-Go-Go on Sunset Strip, and the night turned into a total L.A. experience. After the show they did some barbecue at a joint down on Vermont Avenue that looked like something out of a Fred Williamson movie; they scored some coke and chilled out in her Hollywood apartment all done up in glass, chrome, and powder blue fur; got rousted there by some superfly motherfucker who acted like her pimp or supplier and ran him off with a .38 the Korean produced from her handbag; hit the road again in Hortense's baby blue LTD convertible and watched the sun come up freaking in the sand at Playa Del Ray. By then, Elliott was about ready to get back.

For a while, the following fall, he worried that having seen the Mighty T in his native habitat, where he was just another scuffling would-be player, would compromise their thing together. It didn't, but basketball did. As Elliott began working with the team, T grew withdrawn, almost jealous. They still did the weekend thing, but Elliott had less and less time for the radio show. And less need for Tyrone's cloak of darkness. When the season began, he was back in his own world, like two years before at the pit. On the court, he was nobody's baby brother. Nobody's fucked-over boyfriend. Nobody's second-choice son. Nobody's running buddy. Nofuckingbody's motherfucking nothin. He was the boss.

And the team was on fire. In the middle of the season, around the time everyone forgot what the ground looked like without snow, they were running a ten-game streak and climbing in the polls and the papers said Elliott was the reason for the newfound consistency. T, never one to miss an opportunity, announced each win on the air with the Ohio Players' full-funk "Fire," read his man's stat line, and slipped in a promotion for upcoming weekend gigs, where, if the team wasn't out of town, Sweet D himself would be on hand to work the turntable just like he worked the court. Elliott never craved the spotlight off the court, but the tie-in was good for business, and besides, he was just there to be there; it would always be T's show.

Which could cause problems. Because of the way T played to the crowd, he sometimes had to play off a chump whose woman had gotten the wrong idea. Or one of the regulars he'd shown up at cards, pool, or dominoes during his weeknight sojourns would try to make points in front of a crowd. But T was a performer who could handle himself, by being charming, disdainful, or threatening as the situation demanded, and having his hoop star sidekick to back him up didn't hurt. One night during the streak, in a hole-in-the-wall club run by a skycap/handyman/numbers runner, the act wore thin in a men's room squeeze over a coke buy. The funny thing was that T didn't use the stuff much, and Elliott never did during the season, but T figured it was good for the image and therefore for business. This time there was a misunderstanding about money, and Elliott heard a commotion rumbling up behind the B.T. Express shaking the speakers. When he hit the men's room door, the first thing he saw was T's shades skittering across the floor, and he waded in without hesitation. Two on three wasn't so bad. It was like that time he'd saved Quincy's ass in Cambridge, on his last visit. But when one broke out of the john, ran over a couple of dancers, and got the crowd into it, Elliott knew they were in trouble. T's first instinct was to get back to the gear, save the shit and maybe the party. Elliott, knowing what T had been doing, wanted to book. The confusion cost them, because the police showed up.

They sat, not speaking, for several hours in a large holding cell that included one or two other people T knew. T had managed to lose the shit, but the dealer, who was still holding, had fingered them both, and the owner was pressing charges because he hadn't sold enough booze and lots of people were asking for refunds on the cover he split with T and Elliott. They figured it wasn't serious, but it was messy. Elliott knew T was trying to find a promotional angle, but he had sense enough not to say so just then, because Elliott was worrying about a suspension. Besides, sitting there hatless and shadeless with dried blood on his upper lip, he was just Stanley.

Finally their names were called in an order they'd never heard before, Davis and Tillman, and they followed a uniform to the front desk, where they collected their belongings under the gaze of a pouch-eyed white man in a loud sport coat with three hairs combed from ear to ear across the top. "Let's go," he said, and they fell meekly into step as the man turned to T. "Not you, beat it." Elliott stepped forward to protest, but T held up a hand. "It's cool, I'm gone," he said. "Later." In the passenger seat of a new Chrysler with dealer plates, Elliott recognized the angel as a partner of the car baron who had courtside seats, an open door to the coach's office, and a hearty rapport with the players; the guy who'd chauffeured him around town talking up the university on his first visit. The partner didn't say a word till he pulled over at a campus intersection, three blocks from Elliott's dorm, and turned down the Sinatra on the radio. "Lookit, this never happened and it ain't gonna happen again, all right? If you can't remember who your friends are, remember who they're not. Stay outta those rat holes. Your boy's a loser."

Elliott dialed T's number as soon as he hit his room. It was busy, and stayed that way for two days. On Monday night he fell by the studio and T never looked up. "Got a show to do, Bigtime. Catch you on the rebound. Get it?" That was it. For a while Elliott thought somebody had warned T off him and he wanted to know who, but he knew that wasn't it. There'd been some tension with Quince, too, when he'd made all-city and dominated Ma's conversation, but Quincy didn't have to be there to deal with it, and besides, he had a hundred-match wrestling advantage from the days when he was still bigger, and about a thousand other stupid ways to keep him in his place. T didn't have any of that, no claim to lead but Elliott's willingness to let him, and so he couldn't handle it when everybody could see that Tonto had a bigger horse. Fuck him.

He expected to sit the next game but figured out at halftime why he wasn't: that would let everybody know he'd done something wrong and the papers would start looking for fingerprints. Instead, coach did the next best thing, kept him on the floor for forty minutes even when it was obvious his head was somewhere else. He finished exhausted, with four assists and five turnovers, and the streak was broken on a nonconference game. But that turned out to be just a bump in the road. The team, which now had Elliott's undivided attention, built momentum down the stretch and shocked everyone by emerging from the NCAA regionals to make the Final Four in San Diego. They were destroyed in the semifinal, but nobody had expected them to win anyway, and they came home as conquering heroes.

Riding high, Elliott did nothing but hang out for the first few weeks after the tournament. He even made a point of showing up at one of T's campus parties, because he knew T would have to recognize him from the mike, and he knew that would hurt. Then, at the last minute, he settled down to take care of business on his exams, which he could do because he'd never let himself get too far behind. In fact, the academic adviser who traveled with the team was always pissing everybody off by holding up his work habits as an example. She tried to take credit for that, but it was something Elliott had learned long before, back in high school, when doing homework was like being on a date. He knew he was nobody's Einstein, but Glenda had convinced him he could always get over just by plugging away. It wasn't the same alone, but then neither was working on his game.

Nothing was, but he'd gotten used to it. Just like he got used to being in the studio alone when he got his license so he could take over the radio show that summer while Tyrone was trying his luck in New York. Worked up his own sound, too, with more heart than T's—Earth, Wind and Fire's bittersweet "Reasons" was his theme—and a smoother mix. As something of a local celebrity, he conducted a few playground clinics, which were okay for a while but made him wonder how Quincy could stand being with kids *all* the time. And at the end of the summer he attended an all-star camp for potential pro draft picks that allowed him to think seriously for the first time that he might have a legitimate shot if he could stick the outside J deeper and more consistently. It was all falling into place as all the distractions fell away. He was ready for the challenge.

By the time the next season started, he was on top of all his work, including the grad course he was taking; he had improved his quickness on defense to compensate for his size, and he was popping unconsciously from twenty feet. He sprained his ankle in an early game—drew the charge—but that had happened often enough before that the ice and tape and whirlpool routine were like brushing his teeth. The good sign was that the team came back to win in OT even when the trainer wouldn't let him go back in. There was a time that might have bothered him because it meant they didn't need him, but he was past that now. They were playing the way he showed them and they were winning, that's what mattered, and he was anxious to get back so he could keep it going. Like Davis had taught him: be as good as you can, but if you don't win, it don't matter. The first part of the season was like exhibition anyway, you were supposed to pile up the W's and work out the kinks. The ankle didn't come around like it should, but since the book said to play him for the drive, he had room to exploit his increased shooting range and was content to start the offense from farther out. Don't push it, the coach said—because they hadn't lost yet—and he would be fine by the time the schedule got heavy. Elliott knew his body, though, and knew that something was wrong, even though the X rays were negative. The pain and swelling after each game should have subsided instead of getting worse.

The conference opener on national TV in January meant that the time was up for playing it safe. Teams were beginning to pick him up on the perimeter to take away the outside shot, so he drove into the middle like he used to, hoping to draw attention so he could dish off before he had to take it up. By the second half the ankle was talking loud and saying something even with the blood-stopping retape job, but the team was down and he could see from their eyes that he needed to be out there. So with twelve minutes to go and a seven-point deficit and panic spreading from the court to the field house seats right on top of them, he stretched out to pluck away a high dribble near midcourt and accelerated into the clear, using the rising screams of anticipation to cover the hurt. Since he knew he'd have to gather himself anyway for the throwdown everybody wanted, make sure he pushed off the right foot for a change, he slowed to allow the beaten defender to catch him and turn it into a momentum-shifting three-point play. That wasn't a good idea. Motherfucker came down hard with both arms, catching him in midrise and pulling him to the floor awkwardly on the bad ankle. Shot went in, though, prettiest double-clutch underhand flip he ever made, the kind of Pearl Monroe shit he always tried to avoid and the crowd loved. But he had to limp around squinting back tears before he could settle himself to make the free throw, and had to lurch to foul on the inbounds because he never could have made it to the other end. It was dumb luck that the guy missed his free throws—well, not entirely, he knew he had grabbed their worst shooter—but by the time the second brick turned into a break that cut the margin to two, he was gone, hobbled off to the dressing room between shots to an ovation that seemed to him as much pity as gratitude because he knew he wouldn't be back soon.

If ever. Before word got to him that they had suffered their first loss, the doctors had opened his ankle and found a bone chip that needed to be cleaned out—the sprain had actually been a tiny crack that didn't show up on the X rays. The surgery itself would put him on the shelf for at least six weeks, but the bigger question was how much damage had been done to the joint. Nobody wanted to talk about the possible damage to his life.

Elliott was barely off the phone with Boston that night when T called, asking if he wanted to get back on the turntable when he was up and around. Elliott didn't even have the heart to tell him to get fucked. What for? He was just being himself, and he had won. His theory that jock dreams were full of shit had proved correct, and he was back on the high horse. Elliott did say that he didn't think he'd be up for it for a while, but maybe in about a month. T said no sweat, but give him a call anyway when he was moving around. He might have a surprise.

Whatever "moving around" meant to him, it seemed to have slipped his mind that his apartment was upstairs. But Elliott lost the crutches before he was supposed to, anyway, and gimped up to the crib one night after the radio show, when he'd called to request "Fire" for the hell of it. T greeted him at the door like a long-lost brother and offered him some herb. The season was done, probably, why the fuck not? The apartment had two personalities as well. Usually, when Elliott had been there, it was the place where Tyrone went to become Stanley. But this was T time all the way, dim lights, mood music, and his boy in full costume.

"So how bad is it?"

"I'll dance again if platforms don't come back."

"You dumb fucker. You know goddamn well your ass shouldn't have been playing on that foot. You guys, man, you all get to thinkin you're fucking Superman, don't you?"

"You through? What you got to drink in this motherfucker?"

"It hurts me, D, that's all. I just don't like to see my man with his wings clipped." He went to fetch some wine. "But that's okay. You'll fly again once you realize that wasn't you that got left out there. Look at it this way: your name's still good for business, and now you got time to actually show up and shit."

"You're all heart, T. So where's my surprise? What's up?"

"Patience, my brother." A quick knock hit the door, and T checked his watch. "It's magic, what can I say? Right on time."

T opened the door and a caramel-skinned girl with long hair, a leather jacket, and short skirt stepped in.

"Right on the dot. You're good, princess." He kissed her on the cheek and peeled her jacket. "This is Elliott Davis, Sweet D his own self. This is Vanessa."

"How you doin?"

"Great, thanks. I've been wanting to meet you. I heard about your accident."

"Yeah, it's no big deal."

"Come on back here and let me get you hooked up."

As Vanessa slid around the corner, Elliott grabbed T's arm.

"What is this, man?"

"Hey, I said I had a little somethin for you, right? Welcome you back to the team."

"How old is she, anyway?"

Tyrone grinned. "Old enough not to know any better. Relax, D. Have some more herb."

He should have left right then. This shit was too freak. But Vanessa reappeared with a glass of wine and an attitude more smoldering than the reefer she offered him. He sat down. She sat next to him and started talking about watching him play. She actually remembered some of his passes, and the way he wiped his hands on his shorts when he crouched over on defense, looking to make a steal, and pointed to his teammates where to go when he was running the offense. And she'd been to some of their club dates and just loved the way he was able to block out everything and concentrate when T was working the crowd. She didn't seem to notice, or care, how T was working them now, grooving the sides as if he had a mixer, adjusting the lights, pouring wine, rolling joints. He was good. Before long, all Elliott noticed was her lips moving soundlessly and her breasts and legs pressing against him.

Deep inside, her mouth still held a taste of bubblegum, her neck and breasts of sweat behind the scented soap. Her stomach, tight and smooth as the thighs he gripped, fluttered under his lips. The hands that undid his shirt buttons and his fly were small and tender. The lips full and strong.

He opened his eyes to watch her on her knees between his. And saw T standing solemnly behind her, naked and thin as a shadow, pulling at himself, growing larger with each heavy breath. Like slow motion, he lowered himself to his knees, slid down her panties, placed a dark hand on her back, and readied his cue stick. The force of his thrust brought her head up, widened her eyes. She gasped and clutched Elliott's thighs. He lowered her face back onto him, desperate to maintain the rhythm. But as he rose to bury himself in her, squeezed her to him with all his strength, he couldn't see her for the shadow enveloping her from behind, and now falling across his own hands as they held her. And there was a chain reaction: Elliott shivered, she stiffened, and the shadow grew teeth in a widening smile.

Release faded into resentment as the girl looked sweetly up at him, panting and licking his juice from her mouth. She got what she wanted, but it wasn't him. She didn't even know him. She just wanted a taste of that little bit of fame she'd seen out on the court. Before, that had been cool. There'd been some game and party groupies around, but he had picked his spots. Everybody got what they wanted for a hot minute and went on about their business. This wasn't his choice. The part of him she wanted didn't exist anymore. He felt had.

He grabbed her by the throat and squeezed until her eyes got big with fear, which made him big with desire. He sprang forward from the sofa, knocking T back out of the way and sending her sprawling on the floor. When she tried to scoot away he fell on her, pried her legs apart, and forced himself inside. Her high-pitched yelps gave him his rhythm. T squatted beside them, holding her down with one hand and stroking

Elliott's back with the other, and cooed the melody: "Go ahead, work it out, work it out, do it baby, that's my boy." Elliott fired joylessly into her wetness and pulled out.

"So what now?" He didn't hear Glenda returning to the porch from putting Erika to bed, but her voice didn't startle him. It was the next sound he'd expected to hear, cutting through the fog of four years in a bemused monotone. Three syllables to close the chapter and turn the page.

He'd always been straight up with her, no fooling around. She had long ago replaced Quincy as his closest friend, and he talked to her that way. That's why just showing up wasn't enough. He knew that after the first time he'd come over. She wanted more, and she deserved it. So he'd just finished telling her the story of his life from the time she left it—most of it, anyway. He didn't go into detail about that business with the girl Vanessa, or the trouble afterward, or how his helpless anger had finally moved him to pick up the phone. She'd get the idea.

"I believe it's your move," he said, nodding to the chessboard.

"No, I don't think so." She tipped his king as she had always done, win or lose, when she'd had enough. "New game."

Ten

Fontelle

"Look here, Fonny." She saw the bald spot on the back of his head as he sprawled on the sofa watching the late news, his socked feet on the coffee table beside a discarded *Black Enterprise.* "They're still looking for that boy. Shame, but if they ain't got nothin to say they need to let it go by now, know what I mean? Man, if that was a black boy you know they'd have his parents in jail, all his relatives under surveillance, and it still wouldn't be on the news. Been what, about a week now? Biggest city in the world and nothin else happening. Except all that Bicentennial bullshit."

She had paused on her way to the kitchen from the makeshift dark-room in the basement. The same space that had been a Barbie museum, feminist library, and painting studio. The space Daddy had crafted for her out of a spooky, damp corner the summer he'd gone off to the March on Washington, complete with desk, bulletin board, shelves, and a bed covered with Mommy's grandmother's flower-print quilt. The space whose privacy she had sought to secure with a cheap Woolworth's hook lock, which she had only seldom had the courage to use.

"I'm going to clean up the kitchen," she said, her hands on his shoulders over the back of the sofa. "You want anything?"

"Naw, baby, not now, thanks. Might get a nightcap a little later."

She pulled her hands back and rubbed them on her jeans and walked away. At the kitchen sink, she quickly drew water and worked her hands in the sudsy warmth. When she went to remove the dishes from the table, she couldn't help noticing again the flower painting on the wall, carefully preserved with a plastic cover. Her first, which Mommy had been so proud of. It duplicated the pattern of the quilt downstairs. Mommy thought the broken flower was a mistake, then decided it was an artistic touch, which got her excited enough to shop for art courses, which left Fontelle spending more time in the basement room with the door closed and not locked. After a while, she had stopped asking Mommy to come down and see; Daddy said it was too difficult for her, and he was right.

"I'm tired of hearing about those goddamn tall ships already. How's that writer of yours?"

"He's all right. Looks like his book is finally going to get published."

"Oh yeah? Bout time. So he gonna quit teaching and make some money now?"

"I don't think so. It doesn't usually work that way. You know what they say, 'Don't quit your day job.'"

"Yeah, I heard that. I keep tellin you, Fonny, you want to be some kind of artist, that's fine, but you better find somebody making some real money."

"Like an engineer, right?"

"Beats a teacher. Or a sculptor."

"Change the record, Daddy. It's not like that. Quincy's not my boyfriend and never has been. I wouldn't think about marrying him— I suppose that's what you're driving at—even if he did make big bucks. Who says I'm going to get married at all?"

"Now, I didn't say anything about all that. But you gotta eat, papers or no. I'm not going to be around forever, you know. I just want to know that you'll be all right, is all."

"I'm fine, Daddy, and so are you. Please, I told you when I came back I didn't want to go through all this. I just need some time and space and then I'll get out of your way."

"Don't say that, Fon." He stepped close behind her, and her hands moved more slowly in the dishwater. "You know you're never in the way. It gets pretty empty around here since your mother passed." He fussed with her hair. "I'm glad you came home."

"You don't want to miss the weather."

"Yeah, that's right. You can leave that chop out, I'm gonna be hungry."

How lonely was it for Mommy when she went to school in New York? Hard as he had always worked, late nights, going in on weekends, furnishing the house and the lessons and the vacations and the doctors, he had made a great show of being around when he could. But not for Mommy, really; it was for her. Even though there wasn't much for him to do in those last few years. She had a license and the car Mommy couldn't drive, her friends, her classes, meetings, and dates. But he wanted to act like she needed him as she had when she was younger, to take her places, talk to her, go over homework, sit up together and watch TV.

Maybe Mommy didn't mind. Maybe she enjoyed the sound of him in the house. Maybe it didn't matter that when he was there paying attention to her, it took away from the time they, mother and daughter, had together. Time that was quiet and free, not command performances. In the mornings they ate breakfast together before school, after he was gone, and listened to the radio. In the evenings she brought dinner to her mother's bedroom and watched the news while she ate, filling in the commercial breaks with school reports. The kind of information Daddy demanded, then commented on. Mommy just listened. If Mommy felt like sitting in the living room to wait for Daddy, she would come out and do her homework at the dining room table to keep her company. On the weekends, sometimes she'd drag Mommy to the mall and try to get her to do herself up the way she knew Daddy liked. "Gotta put a little life in it, girl, you know what I mean?" she'd say. "Girl, what you know about some life?" An awkward pause, then, "Besides, we got more dresses in the house than we need. Can't get you to wear any, and you're the one could use some making up, with your little hippie behind." Those exchanges were like flashbacks even then, but the timing was off, Mommy showing traces of the busybody she used to be, and her finally old enough to mix it up with a partner who didn't have much left.

When Daddy was home in the evening, Mommy would just stay in the room, and so did she—until he called her out to keep him company. It wasn't the same, which was why by her senior year in high school she tried not to be around much for either of them.

That didn't work. Mommy retreated even more, and Daddy became more agitated when he was home and she was gone. She hoped that when she went away, even if it was just across the river, they'd both stop waiting for her. And realize that they had each other. From what Daddy said when she called, it seemed to be getting better. And Mommy did seem happy—tired, but happy—at the semester break. Maybe they did find each other. Or maybe, by giving up on her, they gave up on themselves, and Mommy was just happy to be left alone altogether. She never could be sure, because afterward everything changed so fast.

The call came just before Valentine's Day. There was going to be a big-time party that weekend, and she and her freshmen partners were definitely going to turn it out because the upperclassmen were just too tired with all the political stuff she'd already gone through like last year's dance step. A few people were in her room, male and female, they all ran together, and he said, "You need to come home right away, Fonny." There was more, but she didn't listen. She never knew if he said she was already gone or that there was still time. She waited until she thought he was probably finished and said, "Okay, Daddy," and hung up. She lit a joint and sat on the bed with her knees pulled up. After a while that could have been a minute or several she felt pain in her fingers like a burn, and the others who hadn't been paying attention to the conversation were around her, holding her and shaking her and asking, so she told them, "I think my mother's dead." She floated across the top of the GeeDub in the backseat with hands on her and people going "shh." Somebody knew the way. She saw both cars in the driveway as she shuffled to the door. And she saw his face in the doorway. He wasn't sad, though he looked as if he had been. Nobody, in fact, had ever looked happier to see her. She remembered that.

She spent the night in his arms on the sofa. Apparently there was nothing to be done. The afterlife began in the morning with a long shower like this one. Her own pallbearers from school had vanished quietly, leaving her with a packed bag, but what she needed was already there at home: a dress her father had bought a few weeks before. She watched him through it all, and she stayed by his side, like a little girl at a gathering of family strangers because that's what she was. Even when her friends, the ones from high school and the ones who'd delivered her from Barnard, appeared at the funeral, she refused to step out of his shadow. He knew what to do, how to be bereaved and cordial at the same time. He took care of everything, and Mommy's friends and relatives took care of the rest. She did wonder, once, as she listened to him describe the last months to a sorority sister of Mommy's at the house after the service, if Mommy had ever had the benefit of his charm since she'd left for school. Or anytime, really, since the time before she could remember. He talked sweet like Marvin Gaye with a little rush in his voice, broke into a helpless, boyish grin sometimes to show that he was all right, and all the time drew graceful arcs in the air with his long, strong hands. Studying him, she felt worst of all about what Mommy was missing. Long before she died.

But that didn't last. The people went away and he broke down. Stayed up all night trying to cry. Wouldn't eat. Couldn't talk. She was afraid to go back to school. But the house was cleaner than it had been, and the women had left enough food for two weeks. She spent a day in the basement sketching funeral faces, then collected photographs of Mommy to work from. She left the basement door open in case he wanted anything.

After two days she surfaced for a shower and fell out on her bed in panties and T-shirt, switching back and forth from WLIB to WABC on the radio. She didn't hear the door open but the rustle of paper broke through her "Rainy Night in Georgia" haze.

"You make these? I went looking for you, tell you I'm okay and get some sleep. You need to be getting back to school. I found these."

"You like them?"

"You know I hadn't looked at the pictures in a long time, but this is even better. It's like you brought her back. With your own hand, you know. And look, see, this one is off an old picture but you made her look more like now, you know, the way you remember her."

"I didn't realize I'd done that." She smelled bourbon on his breath, not a good sign, but at least it had got him moving.

"You realize how much you made her look like you? She used to, but I hadn't seen that in a long time, either. I suppose it was always there. And you found it. I guess that's what they mean about putting yourself into your work." Silence. "I'm going to keep these, if it's okay."

"Sure, Daddy. I hope having them helps you as much as drawing them helped me."

"Yeah."

"You haven't slept either, have you?"

"I'll be all right now." He stared at her and, as she had with the drawings, must have seen something she didn't know was there. "I don't know what I'd do without *you*, Fon."

The emphasis on the "you" didn't hit her until days later, when she was back in the dorm wondering why she needed to make excuses for going home for the weekend. At that moment, when he said it, it brought her arms around his neck and his around her, and they swayed slightly to the music and slumped to her pillow. And she remembered hugging Mommy the last time she'd left for school and all the hugs she'd never get and began to tremble, from fear, not from sorrow, and felt herself about to cry and became aware of his tears soaking through to her breast, and they both squeezed harder. And then he touched her, like he used to.

She fingered the large, notched knob and turned it hard, and her body shivered from the rush of cold water. She found the other and turned in the opposite direction and bit off a scream as it came even colder. Then, gently, she shut the flow and sagged shaking and gasping in the slick, tiled cell. She had come back, twice, three times—what would I do without *you*—never knowing, always expecting, because it was safe, and she made excuses because nobody else, she knew without thinking, would believe so. Sitting on the shower ledge, dripping onto the Congoleum, she toweled herself off slowly, beneath the view of the mirror. The fabric warmed her skin. She rubbed harder until her breath came in short bursts. The next time she had felt less sure; instead of her mother, and the emptiness they both felt, she thought, again, as when she was thirteen, about the flowers in the quilt and what they were supposed to mean four generations later. Something else, probably.

She didn't need the mirror to tell her what she wasn't. Men were so easy to fool; they saw what they wanted, even if it wasn't there. Quincy, too. But she needed it then, he let her be the flower in her own make-believe garden, let her be somebody someplace else. Made it easier not to come back. A good lie, for a long time. She rubbed lotion disdainfully onto the hard, colored-girl knees, up and down the bony, stubbly legs. No wonder. Six years, and she'd blown it in half an hour.

Maybe it was true what he'd said about desire. You get interested because you want somebody, but you don't want to be that blatant about it so you force yourself to listen to their story. Then you become involved, become a friend, and you're stuck with them after you get what you wanted or even if you never get it. Like a lot of the stuff Quincy said, from the very first, it sounded real good but felt bad later, because telling her was like saying it didn't count for her, which meant that she didn't count for him. The more she encouraged his honesty, the more it bound her to him but kept her away. Stuck.

The lie of desire had got her through another year of Barnard, though, and gave her time for the transplant to take. And by the time she got to Brooklyn she was okay. Quincy was fucking everything that moved then, but she didn't need him for that. She knew where he was. And she had her moments. A couple. In the dark.

She cinched herself in a cotton robe and emerged with the towel wrapped around her head. California was going to be different. She was going to bloom in the sunlight, away from home, and away from Quincy too. Even though she went with Antoine—came with him too, sometimes, when he couldn't get what he really wanted—that was just a ticket. So what the fuck was she doing here?

She dialed the number before she knew what she was doing and sat hurriedly to compose herself. On the third ring she snatched the towel from her head and shook her damp hair to get into character.

"Hi, lover.

"What's the matter, is Lady Cronkite there?

"Wait, listen. I didn't mean to put you on the spot or anything. It was good to see you. Old times, you know, I just got carried away. I won't, I mean, if you don't . . . come on, Quince, don't leave me hanging. What I'm trying to say is, that wasn't the way it was supposed to be. It's okay if you don't want me, like that, anymore. I mean, I never thought you meant it anyway. But I still, I still need to talk to you."

She loosened the robe. The coolness calmed her.

"It was awful. I mean, it was okay for a while, everything went pretty well. No, he went off . . . Don't say it, okay, I know. I knew. But it was good.

Yeah, that too. You'd be surprised. But even after, it was okay, cause I made good contacts and got into the photography. But then I started getting these letters, from home."

She shrugged the robe from her shoulder, and one hand drifted from the receiver to her nipple.

"Yeah. I didn't want to come back, but nothing was happening, and I didn't know what else . . . and I figured I could count on you to . . .

"Dammit, Quincy, will you listen?"

She tugged through the wet kinks in her hair at the base of her skull.

"I need you. I can't . . .

Okay. Sure. But hey, call me, okay? Please?"

She held the base of the phone clenched between her thighs and hunched forward to whisper feverishly.

"Night, Crawdaddy. I love you."

Balled up wasted in the stillness amid the phone cords, soggy towel, and twisted robe, she heard the tinkling of ice in the distance like an alarm. Without looking she found the radio dial, turned it on, and eased up the volume. Then, aware for the first time of the thin beam of light piercing the darkness, she rolled from the bed, bounded bare-foot to the door, and nudged it closed. Caressing the painted wood with her body—they'd changed it, together, from pink to lilac long ago, and she herself had later added the numbing strokes of gray—she circled the button lock of the knob with her thumb and slowly withdrew.

From the box in the corner, Diana Ross breathed a slow-building chant:

If there's a cure for this . . .

The sleeveless nylon full-length nightgown was in the top drawer. It felt good sliding down over her. It felt pretty. Women were so easy to fool. Another mirror, over her dresser, confronted her. She faced it, and her fingers found the makeup kit that had fallen to her careless possession after one doomed mall trip.

Don't call the doctor.
Don't call the preacher.
Don't call my mama.

They pushed color onto her cheekbones. They delineated her eyes. They spread a gaudy gloss onto her mouth and, willfully, scrawled her Fox signature across the glass of her self-portrait in some passion-purple fashion fair tone.

She turned from it, absently licking the color from her stub-nail fingers, closed the drapes, and stretched out under the covers of her bed.

I don't need no cure.
I don't need no cure.
I don't need no cure.

Bright, exotic, tropical flowers blossomed like fireworks in her head, one after the other, bigger, bolder, louder, filling her black canvas that expanded infinitely. The door clicked open, and the flowers faded in the dim hallway light.

Eleven

Delphine

Delphine felt entirely stupid, but hey, it wasn't the first time. Might be the last, though. Chris refused to come early, just absolutely refused, and she wanted to hate him for it but she couldn't afford to be hating him right now and she did understand. He'd be miserable. So was she, but it was her idea, hers and Beth's, so she had no choice. There wouldn't be time to go back home and change, and she'd never get her hair right in some hotel bathroom. So here she was getting dropped off at her senior prom by a big brother in a warm-up suit, wandering around alone looking fabulous and already starting to sweat.

The timing wasn't bad, anyway. Easing into the ballroom, she saw what looked like the last hoedown. The band was playing K. C. & the Sunshine Band—"Get Down Tonight"—and that's what everybody was trying to do. Looked like that's what they were always trying to do, except they'd never admit it. That's probably why they didn't want the blacks around, so they wouldn't look as foolish as they did trying to act black. Suppose the brothers playing horn in the band didn't count— even they looked funny up there, two-steppin side to side in their white coats, careful not to be too cool for the rest.

Now how was she supposed to find Beth in all this pink and blue and blond? They should have set a definite time to meet at the door or something, but who could tell when Bubba was gonna get it in gear? As she crept along the wall peering into the congregation, some cream puff whooshed by patting her hair and almost caught Delphine in the head with an elbow. "Damn, knock me down, why don't you?"

"Oh, Delphine, I didn't know you were here." It was this horse-face child from math class. Delphine turned away. Didn't need to be gettin into any little stupid mess now, with some flat-ass, birdbrain heifer.

"There you are! Hey, you look great, Del."

"Don't I, though?" she responded to Beth, who had appeared from nowhere. "You look good too, girl. I'm glad you found me cause I don't know . . ."

"Well, it wasn't that hard."

"Yeah, okay. I see what you mean. How's it goin?"

She could see as they worked their way to Beth's table, though, that everything seemed to be okay.

"You know, I think it's gonna work," Beth said.

"Couldn't have done it any other way."

"Come on, slap me five."

"You've had too much champagne," she said, obliging self-consciously. "Let's get to work."

"Don't go way, Brian," Beth called to her boyfriend.

Delphine hated the way Beth got all cutesy-clingy around him, but she was used to it. She met Brian hanging around practice, treating Beth like some kind of princess although he spent too much time looking at her too. They had a long conversation once—long, about ten minutes maybe—about busing while waiting for Beth. He said he thought it was a good idea. He was doing the talking, she bit her tongue cause she knew if she led him far enough he'd say something stupid enough to make her hate him, and she didn't want to do that. He wanted to be right, he just didn't know how. She did cut in, though, once when he was babbling about opportunity, to let him know they were okay before and in fact this wasn't exactly the promised land, just someplace else, and they'd all have to make do. He hadn't thought of it that way before, he said, and that was something, she supposed.

He thought he looked good, with his dark brown wavy hair and little-boy swagger, and Beth swore they just broke the mold and whatnot, and to tell the truth she could sort of understand. Because the swagger wasn't set yet, his eyes gave away that he was still pretending, and searching, like he wasn't altogether responsible for the way his body acted. She knew if they were all black, which didn't make sense, and if Chris weren't around and if Beth wasn't her friend (she had to admit that's what she had become), or even if she was, she could go for Brian. She knew it, anyway, the morning she woke and realized the dream she'd had about Chris turned into Brian when he touched her and the vision of their bodies together shocked her awake. That was Quincy's scene, or had been for a while anyway. She steered clear of Brian, and that weekend at Chris's house with his mother out she almost let herself go completely with him—actually she did, but just not inside her—so that her dreams would come out in the right color.

The whites were leaving right on cue. Beth held the band strictly to the ten-forty-five cutoff, and once the music stopped the people couldn't get out fast enough. Most, Beth had said, were off to a bowling alley, but Delphine didn't care where they went, just that they had been there and gone. She gave the black band the signal to move into place and made sure the kitchen was getting ready for the next shift while Beth pestered the cleaning staff.

"Woman power!" Beth said, grinning, as she and Delphine completed their rounds in the fast-emptying room. The high heels and the champagne worked a hardship on that little bouncing gymnast's walk of hers, but she managed. She really was too short for the drill team, but Delphine had needed her energy. And as it turned out, she needed the mix and she needed a friend, and Beth was willing. There was more to her pixie ass than Delphine had thought. It was her holdout, and Brian's good-natured cooperation, that had made sure they got a decent turnout.

"Yeah, but you got all those promises to keep now," Delphine said. "You know that bowling isn't gonna hold em off for too long."

Beth looked over her shoulder to Brian waiting by the door and sighed with mock despair. "Oh well, what can I say? Girl's gotta do what she's gotta do."

They both giggled.

"Shit, I'm ready!" Beth declared, almost too loudly. "Who wants to go bowlin anyways?"

They embraced and started walking toward the door.

"Have fun, girl," Delphine said, and added in a whisper: "Don't wear him out."

"I'll call you tomorrow."

"Make it late."

"How bout Sunday?"

"You got it."

"Bet you two are pretty proud of yourselves," Brian said, pulling Beth to his side.

"Course we are." Beth put her hands on her hips, colored-girl style. "*You* said it was a dumb idea."

"It was. But you pulled it off."

"We couldn't have done it without you . . . guys." Delphine tried to pull it back when Brian's eyes fixed on hers, but it was too late.

He took her hand and squeezed it. "Well then, I guess we all oughtta be proud, huh? I had a great time. I think everybody did, but they'll never tell you, so I am. Thanks."

Delphine reclaimed her hand and scanned, over Beth's head, around the room.

"I better make sure everything's ready."

"Relax, Del, they got it. Time to have some fun yourself." Beth circled Brian's waist as she said it.

"You want us to stick around awhile?"

"Oh no. Folks should start arriving any minute. I'll just wait here for Chris. I'll be okay."

"Well, I'm gonna dash off to the little girls' room."

"Too much champagne, huh?"

"Yeah, you wish."

They both stood dumbly and watched Beth bounce away around a corner. Then looked at each other. For a second. Delphine's eyes zoomed down to her shoes, and she fretted that she didn't have anything to do with her hands.

Brian changed position a couple of times and finally asked, "So how come Chris ain't here?"

"Oh, he . . . he didn't wanna be bothered with the cleaning up and all. Figured that was woman's work, you know. He had some other stuff to do anyway. My brother brought me."

"Oh yeah, I heard about him. He's supposed to be a pretty good basketball player, huh?"

"Well, he was. Messed up his ankle, though."

"Tough break. So, what're you doin next year? College, right?"

"Yeah. BU. I told my parents I didn't mind stayin in town, but I didn't wanna live at home."

"Yeah, I know what you mean. Me, I'm goin in the navy. Gotta get outta here."

"Thought you liked it here," Delphine said. It felt strange to talk about the place they'd both spent their whole lives like it was his home and not hers. But she knew what she meant.

"Yeah, I'll probably be back, I'm sure, but it gets boring doin the same stuff all the time, you know? I mean, there's more to life than what you know. That's why I guess I'm kinda glad you guys came in. I know it was a lotta problems and all, but I never woulda thought about all that stuff otherwise, know what I mean?"

Delphine wondered if there was a time black folks had the luxury of not thinking about whites. Back in Africa, maybe. "Yeah, I know," she said.

"Tell you what, sounds funny, but I wouldn't mind stayin for the rest of it. I think it'd be a blast."

"Don't press your luck."

Brian looked at her as if he didn't have any idea what she meant, a look that was so absolutely innocent that it kind of appealed to her and scared her at the same time. Where had this guy been for the last two years, for the last eighteen, for that matter? He really didn't get it. He shouldn't even be standing around here talking to her now.

"Maybe I better go make sure Beth didn't fall in or nothin, huh?"

"Yeah, maybe you better." Delphine smiled to cushion the blow of reality. "Thanks again for your help, Brian."

"Don't mention it." He stuck his hands in his pockets like he didn't know what to do with them and kind of bowed with his shoulder. "I'll see ya, okay?"

"Sure."

Delphine wandered a few steps into the dining room and looked around. Beth was right. Everything was under control. She probably hadn't needed to come early, but she felt a personal responsibility. Suppose she hadn't and the whites didn't leave? When the tribe showed up it'd be like *West Side Story* or something.

She drifted down to the lobby in time to see Beth and Brian strolling out with their arms around each other and wondered, from the look of them, whether they'd make it to the bowling alley at all. Then it occurred to her that Chris would be expecting a payoff too. The prom had been a shaky excuse—white women's lib bullshit, he called it—but it bought her some time. She understood how Beth felt after the last few weeks, not that she and Brian hadn't done anything already. That's why Beth left the Catholic girls' school in the first place. Delphine was ready, too, but she didn't think she should be. It wasn't the same. Beth wasn't even going as far as BU, and Brian would be back if she let him get away at all. If she got stuck, well, the odds were better. Not that Chris wasn't responsible, and not that Daddy wouldn't be after him and all, but they had more to do. This was a beginning, not an ending. Like they say, commencement, time to commence getting on with life, not settling in. And hell, look at Bubb and Glenda. Erika wasn't his child, but Glenda was his girl. And they still didn't have it together. Maybe Quincy had the right idea, to keep moving.

Still, she had this warm feeling, like she'd been drinking the champagne. She stepped outside to make Chris come faster, and when that didn't work she paced to the parking lot on the corner, excited and weary at the same time.

"Hey, cleaning lady," somebody called.

"C'mon, I got a spot on my pants I want you to brush off."

A group of boys from the prom who were gathered around a car began moving toward her. Where were their dates? Delphine stopped, glanced over her shoulder for Chris's car, and reversed her direction.

"So you wanted to get all dressed up like white folks. This oughtta be good."

"Have you seen Beth and Brian?" she asked in a loud voice as they drew closer.

"How you gonna do all that nasty nigger dancin in them fancy clothes, huh?"

"Yeah, I thought niggers liked to dance naked so they can fuck right there."

"How'd you like to do some nigger dancin for us, bitch," one said, catching up to her and grabbing her arm. The other two blocked her path on the sidewalk.

"Get your hand off me, motherfucker. Leave me alone, I'm goin inside."

"You ain't goin nowhere till we see how good you can dance."

"She gotta get naked first though, right?"

She slapped the closest one, a tall blond, as hard as she could. He grabbed her wrist. She spat in his face, pulled her arm free, and started to run.

"Where you think you're goin, bitch?"

Captured, she screamed. Where was everybody?

"C'mon, get her back to the car."

"No! Get *off* me, goddammit. I'm not playin with you fuckers. Let me go!" She reached for a shoe and started stabbing with the heel as she felt herself being lifted and pulled. No good. Too many. Too fast. She could hear cars passing on the street but she couldn't see, couldn't get loose. The hotel sign loomed in the near distance, mocking her as she was pulled into the darkness of the lot. In senseless desperation, she heaved the shoe at it. "Fuck you!" she screamed.

Twelve
Glenda

"There he is. You happy now?"

"Hi, Elliott. You wanna play?"

"Not right now, munchkin. What's she doin up this late?"

"She's waitin for you. You said you might come by. She keeps thinkin you're gonna teach her to play ball or somethin."

Elliott looked at Glenda like it wasn't his fault he was there. Maybe, she thought, that's what happened when you were used to getting all that attention. Can't even tell when you're asking for it.

"You drop Phine off?" she asked.

"Had to. She was drivin me crazy. Hate to be around when she gets married, boy."

"Bet she looked real pretty."

"Yeah, she did, actually."

"Who?"

"My sister, Delphine. She got all dressed up to go to a big fancy dance. Looked like Cinderella at the ball."

"I wanna go too."

"Not this time. The boys couldn't stand it. You'd knock em all out."

"Yeah, I knock em out like Mommed Ollie."

"Easy, champ. Yeah, she looked good all right, but it sure seemed like a lotta work. I couldn't get into it."

"That's cause you never went to your senior prom."

"Yeah, why not? Oh yeah, that's right. Listen I gotta talk to you about somethin."

"Yeah?"

"Later. After Cinderella Ali here goes to bed."

"Why I gotta go to bed?"

"It's late, Riki."

"So?"

"Hey, now. That's no way to talk."

"Come on, kiddo."

"You said we play a game."

"You heard your mother. It's late. I forgot I had to take my sister to her dance. We'll play another time."

"Tomorrow."

"Okay, we'll play tomorrow."

"You read me a book tonight?"

"Erika."

"If it's okay with your mother I'll read you a book, a short one, after you get ready for bed. Okay?"

Glenda set down the book she had been reading and collected Erika.

"What are you reading?" he asked.

"*Sula*. Toni Morrison."

"Yeah, Quincy's always talkin about her."

"You should listen to your brother. He has good taste."

"Yeah, but he's weird."

"He's not weird. He just doesn't worry so much about what everybody else thinks."

"You never even met him."

"Known him long as I've known you. You talk about him enough. If he's weird, what does that make you?"

She took her time brushing Erika's hair. Braiding it. Like she did every night. Winter and summer. Work nights and weekends. Before her mother gave up and moved South with her kid brother. Making the two of them their own family together. While Elliott played ball and went to college. While Walter came and went trying to figure out what his place was because he didn't have one. While Phine finished growing up and now was graduating high school. And now Elliott was back, maybe, but that didn't change anything. Her and her baby. A family. Every night. Just like this.

"Let's go brush your teeth."

"Elliott, I'm ready!" she sang when they finished.

He stepped into the room and looked over her little library.

"How about *Peter Rabbit?*"

"Yeah! I like that one."

"Short one, huh?"

"It's not so bad."

"Glad you think so. Say your prayers first, Riki. Case you fall asleep."

"I ain't gonna fall asleep."

"You're *not* gonna fall asleep."

"That's what I said."

Elliott situated himself in the high, fluffy bed, where Erika could lean on him and see the pages.

"'Once upon a time there were four little Rabbits'—"

"'Flopsy, Mopsy, Cottontail and Peter!'"

"Hey, that's right. You read this already? You wanna read it to me?"

"No, you."

"Okay. But you can help if you want."

Glenda sat in the rocking chair folding the laundry she'd done earlier in the evening. And listening. And watching. Walter had tried this too, once. She'd stayed then, too, so Erika wouldn't think this was a new routine. The way it was supposed to be. Or would be. Every night. Erika was younger then, though. And she could tell Walter had never done that before. Elliott had Phine. She knew he'd helped take care of her, some. Even though he was only five years older. He turned the page back when Erika asked so she could compare Peter's blue jacket with his sisters' red ones. He repeated words. He answered questions. How come the mother was wearing blue? He did voices. Glenda stood from the rocker. This could take all night. She paused in the doorway. Erika didn't look up. Or ask her to stay.

She went into the kitchen to warm up some food. Then sat down at the table, in what used to be her mother's seat, to look at the paper. The words "Stop, thief!" in what must have been the Mr. McGregor voice startled her. Girl'd never get to sleep that way.

That was where she'd found her mother every day when she came home from school or finished her homework. And in the summer, when she came back from playing basketball or shooting pool or going to the movies with Elliott. Or baby-sitting Phine. Her brother would be in the living room lookin at TV. Boy never did nothin but look at TV. And her mother would just be sitting there. Waiting for everything to happen.

Waiting for her father to come in and act a fool. You'd think he didn't have a job. Didn't have his own home. Didn't have a family. She knew people got like that when they didn't have nothin. Had reason to get like that. The white man could mess with you all right. She didn't have any problems understanding that. But if he could get you to mess with yourself, he didn't have to. She didn't understand that. The white folks gave him a hard time on the T. Maybe could've paid him more. Could've promoted him. Maybe there was other stuff he might've done. So? Who was stopping him? Not her mother. Look like movin away was the only thing she ever made happen. Marrying him probably wasn't even her idea. Not her brother. All he wanted was a TV. Didn't cost that much. All Glenda wanted herself was a roof and food, and she hardly ate anything anyway. And a mother and father, maybe, but you take what you can get, and she knew even before she met Elliott not to expect but so much from them.

If he didn't like it, he could've done somethin else. He could've done nothin. He could've turned off the doggone TV and read to the boy. He could've taught her to play ball. He could've got his wife up outta that seat and taken her to the movies. Her mother could work. Glenda could get a job. They'd be all right. It was nothin but money, and if you didn't need much, the man couldn't make you do nothin. Couldn't make you hate so bad that you hated yourself and your own. You had to do that yourself.

Elliott had only been coming by a little while. Maybe a week, after they finished the science project. She was happy that she had somebody to talk to when her homework was done. Somebody to talk to while she was doin it. She knew her father wouldn't like it. He didn't like it when anybody was happier than he was, and that only took a little bit. He'd been getting worse for a year. Mad about stuff that didn't even have anything to do with him. Mad about Malcolm. Mad about Louise Day Hicks. Mad about whatever. She saw the way he looked at Elliott when he came in and they were out on the porch playin chess. Elliott spoke. He didn't. She told him not to worry about it. He never said nothin about her father bein a drunk fool. What could Elliott say? He was probably scared. Should have been. He came back, though, like she wanted, and she didn't say anything either. As long as they could both ignore it for a couple of hours and talk and play chess, she'd be happy.

But he couldn't let that happen. Next time he stopped on the porch and looked at her hard. Elliott had his back to him. Started to turn and speak. Must have seen her face and went back to the board. She thought her father was gonna do somethin. She wasn't scared, but curious. When he went on inside she forgot about it. One more night she could play. The voices came out like always. Complaints. Why this? Why not that? The excuses. Happy sounding but careful. She watched Elliott watch the board and try not to act like he heard. Like it bothered him. She couldn't say anything to make him know it was all right. It would come out like her mother. She looked at his long lashes, blinking in confusion. His wide, bony shoulders rocking nervously. His hand held out over the board like it could it grab everything and hold it tight, if it knew the right move. She looked at him so she wouldn't hear. Held her breath till the moment passed.

The voices didn't stop. Elliott couldn't move. The sound of a plate crashing on the kitchen floor made her draw breath. She got up to go inside. She sensed Elliott about to rise and touched his shoulder to say no. Standing in the kitchen doorway, she saw her father standing over her mother, who was on her knees picking up the plate.

"Why you always trying to keep me quiet with some damn food? This is my house, dammit, I'll say what want."

"Stop it."

"I told you I didn't want that boy hangin around here. If I hafta tell him he won't be hangin around nowhere. You let that girl do whatever she wants."

"Stop it."

"I'm out here takin shit all day and what are you doin? The house is a mess. The boy is an idiot. Now you gonna let that smart-ass little girl run around and be a whore like you."

"Stop it!"

He bent down and yanked her mother to her feet. The plate fell again. He was in her face.

"Dammit, look at me when I'm talkin to you. You hear me? Say something."

"Stop it!"

He turned at the sound of the meat cleaver smacking into the table. Noticed her for the first time.

"I'm right here. Talk to me."

He looked at her like he didn't know who or what she was. Looked at the cleaver tomahawking out of the table near her hand. Didn't look at her mother gasping and sighing. Didn't shift his eyes at the sound of El-liott stepping in behind her.

"Glenda, no!"

Her mother threw her arms around him when he shifted, made a step in Glenda's direction. He pushed her back against the refrigerator.

"Who the hell do you think you are?"

He came toward her. She tugged the cleaver free with both hands and held it in front of her. He stopped. Saw Elliott lingering in the shadows.

"Oh, I see. Jumpin bad cause you think this punk's gonna back you up. He put you up to this? You all in this together? Tryin to rule me in my own house? Whatsamatter boy? You scared to do it yourself? You gonna let this little heifer do your fightin for you? You want some of that, you better come get some of this."

He moved forward again. She stepped in front of Elliott.

"Well, I guess she wants it more than you do. Move out the way, you little hot-pants bitch. I'm gonna fuck up your boyfriend here. And then I'm gonna teach you some respect."

He stared at her. He was breathing heavily and sweating. Eyes were big. Almost smiled. She felt her arms begin to drop. He saw it.

"Gimme that!"

His arm came forward. Hers sliced upward. Blood dripped from his arm. He fell back and said nothing. Studied her again. Raised up his other arm. She raised hers. Felt Elliott grab hold of the cleaver. Snatch it away from her with one hand and push her aside.

"You better go now," she said. To her father.

He straightened himself clutching his bloody arm. Looked from her to Elliott to her.

"You wait. This is my house."

Her mother made some noise. Didn't say much. Crept toward him sobbing no, no.

"Let him go."

He studied all of them. The television got louder.

"My house."

He staggered out the front door. Her mother sat back down. Elliott put down the cleaver. She went to the porch to watch her father go.

"You okay?"

She drifted away from him. Still watching her father disappear down the street. Elliott looked around. Didn't know what to do. Took a step toward the door and acted like he wanted to say something.

"You don't have to leave," she said.

The asking look on his face made her turn her back. She nibbled at her finger.

"You don't have to stay, either."

His hands grabbed her arms, turned her to his chest, and held her tight.

"'But Flopsy, Mopsy and Cotton-tail had bread and milk and blackberries for supper.'"

Erika snored softly into his chest. His long lashes were lowered. He stroked her braids and held on to the book like maybe he thought there was more. Finally he eased her head onto her pillow with one large hand and swung his legs off the bed.

"I'm impressed."

"She was asleep for the last three pages. But I wanted to see how it came out." He whispered. "Maybe I'll try Toni Morrison next time."

"You hungry?"

"I could eat."

"So?"

"So what?"

"What did you want to tell me?"

"Coach called me today. I got invited to a tryout."

"Where?"

"Seattle."

"Seattle?"

"Yeah, up in Washington State."

"I know where it is. Didn't know they had any black folks there."

"Well, they got a basketball team."

She got up, poured a drink of water. Stood.

"You goin?"

"I don't know. Not sure my ankle's ready. Or ever will be. And I'd have to see if I can delay my answer on this job."

"NBA's all you used to talk about."

"I was a kid then."

"You were a kid, but you were never a fool, Elliott. What did you think you were doin the last four years?"

"Good question."

"You got your degree anyway. What've you got to lose?"

He fingered the old crack in the kitchen table. It was smooth now.

"How can you ask me that, Glenda? I just got home."

She shrugged slightly. Put her glass in the sink.

"What do you think?"

"How should I know? Look, Elliott, it's your life. You do what you want."

"I see." He stood up. Slowly. "Look, it's late. I got some things to do in the morning."

She crossed her arms, looked down, and began to chew her fingernail.

He turned to go.

"My father," she said, and moved toward him. Through the space of that night nine years before. He waited as she came to him and looked up into his face. She wanted him to see the scene, too. "He hated us because he thought we made him live a life he didn't want."

He smiled sadly. The flutter of his lashes made the steadiness of his voice a surprise.

"I'm not your father, Glenda." He touched her hair and her eyes closed. "I thought you knew that by now."

"Elliott?" She opened her eyes and grabbed his hand as it left her head. "You don't have to leave."

Thirteen

Quincy

Quincy stood at the window looking out over Morningside. He didn't know how long he had been there. The call from Renée, Max's old roommate, had come just after nightfall, telling him what he needed to know. It wasn't too late, but it would be before the sun went down again. He had tried lying in his bed for a long time, planning strategy, wondering whether or not he should do anything at all. They were all there with him, telling him not to bother.

Renée herself, sweet freak of the endless legs, who had served herself up as the tastiest meal in Max's absence until his tongue was sore. She didn't have to call back, and obviously didn't understand why he wanted to know. He wasn't sure that he understood, either. She did it for Max, not him, he knew, because she thought it was crazy for Max to let that happen to her. Thought she was shaky and he would make sure she went through with it. He'd listened for the hint of an invitation— that wasn't on the agenda, but he couldn't help it—and heard none. He thought she might have gotten married, not that it would necessarily matter; a man answered when he first called to ask about Max. Must have a steel-belted tongue.

Mariela danced by, naked, a sad look on her face but the faintest glint in her eye. And Bernie, laughing as always. He had seen her faintly and heard her clearly and remembered her predictions lying in bed with Max watching *Saturday Night Live*. She even managed to joke when he went with her to the clinic and had him wondering whether it was he or Carlos whose sword had struck home. (Would that count as some kind of nephew? Grandson?) In any case, she had gotten into the cab afterward, still smiling, it seemed, and disappeared by mutual agreement. By now they were all growing faint, having been banished by Max but making a special effort, this night, to remind him of the way it used to be, and could be again. If only he would just lie there and do nothing for twelve more hours.

The clearest was Fontelle. The one that came back, like Max, but got away. The one who never left—it was her image of him, after all, that greeted all the others—and who still didn't quite belong. Whose departure, just recently, had saddened and mystified him and left him unsatisfied for brand-new reasons. Something was wrong there, something he didn't want to think about right now, but she kept staring up at him fully exposed at last, no shields, no veneer, nothing but raw, frightened yearning. Trying to shake her, he had jumped at the sound of the phone, and there she was. Unnerved, he'd tried to replay old conversations, but she couldn't. Tried to distract them both with talk of her California exile, maybe hit on an easy answer that could be dealt with another time. But she wouldn't stay there. She was here. He didn't need anybody else here now, though, not until he figured out what to do about tomorrow. *I love you, Crawdaddy.* Damn you, girl. I love you, too. But I can't. I'm busy. She had already hung up. Six years late and one day early. Goddamn.

He picked up his copy of the book, fingering the smooth paper cover, and held it to his naked chest. The only thing he had ever created and kept, been able to hold in the night. In the unshaded light from the street lamp outside he looked again at the photo on the back. He, at age eight, stood somberly in a short-pants baseball uniform that even then had looked like it was from a previous era. His left hand held a bat that was propped on his shoulder; his right was draped around four-year-old Bubb, who was drowning in his uniform, big, long-lashed eyes staring out from beneath a droopy, backwards cap. The kid almost looked scared, but it wasn't that. It couldn't be, not with big brother on the case to protect him, to use that midget bat to swat away anything that could ever hurt him. They both believed it then; Quincy still did, even if he hadn't knocked any obstacles from the kid's path in a long time. Even if Bubb had grown tall and graceful, the athlete, and Quincy couldn't swear that he had ever lifted a bat again after that day posing for Davis, who was trying to get into their hearts as he had their mother's pants. Tall, but lost, Bubb still had that wide open look like he hadn't made up his mind yet about how to handle whatever was coming at him.

Still, Quincy had done his best to raise him, teach him, and protect him, by absorbing Davis's wrath and finally by sacrificing himself for the peace of the family. By running at life recklessly to leave a calm wake behind. He'd tried to do the same for Phine, although he had less control there. He had given her the gift of the word and fed it all those years, after he was gone, with the monthly letters no one else knew about. No-bullshit stuff about life, men and women, things that nobody else would ever tell her, certainly not her father, until it was too late, laying himself open so that she could find for herself anything worth repeating, and know through his own example what to avoid.

He hadn't done such a bad job with Carlos, either, all things considered. He could even take some perverse pride in the fact that the kid was about to piss away everything because Glory, truthfully or not, had him by the balls. Quincy should have seen the trap coming, or at least known that Carlos was vulnerable. He had given Quincy big shit once he found out what went down with Bernie. At first Quincy thought Carlos was simply upset because he missed her company. But that was an underestimation. Carlos could not understand how Quincy could let that happen to his own child, his own flesh and blood. It was murder, he insisted, somehow not sounding like centuries of half-ass Catholicism or a right-wing lunatic. He sounded like a kid who knew the odds and didn't like them, who understood that his own existence might have been at stake. Maybe, too, he really saw something worthwhile in Glory. Or maybe he just saw something fucked up in Quincy.

Either way, it didn't matter. Being a teacher, like being a parent, meant setting yourself up for rejection. That was the whole point. When they say fuck you and walk away, they're done. His father had prepared him for it, even though neither of them understood and the time came early, so early, and unexpectedly.

In the dark, Quincy reached for another book on his shelf, *Captain Blackman,* slipped out the photo he kept inside the front cover, and sat at his desk. Clicking on the desk lamp, he shut his eyes against the sudden brightness and the fear of his own emotions. When he opened them he was in the arms of his father. But no, not this time. There was a child, who had been him, in his own arms. And the child had none of the studied responsibility in the face captured six years later, preserved on the book that lay beside the picture. He had the bright-eyed innocence of Bubb in the falling-down cap. But he was happier, because he believed in a way that Bubb never did, really, that his protector would continue to hold him for all time. Because he didn't know that he would become the man. So soon. *You got it now, little man. I want you to take care of everything, hear? I'm counting on you.* The little boy in the baggy baseball suit in the grainy picture on the shiny book seemed to smile the smile of the baby in his arms in the photograph, and ran across the street laughing in a blue baseball jacket. *I don't care what you say, man, that's like murder. I ain't never gonna do nothin like that, man.*

Okay, Daddy. I'll try.

Fourteen
Fontelle

He closed the door so gently that at first she thought he had not entered. Then, in the small space between the end of the record and Vaughn Harper's voice like smooth, unsweetened chocolate, she heard him breathing. Having heard it, she could not shut it out, even when the next song began and she tried to fly away with the strings, hide behind the beat, and push the voices out between them, an obstacle course to confound him. The breath pursued her like a serpent, gliding over, under, and around her defenses until, weary and entranced, she opened her eyes.

His silhouette was young and narrow, an athlete's, looming above her in boxer shorts. She raised her eyes to his and he wavered, returning a look of desperate tenderness that paralyzed her. He bent close, breathing bourbon in her ear, and slid himself beside her. Large, hot hands grasped her shoulders; mustache, lips, teeth, and tongue tickled her neck and nipped at her throat. She tried to find her way back into the music as the straps came down her arms and the gown fell away and her hands touched his heavy face, but it found her nipple and drew her back out into herself and into him. The deep tingling gave her voice but would not let her speak. His weight surrounded her.

She heard a sound that was her and felt a shiver that left her still. Her own breathing, high pitched and bluesy, made the music go away. He found her hand, foundering aimlessly, and brushed the length of his body with it, still tickling her with his tongue, and placed it on the fabric of his shorts. She found him there, hardening, and as he groped for the hem of her gown, she reached with her other arm, pinning him with her elbow. She seized him with both hands and began to stroke. He tried to reach for her one more time but fell back, yielding to the grip of her powerful fingers as they rubbed and squeezed, forming the clay that had formed her. It was her breath that she heard filling the room and overpowering his, her breath that came in wet, growling spurts on her hands and on him until her sculpture came to life and her color-smeared lips reached out to taste it as if to swallow herself at the moment of creation.

His groans disappeared into the music. She lapped at the thick juices running down his shaft and clinging between her fingers until it was all gone. And wondered why she was still alive.

But she was, and that was the truth. Rum and reefer had often helped her disappear, at least partially; even being with Quincy, finally, had been a fleeting escape from this, the feeling that brought her sticky fingers up under her gown. Killing the fire by fanning it. And she knew she was in that place Quincy had described, where you feel so good it's bad, or so bad it's good—it didn't matter—and the joy and the shame are so mixed up, and so strong, that you want to burn yourself up. Like a piece of paper. Just burn bright and die right there.

He saw and began to reach for her; a feral rasp froze him. She smiled and her head rolled back. The sight of the creator confused, captured behind her tainted eyelids, gave her the fuel she needed to ignite. Her cries, and curses, contorted her body as she left it, and spiraled slowly beneath the rhythm of the radio that had not been very loud after all.

Dead at last by her own hand, she raised up to confront him, one ghost to another, and told him in a grim-smiling whisper that came from another place to leave her, and never come back.

Fifteen

Delphine

The world turned upside down. She'd felt that way before, sort of, during the lifts and tumbles she'd choreographed for the team. But it wasn't the firm, supporting hands of her sisters that were pulling and clutching her with rough, pink fingers. (She had wondered, during the first practice, if she could count on Beth's pink fingers to hold on.) She should keep shouting, but all she could manage was grunts and snarls to keep from crying and keep from hearing their goddamn lynch-party laughter. Her legs kept churning and her hands kept pushing, but inside she was starting to give up. And that surprised her. All of her athletic training and all of Bubb's game time clichés were no good. Instead, she began to understand Quincy's warnings about the cruelty of men, that fuck-it-all animal thing that wasn't love or even lust. How sometimes, even a woman he thought he cared about turned into a lump and he could see in her eyes that she didn't want it but she couldn't stop him and he couldn't stop himself. That's how he knew he could understand war and lynchings and rape.

Her body slammed onto the trunk of a car, and she felt the cold metal on the side of her face after the breath left her body and before the pain replaced it. On the other side somebody pinned her arms outstretched. At least the car was clean. Oh, Jesus, no. They were pulling up her gown from behind. Her mind said "please" but her mouth changed it to "fuck" mumbled into the silver, polish-smelling surface where bloody spit dripped a puddle. Her face throbbed. Her knees hugged the side of the car. Her feet kicked weakly. She heard a zipper, like a whisper, then felt a scratch as a hand grasped the top of her panty hose. No Jesus. Fuck no.

"No!" The blunt flesh prodding her behind brought back her voice. Shocked her into yanking an arm free and twisting away. Clawing through a forest of white and powder blue jacketed arms. Shrieking in tongues into the purple faces that made angry noises she'd long since stopped hearing. Flailing like a cornered cat so that the light suddenly engulfing them seemed at first to come from her, like the shining glow of her own fear and rage. So bright she couldn't see the other set of arms pushing into the forest.

"Delphine, get down."

More white hands from another white jacket. She struck at them, too, and at the smaller ones reaching for her from the other side of the car. But those held on to her, not roughly, and turned her from the glare of the headlights of the second car that had pulled up.

"It's okay, honey, come on," Beth said, and Delphine tumbled from the trunk of the car into her supporting grip. She hobbled toward the second car, one shoe still on, as the pushing and yelling sounds clarified behind her then began to break up into isolated curses. Lots of car doors slammed, and she heard engines running. She was in a backseat with Beth in her arms, and all she could say was, "My shoe." "It's okay, it's okay," Beth kept saying, and she thought she was crying now because her body was sobbing, but her face remained dry. A car door opened and she jumped. "Brian, look for her shoe, all right?"

Maybe she passed out. She couldn't feel anything or hear anything and then the shoe was in her face, held by a white hand connected to a sweating white face that said simply, "You okay?" and reshaped when she snatched the shoe. "You want us to take you home?"

"No," she said. Was he crazy? Chris was coming. She was going to the goddamn prom. She slipped on the shoe, tried to smooth her dress, and fumbled for the door handle.

"Del, wait. You don't have to."

"I know what I have to do, Beth." She opened the door and found herself flopping back to take a deep breath. "Thanks, guys, I . . ." She looked at their faces, cute faces, both of them, really concerned and flushed with the effort of saving her, and she tried to focus on the humongous fact of what had happened and what hadn't, but still it was their pink faces that pushed her back out into the night. "I gotta go."

She left the car door open and moved stiffly toward the still-mocking sign.

"Delphine."

Chris was there, just suddenly there in front of her, pausing to see whatever her rumpled form showed. She fell into him the way she would a teammate's arms after a brutal half mile.

"What is it? What happened?"

She heard Brian's car drive away behind her and knew he was looking and wondering. She shook her head and nudged him backward until they were both moving toward the hotel. She knew she should tell him everything. She wanted to.

"Let's go inside," she said.

He wanted to kill somebody after she told him, sitting on a sofa-bench thing in the hall outside the ballroom with the tribe filing past in googobs of color and style that she couldn't help noticing proudly even though it frustrated him because it slowed down her story. His eyes got smaller and it was like he got bigger and even darker, like he was going to turn into one of those hero monsters in Bubb's comic books. But he held on to her hands the whole time, tight but not hard. That was nice. He wanted to know who, of course, who to kill. She wasn't sure. She thought she might recognize one of them, she had to give him that much. Brian probably knew who they were, but she didn't say that. What she said was that she had fought them off before Brian and Beth got there. Maybe because that's what she thought she should have done. What she wanted, and Quincy and Bubb and Daddy would have wanted. Not to be a lump, a victim, like she thought maybe Chris wanted so he could become a monster and kill somebody for her. He wanted to take her home, too, everybody wanted to take her away, like it had really happened, but it hadn't. She was there, she really was okay, and what she wanted was for him to take her inside to the party she had made happen. To be where the animals didn't want her or any of them to be. Just for a little while. Please.

She found a girlfriend to help her fix herself up in the ladies' room. She wasn't that far from looking publicly presentable, just a long way from prime prom quality. She just told people she'd had an accident, fell down or something, and they thought it was a shame but were so into how they looked nobody minded not having the competition. Underneath, though, she must have been in good shape because she was sore but able to move around pretty well. And that's all she really wanted to do. Since she wasn't going to win any beauty queen contest she just wanted to be out there with all the pretty people and move. Chris was cooler than normal, cooler even than you'd expect with the jacket and bow tie and starched shirt and satin-striped pants. That was because of her, she knew. He was looking at her like a china doll that had already been broken and glued together once and might come apart again any minute if you looked at it too hard.

But she didn't feel that way. There had been a low vibration in her body—she realized it when they first got up to dance. A rumbling, shuddering feeling like before an earthquake or maybe after. But once she was into the ritual, that shudder turned to bass. A thumb-stroked throb up and down her spine that kept her erect. Some chicken-scratching rhythm guitar pepped up her feet, and the horns and party lights lifted her right up out of herself where pain and shame couldn't find her if they dared to look. She swooped around that way for a while, free of Chris's care and vengeance, too, and absorbing the spirit of everyone who didn't know what did or didn't happen to her and maybe didn't even know or care about all the trouble that went into this thing. Then they all came together for a bus stop that was for her a dance of conquest. In perfect rhythm, like a great big drill team, they stepped and twirled and rocked and snapped and clapped and smiled. Her tribe celebrating its survival in the new world. Even their cotillion getup was part of the victory, adapting the other folks' costumes for their own private celebration. When that dance ended, she told Chris she was ready to leave.

It didn't matter that they'd only been there awhile and there was a lot of prom left. They did their slow dancing in his car, where she could be sure the exhaustion she finally allowed herself to feel was from happy and excited, not scared and angry. The dancing was more with their minds than their bodies, though. She curled into him with his arm around her and her legs drawn up on the seat, and she rested her aching face on the still-cool fabric of his dress shirt. And he held her hands like he was checking each small bone to see that it wasn't broken, and being a china doll, right then, wasn't such a bad thing. Not bad at all, and she started to cry, but it wasn't the big what-are-they-doing-to-me cry she'd been holding in so long. It wasn't that at all. More like an I-made-it-and-don't-he-feel-good cry. And he just let it come. Didn't get scared or nervous or try to smother her with a handkerchief like she thought he might. And when he had touched her softly to make sure that all the pieces were together and her crying was down to a kind of moist purring, he kissed her. It was like it could have been the first time, it was so different from any other kiss—even the night she'd pulled on him till he spurted all over her wrist, and he'd shocked her by reaching into her pants and finding an electric button. But at the same time it was like they'd both kissed a hundred different people and knew that this was the way it should be done. And that they were the people they should be doing it with. So good that she knew right away she'd never tell anybody but Quincy how it felt. How she understood now the good feeling that was the other side of the bad one he'd warned her about and she knew now, too. So good—and this surprised her—that it was good enough. Not that they stopped or anything. They kissed and kissed and kissed some more, and knowing that she wouldn't break, wasn't a china doll, he acted like she was a lamp he wanted to rub the genie out of. And she checked him over pretty good for cracks, too. They didn't stop, she thought and hoped they never would, but he didn't really start, either. And he could have. After all, the next best thing to killing would be to claim the thing you wanted to kill for. And she wouldn't have minded, not really. She thought she would have an hour ago, but if he had tried to take advantage of her, if that's what it was, she would have thought it better to replace the fear with something better. She would not have become a lump. She couldn't afford that. If he wanted it, she would have wanted it too, just because.

But he didn't. Or even if he did, he didn't. And she loved him for that. Maybe not a forevermore love or even a next-year love. But a right-now, hallelujah-goddamn, I'm-gonna-remember-this-and-get-me-some-more-someday love. The kind of love that made the kisses so good they were good enough. Because they showed how much more there could be.

Not now. But definitely. And soon.

Sixteen

Glenda

If she held her breath, the snapping of her bra would make no noise. Her heart was already louder than the television downstairs. The creak of the extra set of footsteps on the floor and the surprised squeak of the overpowered bed became part of the cartoon sound effects. He wouldn't care. She brought him a big bag of potato chips and some orange soda, the noisiest snacks she could find, to distract him while Elliott eased upstairs. Then said she was going to do some exercises before she started her homework. And turned the TV up for him. And opened the front window to let in the traffic sounds. Because he wouldn't care, he couldn't be trusted not to say something by accident.

Her father had been gone for a couple of months. Been back a few times. Late at night or when she was at school. She hadn't seen him but she knew. Those were the times her mother seemed to have money to spend. And when she looked less agitated. Probably wasn't cause they'd been doing it, even if they had. She just always calmed down when she knew where he was, even if he looked like shit or treated her like shit. Like she could relax as long as she knew. But she hadn't relaxed in a while. First she spent more time cleaning the house, so he'd like the way it looked and stay and she could sit down again. When she had the money she spent it on food and cooked it all up so he could eat it when he came back. One of those times when she was on her feet she must have noticed her son, and some of the food turned into toys to lure him outside where he could meet and act like people. And Glenda started getting a little piece of allowance money she could save for books and records. And finally her mother got so unrelaxed she started looking for work.

In the meantime, Glenda had come to understand that agitated feeling. The nights Elliott didn't come over she sat around feeling stupid for feeling lonely. Since nobody was keeping track anymore they stayed on the phone after they'd talked through their homework, on some nights watched TV together, and even continued chess games on the phone. After school and on the porch he held her hand a couple of times and kissed her a couple more, but that never seemed important and not nearly as good as when he wrapped her up that first time and she could hear her name echo through his ribs. It was the grip of his hands that relaxed her to the point of uselessness. But she didn't mind. School was almost over and she knew she could pass without concentrating. After that she'd be okay. Everything stopped in June and she expected he would, too. Her mother was on her first week part-time at Filene's. It was a start. No telling how long it would last, but at least a week. Time enough for one serious grip to relax her good into the summer, when there would be nothing left to hold her but the memory of it.

There was a moment when she let her breath out. When her clothes were in a pile on the floor beside the bed and he was pulling his pants down. Just a moment, before she scrambled under the covers. For him to see her. To make sure he knew who she was. It wasn't for approval. At least she didn't think so. But it was important for him to know. And remember. He saw and seemed to like it. He leaned over and kissed her. She was glad, but that wasn't what she wanted. She held her breath again and pulled the covers up while he played with the rubber. The bed screamed once more when he got on his knees between hers. There was some kissing and grabbing, but he was paying more attention to what he was doing than he was to her. She spit out a puff of breath when he eased up to the spot, started panting in time with him while he worked up a little rhythm to smooth the way, then shouted an "ouch" her brother must have heard downstairs when Elliott pushed through. His mouth fell onto hers, to shut her up, and his hands gripped her but wouldn't stay still. "Shh," he breathed over and over as he rocked up and down and she tried to press him close. Every time he pulled back she rose to meet him. That only made him rock faster until "Shh" turned into "Shit, aw shit" and he was the one whose mouth had to be covered.

Then, right then, he was hers. Just like she wanted him. His weight sagged and oozed all the breath out of her body in a sigh. His arms wrapped all the way around her until there wasn't any him. Just a bigger, better her, safe and strong as she always believed she was.

Now she held her breath again so they wouldn't wake Erika. His hands had grown large enough nearly to pick her up by the waist with just one. Large enough to give her the feeling of being held just by passing over her body. He wasn't in a hurry anymore, and neither was she. When her clothes were off she paused again, longer this time, with his hands still on her, to let him see her and remember. He still liked it, and she was still glad. Because, like the first time, she expected it to be the last.

"So whaddaya wanna do this summer?" he'd asked the first time, separating himself from her and breaking the spell.

"After school's out?"

"Yeah, we can spend all day together."

She started reaching for her clothes with a confused look on her face.

"What's wrong?"

"You don't have to lie to make it all right, okay? You never said nothin about summer before."

"It wasn't time. It's only a couple of weeks away now. You like to swim?"

"Don't mess with me, Elliott."

"What? What I do?"

"I don't need your pity, and I don't need to be sweet-talked. You got what you wanted, now get dressed and go. My mother'll be home soon."

She didn't speak to him for three days, until she called and asked him to come over. Because her mother was beginning to wonder if something had happened. So she wanted her to see him to prove that he hadn't taken advantage of her and dumped her. They sat on the porch studying for finals so her mother could get a good look. But she didn't talk to him much. And it didn't seem to matter to him. He left with the same cheerful "See ya tomorrow" he always did. By the time he got home she was ringing his phone.

"So where you thinkin about going swimming," she asked.

"You're crazy, girl, you know that?"

They swam, they played basketball, they did just about everything together but make love. There was more of that later, much more, but only after long hours over the years of touching and holding. When he learned to let her open his shirt, as she now unzipped the double-knit warm-up, and explore the length of his chest and abdomen. When he learned to caress her back and neck and hips like he was kneading dough for drop cookies and stealing a nibble on each one. To smother himself into her—just like this, goddamn—so tight she didn't even think about breathing anymore and she could feel their bones grinding together. Before he ever pulled his pants down.

They'd learned so well that by the time he left, went up to school, she forgot about the learning part. Thought it was natural, automatic. That when those swishy girls up there called, he loved them just as good. Without even loving them. Take their breath away. Give them his strength. She didn't hate him for it. He couldn't help it. Just thought it was a waste. That they didn't need it like she did, or they wouldn't be up there. That was the only surprise. She'd had him so long she didn't know she'd gotten to need it. That the agitation that kept her moving could wear her down if she didn't get to relax.

That's why she finally went along with Walter to his apartment, even though Elliott was coming back soon. She'd be doing him a favor, in a way, getting rid of all the agitation that had built up. Like getting a massage. Soon as he lunged over to kiss her, though, she knew she was wrong. It wasn't automatic. She tried to slow him down. He sped up. Grabbing and pulling like she was something wrapped in a box. She had to push him. Slap him. Said no. He kept on. Pulled her apart right there on the couch with the Lakers and Knicks and poked at her. The only person she had to be quiet for, that time, was herself. If she couldn't stop him she didn't want to bother her own self about her mistake. Just go on then. Didn't want him to touch the rest of her. He didn't have any strength to give. That's why she'd never thought of this before, it occurred to her only then. He'd always been nice and polite. Because he needed her too much. The game, she noticed, had gone into overtime. But it was over before it was over. She didn't think he'd been there long enough to make a mark. To leave something behind. She knew, had known, that he'd never replace Elliott. Even if he'd done it right. Just a massage. But what he left behind would have to.

She knew that when she knew it was there. But hoped, maybe, she wouldn't have to choose. More of her, like she said. What they wanted anyway. But just saying the words she knew he wouldn't hear it the right way. Knew it was time for the leaving she expected that afternoon with her brother downstairs watching loud cartoons, the leaving that had started when he went to school, even though he managed to convince her that it wasn't that. Knew that her strength and her relaxation would come from what was inside her, for the rest of her life, like she knew it would before she felt his big hand pull the cleaver from hers and guide her face into his chest where she couldn't see anything and lost her name in the echo of his body.

But what he have to come back for? She was ready to go on and sleep there in that strange room where he had a life and she didn't belong. Didn't mind that he had left her alone. Didn't even wonder where he was going or who with. She was glad he came back, though. Even though he didn't say anything different. Even though it made everything harder. At least they had a chance to talk about it, the way they talked about everything. Like they were making plans for next week instead of forever. Okay, I'll go home and keep the baby and you go play ball and we'll just forget about everything. Just like that. And then she curled up on that chest in the dark one last time and he fell asleep. And she decided, since he was there, to take something for herself. It was easy enough, once she worked him free, to bring him to life and straddle him. His unconscious hands reached for her hips, but this time it wasn't his hands that she wanted. That part was over. She wanted to make him water the seed he hadn't planted. Add something to the mix so that when the small hands touched her she'd think of the years of squeezing instead of the minutes of grabbing. It's all she figured to have, and he owed her that much. He knew it, too. His eyes blinked open in the dark, but he lay there and let her do what she wanted. Let her practice flying solo. When she finished drawing him up into her, feeling a faint shudder of pleasure and a weary release, she reached up to stroke the long lashes closed again and collapsed onto him till he went back to sleep.

"I can't do it, Cooz."

The rumble in his chest was deeper than she remembered. And she had forgotten how the tickle of his lips on her neck when he finally spoke sent an aftershock through her body. Their body. She dug her fingers into the back skin made soft by sweat and ignored the voice. To make it come again.

"It's been too long. I know you don't need me, but I can't go. I can't leave you again."

The trembles turned to alarm. She lifted his head by two handfuls of hair to confront him.

"How you gonna tell me what I need and don't?" she demanded.

"Ouch. Wait. I'm just sayin it's for me, all right? I need to be here. Even if you don't want me to stay."

She put her hands on his chest to push him away. It took all her strength, and not just because he was so much bigger.

"Uh-uh, Elliott, that's bullshit. You ain't puttin that on me. You think I want some fat old man sittin around here lookin at TV talkin about that coulda been him?"

"I wouldn't do that, Cooz. That's all done."

"Yeah, that's what you think. You get off me and take your ass to Seattle or Alaska or wherever you think it needs to go."

"But what about us?"

"What about it? The only us I know is me and Erika. Now go on, dammit."

"Shit, I must be crazy as you are." He angrily pulled on his sweats and sneaks. "You're full of shit, Glenda. You say you know what you want, you ask me to stay, and then you tell me to go. Maybe you just want to be left alone after all. All right, then. Fuck it, I'll go. You happy now?"

He stood there like he wanted a response. Like always. Couldn't just make a move and be done with it. So she said, "Don't forget to go to your left," and turned away. To make him leave. So she could breathe.

Seventeen
Maxine & Quincy

Maxine Love awoke that morning knowing that nothing would ever be the same again.

How's that for a melodramatic lead? Could go either way, too, pro or anti. Sponsors would like that. Good Sunday night feature, or maybe a piece of a half-hour local special for the next *Roe v. Wade* anniversary. Could even be Mother's Day, but nobody would buy that. Not about politics—the story of a woman with a decision to make and the courage to see it through.

Shit.

Maxine Love was glad she'd gotten any sleep at all to wake up from. Not because of any decision. You didn't get to make those. That's what the stories can never say. Your whole life makes those for you. The church, your family, your job, the man you got or the man you don't. Of course you're going to have it. That's what we do. Or, what the *fuck* you gonna do with a goddamn baby and half a career and a baby-machine sister you've been telling is wrong about everything and a four-year so-called relationship that's about as solid as the city's budget?

No, what she thought was going to keep her awake but didn't was fear. Fear of the whole goddamn procedure for one. Many times as she'd told people to do it, including Brenda, she'd never been there and absolutely freaked at the thought of going to sleep while somebody used some unseen equipment to go inside her and fix what some man had done.

And, two, fear of what came after. That wouldn't be in the story, either, because nobody, including her, wanted to think about it. How would people look at you when you tried to carry on afterward? She knew what she thought about others, when she knew, and didn't like it. Like the way you look at people whose battlefield courage you respect—they did what they had to—but pitied anyway because something was missing and you're glad it's not you. And then, do you get close again? Do you come again? Or deflect all your energy into a force field to keep it from happening again?

That was it, the scariest part. Keeping on at work, she knew she could handle, even if she didn't like it. They wouldn't see it the way she would. Shit, she was probably the only one at the station who hadn't had one, before or after it was legal. But as determined as she was to establish her career, as scornful as she was of her mother's and sister's traditionalism, she never really thought she might have to choose. Ever. Not until he went crazy. Even then, at first, she thought he was just overreacting, scared of commitment and all that shit. By the time he put her out—son of a *bitch*—she knew it was way past that; she was slow but she wasn't stupid. Yet it was only last night, fighting the urge to call him and tell him to go fuck himself in hell, fantasizing about having the fetus shipped to him, maybe at school, that the full impact of what he had done to her hit home. It wasn't about not trusting jive, self-absorbed motherfuckers—who ever thought you could? It was about trusting herself. Her own body. She thought he'd be good, that they could make a life together because if anything went wrong she'd be okay. Be able to walk away and move on. Take care of herself and find somebody else. But it wasn't that easy. If she was reluctant to take a chance, afraid that a mistake might ruin both the relationship and her career, she'd never be free. Because of him, and because of this, she now had to face the possibility that she might in fact become what her mother said she would: lonely and bitter.

She sat on the radiator under the front window and inhaled the aroma of the pot of coffee she'd put on. She wasn't supposed to drink anything, but the smell gave her the best of the flavor and enough of a contact rush. Too nervous to look at the paper, she listened to WCBS for her other morning fix, just in case there'd been an earthquake someplace or a really bizarre crime that hadn't come over the wire before she left the station. Or any news of the kid. And she looked out at Seventy-seventh Street wishing that Julio would hurry up.

An unlikely choice for an escort. That's how she'd describe it, but in fact he was the perfect choice. The only choice. She had to admit that between the job and running up to Morningside, she'd let her social life lapse into what could most politely be called oblivion. There was Renée, of course, she had to tell her. Despite the ironies. She had never forgotten the way he was looking at her in Mikell's that night when girl-friend picked up her cues to reel him in and disappear. And she hadn't forgotten that one phone call in Cleveland, when it seemed like she was trying to tell her and not tell her that she'd finally finished the job. Wanted to gloat, but had second thoughts. Neither of them knew, then, that she'd be back in the city and might need to reheat the embers, but Renée made her point, planting the doubt, warning her, subtly, that he couldn't be trusted. That wasn't news, and she knew when she did come back that that wouldn't be a problem—and hadn't been, she was cer-tain—but she appreciated the signal. Anyway, something about Renée's eagerness and certainty when Max told her of the situation she was in now put her off. It wasn't about ulterior motives. She just didn't like the idea that somebody else—somebody who'd given away as much as Renée, bless her heart, and was still doing it despite her marriage—might presume to know what was best for her.

Like she did with Brenda. That one was easy. They talked nearly every week, briefly, but she wasn't about to give Fertile Myrtle a chance to lecture her. Forget Mom, and Dad still tried to believe she'd never done it at all, a lie he'd been practicing since he let her convince him nothing happened with that boy in eleventh grade. And sisterhood be damned, she wouldn't give those crazy white bitches at the station the satisfaction. So that left Julio, as both confidant and escort. And why not? He knew the routine well enough, and his very boastfulness about his wild exploits, some of which she knew he made up, made her cer-tain he could be trusted with something real and personal.

Still, looking out the window, it wasn't Julio she imagined turning the corner in a slow rolling walk or uncoiling from a cab. It was him, mov-ing into view for a last-minute rescue. Like Lancelot coming for Guin-evere. Of course, he was also the Arthur who had condemned her. It didn't make any sense. What could he do, what could he say that would make any difference now? He didn't want the baby and she didn't want him. She didn't expect him to appear, and she didn't even want him to. But when she saw that Julio had finally emerged from a cab and was, characteristically, smoothing his hair as he glanced around for admir-ers, something in her couldn't help being disappointed.

• • •

He hadn't slept. And by the time the sun came up he was moving to meet it. Way early, but if he sat around waiting he might keep sitting until it was too late. It was cool and muggy as he headed down Amsterdam, everything quiet near the campus. An ambulance shrieked into St. Luke's, and nurses, like the city itself, changed shifts. At some spots, it seemed quieter now than in middle of the night, though that was not exactly true. Ebb tide. And the street is very still once more. The time when accidents happen because everybody's guard is down. Feelings get hurt, because the cover of darkness is removed, the heavy action over, but the daytime armor for coping with 8 million crazy motherfuckers is not yet in place. When you face the fact that last night was a mistake, but too good a mistake to have quit before seeing time. And you leave or she does, but not before a self-conscious silence like the kind at a restroom urinal—private business hurriedly carried out in public—or angry recriminations to preserve self-respect already lost. And sometimes not before it's too late, because the accident has already happened and will never be undone.

He had always assumed that this was the route that had been taken after his accident, on a city-hot summer night after Max had left for Cleveland. The woman didn't seem the cab type. And it would have been about this time. They hadn't found each other till closing time at the club, though she said she'd been watching him. He had seen her, too, all big legs and butt, no business at all in that mini but impossible not to notice; it seemed so comic, almost, that you ended up admiring her chutzpah. And thinking, or at least he did, briefly, before concentrating on better suited prey, about some no-talking, funky-sweating, jungle-boogie fucking. When the number he'd been playing most heavily failed to come out, and he began to drift toward the exit, she appeared before him as the answer, literally, to the question What the fuck?

It wasn't that easy. It never was, but this one should have been easier than most. No talking? She annoyed him with that Greyhound-from-God-knows accent all the way up in the cab, which seemed for her to be an unexpected way to get there. In the room he shut her up long enough to take care of business. But it was gentler than he had thought, his sympathy raised by her clear inexperience at being as drunk as he was, and by the sheer awe with which she held everything about him. The tenderness brought another wave of conversation, this time about her life, which in turn brought him to her again with an affection that completely astonished him, but not her. And then she vanished into the sunrise, transformed into the conqueror, and left not a trace of herself as she marched down Amsterdam, no longer laughable or needy, maybe even haughty now in her satisfied sobriety, and caught the 110th Street crosstown home for a quick change before work or church, whatever night that was. And kept what she stole from him. What he hadn't known he'd let her take. What he thought would never matter because Max came back and he wasn't giving anything away anymore. Everything he produced, he would be able to keep.

But not unless he got downtown in time.

So it's like this, is it? No receptionist, just everybody sitting around like at some secret meeting: if you have to ask you don't belong. The room is closer to an emergency room (a matter of life and death) than to Joy's understated-posh outer office. The sound level is in between, too, the more open, business-as-usual noise of a clinic muted by a tension that might have come from disappointment or embarrassment. She and Julio find seats, thereby declaring themselves members of the cell. The reading is almost strictly bring-your-own; the few magazines are scattered and worn, fat from constant, careless use. But several copies of the day's *Times* form subwaylike fences between the members and the activity of the room. A worker appears from nowhere to ask her name, then briskly disappears. Julio goes over to use the pay phone on the wall, just beating out a young doctor who doesn't seem to be in a great hurry, anyway. Instead, he briefly surveys the field and glances at his watch, looking up to feign horror at the sight of a young woman dressed for surgery who pads out to the waiting room.

"Escape!" he says, smiling.

"No way." She plunks down next to a woman, presumably her mother, who looks concerned. "This is taking forever. Might as well read the paper." The mother glances over at the bronzed Kildare, who with a quick hand motion indicates that this is okay.

"Weekend rush," he says with light shrug. "Won't be too long."

"Yeah, right," says the young woman. Home from college, maybe. Made all the arrangements herself. Mom, who doesn't work, is there for moral support; they'll do Bloomie's after. Dad doesn't know. That's one story line. The room is full of them, and Max can imagine how they would go.

Rita (not her real name) fingered her wedding band nervously as she waited beside her husband, who turned every few minutes from his paper to smile reassuringly or touch her hand. In their late thirties, this pregnancy had come as a surprise to both of them. But it was not the unmixed blessing so many childless couples pray for. Rita had already borne four children, the youngest nearing his twelfth birthday. A history of troubled deliveries, coupled with dicey finances that had forced her to find work after twenty years, had brought her to this moment of decision.

Darcel (not her real name) had forgotten the wisdom of her mother and ignored the warnings of her girlfriends. No married man, they had said, will leave his wife for you—even if you have his baby. Desperately facing thirty, Darcel had gambled and lost. For her, this passage is one of sobering realization—and an ironic kind of triumph. Reconciled at last to past failures, she will, after today, seek happiness from the only reliable source: herself.

Linda (not her real name) picked up a discarded copy of the paper, turned it inside out as if she were looking for a prize, and let it crumple into the empty seat beside her, along with the six-month-old *People* magazine that had brought no relief, either. She chewed her nails and recrossed her legs and silently dared anyone to say anything to her. But both the restlessness and the hostility masked her truer feelings: Linda was afraid. At sixteen, she carried falsified proof that she was two years older—and her presence here indeed suggested experience beyond her age. She had been sexually active for more than a year; she had been careless, and she had been lucky, until now. The consequences of her irresponsibility had never occurred to her before. Her boyfriend had deserted her, as she knew her parents would if they knew her condition. Only the aunt who had given her the money and the referral offered her any support, although she, too, had declined to accompany her. Afraid and alone, Linda fidgeted as she waited. Waited to get the whole ordeal over and done with. Waited for everything to get back to normal. There was another boy she was eager to go out with; she'd have to wait six weeks for that, too.

Maxine Love, twenty-seven, had never particularly wanted children anyway. She was too busy. At one time she thought she might, but only as a joint project. Only with a man as ambitious and progressive as she would she be willing to share the inconvenient adventure of child rearing. There would be no sacrifice, no career hiatus, for either of them; together they would disprove the stereotypical and self-defeating notions that had stifled women and cut men off from their families for years. That would be the only way. Because of a lapse of judgment, a momentary loss of concentration, Maxine had believed her conditions were about to be met. But that had not been the case, and so she was here to cut her losses and get back on track. Her only concern, at the moment, was that the doctor was running late, and she had to get back in the office that afternoon.

"Maxine?"

She follows the woman who had first taken her name out of the waiting room. Julio, just off the phone, reaches for her hand with both of his. She smiles bravely and lets him squeeze. All right already. Inside, sitting across a metal desk from the greeter, she breaks herself down into answers for a standard form, like central booking.

Kildare saunters in, smiling, and identifies himself as the anesthesiologist, Dr. Silver. Hi-yo. He takes her hand, too, more gently than Julio, but that's what he does. Suave you into semiconsciousness; the drugs just finish the job. She notices his gold bracelet; she'd been told to leave her jewelry at home. There are more questions from him, some of them the same: did you eat or drink anything this morning, any history of heart problems, diabetes, any allergies, do you smoke, do you drink?

"Sure, what've you got?"

He likes that, and so they are both smiling when Joy, Sisterdoc, pops in to ask if there is anyone in the waiting room she should let know. The implied danger of the question skips past her at first—let know what?—because she knows Joy will recognize Julio's name and fears she might reach the wrong conclusion. Of course the recognition doesn't register. Straight, smooth, and hard as an African sculpture, Joy gives away nothing. But that is definitely something to be straightened out at her next office visit.

Into the operating room, finally, she listens to the West Indian nurse talk, primarily to herself, about how busy it is this morning, as she takes her blood pressure and hooks her up to an EKG. Silver glides back in looking as if he has lost, and now found, the love of his life; he's good. "Just a teeny pinch," he says as he puts in the IV. "Should I count backward?" "Who started that? Everybody always asks that. If you want to count, try forward; no sense making this complicated." An oxygen mask is placed over her face. She sees Joy and notices the clock on the wall: nine-fifty.

Damn, this is too much—talks, reads, writes, and fucks too. Lots of practice. That's okay, it wasn't wasted, and he can get lots of practice right here right here right here. Yes, this is good, this is what you want, you need me, don't you, say it and I'll stay with you, I'll give you all you want. Yes! Shit! Take it, tell me what you need, tell me what you see.

Should I say how much I missed this, needed this, no, you can see it, don't you, hear it, feel it, yes, baby, I'm back, it's for you, I told you it would be good, we'll keep it just like this, just like this, it's good, isn't it, I told you, give it all to me, baby, I'm here, I'm here.

I told you I know what you want, I've got what you need, not her, can't you feel it, it's right here, it's in me where you put it because you know this is right, this is good, it's been so long don't stop, this is it, we're almost there, yeah, get it get it, I got it, I got you. Shit.

Must be expecting some kind of attack; the place is hidden well enough. Twice around the block, check the lobby directory—okay, so this has to be it. He looks around for someone to ask, but everyone is just sitting, waiting to be taken away. He starts to investigate a passageway when a hand catches his shoulder. Julio Lopez, *Channel 6 News,* investigative stud.

"What are you doing here?" Julio asks.

"Where is she?"

"I don't think that's any of your concern now."

"The hell it's not. Where is she?"

"Look, let's step outside and talk."

"Fuck you. Get off me. What are you doing here, anyway? What she do, fuck you and say it was yours?"

"Come on, man, let's go."

The greeter emerges from the passageway, hands up and mouth pursed in shushing gestures.

"Help me. I'm looking for a woman named Maxine Love. Is she in there?"

"I'm sorry, you're not allowed."

"Not *allowed*? I'm the father, dammit, *she's* not allowed. I have to talk to her."

"Please. If you won't leave I'll have to—"

"Fuck that. Where is she? Max?" He passes the woman and charges into the passageway. "Max!" It is a labyrinth lined with doors. Locked. Empty. Somebody else. The woman is following, calling for someone. Julio closes in.

"You crazy, man? Get the fuck out of here!"

"Go get your camera, boy. I got a story for you."

He pushes off and runs, pounding on doors as they fly past, no time to turn knobs.

"Max, stop! Wait!"

He speeds around a corner and something hits him from behind, carrying him hard into a wall and down to the floor. Julio again.

"Get off, motherfucker!" He feels pain in his side. A hand covers his face.

"Shut up, fool. You're goin out, right now."

He bites the hand and tastes blood. Hears a scream. Twists the weight off his back. Sees two pairs of gray-striped legs around him. Feels himself yanked up.

"Let's go, asshole."

"Kiss my ass."

A forearm closes his throat as his own arm is pinned to his back. His free arm reaches out at the face of a black man in a uniform—a man old enough to be his father—but can't reach. *Please,* he tries to say. Nearly off his feet, moving dizzily back through the maze, he struggles and sputters against the angry voices that are beginning to fade as if they were under water. Tries to see through the arms and faces to any door that might open, still. Moving too fast. The faces blurring.

"My baby," he croaks, and the forearm tightens and darkness falls as he is carried away.

Ten-fifty.

Not quite the hospital scene from *Gone With the Wind*. People lying around groggy, recovering. Nurse asks if she wants juice, apple or cranberry. Remembering Silver's questions, she mumbles that she really wants a drink, and the nurse fixes a cranberry–ginger ale cocktail. Joy comes in to explain that everything went fine. This is the moment she chose her for. Okay, she's got to keep the detachment before the procedure, but now that it's over a sisterly hug, a warm smile, an irreverent comment—girl, we dodged that bullet—would be nice. She can't. She never could. The qualities that get you over, make you tough enough to succeed, always take over, and so the advantages of being you doing that, instead of somebody else, tend to get lost. A lot of the time, anyway. And that's really why she picked her, after all; she's always known that. Brenda and Renée are for hugs; Sisterdoc's for taking care of business. Like presenting this no-stick pad that looks like a disposable diaper. And responding to her questioning face by saying: "It's easy, you walk like one of those geisha girls." Then, finally, the smile. "See you in a few weeks. Take care of yourself." It's enough.

A bite of a blueberry muffin in the next room makes her nauseous. But clears her head and leaves her anxious to be done with these assembly-line stops. Nurse takes blood pressure and temperature. She's still alive, so she can get dressed, put on a real pad, and make one more stop, for final instructions. She's glad, this time, to see Julio when she returns to the waiting area, because that means it's all real and it's over. And now, maybe, she can start thinking about Washington. Not a bad idea, on her own terms. A clean finish to the story. A vacation is definitely in order, and possibilities can be investigated.

"Okay, we got it," she says. The piece is wrapped. "What's wrong with your hand?"

Pulling furiously on a succession of Trues and pacing the sidewalk, he reminded himself of an expectant father. Irony is a bitch. The security guard lingered in the building lobby. Julio must have called them off after they put him out. No cops, no press. His neck was sore, his ribs ached, and his shoulder remained tender from the guard slamming him into a brick wall outside. What goes around comes around, at least he had his clothes on when *he* got put out. But maybe. Maybe she heard him and changed her mind. But then what was taking so fucking long?

They pushed out from the door and walked swiftly toward the corner. They looked like a smartly dressed pair of thieves.

"Max!" He flipped his cigarette at a cab as he skipped across the street in front of it. Julio gripped her arm, keeping her from turning to see him. He jogged almost to within reach. "Max, wait. You didn't—"

"Hey, I told you to get lost, all right?" Julio said, turning to face him. "Don't push your luck, man." Julio stiff-armed his chest with one arm and signaled to a taxi with the other.

He swiped the arm away and reached for Max, who had stopped, turned halfway around, and was staring at him with an expression he couldn't comprehend. "I tried to get to you, Max. I changed my mind. I'm sorry, can we . . . I need to talk to you."

"You've done enough, man. Now back off." Julio popped him with two hands in the sore shoulder, knocking him off balance.

He recovered with a right to the macho-pretty face. Moved in for a second shot and got caught in a bear hug that awakened his ribs. They wrestled into a wall, knocking over a garbage can.

"Changed your fucking mind?" he heard Max saying. He freed himself from Julio and stepped to her. She slapped him in the ear and grabbed at his throat. Julio grabbed her from behind.

"You jive, arrogant son of a bitch!"

"Let's go," Julio said. "Forget about it."

"Forget?" Her voice was low. Her eyes were wild. "You think I can forget this? Listen. I'm glad I got your poison out of me, you hear? You got to be a man to be somebody's father, boy. Look at you. You ain't shit. And you ain't got shit. And you never will." She started to go, paused, smoothed her skirt, and turned again. The no-nonsense Carole Simpson voice she never got to use on the air froze him. "If you ever come near me I swear I'll kill you," it said. "Just like I killed your child."

Interlude

Interlude

Clarence Crawford

CENTRAL KOREA, DECEMBER 1952

It was cold. No, that wasn't even the word for it, had to be another one. Cold was December at home, playing in the snow, getting ready for Christmas. Even that would be too much for some of these Southern boys. Forty below was something else again. That was too much for anybody. Especially these refugee kids wandering around the perimeter, even though you'd think they'd be used to it, being Korean. It was their country, after all. Used to be anyway, before the Americans and Chinese, not to mention the British and French and whoever else, started running all up and down it, killing each other and everybody in between. Of course, before that it was the Japanese. In a way, those kids had been orphans for a long time, before they were even born. All they cared about right now, though, probably, was that it was cold. And they were hungry.

It was the one thing Crawford had never gotten used to since he reactivated and joined the outfit as a replacement in the summer. Shot-up bodies, blown-up bodies, frozen bodies, napalm-fried bodies, that all became more or less routine. Even the cold, once it hit, was just there. But the kids always got to him. They just appeared in the countryside like little packs of wild dogs whenever the unit was moving from one location to another. And since they'd been set up for a while in this valley, the kids seemed to be multiplying, scrounging in the garbage for scraps like rats. Some of the guys didn't go for it at all. At least twice he'd had to stop somebody from taking potshots at them in the night. He knew there were stories of the early days, when the North Koreans sometimes used refugees as camouflage, planting grenades on kids and herding them toward the Americans. Because he hadn't been there for all that—the early retreat, the big push, and all the vicious counterattacks in the first year—he sometimes had to be careful that he didn't come across as a naive rookie, despite his rank. But hell, they were just kids.

And they were about to get abandoned again. Word had just come through that the unit, after spending weeks trying to dislodge the Chinese from the ridges ahead, was going to pull back up into the hills. Some said it was a trick; they were going to try to lure the Chinese out into the valley and hit them from above. They were probably too smart for that, although there was no telling when they'd decide that another thousand or so men were expendable in a big rush. Others said that once the battalion got behind the hills they were going to be part of a big swing to the west, more of the constant shifting and reshaping of the lines that never seemed to make sense at the troop level but didn't much bother anybody anymore—just the way it was. Whatever the reason, they were going to move fast, which meant they wouldn't be loading up all the rations stacked in the field. So what the hell, Crawford decided to hand out a few cases of C rations to the orphans. Frozen pork and beans, Vienna sausage, and hash wasn't exactly good eating, but it had kept the army going long enough and might keep these raga-muffins alive for a few more weeks. It was close to Christmas anyway, and it made him feel like Santa Claus, handing out presents back in Boston to kids like his Quincy.

That's when Maynard showed up, the company commander who always reminded Crawford of a bar of soap. The only hard you could see on him were his bars, his gear, and his eyes. The only time he had something to say to you, it was nothing you wanted to hear.

"Just what do you think you're doing, Sergeant?" he demanded.

"Handing out some of these surplus rations to the orphans, sir."

"So now you're feeding the enemy, is that it, Crawford?"

"No sir, not the enemy. They're just kids. They're hungry, rice paddies all tore up."

"We have orders to destroy these supplies before we move out."

"Beggin your pardon, sir, but is that necessary?"

"I don't question orders, Sergeant, and neither should you. I'll be damned if we're going to leave this shit here for the Chinese."

"Well, all the more reason, then. Few cases won't hurt nobody."

"You put that box down right now, mister!"

Maynard's face was starting to flare red. He was a good tactician but wasn't much of a man. Always fussing at guys with his Elmer Fudd self. Crawford had nearly gotten into it with him a couple of times, usually sticking up for the men. Other Negroes, Mexicans, even the rednecks. Maynard never seemed to understand that between the maneuvering and the fighting the army was about people, more than ever since General Ridgway had forced integration of the units in the field.

"Captain, this'll only take a minute. The men are all ready to move out." As they stood there another bunch of kids had appeared beyond the wire, their arms outstretched. Crawford tossed the carton over.

"Goddammit, if you do that again I'll have all these gooks shot and then I'll have your stripes. Do you read me?"

"Yes, sir, I read you." Like a cheap paperback, you son of a bitch.

"Now start pouring some gasoline on these cases and move out."

His outfit was the last to pull back, the rear guard in case any Chinese advanced down from the ridge. Maybe they were expecting an assault, another of those human wave attacks that didn't happen so often anymore since the war had settled into patrol skirmishes and artillery barrages along the line. Only about a hundred yards away from the encampment, they hunkered down behind rocks in the thigh-deep snow and watched as American planes swooped over the valley to drop napalm on the rations, some ammunition, and other supplies they had left behind. More waste. Trudging up and down these hills, scrapping for positions that were later abandoned, the army was forever dragging shit around that it couldn't use up. Crawford wasn't complaining; the army's logistical capabilities made life bearable for the troops. But it also showed up how out of place they were. Instead of arguing about truce lines, if it was up to him, they'd all just go away and leave these people alone.

The fire burned up into the sky that was just growing dark. Like a huge bonfire, with the funny oranges and blues billowing up and taking shapes like living creatures. Crawford forced his attention to the edges, to see if anybody was coming around. What he saw sickened him even more than a Chinese charge. A flock of those kids were rushing the fire, trying to get at the cartons of food. They actually stuck their hands into the flames, screaming like animals but not pulling back. Maybe if he hadn't made them think they were entitled to the stuff, they wouldn't have tried. Whatever the reason, they were going to burn themselves up if they didn't quit.

He thought he was still just watching when he found his legs churning through the snow. After a few steps he knew what he was doing and fired his M1 into the air to scare them off. His platoon surged forward with him, thinking he had spotted the enemy. They were firing too, but he tried to wave them to stop as he kept pushing forward, yelling. *Hey! Get out of there, go on. Get back!* They didn't understand. Neither did the men weaving across the field behind him. When he reached the bright-burning mass, the ammunition was exploding like Fourth of July fireworks. He grabbed and shoved the kids away from the fire, screaming and shooting to send them on their way. One little boy, his path to the glowing food finally cleared, ran up and jumped into the flames. Crawford snatched him by the flaming rags on his body and flung him down into the snow. Before he could fall on the boy to smother the flames, he felt himself being thrown to the ground. Trying to rise, he first heard a ringing nothingness in his ears, then sank screaming from the pain of fire in his own chest. Four other men who had been coming up behind him were on the ground, but moving. A mortar round. With the ammunition going off he never heard a thing but had caught the worst of it. He writhed in the snow, now hoping for the cold to chill the pain burning through him. To stop his dark red insides from sliding away. In a blur, he saw Jackson and Page running at him hunched over. He pointed to the boy—didn't know if he'd been hit, was still on fire. Tried to tell them but couldn't speak. Finally Page went to check him out. Jackson leaned over him, grabbed at his shirt, started trying to drag him, but the face looking down said everything. Crawford pushed him away so he could see: Page had the boy; he was still alive.

With that, Crawford drew a jagged breath and let his head fall back. Looked past Jackson to the stars. His boy, Quincy, liked to sit out on the stoop sometime when it first started to get dark and watch the sky. Looked like he was thinkin about flyin off somewhere, DeeDee said, but she kept a good eye on him. Jesus. She'd have to, now. The sky got brighter. His body seized up, then he didn't feel anything.

He was flying off to meet Quincy.

Oh, man, I'm sorry. You got it now, little man. You take care of everything, hear?

Part Two

Part Two

Eighteen

Davis

Derek Davis arrived in Boston at the age of eight and knew for certain that his life was over. The flamboyant colors of Barbados were already beginning to go dim in his mind as he held tight to his father's hand with his left hand and his brother's with his right and they trudged into a world of gray—gray buildings, gray people, and the gray stuff they said was snow. They shivered and skidded toward the settlement house, where he believed and hoped that he would just die. When he didn't, he decided sometime later it was for the same reason he thought he would: because he didn't belong there. The cold that made him chew his fingers to bring the blood, the wind that made him walk crying with his head down or sometimes even backward, the rude, barking voices that told him to get lost (as if he weren't already) were not his own special punishment. In fact, they had nothing to do with him at all. This was a misery inflicted upon, and caused by, those who were foolish enough to believe that they were entitled to it. If he could only remember the wild reds and the greens of the trees, the pink of the sand and the blue of the water—if he only concentrated on the music remaining in his father's tense voice—he could separate his mind from his body and understand that this was a mistake. You can't die in some-one else's nightmare. Sooner or later, you just wake up and everything's all right.

Soon the process of separation was well under way. He gave himself so freely to the cold that when his little brother, Desmond, lost his mit-tens, just one day's reason for their father's anger, he offered his own, even though he knew that would mean going without for the rest of the winter. And then he became expert at fashioning tight snowballs with his bare hands to hurl at the pig-faced policemen who insulted them. It was only weeks after their arrival that he landed a missile squarely on the face of one fat officer, who had grabbed Desmond for no good reason. He was able to rush in and pull Desmond from the distracted offender and they raced to freedom. Their father whipped him that night for making trouble, but he accepted the punishment knowing he had done the right thing, and that he had earned his father's respect along with the rebuke.

It had made no sense to bring them, but Derek's father had insisted against the wisdom of men and women alike that if he had to leave his family to find work in this place, he would not leave his sons behind. His own father, Derek's grandfather, had escaped the sugar fields to help build the big canal, but the Panama money he sent back until he was killed in an accident never made up for his permanent absence. And Derek was glad, even though he and Desmond spent all their time when they were not in school escaping the supervision of the ancient woman who ran the rooming house until their father returned from work or, more often, from looking vainly from work. He was glad because he knew he was so important that his father could not bear to leave him, and important enough to take responsiblity for Desmond, who was a year younger. Under the circumstances, he was even glad for their father's daily anger, which he knew came from the gray outside, and even provoked it because it was the expression of love and care: the quickened movements and animated voice became this world's replacement for his mother's touch and coo, and at the same time reassured him of his father's protective strength.

When his mother arrived with Mildred and Martha, both grown tall and bossy, and they all moved into a cramped apartment that the women despised but was more luxurious than the rooming house, Derek was more his father's son than he ever would have been had he spent that year under their control. Yet he welcomed their presence because it allowed him to be even more reckless in this hellish place. He now had angels from heaven to remind him that a better place awaited him.

They worried over his hair and clothes and saw to it that he and Desmond got off to school every day instead of playing in the street as they often did before. School there was like nothing he was used to; it was large and loud and closed in and dirty and teeming with the off-spring of both the gray people and other colored people also trapped in their nightmare. When the wops and micks called him a black nigger he knew they were mistaken, that they had others in mind, but he fought them anyway and suffered the attentions and cautions of his mother and sisters that replaced the anger of his preoccupied father. He also fought the real black niggers who had no other true name for themselves and seemed to believe they belonged there, too, and so deserved his scorn as well as the gray people's. And he fought the dark Portuguese, who had their own heaven but were too stupid to know it or claim it. And all the while, he could sense through his father's deepening silence a growing pride in his refusal to accept the perverse and contradictory status of colored American.

According to his father, Jesus Christ was a man named Marcus Garvey, who went to jail because colored Americans could not stop their government from punishing him for trying to help them. But he would be back someday to cleanse them of their sins. And their biggest sin was not remembering. A man must always remember where his home is, and he must always know his own people. The water of his homeland is the blood in his veins and in his family's veins; the land is his flesh and theirs. He who forgets this is a dead man, like these colored American zombies. Derek's father repeated these words many times, usually when the women were in the other room, or when the two of them were out walking. Derek heard the words before he could understand them and after he stopped trying to, after Garvey had died without accomplishing anyone's salvation and after his father himself had apparently given up hope of reuniting their flesh and blood with their native land and water.

After a time Derek could barely remember Barbados. He knew, and could not forget because of his father's words, that he was a foreigner, but that knowledge did not bring him the comfort it once did. Instead, it made him angry and irritable. As his father worked long hours and years unloading fruit boats in the harbor—watching them come and go without him—and the rest of the family, even Desmond, grew progressively settled and comfortable in a succession of South End apartments, Derek became as his father had been but did not remember why. He still fought everyone except other West Indians but most often channeled his aggression through football at the community center and in school. A large boy, he played fullback on offense and linebacker on defense, and the only difference was that sometimes he held the ball and sometimes he tried to knock it loose. Either way, he always ran toward as many people as he could and hit them as hard as could, and for every finger poked in his eye with a growled curse when he was on the bottom of a pile, he silently ground knuckles, elbows, knees, or teeth into someone else, on either team, when he was on top. And the more he hurt people, the more recognition he received, which made him even more angry because he still believed he was not supposed to be there.

At least that was what he thought he believed until he learned he did not have to stay. Midway through the football season in his junior year of high school, his father and mother sat him down to talk to him together, which they had never done, and his first thought was that Desmond or Martha or Mildred, none of whom were in the room, must be dying. But they, mostly his father, talked about war. About the gray people, the Americans becoming foolishly excited about going off to fight their own relatives in Europe. About the Americans foaming at the mouth to kill the yellow people from Japan, and about the stupid colored Americans who would be tricked into joining a family feud on one side and a battle of racial hatred on the other. Derek, of course, knew about Hitler and the krauts and the wops and Pearl Harbor, and he confessed that he felt some of the excitement although the insults hurled at the japs made him uncomfortable. But he did not understand what it had to do with him, so he turned for the first time he could remember to his mother for an explanation of what his father was saying. She told him it was time for him to go home, and he simply looked dumbly around the apartment. "Home to Barbados, baby," she said, and still he sat because he had stopped listening for those words years before. "Good," he said finally and stood. "I'm glad. When are we going?" "Not we, Derek," his mother said, "just you." And he sat back down and looked questioningly at his father, who, he always supposed, had stayed because of him, because of all of them.

"Listen to me, boy," his father said. "You big. You strong, you young. Dem go want you do dey dirty business. You see all dese boys like you, dem runnin down to de recruitin station talkin bout dem gon kill a jap for Uncle Sam. You don't got no Uncle Sam, you hear? You not one a dese colored American fools. You got to go, boy. Get away from here. I not have you spill Bajan blood in Europe or Japan for dat Roosevelt and his pig cousins. No, never! You got to go."

Derek remembered the months he had spent with his father and Desmond, and the joy he had felt knowing they would always be together. And the security he first felt when his mother and sisters arrived bringing all he knew of Barbados with them. The water and land his father talked about had become nothing but flesh and blood. As much as he felt apart from everything else around him, how could he ever be home without them? He turned his arguments voicelessly with a sad face to his mother, who closed her eyes and looked away.

"Derek," his father said, "when you trim branches from a plant and trow dem away, you make de plant proud and beautiful. But when you take a cutting and put it in water to make new roots, den put it back in de soil to grow, you got a strong new plant even if de first one dies. You go back in de soil now."

Two weeks later Derek's mother and sisters and Desmond said goodbye at the apartment, and his father took him to the docks where he had worked when he could since he brought the boys to this cold place, and sent Derek back to the water and the land.

He had always imagined his father as some kind of hero, an explorer who was expected to return with money and stories of survival and triumph. Although he had no money, he was prepared to tell the rest, like a Joseph come back from Egypt, even if he had never believed in the pharaoh's power. But in his mother's house, where he had been sent to stay, his father had no honor; he was considered a foolish and impatient man who had stolen away their daughter and only child to feed his vanity. The disdain had always been there, he could remember now, in the way his grandfather had referred to his father simply as Davis, as if he were an incomplete man from nowhere. In truth, his grandfather was the vain one, a moderately educated cabinetmaker and part-time Methodist preacher who fancied himself quite better than the average Bajan. His home, surrounded by proud banyan trees and a neat wooden fence, had been their family's anchor as they had moved their own flimsy chattel house from site to site in the countryside during Derek's childhood. They had always been welcomed there, Derek realized now, as if to remind his mother what she had missed by marrying into a tribe of discarded cuttings, scattered peasant farmers, and itinerant fishermen. Derek was accepted back by his grandparents as a remnant, a small repayment for their loss, but little more. As far as they were concerned, his life had been wasted in exile, and if he were able to make anything of it at this late date, it would be a great surprise.

He swallowed the lies he had been prepared to tell but refused to admit how unhappy he had been and bided his time as a colored American sinner reclaimed by charity. Most Bajans his age did not attend school, which was a bitter disappointment because he had hoped to finish in his homeland. Instead he worked as a helper to his grandfather and was frequently sent to do odd jobs on the estate of a wealthy Englishman a few miles down the coast. He had little recreation because cricket did not appeal to him; he missed the fierce and exhilarating contact of American football. He spent his free time watching fishermen on the beach and wandering the narrow, crooked streets of Speightstown. Often he would imagine his father washing into town, spotting his mother on Mullins Beach and by the sheer force of will winning her from the preacher's clutches and inventing a family for himself. And then, unable to maintain it, carrying them across the ocean to start over. His mother had obviously believed in the possibility of his father's vision. She never would have taken the girls away if she had thought they would be coming back, because otherwise they should be married off by now. She knew after a year that his father would not be coming home rich and had chosen to give up her own family to preserve his, to cut herself off from this place that was as lovely as he once remembered. Barbados, at least for the Bajans, was clearly far poorer than Boston but never seemed as depressed. The hot sun burning through the solid blue sky, and the rhythmic tide of the Caribbean, made each day fresh and clean. But Derek no longer believed it to be heaven. If it was, he was the victim of a cruel joke, cast out from hell to live alone in paradise.

Letters from his mother gave him hope. His parents had decided to send Desmond to join him the next year, since it looked as if the war would continue, and they didn't want him dragged into the conflict either. Derek was glad of that because Desmond had already begun to grow away from him. He actually seemed to like it in Boston; he enjoyed school, had colored American friends, and never fought with the gray boys. It was their mother, Derek knew, who had trained him to be satisfied, and their father had given him up. But when Desmond came to join him, he would be obliged to join forces with Derek. He would become an outsider as Derek had been in Boston, and with his brother beside him Derek would no longer be an outcast alone in Barbados. They would have each other.

Nearly a year after Derek had arrived, one day when he returned home from the market, he found his grandmother crying and his grandfather ranting. A yellow piece of paper lay on the table near his grandmother's trembling hands.

"Yes, go on, read it," his grandfather commanded.

"What does this mean?" Derek asked in a small voice. "A fire?"

"Yes! Goddammit, your father do this. He snatch my daughter away from here and now she gone. And the girls and your brother too, all gone."

"My father—"

"And good riddance too. At least the black bastard did not escape from his own hell."

Derek flew at the older man who was stout but smaller than he and pummeled him with blows till he fell to the floor.

"Derek, no," his grandmother pleaded. "He didn't mean it, he's angry. My God, stop it." He pushed past his sobbing grandmother, stepped over his still-cursing grandfather, and ran out the door, through the yard, down the road for half a mile till he came to the beach, and across the expanse of coral sand that was no more to him than a muddy field or snowy Boston street, and plunged into the sea, splashing wildly toward home.

It took three men to pull him safely from the water and return him to his grandfather's house, where sorrow and anger wrestled for dominion for the next several days. Because Derek had nothing more to wait for, he knew that he did not want to stay, even though he had nowhere else to go. His grandmother resisted. She had been kind if not warm and now clung to him stubbornly as all that was left of her family. But his grandfather, like Derek, saw the truth: as a marker for a debt that could now never be paid, the boy was worthless. And so with a mixture of resentment and relief, he pulled together enough money to send the evil young man who had once been his grandson back into the darkness from whence he had come.

Like an explorer on his second voyage, Derek trudged through another gray Boston day clutching his small cloth satchel to the site of his former encampment: the crumbly, brick South End block where a charred three-story building squatted like a rotted tooth. He tried to go inside but the doors were boarded up. He retreated to the sidewalk and stared at the second-floor windows. There was no fire escape. Surely Desmond could have jumped from that height, and his father might have coaxed his sisters out. If necessary Derek could have carried them all, one at a time, down the smoky staircase, and if his father was too proud to be carried they would have jumped or remained together, with everyone else safe. But if, on the other hand, they had all been asleep, no one would have moved. They might have all died from the smoke before they ever saw the flame. Even then, he knew, there would have been a moment, one noxious breath when his father realized that it had all been for nothing—but smiled anyway because he knew the transplanted tree would survive.

Derek stood there for an hour feeling the smoke and the flames and the seawater, his blood, closing around him and filling his lungs and finally feeling nothing but the raw cold. And then he made his way, as before, to the settlement house, knowing this time that he would not die but not knowing how he could live.

Within a few days he found his old football coach, who, to Derek's surprise, offered to take him in. He had never thought of him as a particularly friendly man, and Derek had certainly not been friendly to him. But the coach was moved by his plight, by the completeness of his loss. There had not been enough money to send his family's remains home to Barbados, and Derek didn't even know where the bodies had been buried. Perhaps this was an act of recompense. The coach's own son had been killed in the war, one of the foolish colored Americans Derek's father had talked of, and the coach, who had encouraged his son's participation, now shared Derek's father's skepticism and continued his act of preservation. The coach arranged for him to finish school and pay for his keep by working as a janitor in the building where he lived. Derek remained silently grateful.

The following year the coach sent Derek to Shaw College in North Carolina to play football on scholarship. Derek hated the American South. In Boston he had fought openly with the whites who despite their pugnacious arrogance were in fact seeking to convince themselves of their right of place. In North Carolina Derek sensed no comparable insecurity. They believed in the land as powerfully as his father had in Barbados, and their resentment of outsiders, including the colored people who had shared the land for hundreds of years, was brutal and at times lethal. And if Derek disliked the colored Americans of Boston, he despised those of the South, including his schoolmates, who walked the streets with a whipped subservience that surpassed that of his father on the most hopeless of days.

Being immersed in an environment of colored Americans was a new experience for Derek. They dubbed him the Emperor for his proud, aloof manner and mocked his accent, which he in turn intensified. But the taunts did not have the same bite as in Boston; more than anything, his fellow students simply left him alone, which he did not mind. In the tolerant space they left for him, he played football and studied, reading endlessly about their history and politics so he could understand them. Because he knew that when he finished trying to knock them down on the field, he would be left with trying to teach them to stand, like men. Somewhere along the way the obligation he felt to his coach and the anger he felt toward the coloreds as well as the whites became a commitment to the unfinished business of his father. And he knew that when his time was up he would return to Boston to earn his salvation by opening the eyes of others.

After ten years working the wards of the South End, Derek had seen almost everything. The lost jobs, the sudden violence against men, women, and even children, the neglect and abandonment. The city made people even less stable than on the old peasant farms in Barbados. They shuffled around from place to place. Men and women often seemed to change partners for no good reason, and as a result too many children had no idea where they belonged or to whom. That people brought these plagues upon themselves never ceased to sicken him; that the circumstances were imposed from outside enraged him. Attending Boston University part-time to attain a social-work degree had done nothing to heighten his perception of these problems, which he had seen all too clearly his entire life. But it had given him a credential he could wield to help combat them—and it had helped him better understand the trifling bureaucrats and the power brokers with whom he would have to contend. When he went to confront, curse, or negotiate with—never beg—the powers that be, he encountered the same red-legged back-row johnnies and their brothers and cousins whose asses he had kicked in the playgrounds, alleys, and football fields before he returned to Barbados. Sometimes they remembered him, sometimes not. The only difference was whether they used his name and smiled when they said no. And now the stakes were even higher because in those few hours he wasn't solving people's particular problems, he was engaged in the fight against plans for urban renewal—"nigger removal"—that would only multiply all the other problems.

That was the state of his life the day DeeDee Crawford walked into his office and changed it. At first she reminded him vaguely of his sister Martha, the less bossy one, only quite shorter. She was dark skinned and the kind of pretty he had seen only in Barbados, a kind that took itself for granted. She sat and began to tell her story, and instead of instantly cataloguing it as one of the many he had heard a hundred times, he found himself listening. She was a widow with two young sons. Her husband had been killed in Korea, an extension of the yellow war the Americans had continued even after exterminating two Japanese cities. Her own people in South Carolina had passed away, and in any event she did not want to raise her boys in a place where they could not look people in the eye. She had been working as a domestic out in Brookline, but that kept her too long from her sons. Nothing else had worked out. She was behind in her rent. She needed relief. She needed his help. People had told her that Derek Davis, the Emperor, could get things done.

And that was true. Normally, after fifteen minutes of hearing such a story, Davis had suggestions about calls to be made, people to be seen, forms to be filled. Everyone walked away with hope, if not a solution, the belief that something might be done somehow to smooth some of the edges in their ragged lives, as long as they were willing to take some action themselves. But he had no ready-made answers for this woman, whose problems were in fact no different from others he had helped to resolve. When she finished speaking, he asked her to say more. He wanted to know more about her family, her children, her late husband, her ambitions. He didn't want her to go away with a wisp of hope. He didn't want to find a possible solution. He wanted to be her solution.

And he wanted her to be his. Until that moment, he had seen himself as doing for others, taking care of them, teaching and guiding. What he thought he saw when first he laid eyes on DeeDee Crawford, and knew when he heard her story, was a space into which he might fit himself, a space he had been wanting and not seeking since his father sent him away. Only six months later, when they were about to be married, did he realize that the change went even deeper. By joining himself to her, by absorbing her soul and history, he was completing the initial voyage he had taken with his father and Desmond. He was planting himself in the soil fertilized by his family's ashes. He was becoming, once and for all, a colored American.

But at first he wanted only to know her better. He told her to come back the next day, and set about finding her a job. There had been a push to get more colored workers in the schools, and he thought he could pull some strings to get her into the attendance office in a school in Roxbury. She could handle the work, even if she didn't have any experience; she was intelligent and educated. She would damn sure not be cleaning anybody else's toilets anymore. A factory job would pay better, but this would give her a schedule that matched her sons'. Money would not be a major issue any longer, in any case; he would see to that.

The next day he didn't tell her about the job. He listened some more to her plans to go to school and be able to educate her sons, so they wouldn't have to go in the service to better themselves as their father had done. And then he asked her to join him for lunch at a nearby diner, where he did what he had never done before, told his own story. He needed her to know who he was, before he helped her, so that she wouldn't feel obligated to him. He wanted to be sure that she didn't look at him that way only because she wanted his help. But the others who came to him were either impatient or shy. As he spoke to her, he realized that her face suggested that she already knew him, or at least understood the displacement and loss that had forged his sense of purpose. And more than once, they even made each other smile.

After she had started her new job, she called to invite him to her house for dinner. To thank him, she said, which he hoped was a lie. He wore his best suit and made no effort to take off the sunny disposition he'd had on since their luncheon. Her home was clean and neat, as he knew it would be. As his might have been if they had ever stayed in one place long enough; if his father hadn't commanded the impression all those years that they would be going back soon, long after everyone had stopped thinking it.

She introduced him to the boys as Mr. Davis. "This is Quincy, my oldest. He's eight." He looked like his mother. He had dark, sculpted features that would have warmed Garvey's heart, a serious face, and a proud little stance. There was something going on behind his eyes that Davis couldn't read, something more than the awareness he had that it was unusual for another man to be in the house.

"And this is Elliott. We call him Bubba. He's four and just started nursery school." "Hello, Elliott," Davis said. And the little man, who must have taken after his father, beamed, drawing a sideways glance from his brother that he never noticed. Both had close-cropped hair with carefully razored parts on one side, and both wore short-sleeved sport shirts buttoned to the collar, pressed pants, and shined shoes. It reminded him of the fussing his mother and sisters had done over him and his brother, which made him wonder how Mrs. Crawford's commendable devotion was affecting their spirit. She had made them, quite obviously, fine little boys. Who would make them fine men?

Although the question never left him, he did not dwell on it. His purpose was clear, and for the first time in years his own needs were paramount in his mind. Through his work, Davis had acquired many friends and acquaintances; the Emperor was well known in the South End for his effectiveness, his hard-handed compassion, and his political skill. And because of that, there had been enough women to quench his thirsts, women who knew little of him because he did not want them to. In truth, he had been without companionship since Desmond had grown satisfied with America and their father, who would not let that happen to him, sent him away. He would never have guessed that it would be a woman who might take the place of his brother and father, who might share his time, engage his mind, and understand his soul. And perhaps that was possible only because he had packed those parts of himself in the satchel he took to Barbados and left them in there when he brought it back. But it didn't matter. Davis was ready to unpack, and eating roast beef in this sunny kitchen with the clear-eyed woman and her sons confirmed his belief that this was the place to do it.

He called her briefly at her new job the first few days to make sure all was going well, and soon started calling in the evening. She invited him to dinner twice more within a month. They shared conversations about schools, desegregation, urban renewal, and the plight of Negroes in Boston. Her fresh intelligence surprised him until he took it for granted as she did her own beauty. That, he never failed to appreciate, and it captivated him even more as she continued to favor him with her attention. When after several weeks she allowed him to kiss her, he felt as if they had made love.

He came, eventually several times a week, to be with her, but increasingly it was her sons who made him want to stay. Elliott began to turn sullen, but without menace, almost asking him to stay by wanting him to go. Quincy was unfailingly polite but sly—more tolerant and less hospitable. But he was endlessly fascinating, mature and silly at the same time. He was more at ease with himself than Davis had been, at least until he finished college, yet at the same time more rootless than he himself had ever been.

It was a package deal. He knew that DeeDee would not have wanted him if he did not want her sons as well. And as much as he was convinced that he wanted her for his companion, he needed the boys to complete his life. It was not surprising, then, that when he asked her to marry him a few months later, she delayed her response until she could secure their approval. Once they said yes, he took them all out to dinner to celebrate, and they planned a modest wedding at her church. During that discussion he noticed that for the first time she began to defer to his judgment in matters concerning the boys. As they talked excitedly about what they would wear and what they would eat and who would come, she interrupted to say, "Let's see what Mr. Davis thinks about that." Elliott seemed puzzled; Quincy noticed and understood the change immediately.

Davis moved in with them, in their rented bottom floor of a two-family house; his own apartment would not have been large enough and would have forced the boys to make an even more wrenching adjustment. Soon, however, he began to understand that he was sharing that space with four, not three, other people. It was the same house they had lived in since her first husband had died, although he himself had barely been there, and Elliott had not yet been born. For the younger boy's sake, as well as their own, DeeDee and Quincy had casually conspired to maintain a sense of his presence. The closet space available to Davis was limited by the presence of various artifacts—books, papers, records, a suitcase of personal items, even articles of clothing—that had belonged to DeeDee's first husband. At the dinner table, Davis remained consigned to the rather uncomfortable corner chair he had occupied as a visitor, because the roomier and more prominent place between DeeDee and Quincy was "his" seat.

More than that, it was obvious that DeeDee had loved this man in a way she could never love another. Understanding that could not overcome the hurt Davis felt when she resisted his touch in certain ways. Lying beside her in the dark, he had to try to imagine ways to stimulate her that would not remind her of things Crawford had done and would not make her feel that she was betraying him, or upsetting the boys, if she responded. And so most of the time he did nothing but stretch his right arm around her and gently roll her toward him, letting her deep brown softness warm the length of his body. And most of the time, that was enough.

It was enough because they shared another passion, one that he knew he could fulfill even better than her handsome, smooth-faced young sergeant. They both had a hunger for security, a respect for learning, and an uncompromising sense of justice. In his most frustrated moments, he allowed himself to think that she might have eventually outgrown her idealistic soldier and found the need for his kind of strength anyway. In any case, it was clear that while she supported his quest for improvement through the army, his failure to survive suggested, though she would never admit it directly, that he had been mistaken.

Nothing, however, could convince Quincy of that. His father was Jesus and Garvey rolled into one. Often, the boy would make reference to things his father had told him, lessons about life and human nature and race relations, much as Davis's father had taught him. One day, as Davis and DeeDee discussed the lingering Little Rock school desegregation case at dinner, Quincy joined in. "My father says they're just scared because they know we're as good as they are, but they don't want to admit it cause then they won't feel special anymore."

"That's very insightful, Quincy," Davis remarked, amazed by the boy's ability to absorb so much at such a young age—he had been only four when his father died. "I'm impressed that you remembered so well. When did your father tell you that?"

"Few weeks ago."

A sharp look from DeeDee told him to let it go. Later that night, she explained that Quincy had always insisted that a vision of his father had appeared to him the same day, it turned out, that he had died, telling him to look after the family. Ever since, from time to time, he would imagine similar conversations. Davis was astonished and angry.

"Good God, you don't believe that nonsense, do you?"

"No, of course not. I'm not so sure about the first time, though. I've heard about things like that."

"Woman, be reasonable. How can we let the boy continue to go around pretending that he's hearing voices, like he's talking to a ghost?"

"No, Davis, you be reasonable. How can we take that away from him? I decided a long time ago that I'm not going to, and I don't think it would be a a good idea for you to try."

He decided instead to fill the void so there would be no need for spirits. It began with new life: DeeDee became pregnant, which seemed to succeed in legitimizing his presence and inspiring the boys to look more to the future than the past. Then came new surroundings: they moved to a house in Dorchester, where the baby would have his own room and Davis wouldn't have to share space with the ghost of Sergeant Crawford. He even bought a television to give them all something new to do together in the evening, even though he preferred reading and talking to DeeDee.

With Quincy, it worked almost too well. The little box was like a magic window to another dimension, and the boy looked at it all the time. Cartoons, cowboys, clowns, whatever foolishness they put on there, he was transfixed by. As far as Davis was concerned, it was the ultimate in brainwashing, a perfect tool to get all the colored people as well as the gray immigrants to believe they were all red-white-and-blue Americans—and that it was therefore their duty to buy all the things they saw on the screen and couldn't afford. He tried to be patient, but several times a week when he found Quincy, usually with his brother at his side, staring into the box, he would sputter, "Now what is *this* you're looking at?" and move to turn off the set. And nearly every time, DeeDee would appear to say: "Boys, wasn't it good of Davis to buy us that TV?" Without changing their expressions, they would chant, "Yeah, thanks, Davis," and he either stalked out of the room or fell heavily into a chair, loudly rustling his newspaper and giving DeeDee the evil eye as she disappeared smiling.

At night as she put up her hair he prowled around her in his sleeveless undershirt and boxer shorts arguing that she was humoring the boys and undermining his authority.

"I suppose you'd rather have them running in the street picking fights with policemen," she'd say. "It's not doing them any harm, Davis. Besides, Quincy still reads all the time."

He did read extremely well for his age, but the problem, as Davis saw it, was his choice of material: mostly funnybooks, filled with monsters from outer space and gray boys in colorful capes. But DeeDee was right. The TV and the funnybooks weren't affecting his mind; it already ran that way. If he wasn't indoctrinating his brother in imperialistic cowboy games or pretending to have strange powers or chattering about flying saucers, he would have been talking to ghosts or telling grand lies like pool-hall hustlers or running away to join the circus. The boy's habits infuriated Davis, but also fascinated him. Although his own father had suffered delusions about his place in the world, he had taught Davis to see things clearly, to be always aware of life's harsh realities. And his own experience, especially since he had been left on his own, had reinforced the need to take things as they were in order to change them. But this boy Quincy seemed able to float above all that simply by rearranging reality in his head. He had imagination, and that intimidated Davis because he had none. It also delighted him, which he would not admit to DeeDee and didn't have to, and as a result he cherished the boy in a way he never would have thought possible.

That was why it pained him to have Quincy as an adversary, although the conflict was usually indirect. As soon as Delphine, their daughter, was born, it was Elliott who began a career as the troublemaker. He was obviously jealous of his mother's attention, having been the baby all his life, but the more Davis tried to compensate, the more mischievous and disrespectful he became. He never did what he was told the first two times, and then he did it badly if at all. He sulked. He talked back. He dirtied, mangled, or destroyed nearly everything he touched. He constantly provoked Davis and then defied him by proclaiming, "You're not my father." When DeeDee stepped in, to back up Davis or assert her own authority, he ignored her as well, or mumbled that she should go play with the baby. That was the point at which Davis could tolerate no more, and that was the point at which he collided with Quincy.

For all his fanciful notions, Quincy was a bulldog when it came to his brother. The seriousness Davis had seen when he first met the boy had everything to do with his sense of himself as the family's protector. He could live for days in his own world, but the moment he felt his brother or mother or, now, his baby sister was threatened, he became a tree that could not be moved. And Davis learned soon enough that it was pointless to go around him. And so, most of the time, he ended up whipping Quincy for something that Elliott had done. The most outrageous, of course, was the kitchen fire that had nearly got out of control, completely intolerable not only because of the danger but because of the memory it evoked for Davis. Punishing Quincy generally seemed to satisfy everyone, and it was not inappropriate, because both Davis and Quincy knew, as DeeDee and even Elliott did not, that Quincy was the mastermind of Elliott's rebellion. Too preoccupied to challenge Davis directly, Quincy goaded and inspired his brother into acting out, which then obliged him to play the hero. Even though he finally came to understand this drama into which the boy had cast him,

Davis bore him no ill will. He actually respected Quincy's devotion (he would have done the same for Desmond), and it pained him to punish the boy. And he also knew that Quincy, having done his duty, would not hold a grudge as his offending but essentially innocent brother would have.

Davis was also pleased that Quincy extended his influence to Delphine, even though that created the possibility of further conflict between them. He had never imagined that a boy could be so attentive to a baby, a girl at that, but from the time she could crawl he included her in his games with Elliott. He sat her on his lap and explained the things on television, which made Davis finally stop reaching to turn it off. He told her wonderful stories, about knights and princesses and talking animals and distant galaxies. Often, Davis found himself lowering his imperious newspaper to listen and to watch his daughter's happy face as Quincy seduced her with his imagination. And by the time she was four, he taught her to read, by force-feeding everything from the Sunday funnies to the books he was reading in school.

But Davis certainly could not trust Quincy to teach her about her own father, her grandfather, and the world they came from. He wanted her to know about all of her people and their history, to be a knowledgeable, levelheaded woman like her mother. For Halloween, a silly holiday that he rather fancied because it recalled the colorful revelry of Barbados, Davis urged his daughter to become Cleopatra, a striking symbol of African heritage. She went dressed as Wonder Woman instead. For geography homework, he wanted her to draw a map of Africa; she made up a place called Delphinia. He brought home albums of Caribbean music; she listened to Quincy's Beatles records. When he suggested that she could learn from her mother the domestic skills that would be useful for a young woman, she prattled about not getting married and becoming an astronaut.

These were strange ideas, he thought, that would get her into trouble when she was no longer a carefree child. At the same time, he had a more immediate concern: Elliott was getting worse. He carried his disaffection to school, disregarding his work and sassing his teachers. Only Quincy could keep him in line. Much as Davis admired Quincy's willingness to be involved in his brother and sister's lives, something had to change. He had to assert himself before it was too late. He thought he knew what to do.

He had had the idea before, but decided it would be best to bide his time before making his move, and he convinced DeeDee of that as well. But time was running out. Quincy was just sixteen, the age at which Davis's father had cut him loose. Elliott was going on twelve without having calmed down, and he needed more security to get him through the dangerous passage of adolescence. Delphine had somehow turned seven already, and he could only hope that it wasn't too late for her. And so he laid down his hand at the dinner table on a Sunday, the time and place where he had entered their lives eight years before.

"Listen to me now, children," he began. "I have something important I want to say. You know I lost my own family a long time ago, and I had to live for many years on my own. I had to decide how I wanted to live my life. You all have had a grievous loss as well. Now we have found ourselves together for some time. You are all my family now, the only family I will ever have, and I am part of yours, for better or worse. It makes no difference how we got to this point. It only matters that we have chosen to be here, together."

"Can I have the potatoes?"

"Hush, Bubba."

"I am no longer willing to be considered a visitor in my own house. And I want you to know, for all of your lives, that you belong here. This is your home."

Quincy was staring intently, the bark beginning to form around his face. Davis remembered the moment when his parents had sat him down, and pressed on, determined this once to change history himself.

"I have decided to adopt you both, legally," he declared, looking from Quincy to Elliott. "I want you to have my family's name. I want us, finally, to become one family."

DeeDee nodded in satisfaction. Delphine said "Cool" and took another forkful of roast beef. Elliott's habitual scowl began to dissolve into the confusion he used to wear as a young child. Davis followed his glance to Quincy, who sat stone still and silent. And then he dropped his fork and crossed his arms.

"Forget it, Davis."

"Quincy—" DeeDee began.

"What's wrong?" Delphine asked.

"You stay out of this, Phine," Quincy said, without ever taking his eyes from Davis.

"Nice try. I expected that when she was born. Thought by now you'd have sense enough to know that it's a stupid idea."

"Look here, son."

Quincy slammed his hand on the table.

"*Don't* 'son' me. Don't *ever* do that! Everything's fine just the way it is, all right? You may be *her* man, but that don't make you mine."

Shaking with rage, Davis bolted out of his chair and reached past his shrieking daughter to snatch the boy up by his collar. "That's enough, boy. Enough! You apologize to your mother, and you apologize to me. Now."

"Let go of me," Quincy yelled, forcing the panic out of his eyes, which were now inches from Davis's. "We'll kick your monkey ass back to Barbados. Tell 'im, Bubb."

Quincy stopped struggling for a moment and looked to his brother. In the quiet of that second, Davis saw something go out of Quincy's face, leaving an awful, frightened emptiness. Davis relaxed his grip on the suddenly broken boy, his own anger fleeing before the compassion that began to fill him. Now, at last, it was ended. Quincy looked to him like a baby, and Davis could tell his mind was spinning, frantically re-ordering its universe in the instant of re-creation. Exhausted and re-lieved, Davis prepared to embrace him.

"Fuck you!" Quincy spat. He pushed Davis back and looked around the room. His gaze rested on his brother. "All of you. You wanna have a nice, happy family, fine. Go ahead. You can have it without me. I'm get-tin out of here."

Quincy flung his chair to the floor and marched out of the room heading for the front door. Davis slumped into his seat, his heart burn-ing in the spot where the boy had struck him, and dropped his eyes to his plate.

"Daddy, *do* something," Delphine pleaded.

Davis picked up his fork and began to eat.

"For God's sake, Davis," DeeDee said, grabbing his arm.

He yanked it free—the first flash of physical anger he had ever felt toward his wife—and slowly set the fork back down.

"What do you want?" he said softly. "You want me to beg him to come back? I didn't tell him to go."

"That's easy for you to say. He's not—"

"You know better than that, DeeDee."

Another sudden movement claimed their attention; Elliott was run-ning from the room.

"Quincy!" he called. "Quince, wait up!"

Delphine, overwhelmed, began to cry. Davis reached out to her. "It's all right, sweetheart," he said. She spun away and ran around him to embrace her mother. DeeDee leveled an accusing look at Davis, who stubbornly took another bite of roast beef, gagged, and left the kitchen.

For the next several hours he lay in the darkening bedroom. He should have seen it coming, but he didn't. No imagination. He still didn't understand, for that matter, how his unifying gesture had exploded, like a grenade, blowing everything apart into the kind of pieces he had spent his adult life putting back together. He knew exactly what had happened but did not understand why it had to happen that way, or what he might have done differently. Finally, answering a soft knock on the door, he saw Elliott slouching in the doorway. He placed one huge white canvas sneaker inside the room and fixed his gaze on it as if to keep it there.

"Yes, Elliott?"

"You know what you were talkin about at dinner?"

"Yes, of course."

"Well, I guess I think maybe it's not such a bad idea. I mean, if that's what you really wanna do, it don't—doesn't—matter to me. It's no big deal, right?"

"No, not really."

"Well," he said shrugging, "whatever."

"Elliott—stand up straight, son." The boy shuffled his feet and grew, as if he were being measured for new heights against the door frame. "Thank you."

"Yeah, sure," he said and was gone.

For a long time after the brief and sober court ceremony, where the four of them in Sunday clothes tried to ignore the young ghost who haunted them; after DeeDee and Delphine forgave him for what he had done; after Elliott settled into quiet obedience, Davis held out hope for a complete recovery. Quincy came and went, sometimes almost surreptitiously but more often with provocative insolence. And each time he appeared, Davis's heart burned as he watched for a sign of reconciliation. But Quincy never spoke to him directly and referred to him only in the third person in his presence. He told his brother, his mother, and his sister enough to alleviate their worry—he was living with friends in Cambridge, still going to school, working to support himself—but gave no indication of returning home on a permanent basis. None of them, Davis included, was willing to bar the door. Even if he wouldn't stay, none of them could bear the thought of not seeing him. But after more than a year, as the visits became increasingly disruptive, Davis's concern for Elliott and Delphine began to override his own intense longing. And when he came home one afternoon to find Quincy smoking marijuana with his brother, Davis told him not to come back. And Quincy smiled.

But he hadn't won anything except the satisfaction of confusing his brother again. It was a cruel, desperate trick that saddened Davis even more than it angered him. Quincy wanted to raise the stakes so that his brother would join his revolt as he had when they were children. But Elliott could no more endure Quincy's fantasy orphan life than Desmond would have been able to survive in Davis's Barbadian exile, and this was something that Davis had never before realized. And so Davis continued to lavish attention on the younger brother, to compensate for Quincy's thoughtlessness and, finally, for his own father's. Elliott had already demonstrated an interest in basketball, because he was tall for his age and everyone presumed that he could play. Now Davis worked with him intensely even though he never thought much of the game. He hung a basket on the side of the house facing the narrow driveway, and they practiced for hours every day when Davis came home from work and before he went back out to see clients or attend organizational meetings. He signed the boy up for the youth center league, because he didn't have the initiative to seek out pickup games on his own and because Davis believed he should learn to play correctly. He sat Elliott down to watch games on television and carried him to the Boston Garden to see the imperious Bill Russell. (He personally preferred the powerful Wilt Chamberlain, but Russell, the more consistent winner, exuded a prideful attitude that made him a more fitting icon for the boy.)

It was only when Elliott seemed able to sustain his interest in the game on his own, and when he began to prefer the company of his brainy, no-talking little girlfriend, that Davis backed off. And then he discovered his daughter.

DeeDee had been reminding him for some time that he needed to pay more attention to Delphine, who was still under the long-distance spell of Quincy, regularly riding her mother's last nerve and beginning to spend more time with Elliott and his girlfriend. Between working with Elliott, immersing himself in the problems of other families, and organizing campaigns and boycotts to loosen the grip of Boston's racist power structure, Davis had assumed that Delphine, like his own sisters, would somehow take care of herself. The trouble, as he came to see, was that she wanted to do just that. And as she sprouted toward adolescence at the age of ten, he began to heed DeeDee's cautions.

He enrolled her in an alternative school for black children, one of the projects he'd been working on as part of the ongoing fight against the Boston School Committee. He monitored her schoolwork, her TV viewing, and her dress, and he stomped out signs of sassy willfulness wherever they appeared. The junior high school years in public school were particularly stressful. She wanted to be involved in athletics, and he cautioned her that activities such as volleyball and track were not only unbecoming but a distraction from her studies. But when she wasn't preoccupied with sports, she turned to giggling and primping for the benefit of some misbegotten boy or other who had captured her fancy with sly looks and tight trousers. One night he came home late from a rally and found that she had persuaded her mother to let her go see *The Exorcist,* a trashy exploitation film about satanism. Appalled, he took himself straightaway to the movie house, refused to pay the price of admittance, and preceded the agitated usher into the darkened auditorium, where the devil-child on the screen was vomiting on a priest. Even worse, the groans from the audience guided him to the sight of his daughter sitting beside a slouch-hatted boy who had worked his arm over the back of her seat. "Delphine!" he barked, drawing impatient comments and one telltale gasp from the audience. He reached into the row where she was sitting, seized her arm, and wordlessly pulled her back up the aisle. He told the usher who had followed him to stand aside and he would not demand a refund for his daughter's ticket. She stomped into the house and immediately complained to her mother, "Dag, Daddy won't let me do *anything.*" From the safety of the stairs she turned to add: "I *hate* you! Quincy was right. I can't wait till I get out of here!" The rebuke, though it stung, reaffirmed him. This was his own blood child, after all, and a girl, who clearly needed a firm hand. He would not be intimidated again into losing his grip.

DeeDee disagreed. She said nothing then, which was her way, but gradually let him know that he had done enough. That meant she thought he had gone too far, and that the girl needed a mother's sly understanding more than a father's discipline. And, she reminded him, with Elliott gone to college—miraculously, and thanks to basket-ball—they could relax and enjoy each other's company as they never had before. Yielding to DeeDee's wishes, he backed off, maintaining a stern vigilance but never again interfering quite so boldly as Delphine strategically flaunted her dawning independence. Both he and DeeDee were anxious when she began the busing in high school, but Davis was proud that his daughter was a willing soldier in a war he had long pursued. How would it look, she argued, if the Emperor's own daughter refused to participate in the historic desegregation of Boston's schools by sneaking off to some private academy? And though he had deep qualms about showcase integration that only pitted the lower classes against each other, he had to relent. Many a time he threatened to go to the school and kick some second-generation gray ass, but DeeDee restrained him and Delphine diplomatically assured him that she would let him know if she needed him.

And now, suddenly, it was all over. Delphine had made it through, on her own as she wanted, which meant that the last of his children was grown. He sat up in the bed admiring the plump form of his wife, who had long since overcome the inhibitions caused by Sergeant Crawford and even the anger brought on by the exile of her firstborn; she rarely denied him, in part perhaps because he rarely asked for much more, after long days of work, than to feel her warm reassurance. The strong, near-summer morning light brought to life the faces in the pho-tographs on his dresser: he and his parents and siblings in the wrin-kled, brown-toned picture that sat atop the surviving lace-bark doily his mother had brought from Barbados; Quincy and Elliott in baggy base-ball suits, a photo he had taken while courting DeeDee; he and DeeDee and the boys on their wedding day and again, with Delphine replacing Quincy, on the day of the adoption; Elliott's and Delphine's graduation portraits. Greeting them, he wondered as he had each morning for almost twenty years how so many men could walk away from such memories. He heard the stories every day; he knew them by heart by the time DeeDee appeared. He knew even then that it wasn't easy, that fear and anger and hatred drove them to it. But all his ratio-nalizations had grown increasingly hollow since the day DeeDee in-vited him into her kitchen and introduced him to her little men, and all the excuses never seemed more silly than they did today.

Why'd you put up with all that crap anyway? At his most eloquent, Davis could never fully explain the stupidity of such a question. In college, he had wondered the same thing: Why did colored Americans bitch and moan, fight and suffer, as if theirs were the only reality? As if there was nothing on the other side of the Atlantic Ocean. As if Garvey hadn't offered them the solution. They put up with it because they had come to believe, despite everything, that they were already home, and Davis had thought them foolish because of it.

But he stayed because his father had brought him to Boston and because his father had sent him away. Because he had returned twice, to Boston and not to Barbados, like an animal to its spawning ground. Even so, he might simply have walked out the door, as Quincy had, and returned to the life he had before DeeDee walked in. But across town or across the ocean he would not have loved her any less, and he would remain Delphine's father, just as he would when she finally went away. Even if he had never returned after that first Sunday dinner, he would never have forgotten the face of Elliott, who had been waiting for him without knowing it and who was terrified of wanting him to stay. And no time or distance would ever have erased the image of Quincy, who cast himself into the void precisely because he refused to let go of a home and a past that no longer existed. Davis had to give him credit; the boy had gone to look for where he belonged, even if it was all an illusion. That was the difference between them, and that was why it never occurred to Davis to go away. Finally, he could not imagine himself being anything or anywhere else.

So he had stayed till the end, which was now a new beginning that pulled together every piece of his life. Any man who denied himself that could not be said to have had a life. Delphine was going to graduate in another week. He had to be here because he wanted to give her more than his father had given him. He wanted to be certain that if she came back to find an empty shell of a home, she would be able to survive. That, of course, he could never know, so his only recourse was to be there, himself, forever if necessary.

Elliott would probably need him even longer. He was in the other room right now, packing to leave just when he should be unpacking to stay. All his pieces were right here, too. He thought he was following his brother's footsteps, even though he had known better ten years ago. Elliott was like Davis; neither of them could make up a path where there wasn't any. Elliott was running away because he couldn't put up with the crap, whatever it was, which meant that Davis hadn't finished his job. And there was always the chance that Quincy would someday need a father not of his own invention and realize that Davis was the only man for the job.

Davis scanned the photos and thanked the Almighty, by kissing DeeDee's forehead, for giving him a job to do and the will to see it through. Then he raised himself from the bed with the grateful certainty that his life, all this crap he put up with, would continue for another day.

Nineteen

Elliott

Got to go for what you know. That was in a song someplace. And what did he know better than this? Right now, and for what seemed like as long as he could remember. The ball pounding the floor like his own heartbeat, going wherever he wanted it to. Between his legs. Behind his back. Skipping past this dude living off an overblown Big Ten rep. Landing in the hands of a two-time loser back from Europe for a corner jumper even he couldn't miss. Then he followed it the other way. Never let it out of his sight. It knew. In the air again. If it didn't come to him, he called it. And it came, cause the others knew where it belonged too. Eight, nine more quick heartbeats and they were home again. In the air together, but not too high. Spin it up between the arms to kiss off the glass and drop back through the net. Don't go away. I'll be back for you in a minute.

This was the way his life began twice before. Once with Davis grabbing his misses from the side of the house and firing outlets that nearly knocked him down, shouting, "Again! Again!" until he begged to stop. He had never liked doing sports with Quincy, either, but this was different. Quincy just wanted to talk, make up rules, discuss the possibilities, until it drove him crazy; they never got around to actually playing. Davis gave him the ball. Made him do it, ninety degrees in the summer, even in the winter. Made him shovel off the driveway first while he talked some stuff about bare-handed snowballs, and *he* had just come from the tropics. Had him catch and dribble and shoot until he couldn't even feel the ball cause his hands were either numb from the cold or slick with sweat. Until he didn't have to feel it cause he knew what it was doing. Until he knew what he could do. Then Glenda taught him to fly, but that turned out to be a trick cause she kept her own ass on the ground. Wouldn't come with him, wouldn't let him land. Well that's what he was gonna do, fly right on away from all that mess. For good this time, one way or another.

Phine of course had to put in her two and a half cents. *I can't believe she said that. Why would she want you to go? How did she know about the try-out anyway? You mean you actually told her? Well shit, you dumb-ass, what'd you expect her to say?* Good question. That's why he stopped expecting. He was gettin too old for these goddamn games. *Yeah, I told her. And I told her I wasn't gonna go, and she told me to get the fuck out so I ain't gonna fuckin worry about it no more. Sayonara, sister girl. You all can keep this soap opera shit.*

The workouts were hard but good. Lots of running and drills, until his ankle swelled and throbbed. He knew the coaches were watching for that, and he knew that it showed. But he pushed through the pain and held on until the scrimmages, when his eyes and hands could take the attention away from his bum leg. When he could make the ball do whatever he wanted, even kiss the net regularly from eighteen feet when he had everyone expecting a pass. Every move he made, every dribble, bounce pass, shot, and stumble, was pressure.

Everything that had gone before was play. The community center, the park, high school, were all like nothing now, like shooting marbles. Even the big times. The pit and the field house. The NIT and the Final Four. The night Davis and Ma and Phine came to the BC game, and he could hear the Emperor's voice in the crowd just like in the driveway: "Underneath!" "Take it in!" "Give it up!" And the Holiday Tournament at the Garden, when he had the PA announcer introduce him as Elliott Crawford-Davis because he knew Quincy had dragged his ass in from the library or the bars or wherever, and he wanted to let him know they were still cool, and he lit up Clyde Frazier's place for thirty and pointed to Big Bro in the red seats, who was standing and cheering just like he knew what the fuck was going on.

Now, nobody was watching except the coaches and the other question marks hoping to be drafted after the first round, just so they'd have a chance to do this all over again in training camp and try to crack the twelve-man roster and make the club. But he had to admit it didn't look good. He knew he'd made enough of an impression to get picked by somebody sometime, but that was bullshit. If you didn't make the second round, at least, you were just practice meat, and first-round bonus money was the only sure thing. Maybe he should have called T's bluff and gone hardship. *You think your shit so tight, why don't you jump on out there and grab the bucks now?* Before the ankle, and before the merger, when the ABA was bidding up the salaries. Now he was lame and there were all these dudes out here competing for fewer jobs. But even back then it was a sucker bet. He could've caught on someplace, but he wasn't ready yet, and he definitely would've had to buy him a big house with the money cause he wasn't goin back home with no degree (which almost happened anyway). Both Ma and Davis had made that clear the first time he mentioned the money Erving was getting after dropping out.

So here it was, like last-shot time. Turned out Davis was wrong about his precious fundamentals. What the announcers called heady intangibles and the brothers dismissed as white-boy shit. Didn't count for much unless you *were* a white boy. These motherfuckers looked at you and they wanted David Thompson verticals. Awesome physical specimens like that kid in Philly out of high school, Dawkins, who looked like he could lift the whole damn court. Who cared if he couldn't run a pick and roll? He thought Russell, who was head coach here now, might be different, since the old Celts thrived on execution. Even after Cousy retired, K. C. Jones never exactly outran anybody and they still did all right. But this was a new day, and Russell was hardly around anyway, didn't seem to have his heart in it. And here he was in the last day of the look-see still makin everybody else look good. Time for a change.

He half-speeded it up the court, looking over the defense as usual, but juked his man at the top of the key and went straight down the lane. No deception. Ran right at the biggest son of a bitch under there and went up as high as he could off his strong foot, which was attached to the bad ankle. Never made it. Before he even got to the rim the ball was flying back out of his hand and his body was sprawling back toward the floor.

The thud brought the coaches running. "You okay? You okay?" They didn't have any money in him; must be an insurance thing. He got up quick enough but limped as he chased down the ball. "Maybe you better have a doctor look at that." "No thanks. He ain't gonna see nothin I haven't seen already." What he hadn't seen before was the look on their faces. The players too. Not since tenth grade anyway. Like he had some fatal disease, terminal spaz. Like he didn't belong out there. He gave the ball a couple of hard dribbles and looked at it carefully. Felt the texture and shape and heft of it. "Look, don't bother, okay? Hey, it's been real." He flipped the ball over his shoulder to his scrimmage partner, who was standing off to the side of the lane, still waiting for the pass that hadn't come, and he listened for the sound of that last sweet swish as he tender-footed out of the gym.

Shit, that didn't take long. Three days and three thousand miles. If he hadn't tried, at least he could have pretended. But that was her point, wasn't it? No way was he gonna go back and listen to that. He'd already made up his mind, whatever happened, to change his ticket and hop down to the Bay to kick back with T awhile. Figure out what he had left. That first year with T was the last time he'd been anybody without a ball in his hands. Since Quincy took off, and took Bubb with him.

Tell im, Bubb. The last command. He remembered because he heard it sometimes in his sleep, but he wasn't really listening at the time. That's why he never answered. He was watching the two of them frozen in an angry clinch, like Liston and Ali. Watching like a spectator, wondering how it would end, and at the same time knowing that he would be part of the outcome. Then watching Phine and Ma and Davis and not getting any of it until all of a sudden he caught his breath and found himself racing out of the house, just so he could find out what he was supposed to do next.

"Quince! Wait up."

"Took you long enough. What's wrong? What did he say to you?"

"He didn't say nothin. What's goin on? Where you goin?"

"I'll think of something. He didn't get to you with that bullshit, did he? That stuff about bein our father? I know you're not goin for that, you always hated him."

"That's cause you always wanted me to. You said he was taking our father's place."

"Don't you remember, Bubb, I saw him? Right in front of our old place. I looked up and he was right there, just like you are now. He told me to take care of everything, and he'd help. Don't you get it, man? We don't need this guy. He's just tryin to break us up, like always."

"But I never saw him, Quince. I never knew him. It was just you."

"That's always been good enough before. You think I'm lyin about this? What're you tryin to say—you'd rather have *him?*"

"No! I don't know. Why do I have to choose?"

"Because you do, that's why. Because I been takin care of you your whole life and I don't need that old fuck butting in now."

"Yeah, but what about what I need? I don't have to do everything you say just cause you got orders from some ghost. He never said nothin to *me,* man. How come? How come nobody ever asked me what *I* want?"

"Look, I don't have time for this. What's it gonna be, you comin or not?"

"I don't even know what you're talkin about, Quince. This is crazy. I'm not goin anyplace."

"Okay, then forget you, Bubb."

"Hey, c'mon, Quince. All right, go on, you dumb fuck. And hey, man, my name is Elliott!"

"Yeah, Bubb. Elliott Crawford. Don't you forget it."

Of course that wasn't the end of it. That would be too easy. In fact he called the next damn day. Just checkin in, like nothin had happened. Kept checking to see if they were really going ahead with the adoption, like he couldn't believe anything like that could actually happen without his say-so. When it did happen, Quincy floated out of the picture for a while, and Elliott began to not miss him, most of the time anyway. It was like *Leave It to Beaver* went off the air, and they just switched channels to another show where he was the big brother. It was weird how that worked. He stopped goofing off in school, started taking care of business at home, doing his homework, looking out for Phine. Mainly because that seemed like the job description, and somebody had to do it.

Later, in Quincy's last year in high school—in exile—he turned up the heat again, came around more often, and for the first time Elliott almost felt sorry for him, although, like Davis said, nobody had told him to leave and nobody was stopping him from coming home if he wanted. Elliott did the next best thing and went to stay with him one weekend. Ma was a little worried, but Davis thought it was a good idea. Probably wanted to know if he'd come back, and maybe thought he could talk some sense into Quincy too.

But Elliott wasn't about to be anybody's spy. That would spoil everything. All he wanted was to see what this other, secret life was like. He knew Quincy had stayed for a while with a friend from school, but then he had started hanging out with some college students and even moved into an apartment in Cambridge. No parents, no rules—Elliott wondered why he even bothered still going to school, but that was Quincy.

They hooked up after school and took the T to Harvard Square, which looked like Paradise Island. Like a whole little town of people who weren't much older than Quincy, all on their own, almost all of them white, and even though some of them looked kinda scraggly, it was on purpose, not the way poor folks Elliott knew looked. He felt at first like they ought to get in disguise so they wouldn't stand out. But Quincy already fit in, looking the kind of college-sloppy that would have given Ma a stroke, with a wrinkled, paisley shirt, bell-bottom jeans, and long hair not combed too good.

As they walked around Quincy started talking about Malcolm X, saying that he used to hang out around there in his days as a hood. Elliott remembered Davis saying some good things about Malcolm, which confused him cause he thought he was just some crazy guy who hated both Martin Luther King and white folks, and in the end even the Muslims around Boston were calling for his head. But Quincy had just read the book, of course, so he had all this stuff to say about stolen history and institutional racism and doo-dah doo-dah. Made sense, but it was too much to take in all at once. Elliott did ask about the X. Quincy didn't go for that part at all; said it was supposed to replace the white man's slave name but as far as Quincy was concerned he didn't care who had it before, it was the name his father gave him and that was that. Elliott changed the subject.

They ate at a Chinese restaurant a couple of blocks from the square. Elliott had never eaten any foreign food, if you didn't count spaghetti and Davis's peas and rice. He squinted at the menu for a while thinking about pizza and Quincy told him to try the almond chicken, like he was some kind of Oriental gourmet. But it was pretty good and so was the pork fried rice, even though Quincy had to show off with the chopsticks and gave him grief about using a fork. Quincy paid with money from his part-time job in a bookstore. The idea of him actually working seemed like a joke to Elliott; Davis had to hound him out of the house to get a summer job at the rec center. But with this one he probably just hung in the back and read all the time, and besides, Elliott knew their mother was still smuggling him rent money.

Quincy pulled out a pack of cigarettes and lit one, measuring the surprise on Elliott's face, and talked about his plans for college the next year. He had gotten a full scholarship at Columbia because he had applied as an independent student with no family support. They were starting to recruit poor ghetto Negroes, he explained, and so being on his own was actually an advantage. He'd be heading down in the summer to attend a special orientation session. The news hit Elliott funny. Not having his brother around all the time wasn't so bad, it turned out, but this would be different. He was really going away this time, and it was like Elliott's childhood was slipping away.

"So what's going on with you? Davis still tryin to turn you into a Harlem Globetrotter?"

Elliott didn't like the question or the tone. It was like he was putting down him, Davis, and basketball all at the same time. Even if he still hated the practicing, which he didn't anymore, he wouldn't have admitted it. "It's not so bad," he said. "I think I'm gettin pretty good. I'm gonna try out for the team next year in high school."

"That's cool. Knock yourself out. You got a girlfriend?"

Elliott had just started hanging out with Glenda and liked her a lot, but something told him not to mention it. Partly it was because they played chess, and he didn't want to give his brother the satisfaction. But also because he wanted to keep something to himself when his brother went off to have his own life, something he couldn't make fun of like basketball by calling up from college and asking something stupid like, "How's your little friend?"

Instead Elliott asked him about girls and parties and stuff like that. Even though he'd never thought of his brother as the fast type, there ought to be some benefits to being on your own. Did he stay out late all the time, get high, and get laid? Could he get in on some of the action? Quincy just puffed and grinned and said Elliott was too young for all that, which pissed him off because it probably just meant he wasn't getting any either. But he asked if Elliott wanted to go to the movies. It wasn't as good as getting laid, but it wasn't a bad idea. That had got to be a regular thing with them on Saturday or Sunday afternoons before Quincy left, and at least they didn't have to worry about finding some dumb cartoon that Phine could go along with. Elliott chose *Bonnie and Clyde* because Davis had denounced it as a cracker shoot-em-up and because it wasn't James Bond, which Quincy always picked when they got away from Phine. The movie was good, and funny in parts, and he liked the idea that Clyde (the younger one) and his brother had their own gang and did what they wanted. But the ending was not what Elliott expected. Instead of the heroes riding away together laughing, even though they were outlaws, they all got shot to hell, really slaughtered. What was the point of that?

It left him tired and irritable but also hungry even though he had a bucket of popcorn and goobers, so Quincy agreed to go by Baskin-Robbins for ice cream, another treat he had a hard time getting out of his parents. The place was bright and crowded, which was a surprise because he didn't think college kids ate that much ice cream. On their way out, as Elliott clutched his Mexican sundae, he turned to look at a cute girl in a bulging halter top. He didn't realize he'd bumped the arm of the guy in front of him till he heard a cone splat on the sidewalk.

"Jesus! Watch it, willya?"

"Oh, hey, I'm sorry. Can I . . . ?"

The backhand caught him by surprise. He staggered back a few steps, blinked, and held onto his sundae.

"Why don't you guys just stay the fuck away from here?"

Because the words were so unexpected, Elliott had to play them back in his head to make sure he heard correctly. That's when he saw Quincy's arm make a sudden motion, and a glob of chocolate was oozing down the side of the white guy's face.

"He said he was sorry, asshole," Quincy was saying. "It's a free goddamn country, and we'll go wherever the fuck we want to."

In a blink, Quincy and the guy had each other by the collar, grappling. But another one was moving in. Elliott lunged forward and caught the second guy around the waist. They all went down in a heap. Quincy must've got up first; Elliott saw his foot whomping into the first guy's midsection. He realized it had gotten quiet but the noise level was building. Others were crowding around.

"Come on." Quincy grabbed his arm and lifted him to his feet. Elliott paused, waiting for the others to get up. Quincy tugged his arm. "Let's go." They scrambled around the corner and down a narrow street, heads bobbing like Clarence Williams in the opening from *Mod Squad*. At the next corner they slowed down, and soon they were at the entrance to Quincy's basement apartment.

"We shoulda finished em off, man."

"Yeah, right. You see how big that second guy was? You were lucky to get him down the first time. He coulda broke your narrow ass like chopsticks."

"I had im down, though, didn't I?"

"Yeah, you sure did. Good work, Robin," Quincy added in a deep voice, rubbing Elliott's head.

"Quit. Hey, is this all yours?" Elliott asked as they moved through the apartment, turning on lights.

"No, just the back room. I told you I share it with a couple of college students."

"Cool. How come there's only two bedrooms?"

"Cause this is mine and that's theirs, fool. Hey, come out of there."

"Hey, you mean a girl lives here with you? They sleep together? Can you hear em doin it?"

"You're such a moron, Bubb. What's the matter, didn't you ever hear Ma and Davis 'doin it'?"

"That's gross. Where's the TV?"

"Don't have one."

"Well what do you do all the time?"

"I live. Go on, make yourself comfortable."

Elliott flopped onto Quincy's messy bed and was surprised to find a stash of recent comics nearby. He grabbed one and started to read it, and the sound of crinkling pages brought a sharp look from Quincy. "Yeah, okay, okay," Elliott said without prompting. Quincy had this thing about not folding the pages back and creasing the binding the wrong way. He was a real pain in the ass about that, and got to the point where he wouldn't let Phine near the books at all, after he had Ma iron out a stack she had gotten into and wrinkled up. You'd think they were leather-bound encyclopedias instead of twenty-five-cent comic books, for crying out loud, but there was no point getting into it now. The best part, anyway, had been going together to the cigar store after school, where all these old guys stood around talking about baseball, buying the racing form and checking out the girlie magazines, while they spun the racks plucking out the latest shipment of Spiderman, the Fantastic Four, Batman, and the Justice League. Elliott peeked around to see if Quincy had any copies of *Playboy* but didn't ask. He wondered if there'd be any crease in those.

"You know, if you had kept your promise and come up with a formula for super powers by now, we could take care of guys like that in no time."

"I invented the spiderweb, didn't I? You didn't want to use it."

"That's cause I broke my ankle."

"Wasn't my fault. The web worked, you just landed wrong."

There wasn't much in the room: the bed, a desk and chair, a dresser. But Quincy had got hold of a record player somewhere and built up a decent collection to go along with the piles of books. You had to do something with no TV. Quincy played the Temptations' greatest hits and some jazz stuff and sat at the desk reading a real book—homework, he guessed—while Elliott got sleepy on the bed and they interrupted each other every so often with whatever popped into their heads: *I Spy,* Aretha Franklin, Vietnam, whatever. It was a lot like the way they had spent evenings at home after they'd been banished upstairs from the TV to do homework.

But there was one thing that had never come up then, that Elliott had to ask.

"You really believe that stuff about Daddy, don't you?"

"Well, you believe in Davis, right?"

"I don't know what you mean."

Quincy closed his book and came over to sit beside him on the bed.

"Look at it this way, Bubb. Believing in fathers is like believing in magic anyway—it's all a leap of faith. You always know who your mother is. You came out of her, there's no question. You're connected from birth. But fathers are different. Some guy says he plunked your mother, so you're supposed to love him. But how do you know? Or you're supposed to accept somebody because he's plunking her now. Either way it's a choice. I know our father is real because I saw him and I still feel him with me. That may sound crazy to you, but it's no crazier than latching on to whoever comes out of your mother's bedroom."

"Yeah, but it's more than that. I mean, he takes good care of us."

"Okay, then he's your father. Presto. Hey, don't worry about it, all right? It's cool. Get ready for bed, you look whipped."

Later, in the dark, he heard Quincy's voice from the floor, where he had stretched out on a blanket so Elliott could have the bed. "If you want," he said, "you can come down and hang out with me in New York sometime. After I get settled."

"Sure, that'd be great. Don't forget, you owe me a sundae. I only got one bite, and it looked good, too."

"If you'd kept your eyes on the ice cream instead of on that girl's tits you would've been able to finish it."

New York never happened, though. Quincy disappeared into the city like he'd done when he first got to Cambridge, and Elliott got busy playing ball in high school and being with Glenda. Then Quincy got finished with college and started teaching, and Elliott went off to school, and Quincy went back to grad school, and getting together for a sundae in New York got to be one of those things they said to each other a couple of times a year and that was that. In fact, nothing like that night in his room ever happened, except for the time Quincy drove up to Amherst to give him a pep talk.

The very next time they saw each other was a completely different vibe, when Quincy came by the house one afternoon and started smoking reefer. Elliott wanted to try some then, but Quincy wouldn't let him. Just kept puffing away and filling up the room with that smell until Davis came home. It took Elliott a while to figure out that he was trying to get caught, wanted to get put out so he could make the break to New York with a clear conscience and a chip on his shoulder. He had brought his graduation-cap tassel and told Elliott to give it to Phine; he hadn't invited any of them to the ceremony. Four years later, Elliott had asked to come to New York for Quincy's graduation from Columbia, but Quincy brushed him off, said he wasn't even going himself—and then showed up like Zorro in the back of the auditorium when Elliott got his high school diploma and left town without ever coming by the house.

None of that shit was necessary, of course, but like he always said, Quincy was a fucking mutant anyway.

Elliott dialed the number from the airport in San Francisco and got directions to North Beach. On the way in, he noticed how different it was from L.A., more like a real city—a foreign city, maybe, with all the old houses perched on hills and the water always in the background. Not as spaced out and desperate as the other place. He got just confused enough about the address that he ended up having to tote his bag two blocks seriously uphill after he left the cab to get to the right house, then locate T's entrance on the side, and climb a flight of stairs to reach the apartment.

"This better be you, motherfucker," he called as he pushed through the unlocked door, "cause I ain't climbin no more damn steps."

"Come on back here, man. Lemme get a look at your ass."

T was sprawled on the bed in boxers and shades. With the curtains pulled, Elliott could barely make him out.

"Hey, now. *Sweet* D!" He held out his hand out for a slap while he boom-boomed the bass line from "Fire."

"T-*Man*. What you doin in bed, nigger? Get the fuck up, it's the middle of the day."

"Middle of the damn day to you. I work nights. Cool out. So what happened, you got that million-dollar bonus?"

"Not hardly." Elliott lowered himself onto the side of the bed. "It wasn't happenin, the ankle wouldn't do right. I just booked."

"Told you to go hardship, didn't I?" T said as he reached to light a Sherman's.

"Yeah, fuck you, you told me a lotta stupid shit."

"Don't go feelin sorry for yourself now. Point is, man, if you'd really wanted the pros you wouldn't've needed me to tell you that. So you took the shot and missed. Hey, it happens. So you end up here sooner instead of later, is all. But I knew you'd be comin around."

"Is that right?"

"Sure, much as we been through. How you gonna keep em down on the farm and whatnot?"

"Yeah, like gettin put outta school?"

"Not you, hotshot. They just told you to stay your ass off campus, but you got your paper. I'm the one got fucked."

"Well it *was* your apartment, and you brought her there. Wasn't like you didn't get none too."

"Whatever. Just remember who went to bat for you, nigger. You used up your eligibility, they didn't give a shit about you. Woulda hung your ass out to dry if I hadn't took the fall."

That was about half right. The coaches didn't do shit, but because Elliott had finished the credits he needed to graduate the semester before, the suspension was meaningless. Tyrone, on the other hand, was skating after five years and might not have finished anyway. He had already made plans to come to San Francisco, and with the radio now off limits the two of them had just hung around and worked off-campus parties until the semester was over.

"Anyway, like the man said, she wasn't a student and she wasn't white, so wasn't nothin but a thang," Tyrone continued. "Fuck that shit. It's bygones. The T don't run backward, you know what I'm sayin? How long you stayin, man?"

"I don't know. I just know I don't wanna think about school, don't wanna think about ball, and don't wanna think about home."

"Well, all right. You come to the right place cause this here is the T place and it ain't nothin but a motherfuckin par-tay, can you dig it?"

Tyrone had been promised a trial radio spot later in the summer by a station that was getting killed by disco and thought the funk-rock mix he'd shown in his tapes might bring back some listeners. In the meantime he was generally scuffling, getting a feel for the music scene and

222   *Dennis A. Williams*

paying the bills with a weeknight gig at a neighborhood club. Elliott
tagged along that night because Tyrone insisted and because he didn't
have anything else to do. The place seemed small, bright, and empty
when they arrived, but it was early. Tyrone walked straight to the corner
of the bar and plucked up a Hennessy in a small glass.

"Right on time, T," said the bartender, a blond man, not quite as
young as he wanted people to think, wearing tight jeans and a sleeveless T-shirt with a bandanna tied around his neck. "Who's your friend?"

"This is my partner, Elliott Davis, from back East. He's gonna help
me in the booth."

"Welcome to the Shaft, Elliott. I'm Steve, what can I do to you?"

"I'll just have a beer. What've you got bottled?"

"Oh, you've got to try an Anchor Steam. It's the local specialty. And
listen, if you get bored up there, just come on back anytime and I'll
take care of you, okay?"

"Yo, T," Elliott said as they went to set up. "Is there something you
forgot to tell me?"

"Well let's just say the Shaft ain't named for Richard Roundtree.
Don't worry, it's cool. You here to watch me work, and I can get a roomful of deaf nuns jumpin."

Actually, Elliott thought as the club began to fill, grow darker, and
seem larger, it wouldn't be that hard. For a mostly white crowd, they
were ready to get down. And it wasn't what he expected, once he found
out what he was supposed to expect. Not freakish like a leather bar or
a bunch of campy queens—though there were a few like that. Most of
them looked like regular guys, or would have, to him, if he'd passed
them on the street. They came in, they drank, they hooked up, and
they danced. In a way, not having women around almost made the
whole thing easier. At parties back in school, especially with the team,
they spent a lot of time talking shit and pointing and showing off for
one another. Sometimes it seemed like the women they were dancing
with just got in the way, although they usually came in handy later.

"Check this out," T was saying. "See, they think they want disco cause
it seems neutral. They don't relate it to a black thing but they still get to
shake their little asses pretty good. Once I get em goin, though, I lay a
little thump on em and they eat it up. Go native and shit. You just gotta
sneak up on em. White folks is like that, even these motherfuckers
think they all hip and shit."

Later on, after a couple more tactful visits to Steve, Elliott needed to relieve himself. T was kicking it with some Parliament—*If you hear any noise, it's just me and the boys*—and he was right, they were going off like the dancers in a black musical. The men's room, which he supposed was the only one although they might as well have two, was lit in red. The smell of reefer made it familiar, but there was also a dreamlike quality to the way people moved around. Standing at a urinal, he heard slurps and sighs and noticed, in the stall beside him, a pair of legs on its knees. Then someone stepped in beside him, extravagantly unzipped, and looked his way. Beer or no beer, it took forever for the piss to come.

"I haven't had that much play since the Final Four," he said when he finally returned to the booth.

"I was gonna warn you, but hey, when you gotta go, you gotta go. Don't be too flattered, though. Some of these cats'll hit on anything, and a lot of em just like to fuck with you when they smell fear, like a dog and shit. Then there's those like Steve that are suckers for chocolate. Tell you what, though, you can say what you want, but they dance their ass off, don't they?"

The next night, Friday, T was off and they went cruising, stopping in at a variety of clubs just to hear what was playing. Not so much the mainstream rock-pop stuff, which was already pretty heavily infected by disco, not to mention the tired-ass Eagles. They sampled some loud, drugged-out costumed rock, real country, and even reggae—stuff that T would never use on the radio, not blatantly anyway, but that gave him a sense for where people's heads were. It was like at school when he would play every stray piece of shit that came into the station once, then file it away in his mind. Now he could do the same thing in person with the added benefit of checking out just who was listening to what. It was research, really. In L.A., it had seemed like they were just hanging out, but now he could see that T was serious about this, which was both fascinating and depressing, because at this point Elliott didn't have any kind of agenda of his own.

Luckily he didn't have to think about it for more than a few hours. By one o'clock, T was ready to stop taking notes, and they settled into a black club where the beat was familiar and there were women to dance with. A good, old-fashioned anonymous boogie, where he didn't have to worry about backing up T or putting up any kind of front for people he knew. That was what he came for, that and a little something extra. Like the tall, dark-skinned, bald-headed woman who slid up to him looking like the freak off the cover of the old Ohio Players albums. She wore a short, clingy, black wrap dress that couldn't begin to cover her sprinter's legs, and best of all, as he discovered when they stopped dancing, she had a friend who gave off the same vibes. He caught T's eye and nodded him over to the bar, where they could do some nego- tiating. No need to share this time, not that that had been his intention before. That was an accident, at least as far as he was concerned. This was more like it, no children, no surprises, no history, no future. And it didn't take long. They had a couple rounds, talked some shit, and as soon as T mentioned that he had some coke back at the crib they were in a cab.

He woke up early, wired with the feeling that he had just gotten to sleep but that everything had happened a long time ago. They had done a couple of lines crowded around the bed in T's room, using the cover of the Donna Summer album while the record played some- where, filling the apartment with grunts and groans. And then they were rolling all over each other snatching away fabric to get handfuls and mouthfuls of flesh. At one point, he remembered, he carried his girl into the living room, while she scratched at him with these bright red cat claws, to get away from the confusion and concentrate on the business at hand. They landed on the sofa and went at it in a dozen dif- ferent positions, just like the shit in *Players* magazine. He grooved him- self up between her tits and into her mouth; he doubled her legs back to her ears and nibbled at her, then pumped in from above; he flung her over the back of the sofa and came in from behind; she pinned him on the floor and squatted slowly up and down, raking his chest and stom- ach with her nails. It seemed like it would never stop, and when he fi- nally shocked himself by coming he tried to hold on to her, if only for a while—there was nothing to say, after all—to acknowledge their amaz- ing performance with a touch of intimacy. Instead, she sprang up out of his reach and staggered bowlegged back to the bedroom for more powder. Apparently, there wasn't any. Both girls reappeared a few min- utes later laughing, cursing, and mostly dressed, as T shouted some- thing at them and he passed out on the sofa.

He was starving now but knew there was nothing around to eat; T hardly ever ate anything. That would have been the one reason to stay in Seattle, at least they fed him good. Hunting up some breakfast might be a good excuse anyway to walk around and see the neighbor- hood—and clear his head—so he started pulling on some clothes. Then he spotted the phone on the floor in a corner of the living room and without thinking went to pick it up. He had been out of touch for a couple of days and should probably let somebody know where he was.

The voice that answered caught him off guard. "Quincy?" he asked.

"Where the hell are you?"

"What're you doin there?"

"Your sister is graduating tomorrow, remember? You still in Seattle? They thought you'd be back by now."

"Naw, I'm in San Francisco . . . checkin out some jobs. Look, I don't know if I'll make it back. I told her that, lemme talk to her."

"I don't care what you told her. Look, Phine's got some problems and Ma's freakin out. You need to get your ass back here, Bubb."

"Aw, man, I'm busy, all right? You're there, you handle it. You're good at that, that's what everybody's been waitin for anyway. Ma don't listen to me no way, and Phine worships your ass. Davis too. Just take care of it, okay?"

"You finished?"

"What?"

"I said if you're finished, you can quit the nobody-loves-me blues and start packin."

"Who the fuck you think—"

"Don't even start that shit, Bubb, this is serious. You need to be here, so just get it in gear, all right?"

"What is it, anyway? I mean, what's goin on?"

"I can't explain now. I'll tell you when you get here."

"Hey, wait a minute. What . . ." The line went dead, and Elliott threw the receiver at the base of the phone. "*Fuck* you, man. I ain't your goddamn dog." Motherfucker just walks out, does whatever the fuck he wants to and don't give a shit about the rest of us, and then just strolls back givin orders like I'm thirteen goddamn years old. Like I don't have a goddamn life. Stalking the room and talking to himself, he began to snatch up his clothes and throw them into a pile on the sofa. This is it, goddammit. Gonna straighten this shit out once and for all. Where's my fuckin bag at? Tired of this shit.

"Who the fuck you yellin at, motherfucker? I'm tryin to get some sleep in here."

On his knees, pulling his bag out from under the sofa, Elliott looked up and saw Tyrone.

"That was my brother. My sister's in some kinda trouble. They want me to go back and help straighten it out."

"So?"

"What the fuck you mean, 'So'? So I'm gonna go and settle this shit."

"Well, what's the problem?"

"They didn't say."

"Man, listen to yourself. That don't make no kinda sense. Somebody's in some damn trouble, and you supposed to do what?"

"Look, you don't understand. I'm just gonna go and see what's up. And tell em to leave me the fuck alone."

"Hell, you can do that on the damn phone. You just lookin for an excuse to run on back home to that sad-ass bitch, man. You need to let that shit alone. You at the beach now, baby, why you wanna go play in the sandbox?"

"I'm not even thinkin about that. And don't call her no bitch, man, you don't even know her."

"Oh, excuse me. She gots a pussy, don't she? She catch dicks in it and make babies and try to fuck with a nigger's head. What you call that?"

"Lay off, T. It ain't about that."

"The fuck it ain't. Get real, D. You think you just gonna show up with good intentions and make everything all right? It don't work that way. They just want you to share the pain, that's all. What you gonna do?"

"I don't know, all right? I'll think of something."

"Shit, you need help your own damn self. Like that shit at school, man, you know what really went down? Big basketball star? That girl's old man was gonna sue your ass off, get a piece of all that big pro money. He didn't know you weren't gonna make it any damn way. But I kept him off you, man. Got some of my local boys to discourage him, you know what I mean? Else you'd be workin in his damn auto body shop right now, payin the motherfucker off for the next twenty goddamn years."

"You did what?"

"Whole damn thing was probably a setup anyway. See, you don't even know what's goin on right under your own damn nose, man. And you gonna go help somebody else? Shit."

"Look, it's my sister."

"Yeah, it's your sister, it's your brother, it's always gonna be some damn body. But what about you, D? Who's thinkin about you? Just hang with me for a while, that's all I'm sayin. You go runnin back now, you'll just get stuck in somebody else's world."

"Like this ain't yours?"

"Oh, I see. Hey, at least I ain't makin no demands. Give yourself a chance. You can be whoever or whatever the fuck you wanna be here."

"Yeah. As long as it's who you want me to be."

"That's bullshit and you know it. I ain't never stopped you from doin nothin. It's not my fault if you don't know what you wanna do, and frankly I don't care. You just have to be yourself, man, take all the time you want. Back there, they want you to be like you used to be, but I know you got more than that. I know you, man."

"Shit, T, you don't even know my goddamn name. I gotta go."

Chris found out. She didn't know how, she only knew that now it couldn't be over, the way she wanted it to be. He wouldn't let it go. "Don't you worry, baby," he said one night as they tongue-wrapped on her steps to Donna Summer playing on his new boom box. "I'm gonna get those guys, you'll see. I swear they'll be sorry they ever touched you." At first she tried to pretend that she hardly remembered, that it was no big deal. That didn't work because he had seen her right after and knew how shook up she was, and she had already told him too much. Then she begged him not to do anything because she didn't want him to get hurt. That was stupid. Making it sound dangerous just got him more worked up, and besides, no guy thought he was going to get hurt in battle for a righteous cause. It was in the blood or something. She told him she didn't want everybody to know, but he didn't care, and that made her mad, almost mad enough to tell him the biggest reason she didn't want him to do anything. If they were going to be punished for what they had done, she wanted to have done it herself. Right then and there. Since she didn't, they'd just have to live miserable lives and die horrible deaths on their own. Having somebody else do your pay-back was okay if you were in the Mafia or something, but she didn't believe in that. She had denied them what they wanted, which was her, so she won and they lost and that was that.

She also didn't want Daddy to know.

He would insist that it had somehow been her fault. For being alone. For making herself too attractive. For being around those people in the first place. For not being home under his protection. He would make a crusade of his vengeance and hold it over her for the rest of her life. Or maybe he'd just kill her for shaming him. She really didn't want to find out.

In any case she didn't know who those guys were, not exactly. She had a pretty good idea and could probably have sorted it out afterward if she'd tried. But she hadn't let herself do that because that way she wouldn't be able to tell Chris, and he wouldn't be able to play Lancelot. But now he knew, and as soon as he mentioned the names she realized she had known all along. They were from Brian's crowd, which was why he'd been able to step in so easily. The only thing left to do now, the only way to get Chris to hold up, was to go to the police and press charges.

Chris laughed at her. Like they might even arrest some white boys for tryin to get into a sister's pants. Hell, the cops were probably their uncles and whatnot. He was right, of course, although he could have put it more delicately. But still, she insisted. Chris said he thought she didn't want nobody to know. She didn't, really, but it was the only way for her now, unless she jumped into a Pam Grier bag, to control the situation. And when Daddy did find out, at least she'd be taking care of business herself. He'd have to respect that.

So the next day, after school, they went together to the station. Chris was jumpy, the way some people get around graveyards. Police station might as well be the graveyard for brothers, he muttered. Or a roach motel, brother check in and don't come out. But she had been there before a few times with her father, when he had come to sic the cops on landlords and employers and even to bail folks out, so she remained steady with Chris's hand tightly gripping hers as they sifted through all the officers who, as Daddy said, should have been out on the street protecting the citizens, and made their way to the desk sergeant.

"Yeah, what can I do for you kids?" he said without looking up.

"I want to file a complaint," she said in a loud, clear voice, just as she had silently rehearsed.

"What kinda complaint? Somebody steal your basketball?"

"No," she said, squeezing Chris's hand to keep him in check, "I was assaulted."

"You were assaulted?" The sergeant finally put down his pen and looked up.

"That's right. I was assaulted and I want to press charges."

"And just when did this assault take place?"

"Last week. Thursday night."

"You were assaulted a week ago and you want to file a complaint now?"

"We just got their names, okay?" Chris said. "We did your work for you, so now all you got to do is arrest the bastards."

"Well, I appreciate your help, sonny, but one step at a time, all right? Now where did this alleged assault take place?"

"In the parking lot by the Parker House, downtown."

"The Parker House? That's District One. You'll have to go down there to make your complaint."

"This the Boston police department, ain't it? Don't you all talk to each other?"

"Sorry, kid, that's the procedure."

"My father is Derek Davis. Do you know who he is?"

"Sure, I know him. He bit me in the leg in a football game in high school, and now he's in here all the time making complaints. I guess you got it natural, but I don't care if your old man's Ted Kennedy. You got to take this downtown."

"All right, I will."

"See, what I tell you?"

"Come on, let's go."

She called home to say that she and Chris were going downtown shopping, and then they hopped the T to the station on New Sudbury. Now that she had started this, she wanted to see it through while she was mad, and before Chris gave up.

They did the same song and dance, but instead of being sent away they had to wait a long time until a youngish, frumpy-looking police-woman came to get them. Then they had to repeat the whole story sitting across a gray metal desk from the cop lady, who was blowing smoke in their faces.

"Now you say this alleged assault occurred after your high school prom?"

"It wasn't an alleged assault. Three guys held me down and tried to rape me. And it was before the prom."

"I thought you said they were leaving."

"They were. The white kids had their part of the prom first. I was waiting for ours to start."

"But you had been inside already?"

"Yes. I was helping to set up."

"Had you been drinking?"

"No. Well, I may have had one glass of champagne, but I wasn't drunk or anything like that."

"Okay, what were you wearing?"

"I was wearing my prom dress."

"Long gown or mini? Low cut? Sheer fabric?"

"It was a prom dress! Just like everybody else's. I wasn't dressed like a hooker, if that's what you mean."

"I don't believe this," Chris muttered.

"I'm just asking. Why were you in the parking lot? Did you go out there with these boys? Maybe to have a drink or something? Did you have any drugs?"

"Look, she's reporting a crime, okay? Why you tryin to get her to confess to somethin that *didn't* happen?"

"I didn't go anyplace with them. They dragged me into the parking lot. I was out front waiting for Chris. Why don't you go find them and ask them?"

"Were you alone?"

"Yes, I told you, I was waiting for my boyfriend."

"Were there any witnesses?"

"Just me and the animals who attacked me."

"I see," she said and turned for the first time to Chris. "You arrived just after the alleged assault?"

"Yeah, I got there and she was all, you know, messed up. Like she'd been in a fight or something."

"Did you actually see this fight?"

"She told me about it. They had just left when I got there."

"Why didn't you do anything about it then? Did you call the police that night? Go after them?"

"Why, so you could arrest *me*? No, she didn't want to make a big deal about it. And she didn't know who they were, their names. I asked around. They were braggin at school, said they did it, you know. It got back to me because she's my girlfriend and all."

"You went back into the prom?"

"That's what she wanted to do."

"Did anybody else there notice your condition?" she asked, turning again to Delphine. "Did you tell anybody else what happened?"

"No. Well, yes, they asked, but I said I fell down."

"I'd like to speak with Delphine alone for a few minutes please."

Chris looked anxiously at her, but she whispered that she'd be okay. An officer escorted him away from the desk, toward another area of the station.

Policewoman waited for them to be out of earshot before continuing. "Chris didn't actually take you to the prom, is that right? You were waiting for him to join you?"

"I had to go early to set up. I was one of the organizers. Chris didn't want to go, not until the white kids left."

"Were you angry with him for not taking you?"

"No."

"How did he feel about you going alone? He seems a very emotional young man."

"What do you mean?"

"Delphine, I know sometimes young girls get into arguments with their boyfriends. There's a lot going on at your age. Sometimes things get . . . a little out of hand, if you know what I mean."

"No," she replied pointedly. "I don't."

"And if you did have an argument, a fight, and told people you just fell down, you might have second thoughts about that."

"What are you getting at?"

"Whose idea was it to come down here?"

"It was my idea. I told him I wanted to file a complaint, so he wouldn't do something—no, not like that. Why you lookin at me like that?"

"Delphine, you're safe here. This is a police station, and Chris is in the other room. If there's something you want to tell me about what really happened, this would be a good time."

"What, you think he attacked me? What kind of fool do you take me for? No, I told you who did it. You get them in here. Chris didn't do anything."

"All right, if that's the way you want it. But I can't do anything for you without witnesses. Are you sure nobody else saw what happened?"

"It doesn't *work* that way. I'm tellin you what happened. Are you saying you don't believe me?"

"I'm sorry, Delphine. We can't help you."

Too stunned even to curse the woman out, she hurried away from the desk to find Chris. She finally saw him through the open door of an interrogation room, sitting glumly with arms crossed as the officer stood nearby.

"We're all through here," she said with an assurance that masked the uncertainty of the situation. It looked like they were ready to slap handcuffs on him.

Chris slipped an icy look at her, like maybe he thought she had set him up or something. She had expected him to jump up mad, talking back as he had at the other station, but she realized that he didn't feel free to go. Only when policewoman appeared behind her and caught the eye of the officer did he in turn thumb Chris toward the door.

"What the hell was that about?" he asked in a voice more scared than angry.

"Shh. I'm sorry," she whispered and put her arm around his waist.

They rode home silently. She didn't even have the heart to tell him about policewoman's straight-out accusation. He probably knew, just from the way he had been sat down in that room without anybody saying anything to him, that he had sunk from troublemaker to disbelieved accomplice to suspect, just like that, just by being who he was. That must have left him too shaken even to hit her with the I-told-you-so she expected and deserved.

It was also clear, suddenly, why Chris had bragged to her about his intentions, had allowed her to talk him into going into the police, and had not actually taken his revenge himself already. He wasn't really a tough kid. He talked a good game—they all did—but if he'd been the type to run out and raise hell, kick ass, or whatever on his own without thinking about it a long time first, she wouldn't have been with him in the first place. And he'd never been in trouble, so it didn't take much police intimidation to knock the smart out of his mouth. The guys who'd attacked her weren't class-A hoods, but they were rough enough, rougher than he was, and the school was their turf. Now she'd backed him into a corner—called his bluff by going to the cops first, and they'd spit in his eye.

In a way they'd never been closer. Everything else they'd gone through for the past two years involved the whole group, but this was personal, almost intimate. But even though she'd kept her arm around him as they left the station, as a gesture of solidarity, she was afraid now to touch him. Afraid that maybe he'd lash out at her for putting him in the position of feeling so helpless. Maybe that was what Daddy meant by provocation. In any case she resolved before they separated in a bunch of shrugs and mumbles that she would make one more effort to settle this thing on her own.

School at that point was a pretty haphazard affair. Final exams had just finished, and people were coming and going just about as they pleased, especially the seniors. From what she understood it used to be even looser, but they tried to keep some semblance of structure now so that the blacks and whites wouldn't get into something and mess up graduation. A little late for that. Because she couldn't count on a class schedule, it took her a while to corner Beth apart from the pink mob.

"Hey, Del. I can't believe it's only a couple more days. You ready?"

"More than you know. Listen, we gotta talk."

"Sure, what's up?"

"Can we go outside?"

They went and sat on the front steps, where the long driveway curved around a patch of green centered by the big flagpole. In the beginning, the tribe wasn't even allowed to come in that way, where the natives habitually hung out before school; instead, they were snuck in through the back parking lot. That had proved to be a good strategy when the first few days through the front door brought shouted insults, bumping and shoving, and a dozen personal confrontations that could each have triggered a full riot. That seemed a long time ago. Delphine felt perfectly comfortable now sitting out in the bright June sunshine, even though they weren't exactly alone. She felt a lot less comfortable, though, about what she had to say.

"You know, you were the first white person here I trusted," she began, looking toward the flag only to keep from looking at Beth. "I was ready to spend the whole time all knotted up. This place nearly gave me an ulcer. After you came out for the drill team, I thought for the first time that maybe I'd be able to relax and almost be myself. I want to thank you for that."

"Oh, hell, from the look on your face I thought you had bad news," Beth said. "I don't know what made me do that, but I just, you know, thought I should try something different. I felt kinda the same way. I was real scared of you all. I heard so much, about what you were like and how all this was gonna mess up our school, and I just had to try something, you know. I'm real glad I did."

"That's not all," she said looking at her hard.

"Oh, shit, something is wrong. What is it? Is there something I can do?"

"Yes. You know what happened at the prom? When you and Brian showed up?"

"Yeah. I thought that was all over."

"Well, it's not. I went to the police yesterday."

"The police? What for?"

"Because they tried to rape me, Beth, that's what for."

"But they didn't. Brian stopped them."

"It's not that simple. I thought I could just make it go away, but I can't. I can't let them get away with that, Beth. That makes everything we did a lie." The argument was forming as she said it. The frightened look on Beth's face convinced her that Chris had been right all along, and her father too. Getting to the prom and being with Chris afterward had blunted her feelings. But now she was mad.

"I don't understand," Beth protested lamely.

"Yes, you do. I want to press charges. I want those creeps arrested. But the police won't do anything without witnesses."

"But they were just—"

"Just trying to rape me, Beth. They had me on the hood of that car like a goddamn animal, and they were getting ready to fuck me in the ass." Beth glanced around to see if anybody was listening, but Delphine didn't let up. "Do you have any idea what that felt like? Do you think for a minute they would have done that to you?"

"But I know those guys. I went to grade school with them. I know their families, they're not really bad."

"Jesus, Beth, listen to yourself."

"Well, I mean, what they did was awful, I know, what they tried to do anyway, but Christ, Del, those are Brian's friends."

"And I'm your friend. And they *hurt* me, Beth. Can't you see that? I need your help. All you have to do is tell the truth. Brian too."

"Oh, he wouldn't, I know. And he wouldn't want me . . . come on, Del, he's my boyfriend. I might even marry the guy. I can't ask him to send his friends to jail."

"Then you do it."

"Delphine, I can't. You know I can't."

Delphine rose to her full height and tried to stare down the pathetic bundle in front of her. But Beth didn't budge, and Delphine finally looked away, to the flag, the huge temple of a school, the clusters of pink people, the smug houses surrounding them. All the things that gave Beth the idiotic courage to stand there and believe she was right when she knew she wasn't. All the goddamn white shit holding her up when she knew Delphine could haul off and slap the pink off her cheeks and be perfectly justified in doing it.

"Don't be mad, Del."

"What for, Beth?" she answered, still gazing around. "You can't help being a stupid little fool. You've got an excuse. I don't. I was wrong about you, that's my fault. But you know what else I was wrong about? If they'd do that to me, they'll do it to you, too. You just wait till Brian comes home drunk some night and you're not in the mood. Your no won't mean a damn thing more than mine."

With that she went inside to find Chris, to confess that she was out of options—and to tell him that even though he was right, it still wasn't worth getting his butt kicked. Their escape would be their revenge. He wouldn't like it, but that's what she had to tell him. She couldn't find him, though. She'd spent the morning trying to steer clear of him until she had a chance to confront Beth, and now that she was ready for him he wasn't around. Just like a man.

He wasn't on the bus home, either, and she began to get worried. He might have been so pissed off about the police station that he didn't want to face her, or anybody else. Or he was ready to take some action on his own. Whatever his condition was, she didn't like it—and she figured she was responsible. She started trying to call him as soon as she got home. First there was no answer. Then the line was busy. Finally his mother answered and said he wasn't there, but Delphine didn't believe her, so she called back a couple more times and asked her to please have him get in touch when he got home from wherever he was.

After each call in the upstairs hallway she went back into her room quickly and closed the door to avoid her parents. That was why they wouldn't let her have a phone in her room, so they could keep track of what was going on.

There wasn't anything else to do, and that was something new. There had always—*always*—been schoolwork, and when nothing was due Daddy, picking up where Quincy left off when she was a little kid, came up with something for her to read, for her "real" education. When Bubba took off and she couldn't follow him around anymore she hung out with Glenda until track and drill team, and then the new school and Chris took over. Now school was finished, Glenda had Erika to worry about, Bubb had come and gone like some kind of mystery vagabond, and Chris was playing hide-and-seek. This was the time everybody always talked about, graduation was two days away and she had her whole life in front of her, but at this very moment it was more empty than she could ever remember.

She thought about calling some of her girlfriends, but they would want to talk about boys, and with Chris missing in action she didn't feel like playing that. She reached for one of the spiral notebooks under her bed to read what she had written in a random volume of her journal, in order to recapture some of her past life. Of course, she happened to turn to a page where she had written about how this cutesy white girl who had pushed her way onto the drill team seemed to be becoming a friend and how much that could mean to her at that point in her transition, and it was really sickening shit. She started to rip the page out and crumple it but instead just threw the book across the room. Followed by a couple others. Then, because she had to tear something, she got up and ripped down the Michael Jackson poster and the Reggie Jackson poster and the Julius Erving poster that represented both her own past infatuations and the influence of her brother, neither of which she felt like staring at anymore. And since all the records she could see lying around would remind her of Chris or the prom or high school in general, she chose not to put on any music but just sank to the floor to wait for something new, good or bad, to happen to her.

She wanted so much. To put her survival to good use somehow by proving that it meant something. To get out there and show what she had, a bad Bajan princess who had come through the war of integration in what was supposed to be the cradle of America. To strut her stuff around the world, in Africa and the Caribbean and South America and Asia too. And everywhere she went with her New World knowledge she wanted to fall in love with a tall, dark man. With lean muscles and a friendly smile. Someone who would give her all the love she needed whenever she wanted—and never when she didn't—and who wouldn't think that sharing her body and her mind gave him the right to protect her if she didn't need it or to tell her what to do. Whatever she did, wherever she went, her life would be hers. She had earned that independence, and actually it wasn't so much to ask for after all.

She had no idea how long she'd been sitting there projecting herself outward from the dark room when she heard the doorbell and roused herself. It might be Chris, saying that he'd been out walking around all night and had decided to forget the whole thing, and they would sit out on the porch to share their dreams and plan a fantastic summer together that would end with them parting as onetime loves and forever friends to go out separately and conquer the world.

She ran down the steps and saw her mother frozen before the front door and her father rising to join her. At the bottom she saw her mother take a step back to reveal a grinning, deep brown man in a silky shirt unbuttoned on his muscled chest and flared trousers breaking sharply at his bowed knees. She gasped and ran to him, nearly pushing her mother aside and realizing with astonishment that he was barely taller than she was. How could that be, when she could clearly remember climbing his back, bouncing in his lap, listening to his patient voice unlock the magic of letters on a page?

"Quincy!" she squealed.

"Hey, kiddo," he said soothingly in her ear. "I told you I'd be here, didn't I? I came to get my tassel back, now that you'll be gettin your own."

Although she spoke to him fairly regularly and had boxes of his letters under her bed beside her journals, she had not seen Quincy since the day she came home at the end of third grade and Bubb told her she just missed him.

"Well, you sure didn't tell anybody else. Hello, stranger."

"Hi, Ma," he said, bending to hug her tightly. "I asked Phine to keep it a surprise. How you doin?"

"Better than ever now, baby," her mother said, dripping tears. "It's *so* good to see you, I can't tell you."

"Lookin good, son."

Phine saw a flash of uncertainty in Quincy's eyes as Daddy planted himself beside their mother and held out his hand. She knew, because Quincy had told her, that he had thought often about the moment, but the word seemed to have thrown him.

"Davis," Quincy said evenly, nodding and giving the hand a firm, quick shake. "You're holdin up pretty well."

"Got to," he said pointedly, and added with casual significance, "Welcome home."

"Who's your friend?" their mother asked, turning everyone's attention to the pale, skinny girl with the mass of hair, dangling earrings, and armful of bangles who had perched in Quincy's shadow.

"This is Fontelle Fauntroy, a good friend for a long time. She came to keep me company."

Delphine actually recognized her even before she heard the name. She had been reappearing in the letters for years, but the last Delphine heard she had gone off to California and that chapter seemed to be over. She was definitely surprised to see Fontelle with him now, being presented, judging from their body language, like some kind of fiancée.

There were greetings all around and they moved somewhat awkwardly to sit in the living room like company. Quincy played his part well, though. He took in everything, measuring the changes and weighing the time, but didn't try to claim anything. It was so different from the times Delphine remembered, when he was a teenager trying to fill every corner of the house whenever he showed up, silently challenging Daddy for every inch of space. Part of her still wanted him to be that way, to be her prince coming to fight for her, but she was in a way even more thrilled that he would make himself small enough to fit into whatever space was available to him, just so he could be there for her.

"We made a reservation," Quincy said lightly.

"Boy, the only way you're leaving here is over my dead body," Mommy said.

"I wasn't sure there'd be room," he said, vaguely gesturing toward Fontelle.

"You can stay in Bubba's room. Both of you."

"Where is he, anyway?"

"Seattle, Washington," Daddy answered dryly. "At a basketball tryout."

"I thought he was all through with that. Tore up his ankle or something."

"He is, honey, but he doesn't know it yet."

"No, he knows," Daddy corrected. "But he hasn't admitted it to himself yet. We thought he'd be back by now, we don't know what's happened."

"Okay, enough small talk," Delphine interrupted.

"We're discussing your brother, dear. That's hardly idle chatter."

"Whatever. Quince, I gotta talk to you in private."

"You've got all weekend, Delphine. Quincy, I hope you're staying at least till after the ceremony Sunday."

"That's what I'm here for. But in the meantime I'm certainly available for a little counseling. You be okay, Fon?"

"Sure, go ahead. I'm fine. That'll give me a chance to tell your parents everything about you, because I know you've been lying."

Delphine got a kick out of ushering him into the room that had once been his and Bubb's, then Bubb's, and now was hers alone. Right away, of course, he noticed the mess she had made—the ripped-down posters, flung notebooks, scattered records.

"Redecorating?" he asked.

"Kinda housecleaning. You know, getting ready for the next phase."

"I see." He pulled around her desk chair and straddled it backward to talk to her. He probably didn't even realize—and she wasn't going to be the one to tell him—that that was the exact same gesture Daddy used to make when he came into their rooms. "What is it?" he asked as she stifled a giggle.

"Nothing. I just—I can't believe it's really you. You're really here."

He smiled. "Yeah, it's me all right. But you're the one who's changed. Damn, look at you, girl. The pictures didn't come close."

She settled into a lotus position on her bed, wrapped around her oversized pillow. She couldn't have been more pleased if Teddy Pendergrass had come by her room.

"So, what's up?"

She sighed. "So much happening right now, just in the last few weeks. I started to write to tell you all of it, but it was like you said, sometimes you have to let it sit there awhile before you can begin to understand."

"Man trouble?"

"Oh, man. You can say that again."

"Do the folks know what's goin on?"

"I'm still breathing, aren't I?"

"Okay, shoot."

She started with Chris, because that's where it had to start, even though she knew that was misleading because he wasn't really the problem, although right now he sort of was. She talked about how he had helped her find her way in the new school and that had made them kind of partners and going together seemed a natural thing because of that. He was cute and all, and she liked him, but it wasn't until a few months ago that she really started feeling romantic about him—but that was getting ahead of herself. She also figured out while she was talking that because of the way they hooked up, she had let him get the idea from the beginning that he was supposed to protect her. She didn't think anything of it at the time—well, she did like it—but now she understood that's not what she wanted.

Quincy looked real confused, but he was cool. He didn't interrupt with a lot of questions, and let her sort out the story herself. He probably was a really good teacher; she wished she had him.

She was zigging and zagging because she didn't know how to get to the hard part. She told him about all the prom preparations and how Chris probably felt left out by the whole thing and so she went alone at first and there was a moment, not the first time, when she found herself attracted to this white guy Brian and kind of jealous of him and Beth because they were there together and seemed to know what they wanted from each other in life. That's when she wandered outside alone wishing Chris would come and make her feel that way about them. And that's when it happened.

"What? What happened, Phine?"

"These guys," she started, and recomposed herself. It had come out pretty easy at the police station, and that surprised her and made her think she could do this now, but that was a white face on a uniform, somebody who didn't know or care. Telling her brother was not an accusation but a confession, even though she knew absolutely that it was not her fault, and knew that he would tell her so. And he did, when she was finally finished recounting the scene into her now-damp pillow. He eased beside her on the bed and put his arms around her (in a way that nobody had ever done before, like somebody who'd had a lot of practice putting his arms around people) and told her she did exactly the right thing and he was proud of her.

"The funny thing is, I thought about you," she said softly. "You told me how you had done things, got mad, hurt people. And Daddy always says that there's no excuse, that only bad, sick people do that, but I knew that couldn't be right. I mean, if you could hurt somebody like that, too, that means that everybody's fucked up. I don't know, I'm confused. I know I didn't make it happen, but maybe there's something else I should have done."

"No, Phine, you did just fine. Your father's right, there's no excuse. Most of the time we end up hurting people close to us because those are the only ones who can make us feel so bad about ourselves that we just lose it. That's what I was trying to warn you about, the anger that comes with love. And it's worth the risk, believe me. But this is something entirely different. Anybody who'd do what they did to you, strike out at a stranger like that, has problems that have nothing to do with you. And they're not worth your confusion."

But there was still the problem of Chris, which she explained along with the police station and her confrontation with Beth. Now she was back to just wanting it over. Chris getting hurt on her account would only make it worse. She could try to live with what happened to her, but much as she liked him, she didn't want to start a new life thinking that she owed him.

"Shit do get complicated, don't it?"

"But what do you think I should do?"

"First, you gotta tell Ma," he said, and she looked at him like he was crazy. "Don't worry, I'll help you. But she has to know, especially the part about you taking care of yourself the way you did. She won't be mad, I promise."

"Daddy too?"

"I don't know about that one. We'll see. Tomorrow I'll help you find Chris and cool him out. Then we'll figure out what to do about the other guys."

Since Daddy always went to bed and got up first, Delphine went to warm their mother up in the kitchen while Quincy got Fontelle settled in. The girl was much less animated than Delphine expected—she hoped that wasn't some kind of love spell because with all the other problems that came with it, who needed a lobotomy too? Maybe she was just nervous. Anyway, Mommy knew right away that she had come to confess, not only because she'd been locked up with Quincy so long but because she never came to visit with her in the kitchen. Mommy used to see her reluctance as a rejection of the homemaker's role, which it was, but that upset her because she usually worked too, and besides, Mommy said, being independent didn't mean you should resent doing things for the people you loved. They didn't even bother to fight about it anymore. Mommy said if she wanted to go through life not knowing how to cook or take care of a house she'd *better* get married quick, and find herself a good woman to marry, or else she'd live in filth and starve to death.

Delphine smiled to herself about the advice as she hung around, lamely wiping counters and putting pots away in the wrong cabinet

"How long you known your brother was coming, Delphine?"

"Well, he's always said he would. But he just told me definitely a few weeks ago."

"You have no idea what it's been like. I had even forgotten myself until I saw him. It's a terrible thing, but I just had to set him aside in my mind so I could concentrate on you and Bubba. And Davis. But it must be like the way women felt in slavery when their children were sold away. Not that bad, of course. We were able to keep in touch, and I never thought I wouldn't see him again. But as long as he refused to come home and I had all you all here, I just never knew when that would be. And he's my first child."

"So what does that make me?"

"The third. You know what I mean, honey. For a long time, after the boys' father was killed, and Bubba was little, before Davis came along, it was really just him and me. I know that's why the changes were so hard on him. He wanted so much to be the man, and in every other way he was so much a little boy. It wasn't a good situation. I wanted to take the pressure off him, that's why I married your father when I did. But he just wouldn't let go. He couldn't understand that he didn't have to be anybody's father. Certainly not yours."

"He's been a big help, though."

"That's fine. That's what a big brother's supposed to do. I hope he knows the difference now. And I hope you've got sense enough not to put that on him."

"It's just so hard to talk to Daddy about some things. It always has been. He's got these notions in his head, you know. Like everything has to be exactly this or that. No in between."

"And given the kinds of things that go on out here, which he sees every day and you don't have to deal with because of him, can you blame him? Where do you think you'd be right now without those notions, as you call them? Anyway, you also have a mother, which you sometimes tend to forget."

"I know. I'm sorry."

"You don't owe me any apology. You're the one who's missing out, honey."

"Okay, I get it. So listen, have you ever been raped?"

"What?"

"You know. Has anybody ever tried to force you to have sex?"

"Did that Chris—?"

"No, no nothing like that. It's worse, I guess." She took a deep breath.

It turned out to be the hardest telling. She had so long avoided going to her mother with the intimacies of her life, for fear of being seen as weak, or of having her concerns reported to her father. The more her mother comforted her, the more the shame of the attack was compounded by her own shame at not trusting her mother enough to tell her.

"I told you she wouldn't be mad," Quincy said. He had come into the kitchen at some point during the narrative and must have figured she was doing all right because he kept quiet.

"Oh, I'm mad all right," their mother replied. "In fact I'm furious. But not at you, honey. It's those devils we let you go to school with. And those goddamn cops."

She and Quincy both looked at their mother; neither had ever heard her curse.

"You sure you okay, now? You told me all of it?"

"Yes, Mommy. A few scratches and bruises, that's all. Physically anyway. I'm all right."

"Okay. And thank you, Mr. Quincy. I don't know what made this child think she couldn't come to me with this, but I guess you've still got the touch."

Coming out of the bathroom the next morning she ran into Fontelle emerging from her old room in a long T-shirt with a scarf on her head. She couldn't help wondering what had gone on in there, and glancing at the girl's skinny legs she momentarily questioned her brother's taste.

"Delphine. Hi," she beamed and started to look prettier already. Maybe he did know something. "I'm sorry I didn't get a chance to talk to you last night because Quincy whisked you away. I've heard so much about you."

"I've heard a lot about you too."

"Uh-oh."

"You know, Quincy tells me a lot about what's going on with him, and he's always said good stuff about you. Well, usually. So are you guys . . . ?"

"You get right to the point, don't you? I just got back from the coast a little while ago, and I've been staying with Quincy for the last week or so. Until I can get myself together. Okay?"

"Sure. I'm just being nosy, that's what sisters are supposed to do. Tell you what, after you get dressed, why don't you come into my room and I'll tell you some secrets."

Delphine was glad for the diversion. Lying in bed, she had heard a lot of doors opening and closing, and she didn't want to get caught alone with Daddy until she knew what kind of information was being exchanged. Besides, Fontelle was pretty cool. Even though she was older—twenty-five, she said—she acted more like Delphine's own age.

That was different from Glenda, the only other one of her brothers' girlfriends she'd ever really known, who always seemed older, like a little bitty mother you could talk to.

They sat on the floor like Delphine would with her girlfriends, and she showed Fontelle the two Adidas boxes full of letters from Quincy and her own private photo album, which, unlike the official volume, included shots he had sent with a few of the letters—pictures of his classes and his student Carlos, who was Delphine's age, and favorite spots in New York like the view from Morningside Park and Michaux's bookstore and some taken around his apartment—one with Fontelle's portrait of him in the background. Delphine wondered but not aloud who had taken it.

"You must be pretty surprised to see me," Fontelle said. "You probably thought it would be the anchor lady."

"Who? Oh, I know who you mean. Whatever happened to her, anyway? I mean, do you know?"

"Nope. He hasn't said and I haven't asked. She just like disappeared. So here I am."

"Well, actually, I wouldn't have thought he'd bring anybody. But I guess it makes sense. He did say that good friends make the best lovers. You think so?"

Fontelle blushed and looked away. "I wouldn't know. Sounds like it should be true, though, doesn't it? I'm hungry, you think maybe we could go get some breakfast now?"

That must have pushed some sort of button. It ended their chat, anyway, and gave Delphine one more thing to puzzle out over the weekend. When they got downstairs to the living room, Delphine saw her father following Quincy into the kitchen and froze, thinking she should flee back upstairs. Then, as she heard them starting in with each other, she grabbed Fontelle, gestured to her to be quiet, and they crept closer, careful to remain out of sight.

"Whatever it is, I need to know about it," Daddy was saying.

"If she doesn't think she can tell you, I can't help that," Quincy replied. "That's between you and your daughter. And your wife."

"You've got a lot of nerve, you know, coming in here trying to control everything."

"Hey, you the man, Davis. I'm just passing through. You won, remember?"

"Sit down, son."

"You know, I really wish you wouldn't—"

"Stop that foolishness, Quincy. You're a grown man now, we don't have to play these games anymore. There's no time. It's not about winning and losing. In a family situation everybody has to trust that everything's being done for the good of all. These little side contests pitting one person against the other, competing for affection, that just pulls everybody apart. Do you hear what I'm saying?"

"Yeah, okay. Thanks for the speech, but I gotta run."

Delphine tugged at Fontelle and tried to make it upstairs before Quincy realized they'd been listening. He saw them and immediately waved them toward the front door.

"Delphine?" her father called, following Quincy out of the kitchen. "Is that you?"

"She's with me, Davis, we're on our way out. See you later." He shoved them out the door and they all scrambled into Mommy's car before Daddy could call her again.

"You people always go to this much trouble to avoid each other?" Fontelle asked from the backseat.

"It was him," Delphine protested.

"Hey, it's all right. I can relate. I'm still hungry, though."

"We'll get something to eat and then I'll show you around," Quincy said. "And we can try to locate your friend," he added to Delphine. "By the way, while you two were giggling upstairs your brother called."

"Bubba? Where is he? What did he say?"

"He's in San Francisco, speaking of avoidance. He didn't say much, and I told him to get his ass home."

After that the day became kind of a blur. They drove away from the neighborhood, which made sense because Quincy had spent so little time there, had breakfast at a Friendly's, and cruised around pointing out stuff to Fontelle. It was cool—and confusing—watching the two of them together. They weren't intense like Bubb and Glenda used to be, but they obviously enjoyed each other. She wondered if her parents had ever had that kind of fun—not since she could remember, but then they were older when they met, and they had always had kids around, which probably changed things. She did begin to suspect, though, that Quincy was so preoccupied with Fontelle that he had forgotten about her situation, unless he just wanted to take her mind off everything. If so, it didn't work, and she finally asked if they could go by Chris's place.

She left the two of them in the car and ran up to the porch of the house, a little more run-down than hers. She knew Chris was self-conscious about it, thought she was almost white-rich because both her parents worked. But Chris's mother did okay, she was just real busy and wasn't around all the time, which Delphine sometimes envied.

"Hi, Mrs. Higgins, is Chris home?" she asked when his mother answered the door.

"Oh, Delphine, hi. No, he's out someplace. Said he had some things to get done before the graduation, you know."

"I see. I was just worried about him cause I haven't seen him since day before yesterday. And he hasn't called."

"Oh, don't worry, he's fine. I told him you called last night. Who's that?"

"That's my big brother from New York. Okay, listen, I don't want to be a pain or anything. Can you please just let him know I stopped by, and if he wants to get in touch he can reach me at home, all right?"

"Sure, honey, I'll tell him."

By the time she got back to the car, she had half convinced herself that he was avoiding her because he was sick of her. Maybe he'd decided she was damaged goods or didn't feel like playing hero for her anymore. That would almost be a relief at this point—but still, she was pissed that he didn't have the guts, or the heart, to tell her himself.

When they got home Mommy had decided they should all go out to dinner since it was not only her graduation but the closest thing she'd had to having everybody together in a long time. But Daddy wasn't going for it, which told her right away that her secret had been kept and he was feeling left out, manipulated, and generally ganged up on. She hated to see him get that way, when the pride that gave him his authority turned him almost comically vulnerable, and she was tempted to let him in on what had happened, especially since she had basically decided to go back to ignoring it, and she was sure that Mommy would tell him by tomorrow if she didn't. Tomorrow was good enough, she decided. She might be stupid, but she wasn't crazy, and if he was too stubborn to join them for dinner—which probably had more to do with Quincy than with her, anyway—well, he'd just have to stay hungry.

At dinner Mommy talked about the time she told the boys she was getting married, and how she knew right then that Quincy was going to be a problem. Delphine had heard the story before but not for a long time. Fontelle seemed to get a kick out of picturing Quincy as a surly little boy, and in fact he looked like he might have gotten evil again just thinking about it if Fontelle hadn't been there. Of course, Mommy wasn't stupid. Delphine figured it was her way of taking him back to the beginning, like through hypnosis, and trying to get him to see what had gone wrong and that it wasn't really as bad as he thought.

At least he got through it, and he didn't mind when Fontelle told about some of their carrying on through the years in New York, kind of lifting the veil of secrecy he'd draped around himself for no good reason. Delphine had a pretty good sense of what his life had been like, but it was good to hear it from somebody else—and Mommy was downright tickled to be able to nod and say stuff like, "He always was like that." Like Fontelle had brought her baby back. Delphine just hoped that this wasn't going to turn out to be a one-shot deal, that he really was home in a way that mattered and wasn't just using Fontelle as a kind of postcard from oblivion before he vanished again. That would kill Mommy, though she'd never admit it, and considering how good Delphine was feeling right about now, it would permanently piss her off, too.

By the time they got back, though, she had another worry: Mommy suggested in the car in her offhand way that was meant to be taken as an order that she have a talk with her father that night. They must have planned it, actually—the two of them were always conniving even when they seemed to be on the outs—because he was standing there like a bear on its hind legs when they came through the door, pronouncing her name with his accent in full force, which always meant trouble.

"Delphine," he said, turning the second syllable into a dangerous question.

"Yes, Daddy."

"Your friend Chris's mother called. She seemed very upset. She asked for you to call her right away when you got home. Do you want to tell me what that's about?"

Hell no. Why would he even bother phrasing it that way? But she had resigned herself to the fact that she would have to—after she returned the call.

"Delphine, thank God you called, I don't know what to do." Yeah, she thought, that's the way she felt last night when Moms wasn't giving her any help. "Chris came through here a little while ago, and I've never seen him like that. I think he was drunk or high or something, I don't know. He was talking about you, said he was going to finish it tonight. Talkin about pig this and honky that and he was gonna prove somethin or other to you and everybody. He was just talkin crazy. I don't know where he was goin or what he was gonna do. Delphine, I'm scared. What's goin on with you two? What's happening with Chris?"

"I don't know, Mrs. Higgins, but I'll find out, okay? It's all right, I'll—I'll do something. I'll find him. You can call my mother later if you don't hear anything. It'll be okay."

She hung up and looked past the anxious faces of her parents. "Quincy?" she said.

"Let's go."

"Delphine."

"Later, Daddy, I promise. Just trust me, okay?" She kissed his stern face and wished for a minute that she could jump into his arms and cry it all out and leave it to him. But really, she couldn't remember the last time it had worked that way, and this was no time to be going backward. This was her time to take care of herself the way they'd raised her to do, even if they didn't mean it.

"So the game is afoot?" Quincy said as they pulled away from the curb.

"Huh?"

"Sherlock Holmes. I thought you read that. Anyway, where do you think he went?"

"Shit, I don't know. Let's circle around by his place and I'll see if I can spot the car. Damn, I can't believe he's really going to start some shit."

"I can."

"What do you mean?"

"You're worth it, don't you know that?"

"*Quincy*," she whined, then, catching herself, added, "Yeah. Yeah, I do." And even as she tried to gather her thoughts to match Chris's, she reached out to tenderly squeeze her brother's arm.

"Where do those guys hang out?" he asked. "Night before graduation, maybe they're together someplace."

"Good idea. Let's go out Washington. I'll show you where to turn."

Shortly, they turned into a small parking lot beside a corner bar, the ground floor of an old clapboard house.

"Patriot Tavern," Quincy read as they got out. "This looks like the real thing, all right."

"Beth told me about it. Big Hyde Park jock place. Look, there's his car. I was right, he must be here."

"Okay, just stay calm and stick close. All we want right now is to get him out of there."

What was a general hum from outside turned into a blast of sound as they opened the front door. She recognized something by the Doobies pounding in the background, but the real volume came from a room full of white boys and a few girls talking loud. They were clustered at the bar mostly looking up at a baseball game, but they were also spread out at the pinball machines on one side and the wooden tables on the other. She had thought she'd seen them in their natural habitat at school, but this was, as Quincy said, the real thing. Standing in the entrance adjusting her senses, she noticed her brother lighting a match beside her, like it wasn't smoky enough in there. She crinkled her nose disapprovingly, and he gave her one of those barely tolerant, big-brother sneers. While she was deciding whether to call him on it, she spotted a lone dark figure sitting at the bar and pointed him out.

"What's the score, blood?" Quincy said, easing up behind Chris, who flinched. "Be cool. Hey, yo," he said to the bartender. "Gimme a Dewar's, neat, and a 7UP for the lady."

That's when Chris turned the other way and noticed her. She couldn't tell if he was mad or embarrassed or what; happy to see her would not have been the right description. She laid a reassuring hand on his shoulder but didn't speak, either, because she was busy watching her brother acting like a man at a bar ordering drinks with a cigarette dangling from his lips. Cool. Nasty, but cool.

"You with him?" the bartender demanded as he placed the drinks.

"Why you ask?"

"He looks like trouble."

"Tell you what you look—" Chris started, and they each clutched one of his shoulders.

"Tell you what, Paddy," Quincy said slow and Shafty. "Look to me like you got a roomful of thirsty people here to take care of, so you do that, and let me worry about my man here. Okay?"

Chris tried to jump bad again as soon as the bartender turned away. "Man, who the fuck are *you*? And what's she doin here?"

"Shut up, sonny," Quincy said close in his ear. "I'm with Phine, and we're with you. Now you just sip on that beer and do like I tell you."

Chris sucked his teeth and picked up his glass, then turned to her. "You shouldn't be here, Delphine."

"I was worried about you. You don't have to do this."

"Don't tell me what I oughtta do, all right? I've had enough of that shit."

"Take it easy," Quincy said. "Tell me. You see who you came here to find?"

"Yeah, they're here. Over by the pinball. Waitin for em to make their move. I got somethin for em."

"Yeah, okay, you just keep it, hear?" He swallowed half of whatever that was he was drinking and sauntered—that was the right word—over to where they were. He lit another cigarette and leaned against the machine where one of them, tall and blond, was playing. She wished she could hear what they were saying, but the place was so loud and she wanted to make sure Chris stayed put. The player turned to look at her, said something, and laughed. Quincy just smiled and said something back, and they laughed some more. Nice that they were all having a good time together.

"This is stupid," Chris said and started to get up.

"No, wait," she pleaded. "He's my brother, let him handle it." Chris started to protest, but something else caught her eye—a familiar bouncing movement coming through the door, with its inevitable dark-haired shadow. She straightened and locked eyes with Beth.

"You guys get out of here," she said, hurrying over to them.

"Hi, Del, what's goin on?" Brian asked. "What brings you here?"

Beth hadn't said a goddamn word, she knew.

"I couldn't," was all Beth managed to say, glancing sheepishly at her confused boyfriend. Simple-ass bitch.

But she'd wasted too much time with them already; Chris was up and moving toward the pinball machine.

"What is this, Soul Train?" the player asked, looking up without stopping his game. One of his buddies started forward. Quincy tripped him and shoved him to the floor. The player rushed Chris and they started to grapple. Quincy stepped in to separate them. That drew the crowd's attention and others began to pile in. Delphine sensed Brian moving forward and blocked his path, because she didn't know which side he would be on this time. Next thing she knew the bartender was in the middle of it, like a referee at a hockey game, sorting out the pile. Quincy dragged Chris away, clamping a hand over his wrist as Chris was reaching into his pocket.

"Okay, that's all," the bartender was saying. "You boys gotta go. I don't want no more trouble in here."

"Sure, Casey," Quincy said, lighting up again and keeping his body in front of Chris. "But not unless our friends here come with us."

The bartender scratched his head and figured the odds. "There's three of you, right?" he said to the goons. "Go on, take it outside, I can't have this in here. The rest of you stay put, you hear me?"

Quincy patted him on the shoulder and eased back to the bar. "Good call, Mickey," he said, finished his drink, and laid a bill on the counter. "Gentlemen?"

Brian looked like he wanted to say something to her, but she ignored him. Quincy calmly filed past with Chris in tow. Great. Now they were into some ritual male combat shit. She endured the smirks of her three attackers, took a deep breath, and followed.

"You know, what you all did to my sister was not only criminal," Quincy announced in the doorway, "it was a goddamn cliché. I really hate that. Any of you boys know what it means?"

"Shit, let's do it, Buckwheat," one of them said as they stepped into the shadows of the parking lot. Chris, predictably, whirled and went at him. Quincy grabbed hold of the other two and pinned them against a car. Before she could even say anything, Chris was on the ground. Nobody was paying her any mind, so she looked for a big rock in the gravel driveway to do some damage. Instead, she saw something that had fallen from Chris's pocket. She scrambled for it and pointed it at the tall kid who was kicking at Chris.

"All right, back off. Now!" she yelled, trying to steady her grip on the first gun she'd ever held. She had no idea where he had gotten it or why he had been stupid enough to bring it. Or what she should do with it. "Everybody, just quit!"

"I got it now, Phine," Chris said as he got to his feet. "Here, lemme have it."

"No," she said and edged away from him. She didn't really want it, but she didn't want him or anybody else to have it either. "You've done enough."

"Yeah, come on," said the leader. "What you gonna do, girl?"

"You shut up, asshole," she yelled.

"Quit playin, Phine. Gimme the piece."

"I'm not playing, Chris," she said.

He reached for the gun and she pushed him away. He looked for a second like he was going to come at her; she almost pointed the gun at him before she realized what she was doing and turned it again on the blond kid in front of her.

"That's all, Phine, put it down," Quincy said, stepping between her and her targets.

"Not until they say they're sorry and leave," she said. She was trying desperately to think of some purpose to all this, some way to make it end.

"Delphine."

"Please move, Quincy," she almost whined. She did trust him, more than she did Chris, and she definitely didn't want the damn thing. But there was no reason to trust anybody, to take any chances, if she could make it stop herself. "I want to hear them say they're sorry."

"You can kiss my ass, bitch."

Quincy turned and slapped the one in front. "She told you to shut up, didn't she?" Quincy said. The kid looked nervously at her and didn't retaliate. She liked that.

"I'm gettin outta here," one of the others said and retreated into the shadows. But something, somebody, ran into him and knocked him to the ground and started beating the crap out of him.

Chris charged forward into the confusion and tackled another one. Like he just had to hit something if he couldn't shoot it. Only Quincy kept his cool, restraining the tall blond at whom she was still pointing the gun.

"Stop it, all of you!" she screamed, but nobody was listening anymore.

"You give me that now, girl, before you kill one of your brothers."

"Daddy!" she said, letting go the gun and giving him a quick hug.

He patted her back and walked calmly to the leader, who was still struggling to get free from Quincy's grasp. "Tell me," Daddy said, "what do you want me to do with this trash?"

"Fuck you, nigger," the boy spat.

Daddy put the gun to his head. "What's that you say now?"

The kid flinched, then tightened his jaw and tossed his blond hair. "I said fuck—"

Daddy whacked his head with the pistol. "I've been watching punks like you make trouble for me and my family all my life," he said. "I've beaten them and I've had them put in jail, but I've never had the ultimate satisfaction. You want to be the first, boy?"

"Let me go," he mumbled.

Delphine stepped forward and kicked him in the balls; he screamed and sank from Quincy's grasp.

"I think he said he was sorry, Phine," Quincy said.

"All right," Daddy said. "Leave him here. Quincy, go get your brother."

It was Bubba who had restarted the action and was still whomping away when Quincy pulled him off the kid he'd knocked down.

"Damn, Bubb," Quincy said, trying to settle him down. "Ease up, man." He looked crazed, like she'd never seen him before.

She went to help Chris to his feet; the kid he'd been wrestling with had gotten loose and was scurrying across the parking lot.

"All right, children, let's get out of here," Daddy said. "I'd better hold on to this, young man."

She ended up with Chris in the backseat of his car. Quincy was driving, and except for her giving him a few directions, nobody was saying anything. Fine with her; she couldn't help thinking about everything that had just happened, but she didn't want to have a conversation about it. Problem was, like on the T the day before, she didn't know how to start any conversation with Chris. She thought she should probably be grateful, but she was thoroughly pissed.

"I knew you'd try to talk me out of it," he finally said in his sulk, responding to a question she hadn't asked. "But I had to, to do something. It almost didn't have nothin to do with you, you know what I mean?"

"No," she said. "It didn't. And that's bullshit. Where'd you get that damn thing anyway?"

"It's my father's. I went by to see him and took it. If you all hadn't come I probably woulda used it too. I guess I'm glad I didn't."

"You guess?"

"I just get so sick of all their shit, man. Motherfuckers think they can do you any way they want. I'm tired of it, Phine, that's all."

"I know, Chris. Me too. Look, it's all over now, okay?" She kissed him even though he was dirty and sweaty and smelled like beer. Because he looked like he needed it, and she wasn't sure she would ever want to again.

They got Chris home, and he didn't want Delphine around while his mother made a fuss and then went off. So she joined Quincy at the curb as Bubba pulled up in his car. He must have driven Daddy, who took their car back home, or something. It was all too confusing; she just wanted to get in and go.

"Took you long enough to get there," Quincy said to Bubba as they piled in.

"I knew I was gonna end up doin all the work anyway," he replied.

"Please don't start," she said from the backseat. If Bubb was still in his trance and Quincy started messing with him, there was no telling. Bubb turned up the tape deck in the silence that followed.

"What is that?" Quincy asked.

"Herbie Hancock."

"That's not bad."

"I told you that when it first came out. You said it was artificial crap. Obviously you hadn't heard it."

"So?"

"So you like it. So I was right."

"It's okay, I won't tell anybody. Oh, don't let me forget, I've got something for you back at the house."

"What's that?"

"My book."

"Your book?"

"Yeah, motherfucker. I wrote a book and I got it published."

"Really? I thought you were just bullshittin about all that. I guess I'll read it one of these days. After I get settled, you know."

"Fuck you."

Delphine didn't know what they were talking about and didn't care. She couldn't remember the last time the three of them had been together but closed her eyes and smiled, knowing she would remember this.

Mommy hugged Bubb as soon as they hit the living room. He seemed more relaxed now. Quincy, looking satisfied but subdued, sat beside Fontelle and she stroked his back. Delphine plopped down on the arm of Daddy's chair.

"Nice kick," was all he said.

"That's what Mommy taught me. I tried the first time, but it didn't work. Guess you think I'm a pretty bad person, huh?"

"No, Delphine," he said and took her hand. "What I think is that I shouldn't have to wait a week to find out that my little girl's been hurt. Especially when everybody else in my house seems to know about it."

"Daddy, I didn't want you getting into fights with boys in bars. I mean, you guys were great, but none of you should have to do all that."

"Who's supposed to do it then?" Bubb asked. "Your boyfriend, who was about to get his ass kicked? That's our job, Phine. If I'd known about this last week, I never would've left without taking care of it."

"*You* never should've left anyway."

"Hey look, don't start that again. I just came all the way back here to help you out."

"I don't want you to hang around on my account, that's the point. Daddy, I'm going to call Howard on Monday to see if they've still got room for me."

"I thought you decided you wanted to go to BU."

"No, you decided. But I've had it with Boston, I gotta get away from here. And I don't want to be rescued anymore. Not by you or anybody else. You understand?"

His grip tightened on her hand, and his face clouded. He closed his eyes, shook his head faintly, and took a breath, about to say something.

"She's right, Davis," Quincy said. Well okay, one more rescue.

"This doesn't concern you, Quincy."

"Yeah, it does. In fact, I'm the expert. You've done it all, man. Look at her. She's magnificent. She knows what she wants to do, and trust me, she's gonna do it, because that's what you told her to do. Even knucklehead over there had sense enough to come back. Not because I told him to, because he knew he should. He got that from you, Davis. That's it. You're done. Time to let go."

She squeezed her father's hand, kissed his forehead, and followed his eyes to her mother nodding yes across the room.

"You pick a fine time to start making sense, Mr. Crawford."

"Maybe you never listened before."

Delphine dug her nails into her father's hand to keep him from starting an argument.

"Maybe you're right," was all he said.

"Good, can I eat now? I been on a plane all day."

She got to share her room with Fontelle that night, and she was going to be careful not to push her too hard because whatever was going on between her and Quincy, she didn't want to mess it up. He needed somebody like her. The boys—Mommy loved the sound of that, she used it every chance she got—had to fight over the bed in what used to be her room. But they probably weren't going to sleep anyway once Quincy got in his business. That would be good, too. Daddy was too nice with Bubba, but Quincy would put him straight. One more phone call in the morning ought to help, too. It was going to be a busy day. The ceremony would be a trip, with her white cap and gown, like a wedding but better because she wouldn't have to share the spotlight with a husband while she rubbed her success in all those pink American faces. And then the black parents' reception. But nothing would be better than tonight. Last time she peeked, before she got in bed, Mommy and Daddy were just sitting downstairs to-gether listening to the floors creak with the four of them walking back and forth to the bathroom. That seemed to make them happy, and as stupid as it seemed, she could understand. She felt pretty god-damn good herself.

Twenty-one
Fontelle

That was a trip. She'd never seen Quincy like that. He sure did love him some baby sister—maybe that's why he treated all his women like shit. And the way he kept picking at his brother and talking in code made him seem more like one of his high school students. But the big thing was his father, or stepfather or whatever. She knew he was the reason Quincy had never wanted to go home all those years. Quincy was actually afraid of him, but not because he was some kind of monster like she'd figured before. It was more like Quincy was afraid he'd like the man and that would blow his whole game.

True, Davis wasn't very charming, or even friendly. He put out these vibes like a force field that kept everybody at a respectful distance, including his wife and children. But it worked both ways. She knew from watching him, and from seeing how he was with his daughter, that if you got inside that field you could feel safe forever. Nothing outside could hurt you, and he never would either. Nobody asked her, but she thought Delphine was crazy for wanting to get away from that. Fontelle knew that she herself would never want to give up that protection if she had it.

But she didn't. She had never really been safe. That's why, at last, she had turned up on the stoop of Quincy's building with two packed bags, prepared to wait as long as she had to until he got home, so she could ask him to take her in. She'd tried to make him understand, but when she called the night before he was too preoccupied to listen. So she just went there and waited. She would have waited through the weekend. If he had been hit by a bus on his way home, she would have just died there. Because there was nowhere else to run, and if she moved from that spot, she would have gone back home and never escaped.

When she saw him rounding the corner, hours before she expected him, she came alive and started rehearsing a dozen scenarios for greeting him, none of which reflected how desperate she was. But as soon as she saw his face, she knew there was no use faking it. He looked even more lost than she was, if that was possible. It wasn't just that his clothes were rumpled, as if he'd been wrestling with someone—unless it was the devil himself who'd beaten him and taken a piece of his heart as a trophy. She simply stood as he approached and said nothing, offering her own meager presence as a consolation for his unspoken loss. He looked at her and knew, like they'd been running circles around each other for years to get to this spot where all either one of them had was each other. He picked up one of her bags and they went in to his apartment.

Inside, what had happened that morning and, she later understood, the dread of going home left him absolutely unreachable. In the old days, whether he was wrapped up in some political event at school, or when he was writing seriously or preparing to teach—or when there was some new woman—always there had been part of him she could touch, when she could catch him. Now that she was right there and had him, at least for the time being, all to herself, it was as if she weren't there at all. He got up and left for school in the morning and left her lying there; she was awake but pretended not to be, because there was no point in being awake. He returned in the late afternoon and graded homework—his school still had two weeks to run—and read some and jotted down notes and watched TV. He spoke but never talked.

But it wasn't a hostile indifference; she never felt unwelcome. In fact, knowing how he treasured his solitude, she felt flattered that he allowed her to share it. They both understood that she needed to be there, although she didn't say why, and so this was an expression of real trust. She also believed, considering his state, that he needed for her to be there, though she didn't know why. So they were helping each other, as they always had in funny ways, even though she had never anticipated this and was certain he hadn't either.

Finally, after nearly a week, he turned to her in bed in the dark with "Corcovado" playing off his old Stan Getz album and asked if she wanted to come to Boston with him to visit his family. "If you're going,

I want go," she said. And then he smiled for the first time because he knew she wouldn't leave him and she knew she was right about his needing her. He put his arm around her shoulders and she let her face melt into the luxury of his dark chest. It was amazing that she had never been in that place before in all those years; he hadn't touched her in the days she had been there.

"Sweet dreams, Fox," he whispered.

"You too, Crawdaddy," she whispered back.

As soon as they got on the bus to Boston, he began to turn back into his old self: teasing, funny, and confident. But over the weekend, there was something else, too, an attentiveness that was new, maybe because they'd never been together around other people he cared about. But really, as far as she knew there weren't any other people he cared about, except maybe his students. She also noticed, though maybe she was stretching, how much he was like Davis. In different ways, they both provided comfort that came from an overwhelming sense of loyalty. Whatever the reason, she felt herself falling in love with him again. Almost for the first time, because even when she had thought about him all the time at other times and tried desperately to imagine him making love to her as he said unconvincingly that he wanted to and she looked forward to seeing him and talking to him, even after months sometimes—with all that she had never said to herself, I am in love with this man. At least not until just a week before, when she had blurted it out over the phone in a panic. But looking at him through his sister's eyes, and his mother's and father's and even his brother's, she knew that she had never been anything but in love with him.

And he was in love with her. She knew that when she realized that he treated her the same way he treated his sister, with casual tenderness and respect and less self-consciousness than before. And because he wasn't constantly hinting about sex—that had suddenly just stopped— the tension she had always assumed held them together relaxed into something she could identify only as genuine affection. That would have been amazing enough if it had lasted only the weekend, but it continued when they returned to New York. He never said that he loved her, and if he had, that would have spoiled everything. He didn't even say that he needed her; he didn't have to. She knew that she was, finally, what he wanted. It was obvious every night when she nestled into her spot and breathed him in and watched the streetlight brighten the ceiling and drifted into the music on the stereo and waited to speak the prayer that was the answer to hers. *Sweet dreams, Fox. You too, Craw-daddy.*

They were sweet. The light on the ceiling, as her mind separated from her sleeping body, became a portal to an endless, sunny garden of wildflowers taller than she. She danced through the colors barefoot, feeling that nothing bad could ever find her, moving toward a voice that was reciting poetry, song lyrics, and stories somewhere on the far side of the garden. The voice didn't call her, and she wasn't in any hurry, but she knew it was waiting. As she came closer, the thrill of anticipation was so great that she fell out to prolong the moment, her face lying against the strong, dark earth, while the music of the voice vibrated through her body until she had none at all.

By the time school was over, he rose every morning to work on a new children's story that he insisted she would illustrate, with drawings or watercolors or photos—it didn't matter as long as she was part of the process. In the evening, she would sketch drawings of New York as she pictured it, the hopeful faces of people from all over the world striving in small ways for freedom from whatever pasts tormented them. And in the days they set out to find the people she had envisioned and captured them on film—on color slides instead of the black-and-white prints she'd been working with before. They found the faces in Harlem, and also in Little Italy and Chinatown and Delancey Street and the Village and even in midtown, where a straitjacketed executive would occasionally pause on the street to notice the blue stretching between the tops of the towers above or the face of an out-of-town child discovering the magic of a window display, and in that moment free himself to connect with something he hadn't known he'd lost.

It may have been the boy at F. A. O. Schwarz or the Mulberry Street confirmation or the fire-hydrant kids around the corner—or something else entirely that moved him—but Quincy began to focus their excursions on playgrounds. The children they found there, identical despite color or language or dress, represented not just freedom from the past, he explained, but from the future as well. The city rose above them like prison walls, containing them and separating them and channeling them from birth into predetermined directions. But they didn't know or care. They maneuvered through the jungle gyms as if escaping through cell bars. They flung themselves upward on seesaws and swings as if they believed they could launch themselves from the surface of the planet; they threw themselves fearlessly down sliding boards just to prove that the ground, having recaptured them, couldn't hold them down. They ran circles around life itself. He told her about a comic book character who could run so fast that he could propel himself around the world in seconds, even run back or ahead through time; he could be anywhere or anywhen he wanted to be. The mommies and nannies and sitters and grandparents and occasional fathers who watched them believed they had the children under control, but they were only fooling themselves. The kids belonged to no one or no place, until they stopped moving and gave up. Somebody ought to tell them that, Quincy said. Somebody ought to let them know that they were free.

He tried to do that. Ignoring the disapproving stares of the grownups, he pushed and lifted and chased and let himself be chased, anything to encourage the squealing frenzy around him. Having her there with her camera helped, because most of the grown-ups believed he was safe and part of some theatrical or publicity stunt. Some even smiled and relaxed, thankful for the distraction or hopeful that maybe the kid would be discovered. But the camera obviously wasn't necessary. Several times in the early evening she stayed home to sketch and he went out to play Pied Piper on his own.

But she wanted the two of them to play, too. The photos were fun, but for her they were also work; she wanted to celebrate her liberation more energetically. Going home had seemed to free Quincy up from stuff he'd been carrying around as well. For sure, the kids in the playgrounds had nothing on them as far as laughing at the future. She didn't have the slightest idea of a hint of a prospect of a job—and every hour that she stayed with Quincy was like sailing to the edges of a flat world. It wasn't that they thought they'd fall off, but neither of them had ever been that way before.

She hadn't been to Coney Island since she was twelve and her mother watched her ride all the rides with her father. She remembered three things: "My Boyfriend's Back" blasting hey-la from all the loudspeakers, which was the first time she'd ever heard the same sounds from her transistor radio played loudly in a public place like it wasn't supposed to be a secret; her father's shoulders and arms and thighs banging her and cushioning her at the same time as they whooshed and dipped and swirled; and the half-formed idea, like something you were about to say but forgot, that maybe by now she should be having that fun with somebody her own age.

Well, it wasn't too late. Back then, though, the park and the beach were full of people her age; it was an assembly, a convention, a *colony* of twelve-year-olds, like every zit in the universe. It was still like that. She just wasn't her own age anymore, which actually kind of surprised her at first. (She could see now that there were more adults than she remembered, probably because they weren't in motion.) After she got over that, she really didn't mind. She only needed one playmate, and this time the arms and legs that surrounded and pounded her on the still-thrilling curves were definitely the right ones. "I'll Be Good to You" was the tune that stood out, like the park itself making her a promise.

"I think I've been waiting half my life to ride the Cyclone with you," she said as they wobbled to Nathan's for franks and fries.

"You haven't known me for half your life."

"Yeah, weird, isn't it? Sort of a kismet kind of thing."

"Or maybe you're just dizzy."

"Of course, but today I have an excuse."

"They call this place Astroland, right? That fits. You are my starship, baby."

Later she took him up to the parachute drop, a bad move so soon after the fries, but she wasn't about to puke and spoil the fun the way she did last time. She was determined to hang until the sunset she missed before. They caught it creeping down toward the cliffs of Jersey, the faraway kingdom from which she'd escaped, while they stood on the boardwalk among the lingering holiday weekend crowd.

"Do we have to go home?" she asked, intoxicated by the smells of food, sea, and humanity.

"School's out, we don't have to do anything," he replied dreamily. "Far as I'm concerned, we're home right now. You're here, I'm here, what else is there?"

"Good, then we can go anyplace. South America, Australia . . ."

"Jupiter, Mars."

"Sure, I'm game. We can set up a school for alien orphans and you can teach them writing and I can teach art and we can make up our own holidays and myths and train them to come back and colonize the earth."

"And get it right this time."

"Exactly."

"I've got a better idea."

"I bet it's not as much fun."

"Probably not, but maybe mine'll work."

"This is a fantasy, Quincy," she pouted. "Who cares if it works? Okay, so what's yours?"

"Can't tell you yet. It's not time."

What they did the next night wasn't his big idea, but it was fun—and it was his idea, so she had to give him credit. They hadn't gone out dancing or anything like that. It had too many negative vibes since the last time, when she'd just got back in town, and it was also too much like the kind of hanging out they always did before when they were just orbiting around each other. But dancing on roller skates—that was something different.

They clattered on the D train to Brooklyn, to the most happening roller disco in town, according to his students. It had all the charm of a high school gym, with the same sort of clientele, the other extreme from the profiling phonies at Deuteronomy. They looked worse than the kids her father hadn't wanted her to hang around with, which she'd always resented even though she wouldn't have been caught dead with them anyway for fear of being caught dead with them. But the music and the motion turned the musty old barn of a place into a palace where she knew right away she was going to put on a show. Quincy could tell. As they laced on their rented skates he gave her his old go-for-yourself, I'll-catch-up-later look.

That's exactly what she did; they were celebrating independence, after all. She started easy on the first few laps to get her balance, but it came back to her quickly, even though it was nothing like the driveway or schoolyard in Englewood. The speed made it more like the roller derby she and Quincy had sometimes watched on Saturday mornings after not spending Friday night together. But with more style: Chaka Khan as Bay Bomber. They played the same song from Coney Island and she started to swoop. Tonight she heard it differently, her own promise to be good to herself. A little Parliament and Earth, Wind and Fire and didn't hurt: tear the roof off the sucker and get away. A gap-toothed brother in a black T-shirt rolled up and tried to talk to her in what sounded like a foreign language, just because it was Brooklyn and he was maybe twenty but looked sixteen. She wasn't into conversation and anyway he did his best talking with his body in a series of jumps and turns and splits that would have looked good in the *Ice Follies*. She couldn't match his athleticism, but she worked the show with grand gestures and subtle swerves like the superstar she knew she could be.

She was her own ride, spinning and gliding with the hum of the skates on the wood floor as a bass line and the ceiling just an illusion, and a line of followers fell in behind her like a male chorus line or native warriors escorting her on a ceremonial procession. She was so into it that she almost stumbled when one of them surged forward and grabbed her around the waist. When she realized that it was Quincy—he had caught up to her after all—she did stumble but he held her steady and took her hand as they promenaded around the track into a world all entirely of their very own. No one could have told her, in fact, that they didn't come barreling around the turn and propel themselves out across Prospect Park, over the East River, and above the lights of Manhattan, cruising down through the cool, dark space of Central Park and then gliding up Morningside to float in through the window on the beams of the streetlight before settling exhausted and triumphant into bed, where she felt for the first time that she really wanted and needed to keep dancing cheek to cheek, belly to belly, legs entwined till sunup or death did they part, whichever came last, and feel the smooth rocking motion all up inside and through her the way she used to dream it could be, the way he described it with others not knowing that she never really knew. They did ease to a stop finally, anyway, in something like that configuration; he ended up a whole-body pillow, both harder and softer than the mattress, holding her up and holding her down so she could feel him everywhere but inside. Close, but not quite, and that was all right, because anything short of impossible perfection this time would have killed her for sure.

She awoke to the smell of coffee and reefer and the sound of the radio news.

"They found the kid," Quincy said when she was able to focus on him standing naked by his desk.

She wished he wouldn't do that. If he was going to go around without any clothes on, at least he could have an erection to flatter her.

"The missing Katz kid," he added when she didn't quite get it. "Dug him out of a dump in Jersey. They think the doorman did it."

Why did it always have to be Jersey? At least it wasn't his father; that had been her theory.

"And the South Africans killed a bunch of school kids in Soweto. It's all the same shit, really, kids getting fucked over. But you won't hear anybody make the connection. You want some?" He held out the joint.

She groaned and shook her head no. He also had a cigarette going.

Or two. He'd been getting better since Boston, but the news must have really thrown him. So much for their almost-enchanted night—she was going to have to work to bring him back.

"You still wanna do the tall ships?" she asked.

"Sure, why the hell not? It's a great day for freedom."

"Keep the coffee warm, okay? I'm gonna get a shower." Her caffeine intake had increased with his nicotine reduction. But she hated to get up when he was standing there. She usually slipped into the bathroom when he was in the kitchen. Undercover naked was one thing, but she couldn't help feeling that he would judge her negatively in the daylight.

It was hot and cloudy as they strolled down by Grant's Tomb on the river. She had never seen it like this. The West Side was usually deserted on a holiday, what with people at the beach and in the country. People were everywhere, all over Riverside. On the roofs, hanging out the windows. Quincy, still in a sour mood, carried on about white folks getting religion. All the great Communist minds of the Western world, he said, come to bow to Old Glory, probably in a military mood because of the Israeli raid on Entebbe last night. She decided she had to reset the radio for WBLS, or wake up first or just unplug the damn thing.

As it was, she would only be asking for trouble to admit that she was really excited to see the stately procession of high-masted sailing ships from different countries, built to resemble the real things from the old old days. Although, it wasn't like they hadn't planned to do this. He got better when they settled into a spot in the park and they tried to guess the countries by the ships' flags. She spotted one from Portugal, and that set him off again.

"Oh, I get it now," he said. "I don't know why I didn't think of this before, except that I was trying not to pay too much attention."

"What?"

"What do those remind you of?"

"I don't know. Columbus, maybe. Like a coming-to-the-new-world thing."

"Yeah, and you know what that means. Shit, the Spanish and the Portuguese too? Those bad boys were full of *us* the first time they came around here."

"Then maybe that's like the grand finale," she said, trying to lighten him up. "They'll bring the cargo up on deck and have a big auction. Maids and nannies and doormen for sale."

"No, I think it's gonna be the other way around this time. They're coming to take us away. That's why everybody's out here cheering. Can't wait to see us go. Swing around by Brooklyn, pick up all those brothers from the roller disco, Bed-Stuy, Bushwick, and whatnot. All of Staten Island and Bay Ridge will be out on the Verrazano throwing roses as the ships head out to sea."

"They better have lots of guns, because I'm not going anyplace."

"Maybe it's time to be gettin back. This shit ain't workin."

"So we do better, that's all," she said, exasperated. "Honey, we are orphans. We are stuck here. I'm not going to live in the jungle or the desert or the mountains. I know it's modern, and I know those are my people—or at least they used to be. But all the black I know is right here. They may think they don't want us around, but they're just kidding themselves. I mean, look at these people. If they're not trying to be hip like Richard Pryor or funky like James Brown or studs like O. J. Simpson, it's divas like Diana or independent women like Cicely. It's all about us, they just don't know."

"Whoa, okay. You win."

"What's wrong with you anyway? I mean, I know you're bummed out, but let's not get carried away here, sweetie."

"Yeah, I know. I'm just feeling a little out of place right now. It's gonna be all right, though."

She wanted to ask more. This was the first time he'd slipped back into a funk since they'd been back from Boston, and she didn't want to go through that again, although she would if she had to. But he took the edge off by rubbing her back, smiling, and leaning over to rest his head in her lap.

"No more slave-ship talk, okay?" she ventured.

He nodded, closed his eyes, and lay peacefully for a long time. That allowed her to sit back and enjoy the spectacle—the colors of the ships, the park, the water, the happy faces of all the people—without any irony or cynicism.

When he finally came back to life, he stood and stretched and lit another joint, which they shared. A young Puerto Rican couple shuffled by, the man pushing a stroller with a sleeping infant, the woman carrying a tote bag of baby stuff with her other hand in his back pocket. Quincy stared at them until they were out of sight.

"What do you think of that?" he asked.

"It's kind of sweet, I guess. They're awfully young, though. I don't know when I'd ever be ready for all that."

"You'd be surprised."

"What do you mean?"

"We could do that. It's like your alien orphanage thing. We've got a lot to give."

"Quincy, what are you getting at?"

"I think you are ready. I know I am."

"Ready for what?"

"To be like them. You know, have a family."

"What, right now?"

"Yeah, right now," he said, and stubbed out the remains of the joint. "Come on."

She hadn't formed a thought yet, but judging from his reaction she must have looked horrified.

"No, not like that. Let's go, I got a story to tell you."

He took her hand and led her away from the park, talking just loudly enough to be heard through the crowd but not looking directly at her—more like a statement than conversation. He told her that right after she called him that first night she got back into town, Maxine had told him she was pregnant and he freaked. Couldn't deal with it, because he knew he didn't want to be with her anymore. And, he said, he'd made that mistake once and didn't want it to happen again. He already had a child, a son.

He said this like he was talking about some book on his shelf. She tugged on his hand then, tried to stop him in his tracks right there. That couldn't be. He wasn't the kind of guy who went around making babies, even if he was sort of a dog at times. She knew who those guys were, and they weren't him. Besides, he'd never told her about it. She couldn't even form her mouth to ask all the questions. He kept pulling and kept talking.

A one-night stand, he explained, the kind she always accused him of having but that really wasn't his thing. Didn't even remember her name. The summer after Maxine went away and she hooked up with Antoine. Never gave it a thought till he saw them on the street more than a year ago. Tried to deny it, ignore it, pretend it didn't have anything to do with him. Then Maxine tried to get him play daddy. Told her she'd have to have an abortion but she refused, so he threw her out.

That would have been the night, she calculated, before they met at Deuteronomy and she got drunk and made a fool of herself. And he'd never said a word.

After a few days, he said, he changed his mind. Tried to stop Maxine from getting the abortion, but it was too late. That was when he found her on his stoop. Didn't know what to do. Now he did. She was the one. And it was time.

She grabbed his arm with both hands then and forced him to a stop under the elevated tracks on Broadway. She put her hands on his shoulders and stood in front of him.

"Quincy, love, listen to me. I don't know what you're thinking right now or where you're taking me, but we ought to talk about this. I mean, this is some heavy shit, you're starting to scare me with all this. You don't want to do anything crazy now."

"Fontelle, I've never been more serious in my life," he said calmly. "I don't know, to tell you the truth, if I've ever really been serious about anything before now. I know exactly what I'm doing. You've gotta stay with me on this. Please. I need you."

She sighed into an embrace that she could only hope would convey her fear—and her helpless trust. Then she stood back and gave him her hand, and they walked silently through the empty streets, each step carrying them more deeply into his sudden obsession.

At Lexington the sky was ready to burst, and they paused under a bus shelter. Inside one glass panel was an ad for WBLS, with two gorgeous and sophisticated black models. On a second panel was an ad for Wild Irish Rose, and on the third a cigarette ad in Spanish. That was pretty typical of the commercial images presented to Harlem, she thought—smugly, because it occurred to her before Quincy had a chance to say it. She was glad for the break, though; it might bring him to his senses. And she was tired of walking. They just made it. The rain poured all around them like the air had turned to water, and within minutes somebody's wide-brimmed hat floated by on the small river that had already formed along the curb.

She noticed that Quincy was sweating heavily, not so much from the walk as from the standing-still humidity. She took the scarf from her braided hair and began to dry his face, which had grown so solemn that she felt like she was retouching the portrait she'd painted way back when they first met. She remembered wanting to capture the face she hadn't been able to get out of her mind. She knew then that she wouldn't need to keep the painting. Just the act of re-creating the face would keep it with her always, and letting him keep the portrait would be a way of reminding him that she'd been the one holding the mirror.

It had worked better than she could have hoped, because here they were six years later, face-to-face, maybe for keeps this time. She dabbed the tiny beads of water in the mustache following the insolent curl of his top lip. Then the eyebrows over his deep-set eyes that were watching her more intensely than on that afternoon in the studio. Down around the cheekbones and jawline, where he hadn't shaved that morning. When she reached around his glistening neck his hand caught hers and held it fast. With his free hand he took the other end of the scarf, looped it around her neck, pulling her so close that their eyelashes were nearly touching and she never saw his lips reach out the half inch to find hers. And then all she saw was pieces of his face—she forced herself not to close her eyes—and all she heard was the endless water all around them and their own gasps and purrs. She clutched his neck, his head, his shoulders, and his back, and everywhere she could get a hold so his face wouldn't slip away from hers, even though he was holding her too, so powerfully that she could lift both legs from the ground and know she wouldn't fall, not ever.

The kiss lasted as long as the downpour. The torrent of rain had slowed to distinct drops when she steadied her feet on the ground and stepped back.

"Ready?" he asked.

Ready to run back to the apartment and do what they'd never done. Or even right here, she thought as she let her hand slide down his chest. But, since that was obviously not what he meant, she was also ready to follow him on this strange crusade. She wouldn't let him go alone, and she couldn't let him leave her.

"Okay," she said.

Skirting puddles and jumping streams at each corner, they soon arrived at a red-brick compound of tall buildings between First Avenue and the FDR Drive. She'd seen flashes of it, or some other just like it, bouncing up the highway to the George Washington Bridge after excursions to the city for most of her life. Except for a few childhood visits to her mother's relatives in Newark, which were uncomfortable for everyone, she'd never been inside such a place, and frankly she had a hard time picturing Quincy hanging out here. Where did he meet this woman? How could this have happened?

They lingered by the edge of a courtyard that was slowly filling up with people who had been driven inside by the storm and were anxious to catch a breeze. Among them were ghetto characters she'd seen on the edges of Barnard, when she was living in Brooklyn, and even in sections of Englewood. But not concentrated like this. She understood that most were simply poor, hardworking folks—the People—but the prevalence of men who looked like winos and junkies, boys who looked like hoodlums, and mothers ten years younger than she was made the whole place seem tacky.

Quincy had his attention fixed on a climbing structure in the shape of a curved centipede, potentially an interesting idea if anybody noticed. About half a dozen kids were beginning to cluster around it, dodging a boy on a skateboard.

"She usually lets him out for a while after dinner," he said. "He goes to that playground and she doesn't watch him too closely."

That was he first time she knew for sure he wasn't making this up entirely. He had been there before, maybe when she was home sketching pictures of other kids. Maybe he'd been coming there a long time.

"Aren't you going to talk to her at least? The mother?"

"Not now. Wait here."

He eased over to the playground, and as he stepped away from her he began to seem different. He didn't exactly fit in, but he was not altogether an outsider either. It was the kids. He connected with them as he had in all the other playgrounds they'd visited. Joking around, lifting up, tying shoes, acting like everybody's uncle or big brother. Or the kind of daddy that she took for granted in the suburbs and that wasn't much in evidence here.

A little boy entered the frame, kind of gallumping across the courtyard in a Mickey Mouse T-shirt and too-big shorts that flapped around his bowed knees. He looked like he might have to run into something to stop himself. What he ran into was Quincy, who greeted him, slapped five, tickled him, and picked him up. The unlikely familiarity of it all made her glance around nervously to see the reaction of parents and other residents. Quincy seemed invisible, however, to the women sitting on benches nearby, and she took a step or two back into the shadows, feeling that she was somehow intruding. And then she saw him motion to her.

"Create a diversion," he said when she approached.

"Huh?"

"Go over there by that entrance and strike up a conversation. Come out on the other side. I'll meet you across the street."

She nodded and walked as inconspicuously as possible around the courtyard toward two women chatting by a low, chain-link fence in front of one of the entrances. Both wore sleeveless tops and shorts. One was young and fairly attractive, maybe twenty, while the other was stout and looked a bit older than she probably was. Fontelle couldn't help wondering which was the one as she interrupted politely to ask for directions to the nearest subway station.

"Ain't no train over here," said the younger one. "You got to get over to Lexington and 103rd, over that way."

"Where you tryin to get to, honey?" asked the larger one.

"Um, 125th Street."

"Well, you might just as well take the bus out here on First, time you get over there and wait for a train on Sunday. They got some kinda parade or somethin goin on up there? I seen all them boats come round by here yesterday. That was somethin, wasn't it? Don't know what they wanna celebrate the Fourth of July in Harlem for, though."

"I know what you mean," added the younger one. "I don't even get the day off from the store tomorrow. Be even worse than usual with all these tourists runnin around."

"Okay, well, thanks a lot. Sorry to disturb you."

"Shoot, ain't no disturbance. We just out here passin the time is all. You take care now."

"You, too. Bye."

As Fontelle walked away she heard the larger woman, who had done most of the talking, call out, "Willie!" and ask loudly, "Where that boy done got to now?" As soon as she turned the corner of the building, she ran, frightened, to the street, looked about frantically, and then saw what she feared on the far corner: Quincy and the little boy in the Mickey Mouse shirt.

"What the hell are you doing?" she yelled when she reached them.

"Good timing. The bus is coming. We can take this over to Second."

"But you can't—"

"Take it easy, it's all right. Get on, we're going for a ride."

Flustered, she boarded the bus and stalked to the back, not even bothering to drop in the fare. Let him worry about it. He followed smiling with the boy in his arms reaching at the metal rings above the seats.

"Do you mind telling me what this is all about?" she demanded.

"Sure, this is my man Willie. Willie, say hi to Fontelle."

"Hi," he said and reached for her dangling earrings.

"Is he—"

"Yup. See that somber thing he's got happening around his eyes? Nice work, wouldn't you say?"

"Jesus, Quincy, this is *kidnapping*," she whispered.

"No, it's not. He's with me. I'm taking him to see the fireworks. Right, buddy?"

"Fire!" the boy shouted and made explosive noises.

"You got it."

"His mother is looking for him."

"See, he likes you. Don't worry, I'll let her know what's up. Come on, let's change here."

After a nervous wait, with Fontelle looking for the mother to come charging around a corner calling the boy's name, they boarded a downtown bus and settled into the same seat in back. Willie stood on Quincy's lap and looked out the window. Quincy took her hand and kissed her on the cheek.

"You know what you said about waiting for me to ride the Cyclone?" he said. "This is the thing I've been waiting for. Okay?"

"You don't go to jail for riding a roller-coaster."

"Fontelle."

"All right, I give up. I'll just say you kidnapped me too."

Willie looked out the window for a long while, played with Quincy, crawled back and forth across the backseat of the bus, played with her earrings, and looked out the window some more, all the time making little singsong noises and chattering in a language Quincy apparently understood, though she could make out only every third or fourth word. Just watching him was exhausting; Quincy seemed exhilarated. Finally, he started fussing, and all the things he had just been doing no longer pacified him.

"Baba," he whined over and over.

"He must want his bottle," Quincy translated.

"Oh, and we didn't kidnap any supplies, I see."

Before Quincy could answer—not that there was anything he could say—Willie stepped into her lap, and he and Quincy both looked to her chest at the same time.

"Hey, don't even think about it. It ain't happenin, fellas. Wait a minute, come here." She cradled Willie and got him sucking his thumb. So, he'd need braces; that wasn't her problem. Not yet, anyway. She also took out one of her earrings and held it over his face like a miniature mobile. He smiled and swatted at it while his eyelids actually got heavier and began to droop. Just like in the cartoons. "It's working," she whispered excitedly.

"Congratulations, Mom. I knew you could handle it."

The ride down Second Avenue took close to an hour. The streets began to get congested as they cruised below the Village; a lot of people were trying to get to the Battery for the big show. Somewhere in the financial district, the bus just stopped, and the driver announced he could go no farther because the streets were blocked off. So they clambered off to hoof it the rest of the way. Still carrying the sleeping boy, who had grown far more adorable once he stopped moving, she thought to rebuke Quincy for not stealing a stroller, too. But when he offered to carry Willie the rest of the way she let it go.

It wouldn't have mattered anyway. Standing on some corner, her, Quincy and Willie, abandoned by the bus, she began to feel that she had stepped into a movie about life after the bomb. The heavy skies carried an eerie, after-rain glow that made the empty, narrow concrete canyon feel even more deserted than normal on a Sunday night. Walking down the slick, reflecting sidewalks, they began to merge with others out of nowhere, dozens, hundreds, maybe thousands of people moving like zombies to the edge of the island as if they had all heard the all-clear siren. The lights of the still-standing Brooklyn Bridge off to the side, and the distant twinkling of other lights in the harbor, pulled them all forward without a thought for whatever ruins lay behind them.

It was, finally, the water itself that triggered a different image. As Quincy had predicted, they were all coming to be taken away, like there was something waiting out on that water to transport them to another world, which also meant the end of the world they left behind. No chains, no guns, but maybe that's what it felt like. Only now it was everybody, far more white than black, in fact, which was how it probably should be, and no doubt would be. In an odd way, that comforted her, because if even one of them felt the same thing he would understand what should have been obvious for two hundred years.

Not likely, though. When they reached Battery Park, out of the shadows of the caverns and into the indigo expanse of the rest of the world, the zombies settled into an almost festive mood. It didn't seem to matter that they were packed so closely together that a violent sneeze fifty yards away might send someone splashing into the harbor. So closely that she started to feel trapped by the crowd, which was filling in every empty space as far as she could see. There were people in the trees. She leaned into Quincy to keep her balance, now painfully aware of her feet, and he spread his legs to keep his and at the same time held Willie still on his shoulder. She looked out over the bay to calm herself and saw the sky, which had begun to clear with the sunset, fade to black.

And then jets of light streaked across the endless background, leaving traces of bright color like fine brush strokes. A single white beam followed, rising through and above the others and arcing down like a missile aimed at them before exploding into a hundred raining pieces. The crowd stirred; the show was on. A barrage of missiles overlapped the first, painting a picture of red-white-and-blue willow branches hanging down above them. The explosions woke Willie, who panicked until Quincy—reassuring in his own excitement—could fix his attention on the flashing lights changing rapidly from green to red to purple, yellow again and bright white. The people gasped and cheered.

"Look, it's a star," Quincy exclaimed to the boy. "And that one's like a big octopus."

She saw wildflowers and double-yolk eggs and sparkling constellations. He saw alien probes reaching out to seize them. Willie spotted a dog and a spider. Quincy thought a huge, green ball that came hurtling toward them and flew apart looked like Krypton exploding; it looked to her like the earth being born.

"I want him to know what magic looks like," he said to her. And then, suddenly: "I love you, Fontelle."

A thousand diamonds of light brightened the park. She put her arms around both of them. It was like every dream she'd ever dreamed was coming true right here right now with this man who was her dearest friend and this little lost boy, and she couldn't possibly imagine what might come next if this cataclysmic light and noise ever stopped. But whatever it was would be what she had waited for since the first time she looked beyond her father to the sky and noticed a gap in her world as vast as space itself. And now, at last, she believed she was ready to fill it. First, she would have to tell him what she'd never told anybody, about her father. And if that didn't scare him off, she'd help him be whatever he needed to be for his son. And they'd go from there, somewhere, anywhere; the air was literally bursting with the promise of new life.

A rapid succession of spectacular displays climaxed with the crowd breaking into "The Star-Spangled Banner," prompted by music being simulcast on several portable radios.

"This is where I get off," Quincy said. "Come on, partner."

Willie became restless again as the lights faded and they worked their way back through the dense field. It was almost impossible to break through, but they were determined to get ahead of what would become an even more threatening stampede when the song ended. She grabbed hold of Quincy's waist and maintained eye contact with Willie over his shoulder as they pushed through. Maybe half an hour later they emerged into the air just a few blocks away. Even there, the sidewalks were beginning to fill with stragglers breaking early from the back of the pack. Typical New York: all the people trying to beat the crowd formed a crowd of their own. But at least they could move, and Quincy nodded them down into a subway station as their best hope. As long as they could catch something headed uptown, they should be okay. He set Willie down beside the turnstile while he flexed his aching back and fished for tokens. The boy was sleepy and confused and scared by the strange surroundings and the number of people. Quincy told him to scoot under the old-fashioned wooden paddles, but before Quincy could drop in a token someone else pushed through. When she reached over to catch Willie's hand he had drifted too far out on the platform.

"Stay there," Quincy called and vaulted over the turnstile. Stranded without a token, she hurried to the exit, which always reminded her of a barred jail cell, and opened the gate.

"Hey you," a voice called from the token booth. She turned briefly, shrugged, and pointed in the general direction of Willie and Quincy, as if to explain the situation to whoever was watching.

"Willie, don't move!" Quincy yelled.

She heard a small cry and caught a glimpse of Willie's shirt as he broke into his little hopping run toward the far end of the platform.

"This way," she called out to Quincy, but in the moment she turned to catch his eye she lost sight of Willie. Only the movements of people lining the platform as he galloped around and under them revealed his course.

"I got him." Quincy surged past her heading the other way, following Willie's trail. This time he just barreled into people in his way, pushing them back toward the wall to clear a path.

She followed as best as she could in his wake, running down the platform, dodging and holding up her hands to fend off the angry reactions of those he'd just knocked over. Behind her, she heard someone calling her to stop, probably a transit cop on duty for the occasion. It helped to freeze the others in her way, and she got a clear view of Quincy closing in on the frantic Willie.

A distant rumble became the shriek of a train pulling into the station. She stopped immediately to cover her ears, as she'd always done to block out the piercing sound that once frightened her as much as it must frighten Willie. Her father used to hold her until the noise subsided; a strange hand now seized her wrist. A clot of people farther down the platform stiffened and drew back, pointing. She saw Quincy pause and turn to the tracks. And leap into the air. Like she'd always imagined him, like some kind of superhero. She broke free from the cop and rushed toward him, racing the train that was now making a sound she'd never heard and forced herself to block out. She saw Quincy bending down on the tracks, gathering up Willie. Looking up at her, straight into her eyes, ignoring the engine a few yards away. His mouth shaped her name but she couldn't hear. She opened her arms to him and yelled with all her might though she heard nothing: "Quincy!" It was Willie she felt, though, miraculously in her grasp as she sank to her knees on the platform and held on with all the strength she had left. The screech of the train filled her head.

Hours later she sat numb in a room in a police station. Her braids were heavy on her head. Looking down, she could see her sandals, scuffed and muddy from walking all day. But the feet inside them didn't hurt. They were numb, like most of the rest of her. The large, talkative woman from the projects sat across from her. Willie slept in her arms, holding a bottle she had brought with her. Fontelle hadn't seen Quincy, because before they had removed him from the tracks she had told the policeman on the platform about Willie. She knew that's what he would have wanted her to do, make sure the boy was safe. She couldn't keep him. She didn't even know for sure if he had intended to. But letting go of him had taken the last bit of energy in her. When the woman had arrived, and the policemen had taken Willie away, Fontelle had become hysterical and then passed out. Now she felt that she was awaking in the middle of a conversation.

"That was him?" the woman was saying. "I seen him around a couple of times. Thought I recognized him. We went out dancin once a few years back. I see he got a wide variety of tastes."

"He said Willie was his son."

"He said that? Well, let's just say my baby ain't got no daddy. To speak of anyway, and either way that's for true sure enough now, ain't it?"

"But—"

"Look here, honey, I'm sorry about your friend, I truly am. And I thank the good Lord he saved my boy, but if it hadn't been for him, Willie wouldn't've been on them tracks anyway. I ain't gonna cause you no trouble. It wasn't your fault, and you done suffered enough. I got Willie back, so I guess that's all it is to it."

The woman got up to leave; a policeman was standing by to drive her home.

"Wait," Fontelle said. She reached to her ear. The earring Willie had been playing with had gotten lost. She took out the other and held it out to the woman. "Please," she said, "take this." The policeman stepped between them. The woman looked at her like she was crazy. "He liked my earrings," Fontelle said. "Please?" The woman took it, nodded, and left.

Somebody came and put her in a car to go see Quincy. At the hospital they took the elevator downstairs to a cold room and wheeled out a cart covered with a white sheet. The policeman pulled back the cloth only a little way, revealing his face. Frozen and fierce, just as she'd painted it. Both her hands reached out to touch it. Wipe away some of the smears. Smooth the skin around the eyes and mouth. Already it was beginning to feel like hardening clay. She played with the corners of the mouth a bit; he was never all that serious, not really. Just a look. She knew better. And she smiled a little herself as she got him to smile back at her. All very quickly, because the policeman pulled her hands away and covered the face again.

"You okay?" he asked.

"Sweet dreams, Crawdaddy," she said.

She had already answered some questions about what happened. She thought she remembered doing that, anyway, and he didn't ask any more as he drove her uptown. To their apartment.

Inside she could see the streetlights still shining through the uncovered windows, competing with the blue glow of morning rising above the park. She sat in his fake leather chair at the desk, with the typewriter and ashtray and scattered books and papers. In the month she had been there she had never come to the desk. Never thought about how many times he had sat there smoking with her reflection of him staring down from the wall and music playing in the background, talking to her on the phone wherever she was—Brooklyn, Jersey, California—and some woman in his bed or just out of it.

She picked up the phone and dialed, listening intently not so much for the voice but for her own response to it.

"Hello?" he said.

She said nothing.

"Fonny, is that you? Are you all right? Where are you? I'll come get you."

She hung up. Or somebody who had become her hung up. Without crying or apologizing or reluctantly agreeing to go back. Just put the receiver back in the cradle. Guess that's all it is to it.

She sifted through the papers on the desk, picked the receiver back up, and dialed again. This time she would listen for Davis's voice, and she would tell him what he had to know. Then she would go to sleep, wake up, collect some things, and be on her way. Somewhere. She was free.

On the night of the Fourth of July, they went together—Elliott, Glenda, and Erika—to the Pops concert at the Hatch Shell on the river. It was kinda cool. He didn't know why he'd never thought to do it before. Well, yeah, he did know, actually. Nobody had been around to suggest it before.

That started at Phine's graduation. He wasn't really surprised to see Glenda there, and of course that meant the leprechaun was there too. They'd both been tight with Phine, after all. Afterward, at this black reception in the gym—who knows where the white folks went?—he was on his way to say hello even before Phine started in with the somebody-wants-to-see-you shit. She didn't act like it, but then she never had. Fooled around with Erika's hair just long enough to make him feel like a fool standing there before she looked up.

"It was nice of you to come back for Phine's graduation," she finally said, looking somewhere else.

"Yeah, well, you know there was this situation."

"She told me."

"Otherwise I might not have. I was in California. With Tyrone, you know he's the one—"

"Yes. How was the tryout?"

"Don't even ask."

"They won't draft you?"

"I don't think they'd even sign me as a free agent. No way I'd make the team."

"I'm sorry."

She looked at him for the first time when she said it. Sounded sincere, which he thought was real nice. But no, of course she was sorry. Then she'd have an excuse to be rid of him. The happy expression that had begun to form on his face turned into one of disgust, and he stuck his hands in his pockets and turned his body at an angle to her. Phine swooped by to pick up Erika and shot an angry look at Glenda. Girl games. He looked around for Quincy and Fontelle but didn't see them and suspected they'd slipped out to smoke a joint. He wished he'd gone along.

"No, I'm not," Glenda said, repositioning herself in front of him.

"What?"

"Sorry."

"Can we do this more than one word at a time?"

"I'm glad you flunked."

"Thanks a lot. Mind telling me why?"

"You knew you couldn't play but you didn't believe it. Now you do."

"Like, I told me so or something like that?"

Phine whooshed by again making eyes like she didn't have anything else to do.

Glenda took a deep breath. "Riki missed you," she said.

"Huh? Oh, yeah. Maybe I should've brought her something."

"Maybe you did."

She gave him the chess face, the one where she made a move and waited for him to realize she'd seen his coming half an hour ago.

"What about you?" he asked, finally beginning to read the board.

"What about me?"

He could have strangled her right then. But then he wouldn't have anything to live for.

"Maybe I should've brought you something too."

"I don't need—," she said and caught herself. That wasn't the move she'd meant to make. She just couldn't help it.

"You sure?" he prompted.

She took another deep breath. "Yes," she said.

"What?"

"Yes, I do, and yes, you did." She crossed her arms and went to nibbling the finger.

"Can we just go back and match up these answers with the questions one time here? I mean, is this really that hard for you? I'm hangin out here like a damn idiot, you know."

"Don't mess with me, Elliott Davis," she said through teeth clenched with a bit of fingernail in them. Her glare made him want to hug her.

So Quincy was right again. It wasn't like anybody was keeping score. The night before as they sat up late, Elliott had blasted him about thinking he had all the answers. About everything being so easy for him. Leave home, start a new life, slide off to college, settle right into a job, running around with all these women. It all just happened, like he never had to work at it. Even the book (it was kinda hip, though, and he had forgotten about that picture). And now he got to be the damn hero again while all of Elliott's own shit was coming up raggedy.

That what you think?

That's what everybody thinks. Always has.

You really need to get your head out your ass, Bubb.

Told him he'd been making all the right moves all along. Starting with the day he stayed his ass home, with Ma and Davis, where he belonged. Claimed he left because he couldn't hang, and he'd be leaving the next day because there still wasn't anyplace for him there. Said he'd always admired Elliott's dedication playing ball—loved that night at the NIT. And the way he'd gotten his act together in school; the injury wasn't as big a deal as it might have been because he'd never counted on a pro career and he had his degree. And he had Glenda. Said as long as he'd known Fontelle it had only occurred to him last week that maybe she was the right one and he still didn't have any idea what to do about it. Just making shit up as he went along because he had to, but he'd trade places in a minute if he could.

Elliott didn't entirely buy it; Quincy was always smooth with that shit, and he went to sleep feeling good but wondering what his brother was trying to get him to do.

He was definitely right about Glenda, though. All roads led to her. Otherwise he would have followed Tyrone to the coast right after school and never come back. And gagged on T's shadow. The only question was whether Glenda knew it, too. That had always been the only question.

That afternoon at the reception he thought he knew the answer, or at least felt closer to it than at any time since they'd walked into that restaurant in Amherst umpteen years ago. The day after the reception she called him and started talking about grad school. She had it all figured out. He'd take that job and hang on for a few years and get them to pay for the courses, and then this, that, and the other. Of course T would say he was letting himself be pussy-whipped, going along with some woman's agenda instead of thinking for himself. That's because he didn't understand teamwork and that it was a blessing to have someone who knew you well enough to know what your best interests were and to help you make it happen because you'd both be better off in the end. But that was okay, because T was a goddamn fool anyway.

But just to be sure, he stayed out of her bed. No sense letting extraneous shit get in the way. Sure, they had five lost years to make up for, but they had the rest of their lives to do it if he didn't fuck up first.

He went down for the interview in late June and they loved him. Signed him up on the spot to start in September. His supervisor, a hoops junkie, even wondered if he had thought about playing in the Eastern League on weekends when his ankle got stronger. He hadn't actually thought about it, but he stuck it in the back of his mind. Maybe later, when he was sure it didn't matter. Glenda hadn't seen him play since high school, and it beat bowling for fun.

His only concern was that they seemed to like him too much. And even though it was an engineering outfit, the job was in marketing, not production. So he had to wonder if they didn't really want him for the skills he'd been going to school for, like they just wanted to front him or something.

Glenda said: "So?"

"I don't know, you think maybe they're using me?"

"Of course they are. That's what a job is."

"But suppose they don't really think I can do it?"

"Do you think you can do it?"

"Sure."

"You like the job? Pays all right?"

"Yeah."

"So?"

That was about the time Glenda mentioned that Erika wanted to go to the Fourth of July concert on the river. He hedged; it had always seemed like something white folks did and had never particularly interested him.

"Riki ain't white," Glenda said.

Of course, she had a point. The kid had heard about it and it seemed like fun. She'd never heard Davis's lectures about the bogus revolution, or gone through the busing wars like Phine had, or even been called a nigger—yet—by the upstanding folks of Boston. She wanted to hear the band play and see some fireworks. And why the hell not? But if there was one thing he had learned from Davis—and from Quincy—it was that he had to be cool about how he fit into the kid's life. Coming on too strong would only cause resentment, and Glenda, more than his own mother, was fiercely protective of her. Besides, even though everything seemed to be going well, he wasn't absolutely sure that he was ready to take on the responsibility of imposing himself the way Davis had.

So they went to the concert and had a picnic on the lawn—starting over, just like in the park a few weeks before. They ate ribs; a couple of wise guys beside them were wearing tuxedos and drinking champagne. Erika was having a good time listening to the orchestra and checking out the sailboats and the skyscrapers, and so was he, but it felt like they were at somebody else's party.

"We're here too," Glenda said, reading his mind. "Don't worry about what anybody else got if you don't want it. You want one, get one."

When she said it, it really did seem that simple.

By the time the fireworks and cannons exploded with the music, he was able to see it all through Erika's eyes. Even Glenda seemed moved to excitement, sitting there holding his hand. He'd forgotten how much joy he got from her happiness, because he hadn't seen her that way in so long. And he knew it wasn't just the spectacle. She was never fooled by pizzazz; that smile came only when she was at perfect peace with the world at the moment. Which meant that he must be part of that equation, which meant that nothing could be more important in life than preserving that peace.

Afterward, as he led Erika through the crush of bodies, he thought he saw a bowlegged guy, moved a little like Quincy, heading straight for him in the crowd with his head down.

Do it, Bubb.

"Say what? You hear that, Cooz?"

He could tell she didn't know what he was talking about, and when he looked again the guy was gone.

That's when he panicked. Something was wrong; he had to get home, fast. He started to run, pushing through the crowd, almost dragging Erika, until he felt the tiny tug and heard her frantic crying.

"Elliott! Stop!" she yelled.

He whirled to grab her or carry her or tell Glenda to quiet her. Anything to keep moving.

But she planted her little self and said: "You scared me."

He had seen that face before. He could go or he could stay, but she wasn't going to be pulled through his confusion.

"It's okay, kiddo. I'm sorry, I got scared myself. Thought I saw something." He knelt and kissed her tears and coaxed a little bit of smile back on her face. "All right? Don't worry. I'll take care of everything."

About the Author

Dennis A. Williams is a grandson of Hattie Gertrude Clopton and Ola Mae Jones; a son of Carolyn Clopton and John Williams; brother of Gregory and Adam; husband of Millicent; father of Margo and David; native of Syracuse, New York; resident of the Washington, D.C. area; coauthor of *If I Stop I'll Die: The Comedy and Tragedy of Richard Pryor* and author of *Crossover*.